MAREN MOORE

Cover Design: Maren Moore
Couple Art: Chelsea Kemp
Editing: One Love Editing
Proofreading: Sarah P, All Encompassing Books
Sensitivity Reading: Heather Hopkins-Kirby, LMSW and Maggie Taylor, RN

*For the girls who are a little **Smashing Pumpkins** and a little **Taylor Swift**.*

Who guard their heart like the fortress that it is.

*There is **nothing** more important worth protecting.*

content warning

In my books you can always rely on having ample sugar and spice.

My hope is that my stories are light, feel-good, swoony and fun. Catching Feelings delivers on all the usual Maren Moore banter, heart, and spice, but it does also deal with some more emotional topics that some may find triggering.

Content warnings can be found below. Please note these might be considered spoilers for parts of the story.

Content Warnings

- Past death of a parent (off-page but discussed on page)
- Issue of mental health
- Grief/loss
- Car Accident

a note from maren

Dear Reader,
This book is the most personal thing that I have ever written.
There are many of my own lived experiences within these pages, and I wanted to take a moment to share something with you.
Like Vivienne, I experienced the loss of a parent.
My mom was killed in a car accident with a drunk driver when I was only 3 months old.
She was beautiful, kind, compassionate and I wish I would have had the chance to meet her.
To know those things about her, and not just hear them secondhand.
I wrote this book for her and I hope that it will make her proud.
For those who have experienced the loss of someone they love, I see and understand your pain.
Please know that you are not alone.
All my love,
Maren

thank you

A special thank you to Heather Hopkins-Kirby, LMSW and Maggie Taylor, RN for sensitivity reading this story.

la dictionary

I realized when writing this that some of these terms/sayings/pronunciations may not be known so I wanted to include a Louisiana cajun guide!

*** These are a mixture of my own definitions as well as a few pulled from various public websites.*

Please do not consider this an official translation/dictionary in anyway.

*This is purely for **fun!***

Mardi Gras- the French term for 'Fat Tuesday'. The carnival season varies from city to city, as some traditions, such as the one in New Orleans, Louisiana, consider Mardi Gras to stretch the entire period from Twelfth Night (the last night of Christmas which begins Epiphany) to Ash Wednesday. A celebration of balls and parades center around the holiday.

King Cake- A ring of sweet buttery pastry (similar to brioche) that's covered in lots of icing the topped with loads of purple, yellow, and green sprinkles or luster dust. Sometimes contains a plastic baby. Whoever finds the baby in their piece of cake is traditionally supposed to buy the next cake.

Mardi Gras Ball- A ball to celebrate Mardi Gras put on by each krewe (group of people) The King and Queen of each krewe work all year long for the big, spectacular ball. Their identity is a closely guarded secret and part of the mystique until the night of the Ball.

Second Line- The leaders of the parade carry decorated umbrellas, while the other participants shake handkerchiefs while they dance. A brass band plays some beats that gets everyone dancing and moving. You can often spot the second-line by bright colored suits and banners. (www.neworleans.com)

Roux- a mixture of butter and flour used in making sauces.

Laissez les bons temps rouler- Cajun french for "Let The Good Times Roll"

étouffée; é·touf·fée/ a spicy Cajun stew made with vegetables and seafood.

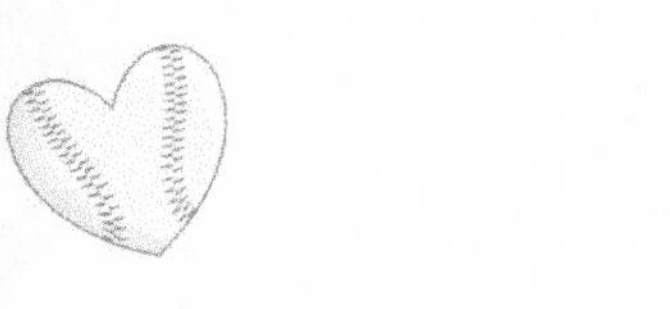

playlist

Scotty Doesn't Know- Lustra
Creep- The Grunge Growlers
1985- Bowling For Soup
Guys My Age- Hey Violet
What's My Age Again?- blink-182
Bullet With Butterfly Wings- The Smashing Pumpkins
Fly- Sugar Ray
Today- The Smashing Pumpkins
Mayonaise- The Smashing Pumpkins
Mardi Gras Mambo- The Meters
Teenage Dirtbag- Wheatus
Dress- Taylor Swift
The Second Line- Stop, Inc
Cardigan- Taylor Swift
If u think i'm pretty- Artemas
All Star- Smash Mouth
Dancing In the Sky- Kristen Cruz
Feeling This- blink-182
Endgame- Taylor Swift
To listen to the full playlist click here.

prologue

Reese

Then

I think I'm in love.

No, scratch that. I'm *definitely* in love with the girl in the middle of the dance floor wearing hot pink cowgirl boots, cutoff shorts, and a scowl.

Okay, fine. It's not love, but it's *definitely* lust, and when it comes to wanting Vivienne Brentwood, I'm a fucking goner.

I never stood a damn chance.

Those tiny cutoff shorts are molded to her ass, hugging the little dips right beneath her delectable cheeks, and I want to groan out loud in the middle of this honky-tonk bar with how badly I want to touch her. How badly I want to run my tongue along the creamy skin that peeks out the bottom.

Is it because the more I flirt, the more I try to charm her with my good looks, the more she dislikes me?

Absolutely.

I'm a bit of a masochist like that. The harder I try to catch her, the further she runs.

And there's just something about a girl who pretends she wants nothing to do with you but secretly wants to bounce on your cock when no one's around.

And trust me, this girl wants me just as bad as I want her.

She can spew all the venom she wants from those pouty pink lips, but I know the truth, even if she's not ready to admit it to herself.

I've been watching her on the dance floor for the last fifteen minutes, and what little amount of restraint I had left has been dissolved by the five tequila shots I downed earlier.

Viv drops her head back and laughs, swaying her hips to the music, her hands lifted above her head, completely oblivious that every red-blooded guy in this building is watching her the same way that I am.

When the white tank top she's wearing rides up an inch, exposing a sliver of pale skin, I'm fucking *done* watching.

I bring the shot to my lips and toss it back, downing it in a single gulp before slamming it onto the table and making my way across the bar toward her.

The dance floor is crowded with people, but the moment I step onto it, her eyes find mine. Even in the dim, shitty light of the bar, I see the defiance flash in her gaze.

Always a fucking challenge, except tonight, the win will be mine. I'm not leaving here without touching her. We've been dancing around it all night. For weeks, really.

Reaching up, I turn my hat backward as I make my way toward her, never taking my eyes off her.

I can't.

Even if I wanted to look away, I couldn't. I'm in a trance, watching her hips sway to the music. She pulls her plump lip between her teeth and runs her hands down her hips.

Almost like she's dancing for *me*.

When I finally get to her, I reach out, sliding my hands along her waist until my fingers dip into the loops of her cutoffs to pull her toward me. Her soft body collides with mine, and her hands fist into the front of my shirt.

"Um… have you lost your mind?" she says, feigning surprise, but doesn't pull away, and *that* surprises me.

I shrug. "Probably. Don't really give a fuck."

I watch her throat bob as she swallows, and her eyes darken as I move us to the music, pressing us tighter together with my hands resting right above the swell of her ass, testing waters we've never been in.

She doesn't respond, simply stares up at me with those wide blue eyes that I feel like I could drown in.

Leaning down, I dip my head to her ear, whispering, "How about for one night, we pretend you don't hate me, Viv?"

"Why would I do that? Hating you is so much fun," she murmurs coyly.

My hands travel lower, an inch at a time until I'm cupping the soft, bare skin beneath her ass, my thigh parting her legs as we move together to the music. Every time the beat hits, my thumb drags along her soft skin.

Her breath hitches when my thigh brushes against her pussy, and I pull back, staring down at her. "Because I know something that would be much more fun. You can even insult me while we do it."

"And what makes you think that I'd ever want to have *fun* with you, Reese Landry?" The sassy tone of her voice reminds me just how much of a brat she can be.

The song slows, the beat lowering with the lights, and we're pitched into near darkness in the middle of the dance floor. The music fades out, the crowd along with it, and all I can focus on is her pressed against me. How I'm surrounded by her smell. Lavender and something fresh.

She lets go of my shirt and slides her hand lower and lower, so fucking low that I feel her fingers dip beneath the fabric of my T-shirt and brush along the trail of hair on my stomach. The muscles contract under her touch, rippling with each brush of her fingers.

Fuck.

"Kiss me." My raspy command has her pupils dilating, and I pull her tighter against me. In the dim light, I can see her rising onto her tiptoes and feel her warm breath fanning along my lips, and I think this might actually be it.

I'm finally going to kiss this girl, and if I have anything to do with it, I'm going to spend the rest of the night kissing her like I've wanted to since the moment I met her. Even though it's only been a few weeks since then, I've been hooked from that very first insult. Her eyes drop closed, and I slide my hands up her sides slowly, memorizing her curves beneath my palms until I bring them to her face and cradle her jaw as I lean closer.

"Yo." A too familiar voice yells from behind us. You've got to be *fucking* kidding me.

Vivienne's eyes snap open, and I groan inwardly when she steps back like she's been burned, the hazy, heavy-lidded look in her eyes vanishing.

Goddamnit.

I'm going to kill him. The minute I get out of this bar, I'm going to strangle him with my bare hands.

My gaze lands on Grant, who's wearing a shit-eating smirk for interrupting what I already fucking know was going to be a kiss that altered my brain. I narrow my eyes as my jaw works. My teeth grind together when he laughs.

"Sorry to interrupt, but I'm heading out. Meeting up with somebody. You two going to be… good without me?"

"Bye, Grant," I say through clenched teeth. He's my best friend, but after tonight, he's going to be my best friend from six feet under after he just ruined that moment.

He chuckles, pulling Viv in for a quick hug, then slaps me on the back and disappears through the crowd.

"Viv," I say, reaching for her. She steps back just as my hand lands on her arm.

"*Clearly*, the heat in here is getting to me because I've lost my mind," she mutters before spinning on her heel and sprinting off the dance floor.

Fuck that. I'm not letting her walk away so easily. She was into this just as much as I was.

I follow closely behind on her heels, calling out her name, even as she busts through the exit door of the bar out into the cool night air.

"Viv, wait. Jesus. Just fucking wait," I say, jogging to keep up with her. "Just talk to me."

Finally, she spins around to face me with flushed cheeks. Her long, dark hair whips in the October wind, and I do my best to keep my gaze on her eyes and not how her white tank top is molded to her curves. Only minutes ago, I had my hands on her, and now she's running away from me.

"What? *Please* do not make this a bigger deal than it was, Reese. We accidentally almost kissed. It was a mistake. Now we're going to forget it ever happened. Trust me, I already have."

Chuckling, I step closer until we're toe to toe, and my head's bent as I stare down at her short frame. "Oh? That's what that was back there, huh? A *mistake*?"

"Obviously." She scoffs indifferently. "I was caught up in the moment. I would've kissed *any* guy in there tonight, Reese. Please don't act like you're god's gift to women."

My nostrils flare at the mention of her kissing someone else. Jealousy unfurls inside of me, and it's not a feeling I'm used to experiencing. Especially over a girl I barely know and haven't even kissed. Yet, it doesn't change the fact that she has me feeling this way.

"Yeah, okay, Viv. And I would've broken his fucking nose, so by all means…" I sweep my hand out toward the bar. "Go back in there and find someone else to kiss. Try me."

Her eyes widen for a moment, like she can't believe that I'm jealous, but guess what… she makes me fucking crazy, so I'm not responsible for the shit coming out of my mouth tonight.

With an eye roll, she pulls her phone out of the back pocket of her shorts and starts tapping at the screen. "Whatever, tough guy. I'm getting an Uber and going home."

"Okay, I'll go with you."

She drags her eyes to mine. "Uh. No, thanks. I don't need a chaperone. I'm a big girl."

"You're not getting into an Uber alone, Viv. You've been drinking, and it's late. It's not the end of the world to share an Uber. I'm a gentleman, and I want to make sure you get home safe."

"Fine, Father." She smarts while she finishes arranging the Uber on her phone.

My lips tilt up at her bratty comment. "I prefer *Daddy*, but whatever works for you, babe."

I pull my phone from my pocket and scroll until the car gets here since she's now ignoring me. I'm not very big on social media, but I try to keep up with a few friends from back home.

After a few minutes of silence, a sleek black Tahoe pulls up to the curb just as I'm shoving my phone back in my pocket.

Viv reaches for the door, but I stop her, opening it. "I've got it."

I'm served another eye roll that makes me want to spank her ass, and then she climbs into the back seat, and I slide in after her.

The driver pulls from the curb without a word and thankfully cranks the music louder, only slightly drowning out the tension that seems to be buzzing like a live wire between us.

It's hard for me to be quiet or still for any period of time, so I only manage a few minutes before I'm joking, "Did we just have our first fight, babe?"

I expect something smart-ass from her, but instead she actually laughs. "God, you're ridiculous."

I decide I like the sound of it way too much.

I shrug, reaching out to brush her hair off her shoulder, and her gaze flits to me. "Ridiculously *charming*, I know." My smirk widens into a smile, and she rolls her eyes again and huffs, then glances back down at the phone in her lap.

Silence once more fills the cab around us, but I never move my hand, the rough pads of my fingers continually drawing circles on her soft milky skin. I expect her to reach up and stop me, but she doesn't.

The further along we ride, the more she leans into my touch until I feel her pressed against my side as she gazes out the window, watching the cars pass by.

I shouldn't love fighting with her, arguing until I want to either spank her or kiss her, but it seems to be the one thing we seem to do well when we're together.

Bringing my hand down to her bare thigh, I brush my thumb along the exposed skin until she begins to squirm against me.

When it comes to her, I've got the patience of a fucking saint, and this time… I want *her* to be the one to give in.

Inch by inch, I slide my hand higher until I'm playing with the rough hem of her shorts.

My eyes shift to hers, and when she catches my gaze, her eyes flicker and drop to my lips, lingering for a brief moment before sliding back up to meet mine. When my fingers graze the skin under the hem of her shorts, her breath hitches, and her pupils go wide.

"Fuck it." The words rush from her lips in a whisper as she climbs into my lap, the juncture of her thighs brushing against my already hardening cock, and her lips slam against mine in a kiss that has my balls aching.

It's messy, and frantic, and fucking *hot*.

Her tongue slides into my mouth, and she moans at the contact, sucking my tongue as she explores my mouth with her hands fisted tightly in the locks of my hair. The needy, desperate sound of her whimpers shoots directly to my dick, somehow making me even harder, arousal snaking down my spine.

Finally, we both give in to what we've been dancing around since the day that I met her, that taut line of tension and pent-up need snapping like a rubber band between us. I've wanted her since the moment I laid eyes on her, and finally touching her, *kissing* her, feeling her grinding against my dick feels like I could lift the goddamn world.

Her hips rock, and she nips at my lips while my fingers dig into the flesh at her waist and she pants against my mouth. When she pulls back, searing me with her molten gaze, I'm scared she's going to flee like earlier, but instead, she slides her hand down my chest to the bottom of my T-shirt and tugs it up. Her hand slips into my jeans and palms my aching cock over my boxers, and an involuntary deep, guttural noise sounds from the back of my throat.

This fucking girl.

Her lips tilt into a smirk when she grips me harder. "See how much fun it is to *hate* each other, Reese?"

There's the softest brush of her lips against mine, teasing, taunting, and then I feel her smile against them. If we were any-fucking-where else, I'd put her on her knees and spank the fuck out of her for being such a little brat.

Instead, I slide my hand into the hair at her nape and tug her head back, exposing the column of her throat to press a hot kiss against her flesh. My teeth rake against her pulse point, and then I suck the spot, soothing it as she whimpers against the top of my head.

"Um. Sorry to interrupt, but like, we're almost to your destination. Am I dropping you both off or is there another stop?"

I'm so caught up in the moment, in *her*, that I forgot we're in the back seat of an Uber and the driver's got a front row seat to what we're doing.

Goddamnit.

It physically pains me to tear my lips from her skin, but I do to keep myself from losing the semblance of control I have left.

That's the effect she has on me. Making me lose my head.

Reaching between us, I close my palm over her hand that's still gripping my cock. "What's it going to be, Viv?" I pause, my gaze lingering on her blown pupils. "Are you going to waste more time pretending you don't want this, or are you going to let me fuck the shit out of you?"

VIV PULLS me into her dorm and slams the door shut behind us with her foot, all while her hands frantically tear at my T-shirt, lifting and tugging in an attempt to get it off me. Her lips move over mine while she fumbles with the shirt until I finally tear my lips from hers to reach behind my neck and pull it off, letting it fall to the floor. Lifting her off her feet, I walk her backward until her back hits the door, my hips pinning her against it. The motion has my cock jutting against the heat of her pussy, causing us to groan in unison.

"Fuck, I want you," I mumble roughly against her skin. I want her so bad I fucking *ache*.

I had no idea we'd end up here tonight when I almost kissed her at the bar, but I hoped that there'd be more.

That I'd have the chance to do this.

To spend the night, showing her that as much as she hates me, she'll love my tongue on her pussy even more.

When I gave her the chance to walk away in the back seat of the Uber, I thought she might take it. It wouldn't have surprised me if she did. The times we've been around each other, she's spent the entire time insulting me yet... eye-fucking me when no one else was looking. So it was a toss-up of what she'd decide.

She pauses, rolling her lip between her teeth as her eyes hold mine, a war with her body and mind raging behind her eyes.

"*One* night. That's it. Then, we go back to pretending the other doesn't exist. That's all you get, All-Star. Take it or leave it." There's finality in her words, and even though I'm not into it, it doesn't seem like there's a choice.

All I've done so far is kiss this girl, and I already know that one night will never be enough. It won't even scratch the surface of the things I want to do to her. But if it's all I get, I'm taking it.

"Fine, but the entire night, you're *mine*."

If she only wants one night, then I'm going to use every single second of it proving to her that no one will be able to bring her pleasure the way that I can. When it's over, I want to walk out that door confident that she'll never be able to forget tonight. Or forget *me*.

With her still pressed against the door, I slide my hands beneath her shirt and yank it up, exposing a lacy, pale pink bra that's only a few shades darker than her skin.

A lazy grin curves my lip up as I lean forward and swipe my tongue up the valley between her tits. "I think pink might be my new favorite color."

"Can you *not* talk? Just keep doing what you're doing with

your mouth?" With a frustrated whimper, she tugs me back to her chest by my hair, and I chuckle against her skin.

Fuck, I love that mouth.

Giving her exactly what she asked for, I scatter kisses over the swell of skin that spills from the cups.

Her tits are fucking *perfect*. Not too big and not too small. A medium size that look like they'll fill my hands perfectly.

I tug the left cup down, and her pert, rosy nipple strains toward me, a beacon for my tongue.

What I didn't notice in my haste to taste her was the tiny little silver barbell through the middle.

Fuck me.

Her nipples are *pierced*.

"Fuck, Viv, these are so goddamn hot," I tell her as I brush my thumb over the metal. She shivers beneath my touch, her back arching against my fingers. "Are they more sensitive? With the piercing?"

She nods.

Just when I thought she couldn't get any sexier, she almost brings me to my damn knees with the sweetest surprise.

When I wrap my lips around the hardened peak, she moans, tugging at my hair almost to the point of pain, and I relish in the sound. I want to spend the rest of my life listening to her whimpers. Hearing her breathless moans. I flick my tongue over the metal, then suck her nipple into my mouth and roll it between my teeth.

"Stop teasing me, Reese," she pants in a needy, desperate tone. "Get me naked and fuck me already, or we're done with this."

I let go of her nipple and pull back slightly to stare at her, my eyebrow arching. "Do you want to come?"

A beat passes, and then she nods, her blue eyes rolling in frustration.

"Then stop rushing me, Vivienne, or I'll leave you just like this. Wet, needy, desperate for my cock. Without giving you any relief."

Her mouth falls open, and her eyebrows shoot up. "You *wouldn't.*"

I lean forward to suck her nipple into my mouth again and tug—hard—before swirling my tongue around the peak. "Fucking try me."

Pulling away from the door, I turn and carry her toward the unmade bed in the corner, tossing her gently onto the mattress. Those pink sparkly cowgirl boots shimmer in the light as she lies sprawled out before me. I pull them off, then toss them to the side, where they land with a thud. Maybe I should've left them on so I could fuck her in nothing but them. Later.

She sits up on her elbows with her dark hair fanned out around her, her cheeks flushed pink, the skin of her tits blooming red from my lips and my beard scraping against them.

I hope her thighs look the same when I'm done sucking on her cunt.

Her heated gaze burns through me, and my cock throbs when she lifts a foot and drags it slowly down the front of my jeans.

I hiss, the movement almost enough to have my control snapping.

My palm wraps around her ankle, and in one movement, I yank her across the bed to me as I drop to my knees between her parted thighs.

Deftly, I flick the button of her shorts open and work them down her hips, leaving her in nothing but a scrap of purple lace.

"Tell me what you like," I say, licking my lips as I eye the damp fabric in front of me. There are a lot of guys in this world who aren't into this and would prefer to get their dick sucked, but I love to eat pussy. I want to fucking *devour* this girl.

Whole.

"What do you mean?" Her voice is breathless as she peers down at me.

"What turns you on? I want to know *exactly* how you like it, Vivienne. Talk to me, tell me how you want it. It makes the entire experience better, and I want us both to leave here satisfied."

"Oh, I... I've never been asked that before." She blinks, then tugs her lip between her teeth. The question obviously surprises her, so she's quiet for a minute as she thinks. I want to know it all, her kinks, what gets her off, how to make her come. "I like it rough. I don't like to be handled like glass. And... I sometimes like a finger in my ass when I come."

Most girls have problems with being vocal about their needs, especially during sex, but Viv tilts her chin higher, and her lips curl into a grin.

I knew she would tell me exactly what she wanted. She's nothing if not unfiltered and honest to a fault.

My fingers grip her thighs, holding them open wider for me to settle between them. Her expression turns molten when I drag the pad of my thumb over the damp spot on her panties, brushing over the hood of her clit that peaks against the fabric.

Her back arches, and her hips come off the bed as she sucks in a ragged breath, her fingers flying to my hair.

So fucking responsive, and I've barely even touched her. That tells me that she's just as wound up as I am, and that only makes me harder.

Fisting the lace in my hand, I tug it down her hips and shove it into the pocket of my jeans, then lean forward, dragging my nose up her pussy. She smells so fucking good that my mouth actually waters.

"Did you just *steal* my underwear?" Surprise laces her tone.

Sure as fuck did, and there's not a chance in hell that I'm going to give them back.

"Yep."

The brat laughs. "I knew you were obsessed with me, Reese, but this is too much, even for *y*—"

Shutting her up, I seal my lips over her clit and suck it into my mouth before circling it roughly with my tongue.

Doesn't she know at this point that her mouthy, bratty little comments only make my dick harder? A special kind of foreplay reserved just for the two of us.

I wet my lips with her, a possessive growl escaping just as she fists both hands in my hair and her hips begin to rock against my mouth.

I'm not sure what I imagined Vivienne tasting like, but whatever it was pales in comparison to the real thing. Sweet and musky and *her*.

Perfection.

Nothing I ever imagined could come close to what it feels like to touch her, to have her hands tugging on my hair when I flatten my tongue and drag it up her soaked pussy.

"Mmm. Is this all for me, baby? I guess hating me gets *you* off as much as it does me. You're drenched."

"Fuck you," she whimpers. Another curse falls from her lips as her head drops back between her shoulders, and the hand that's not holding my face to her pussy travels up to her nipple, pulling at the piercing roughly.

With each rock of her hips, my tongue slides along her pussy, pausing to give extra attention to her clit. I let my teeth graze the sensitive bud when I circle her entrance with my finger, then slide it into her, hooking up to rub her G-spot.

"Right there, right there… *right* there," she chants melodically. Her legs tremble, and I can already feel her cunt tightening and quivering around my finger.

That quick? Fuck yeah.

I smile against her pussy and then flick her clit with the tip of my tongue, teasing and circling until her back is arching off the bed and her arousal is sliding down my hand.

"Look how fast you're coming for me, drenching my tongue. Maybe you *can* be a good girl, Viv."

Goddamnit, this is the hottest thing I've ever experienced. I want her to ride my fucking face so I can *drown* in her.

RIP me, death by pussy. What a fucking way to go.

That's exactly what I want, her smothering me with her pussy. I stop suddenly, pulling my finger out of her and rising to my feet.

Her eyes snap open, blazing, and connect with mine. "Why would you stop when I was about to co—"

I cut her off by flopping onto the bed next to her and scooting up until I hit the headboard, pulling her on top of me in one swift motion.

She looks exquisite with heat in her eyes, her cheeks flushed red, her tits out and on display, and her pussy glistening from my tongue.

"Grab the headboard and ride my face."

Her eyebrows shoot up as if she didn't expect me to want it, but I do, and right the fuck now, or I'll, I dunno… *die*.

My hand hooks around her hip, and I haul her up to my face. After a beat, thank fuck, she springs into action, placing her knees on each side of my head and grabbing the wooden headboard. She's hovering over my mouth with her gaze lingering on mine, so close that I can feel the heat of her pussy, and it makes me impatient. I can't wait another second to swipe my tongue over her swollen folds.

My fingers dig into the soft flesh of her hips as I yank her down onto my face so I can really devour her, sealing my lips around her clit and sucking it into my mouth, alternating pressure. The soft whimper that tumbles from her lips has my cock leaking. I make a vow, right here and now, to spend the rest of the night worshiping her. Getting her out of my system so I don't want her so badly.

I move her hips back and forth, rocking her against my mouth, helping her set the rhythm until she finds her pace and she's writhing on my mouth with her head thrown back in pleasure.

I tease her tight hole with my tongue, groaning when she somehow gets even wetter. I'm having a real-life out-of-body experience right now, and I never wanna come down from it.

"That's it, baby," I praise her. "Fuck my face. Come on my tongue."

I alternate fucking her with my tongue, lapping at her clit, sucking it between my lips and rolling it, then it's only seconds before her entire body goes taut, and she comes with my name on her lips.

"Reese, Oh… god," she moans, dragging her clit over my lips frantically, the friction sending aftershocks through her already sensitive flesh. "Fuck, fuck, fuck."

I can honestly say I have never in my life been so close to coming in my pants until now, and that's just fucking embarrassing since I lost my virginity at sixteen.

Once her movements slow and she's able to let go of the headboard, I gently release her hips, and she sits back on my chest, a hazy, unfocused look in her sated eyes.

"Wow. Apparently, there *is* one thing you're good at."

My lips curve into a smirk. "You're only saying that because you haven't had my cock yet, babe."

Even after the orgasm she just had, her eyes darken at my comment, and her expression turns heated, wiping the grin from my lips. I lean up, sliding my hands along her jaw, cradling it in my hands as I dip my head forward to capture her lips.

Part of me regrets ever stepping foot in her dorm tonight.

Ever touching her, kissing her, tasting her because I know that she'll be stuck in my head like a sickness I can't get rid of.

I should've known better than to agree to just one night because it won't be enough. I'm not looking for a relationship, but what I want is for more than a few hours with her.

There's no way I can play out every fantasy I've had of this girl in the span of a few hours.

My hands slide beneath the fabric of her tank top where it's still halfway on and yank it up, only breaking our kiss to pull it over her head. My fingers reach for the clasp of her bra and

quickly get it unhooked. She pulls back, letting the lace straps fall down her arms, freeing her breasts completely.

I almost swallow my fucking tongue when my gaze drops to her bare tits. I've never seen anything more perfect in my life.

They're even bigger than what they looked like when spilling from the cups. They're heavy and full. Natural. Sexy as fuck.

Pert, rosy nipples turned up, begging to be sucked. Those tiny little barbells through the center. Which is why I immediately lower my mouth to the peak and suck it into my mouth, then let it go with a pop.

She's straddling my lap now, her bare, still-soaked pussy brushing against my cock through my jeans, and each time she wiggles her hips, I find my control fraying at the edges.

"I need you," I pant, pulling back from her chest.

She nods, reaching for the button of my jeans, flicks it open, and drags the zipper down. Together, we work both jeans and briefs down my hips without her ever moving from my lap.

Once I kick them aside, we're fitted together, skin to skin. I can feel the heat of her pussy along the length of my cock, and when she rocks her hips, a whimper sounding from the back of her throat, I almost fucking lose it.

The thick, weeping head of my cock brushes against her clit each time she moves until we're both groaning, chasing the friction. We're frantically grinding like we're teenagers, and yet it may be the hottest thing I've ever done. Her arms slide around my neck as her fingers tangle into the hair at my nape, and she circles her hips.

"Like this," she breathes. "I want you like this. Just like this, Reese."

I nod with my lips against her already sweat-slicked skin, out of my fucking mind delirious for her. She could ask me for anything right now, and I would make it happen.

Her hand trails down between us, and she closes her fist around my cock, using her thumb to spread the precum seeping from the tip.

I'm pretty sure I'm hallucinating when her gaze lifts to mine and she brings her thumb to her mouth, sucking my cum off the pad.

Fuck. Fuck. Fuck.

"Need to be inside you, Viv. Right the fuck now," I groan.

I can't wait another goddamn second to feel my cock inside her.

"I'm on birth control, and I'm clean," she mumbles against my lips.

I trace my tongue along her bottom lip, grazing it with my teeth and then sucking it into my mouth. "Me too. Testing is a team requirement. You sure?" I say between nipping and sucking her mouth.

She nods vehemently and sinks down a fraction of an inch on my cock, causing us to groan in unison at the feel of her tight heat clamping down on me.

My arms tighten around her when she drops her head back, her mouth falling open, moaning soft and so fucking sweet. Sinking all the way down to the hilt. Until her clit is brushing against my pelvis, until I'm so deep inside of her that the head of my cock meets her cervix, bottoming out.

It feels so damn good that my eyes roll back. Being buried inside of her, feeling her sweet little cunt fluttering around me as she rocks her hips is enough to make my balls draw up.

There's no way I'm lasting being inside of her *bare.*

Not when she's so tight she's practically choking my cock. I already feel the base of my spine tingling with the need to empty inside her.

In one motion, I pull out and flip us over, putting her back on the mattress, and making my way back between her parted thighs, fitting my hips between them. I hitch her leg up on my side with one hand and then reach between us, dragging my cock through her silky wetness, rubbing the blunt head against her clit before sliding home again.

"Right there," she pants when I thrust deep, swiveling my hips and brushing against her G-spot. I slowly pull out of her, only to slam back inside, increasing my pace and fucking her harder and deeper. Trying to plant myself even further inside of her with each surge of my hips.

It isn't enough. I won't ever get enough of her, can't fuck her deep enough. Hard enough.

Her nails drag down my back to the point of pain, and it only makes me more fucking insane with need for her. I want her marks on me.

When her head lolls and her eyes drop shut, I reach down and grasp her face, turning her back to face me. "Watch me fucking you, Vivienne. Watch how good you're taking my cock."

She whimpers, her pussy tightening around me, and when my thumb brushes against her clit, her back arches with pleasure. I can feel how close she is to exploding around me, to flooding my cock with her cum.

At the last second, I pull out of her completely, my heart thrashing wildly. Before she even has a chance to protest, I flip her onto her stomach and grab her hips, hauling her perfect, heart-shaped ass up in the air, leaving her cheek pressed into the mattress. Her pussy and her ass on display, waiting to get fucked. I lean forward and sink my teeth into one pert ass cheek, as wetness from her pussy drips down her thighs.

So fucking wet.

With my hands on her hips, I push back inside of her until my stomach is flush with her ass and I'm buried deep. I grip her cheeks, spreading them open so I can watch my cock disappearing into her pretty little pussy as I fuck her. Watching it stretch to take me, swallowing and coating my dick in her arousal.

I use her hips as leverage as I start to move, pounding into her from behind, her ass shaking with each slap of my hips. My thrusts are brutal and punishing, fucking her up onto the bed while she begs.

"I'm going to come, Reese... Please, I- I…"

I gather her arousal on my thumb, pressing the pad of my finger against her asshole, watching it contract as I slowly press the tip in.

Fuck, yeah.

Taking my time, I dip my finger in, then withdraw it until she's relaxed, and ready for all of my thumb. I press it forward as I fuck her, slowly sinking further into her tight hole until it's finally buried completely in her ass.

She cries out, her pussy clamping down on me while her ass is as full of me.

I guide my finger in slowly, using my other hand to hold her hips as I thrust into her pussy in the same rhythm with my dick, my balls pulling up tight.

I'm so goddamn close.

Slamming my hips forward, I push my thumb deeper in her ass one last time, and she explodes, her back arching, her fingers grasping at the sheets, coming so hard that I can feel her wetness against my fucking stomach.

I groan, dropping my forehead against her back, folding my body over her, emptying myself inside of her, the tight walls of her cunt milking every drop from my balls. So greedy, she wants it all.

I can't even form words as I keep rocking my hips slowly until I'm completely spent, and then we're collapsing onto the bed. I pull out of her gently and drop my gaze to where my cum is seeping out of her pretty little cunt in a thick creamy mess, my eyes flaring at the sight. I have the inexplicable urge to gather it up with my fingers and shove it back inside of her.

"Give me five minutes, and we're doing that again," I say breathlessly.

Viv smirks. "Sure you can get it up again that quickly? It's okay if you're a one and done kinda guy. I won't judge you."

My brow rises. "Yeah? Why don't you climb back on my dick and find out?"

She sits up, her blue eyes flaring with determination as she straddles my lap and then leans down, licking my nipple.

"Okay, let's see who will tap out first, *All-Star*."

1 / viv

New Year, Same Bullshit

Now

My idea of a perfect Friday night is one where I'm wearing the same holey, worn Smashing Pumpkins T-shirt I've had since freshman year of high school, bundled up in my bed, under my favorite blanket, watching a cult classic horror movie or a nineties rom-com while I'm snacking on SweeTarts.

Don't get me wrong, I love a good party like the next girl, but I'm an extroverted homebody. I need to recharge after being around people for an extended amount of time, and the best place to do that is the comfort of my bed, surrounded by all the things I love. After a very emotionally trying Christmas at home, I *desperately* need to recharge.

I'm drained. Completely exhausted from being home surrounded by a constant state of chaos, and with the current state of my life, it doesn't appear that anything will be normal for a while.

I'm craving *normal*. Starving for my typical routine. Days

filled with classes, and homework, and binge-watching reruns of *Paranormal Caught on Camera* with my best friend, Hallie. Recording episodes of our podcast *Spaced Out*, diving into the unknown mysteries of the world. Nights spent at my tiny desk in my even tinier dorm, bent over my laptop, pouring my heart and soul into a fictional world that I sometimes wish I could just disappear into.

I miss the comfort and familiarity of my everyday life at Orleans U.

Except, even there, things have changed. After several months of him being her *spicy tutor* and her freaking out about if their relationship was real or not at the end of first semester, Hallie finally admitted her feelings for Lane, who just so happens to be our friend Eli's older brother, after being in love with him for practically *forever*. Fortunately, Lane is just as obsessed with her as she is him, and now the two are officially a couple and so in love that it's sickening. Seriously, my stomach feels like I ate an entire pound of SweeTarts all by myself.

Don't get me wrong, I am so geekily happy for her. She's my best friend in the entire world with the purest heart of anyone you'll ever meet. She deserves the entire universe and more, and even though I wasn't one hundred percent sold on Lane at the beginning, now I know that he'll take care of Hallie in a way that only he can. And I mean… even *Eli* has a serious girlfriend now, Ari. I think she's awesome too.

Which leaves me… single as a pringle.

I'm fine with that. It's just… *so* much change. My head feels like everything is spinning at a hundred miles an hour, and I'm stuck holding on for dear life.

Especially since I found out three days ago that my mother lost her job. *Again*. That's not the surprising part.

Not when it has happened no less than five times this year alone.

The part that completely pulled the rug out from under me is that my mom wouldn't have even mentioned that she lost her job except I got home from the grocery store the day after Christmas to discover a bright-red stamped eviction notice pinned to the front door. Which means every single dime I've been saving for this semester's dorm fees?

Poof. Up like smoke right in front of my eyes.

It's going to have to go to Mama's landlord so she won't be evicted. And now that she's out of work again, I'm going to need to cover her rent until she's employed again.

I have no clue what I'm going to do or where I'm going to go when I'm back on campus. Thank god my tuition is covered by my scholarship, but my housing and cost of living? Yeah, that's all on me.

Sighing, I pull my knees to my chest and rest my chin on top, squeezing my eyes shut.

Most college freshmen only have to worry about their grades, which sorority is throwing the next mixer, where the best alcohol is being served, who their next hookup is going to be.

I *wish* my life were that easy. I wish those were the only things that I had to worry about, but I don't have that luxury, and most of the time, I accept it for what it is. Except in moments like these where sometimes the weight feels too heavy and my shoulders feel like they'll crumble from the pressure.

"Viv?"

My gaze snaps to my mom, who's standing in the entryway to the living room, wrapped up in a thick dark green cardigan that hangs on her small frame, her eyes puffy and her hair knotted and greasy from days without washing it. She's a ghost of the woman she used to be. It's like when my dad died, he took so much of her with him.

"What's wrong, Mama?" I'm already rising from the couch, depositing my favorite blanket onto the worn cushion, and making my way over to her. The entire time I've been home for Christmas, I've been trying to get the apartment clean and back under control, all while taking care of her. Trying to get her to bathe daily, eat at least one meal, take her vitamins as she should.

She sniffles as she attempts to tug her lips up into a semblance of a smile. "I just wanted to tell you… thank you. I'm sorry things are like this, sweetheart. I want to be better, I do. I just… Nothing feels right anymore. I don't feel like me, and I miss your dad so much."

Before she can say anything else, I pull her into my arms and hug her tightly to me as I murmur, "It's okay, Mama. How about we brush your hair? Get you some fresh pajamas? I bet that'll make you feel better."

She nods against my shoulder, so I pull back and paste on a bright smile, even though it's the last thing I feel right now.

I hate seeing her this way. I hate being the parent when I'm supposed to be the child. But this is my reality now.

"Go ahead to your room, and I'll be just a second," I tell her as my phone pings for the third time on the couch.

Once she disappears back through her bedroom door, I pick up my phone from the arm and unlock it, opening the string of messages Hallie sent.

Hallie: Okay, so let's ignore the fact that it's at your least favorite person's house, buuuut tomorrow is NYE Viv and you have to ring in the New Year with your best friend!

Hallie: The party is at Reese's parents' cabin, but it's going to be soooo much fun and I promise to keep at least a six foot distance between you two at all times. Pinky swear.

Hallie: If you don't answer me in the next thirty seconds I'm going to FaceTime you and not let you off until you say yes. 😇😇😇

Laughing, I roll my eyes just as my phone begins to vibrate in my hand with an incoming FaceTime. I swipe across the screen and answer.

A second later, Hallie's dark, curly hair comes into view, pulled back with a neon green headband decorated with tiny purple alien heads. Her unique, quirky style is something I've always loved about her, how she has no problem with her self-expression.

"I'm going to ignore the fact that you answered the phone so fast—it was clearly already in your hand." She sniffs, arching a dark brow. "And focus on the fact that I miss you *so* much. Seeing your face only makes it worse."

I can hear Lane chuckle in the background, followed by an "oof" as Hallie elbows him in the ribs.

"I miss you too, space babe," I tell her, leaning against the hallway wall. "How are things there?" Even if I wasn't feeling the pressure and stress of things with my mom, I would want to be back on campus with Hallie. Being with her makes me happy. A shy smile forms on her lips, her eyes darting to the side where I know Lane is sitting off-camera. "Things are… good. Really good. You could even say great, really." The natural pink of her cheeks deepens as she blushes harder.

The girl is getting the D on the regular, and she has no idea how to even talk about it out loud.

"I'm glad to hear it, Hal." Lowering my voice, I say quietly, "I can't wait to get back to campus. I have a couple more things to figure out here, and then I should be able to head back."

Hallie groans as she runs a hand through her unruly hair. "Viv, I'm pretty sure this is the longest we've been apart since, like… I dunno, third grade? Will you please, pretty please with all of the majestic Bigfoot love on top, come to the NYE party at Reese's?"

The mention of his name makes my stomach clench. No one, and I mean absolutely *no one*, knows about the night we spent together, and every time I'm around him, it feels like I'm waiting for a bomb to detonate. In the form of stupidly attractive, ridiculously charming, and even more annoying Reese Landry.

He's the biggest player on campus, and the fact that he's headed to the MLB after being Orleans U's all-star catcher with thighs that would make any girl's mouth water, well… that doesn't help the girls throwing themselves at his feet. Typical rich playboy persona. Everything's handed right to him on a shiny, silver platter.

Not that I pay attention to him or anything. *Definitely* not. "Hallie, I love you. You know I do, but you know I can't stand that boy equally as much. His living purpose on this earth is to annoy me."

She laughs. "Honestly, you might be right. He does talk about you a lot." My heart speeds up like the silly traitor that it is. "But seriously, it'll just be us, and Eli and Ari and, of course, Grant. A few other people from the team, Lane says. A chill, fun way to bring in the New Year, and I can't do it without you."

My eyes flick to Mama's room as I chew my lip. I don't know if she's ready for me to leave her yet, and now there's the entire new problem of handling her landlord, and also me not having a place to live after next week.

"I don't know. I've got a lot going on here. Just… I'll call you back, 'kay?"

Begrudgingly, she nods, but before we hang up, she stops me. "Viv? You know you can talk to me about anything, right? No matter what it is. I'll always be here, and I love you."

"Thanks, Hal. I love you too." I press the End button,

hanging up quickly before walking through the door to Mama's bedroom. I *want* to ring in the New Year with my friends. I just have to figure out how I can make it happen.

REESE LANDRY IS *DISGUSTINGLY* RICH.

Like having a private jet, yacht vacation, attending the Met Gala kind of rich. The luxurious lifestyles of the Real Housewives of wherever have nothing on him and his family.

Not that I wasn't already very much aware of the fact, but walking into the front door of his ostentatiously large "cabin" that serves as only *one* of his family's vacation homes, it's impossible to ignore.

Not when the looming three-story mansion smacks you right in the face. A mansion is *still* a mansion even if you make it rustic. A cabin is a house made of logs. This is no cabin.

God, why am I even here?

I should've never let Hallie talk me into this. I got Mom situated and was able to slip away for the party at her insistence, but now I'm having major regrets before I even make it over the threshold.

A rush of warmth hits my cheeks as the front door closes behind me, the sound of the heavy door lost in a sea of bodies moving to music booming from large speakers in the corners of the room.

So much for a small, *intimate* party, I see. I should've known that these guys are incapable of doing anything less than larger than life.

Typical Reese. He's the definition of "over-the-top."

Mumbling excuse me's and sorry's, I make my way through

the crowd toward the kitchen, parting the random people until I finally see a familiar face.

"Grant!"

His head whips in my direction, and an easy smile splits his lips as he opens his arms, then pulls me into them. His clean scent surrounds me, and I groan inwardly.

Dark blond hair, chiseled jaw, adorable dimples that always pop when he smiles.

Why couldn't I be attracted to Grant? Sweet, charming, quiet Grant.

He's hot as hell, and you'd be blind if you didn't see it. Trust me, I see it. He just… doesn't do it for me, I guess. Of course, I wouldn't be attracted to the nice and considerate friend of Lane's.

"What's up, gorgeous? I didn't think you were gonna show tonight," he says, bringing the red Solo cup in his hand to his lips and taking a sip.

"Me neither. I just decided earlier today. I thought it was going to be a small get-together? This looks like half the damn campus."

My eyes flick back to the crowd of people, and I wonder how even in this stupidly big house, there are still so many people.

"Yeah, well, you know Reese." He chuckles.

Unfortunately, I know him all too well. Intimately well, but I keep that little tidbit to myself.

Within the first day of meeting him, I knew exactly the type of guy he was. The swagger, the cocky flirting, constantly surrounded by women. I knew a rich fuckboy when I saw one, and ever since then, it's been a constant state of bickering between us. Mostly on my end, since he's unable to take a hint.

"Looks like you need one of these." A red cup appears in front of me, and I take it into my hand, my nose wrinkling with the strong smell of alcohol permeating from it. I wasn't feeling a party tonight, but maybe a party is *exactly* what I need to forget about the shitshow that my life is right now, even if it's just for a night. Before I return to campus and I'm homeless… and possibly a soon-to-be college dropout.

I waste no time taking a too large sip, the liquid burning its way down my throat and immediately making my eyes water. So much for the mascara I applied in the car.

"Jesus, Grant, what the hell is this, battery acid?" I sputter when I finally catch my breath. "It tastes like absolute shit."

His eyebrows wag. "My secret recipe. Like swallowing down fire, but it gets the job done quick. Trust me."

A shiver rolls through my body at the lingering taste on my tongue, and I want to wash it away with almost anything at this point. This is absolutely terrible, but let's just hope he's not wrong about how fast it works.

"Thanks, I think? Oh, have you seen Hallie?"

"She and Lane were on the second floor by the beer pong table last time I saw them." He raises his glass for me to clink, and when I do, we take another sip together, both of us nearly choking.

"God, that just gets worse and worse," I say through clenched teeth. "I'm gonna try and find them. I'll find you later, 'kay?"

He nods and ambles off toward a girl he's been eyeing in the corner, his dimpled grin plastered on his handsome face.

The staircase leading to the second floor is as packed as the bottom floor, littered with couples hanging on the railing, making out against the wall, and sitting on the steps huddled together, making it harder to push my way to the top. But once I do, I immediately spot my best friend and her boyfriend exactly where Grant said they'd be.

"Hallie!" I rush over to her, only pausing to take in the cute-as-hell outfit she's wearing tonight. I am *definitely* going to have to borrow that dress.

Her entire face lights up when she sees me, and then her arms are around my neck, and she's squeezing me so tightly to her that I can hardly breathe. For a second, I pause and sink into her embrace. It's only been a little while since we've seen each other, but the last couple of weeks have been rough, and truth be told, I need my best friend.

I just wish that I could tell her about everything that's happening.

I just… I don't want to burden my friends with my family problems and dorm drama. I plan on telling her, but for now, I'm just going to suck it up, put on a smile, and pretend everything is fine and dandy.

She's so happy with Lane.

After finally getting together during winter break, they're now in the honeymoon stage of their *official* relationship, where everything is fresh and new, and they're madly in love. So, I don't want to take a single ounce of her happiness away. No one wants to be the friend that bursts their friend's blissful bubble. Not after how long it took for them to get here.

And I know Hallie—the moment she finds out something is wrong, she's going to try and fix it, and I just don't want to bother her with my shit right now. No, I'll just figure it out myself.

"I missed you so freakin' much, Viv!" she whisper-yells into my ear over the music before pulling back to look at me. "Okay, I am obsessed with that sweater. I need to borrow it!"

I laugh, glancing down at the distressed black sweater I threw on with jeans, paired with my favorite worn pair of black-checkered Vans. "Ummm, funny because I thought the same thing about that dress! Babe, you are rocking it."

She glances down at it, then back to me. "Really?"

"Yes, really! It's literally perfect for your body." I turn toward Lane and toss him a smile. "What's up, lover boy?"

"Viv." He nods, a teasing smile on his lips. "Been quiet without you around."

Hallie reaches down, lacing our fingers together. "What he means is *boring*. It's been absolutely, undeniably boring without you, Viv. I'm so glad you came tonight! I was worried for a minute that you wouldn't come. You know, because of…*Reese*."

"Yeah, we—"

"Talking about me already, Viv?" A deep, gravelly voice that absolutely should *not* make my thighs clench the way that they do sounds behind me, and I already know exactly who it belongs to before I even turn around.

Because that's the same voice that whispered the dirtiest things I've ever heard in my ear as he fucked me balls-deep from behind.

He drives me insane. Literally, insane.

My eyes flick down his body to the jeans that seem to be made to fit his thick catcher thighs and sculpted ass, back up to the red Hellcats Baseball shirt that stretches over his chest and hugs every inch of the muscles in his biceps, and up to the two dimples in his cheeks.

Those stupid dimples.

And his stupid, stupidly charming smile.

And his unruly hair that he never brushes, I'm sure. Only uses his fingers to run through the strands and keep them off his forehead.

Stupid, soft, perfect hair that I spent one night tugging on, and now I'll never forget how soft it felt between my fingers.

Reese Landry is the epitome of a drop-dead gorgeous, powerful athlete, and it makes me want to hurl.

Everything comes easy to him. He's filthy rich, has the world at his fingertips, and is naturally good at everything. And of course, girls throw themselves at him like they've lost every ounce of self-respect the moment he steps over the threshold.

Easy.

"Wow, it's as if you were summoned. Like a demon or something," I mutter, dragging my eyes away from him to stare at a space on the wall before flicking my gaze down to my chipped lavender nails, feigning boredom.

You see, the one and only time I let him touch me was a mistake. Obviously, a lapse in judgment that cannot and will not *ever* be repeated.

He can't ever know that I still think about that night. He will never know that when I lie in bed and I'm horny and alone, it's his name that is on my lips as I come.

Never.

A secret that will follow me to the grave.

Guys like Reese love the chase. They want anything that gives them a challenge, and that's the only reason he's even interested in me. It's the only reason he acts like a love- obsessed fool when I reject him. But unlike most girls, I know exactly the game that he's playing, and joke's on him—I can play it *better.*

Better than he could ever imagine.

"Viv, it's been too long since you insulted me. I forgot how much I missed it," he says flirtatiously with a wink. When he lifts his hand to brush his hair out of his face, I see a shiny, thin gold chain hanging from around his neck. That looks new.

Of course, rich boy needs new bling to show off his status.

Lane snickers, and I narrow my eyes at him, wiping the smirk right from his face. He drags his hand through his dirty-blond hair, and looks at Hallie, avoiding my gaze.

"Well, please, stick around. I've got plenty of insults ready to ruin your night. You know how much I love bringing your ego down a few notches. Someone has to do it. I may even list it on my resume as my community service."

His smile only widens.

He's impossible. Undeterred.

Things have been even more tense between us since the night we… were *together*… over two months ago. Since then, he's doubled down on his flirting, and I've been doing my best to pretend he doesn't exist.

Impossible when I know that he's this sex god with the dirtiest mouth. But avoidance is my thing, so I'm going to act like it never happened and pray that eventually my vagina will stop throbbing when he walks into a room.

"I need another drink," I mumble, looking down at my now empty cup. "You guys want anything?"

Hallie and Lane both decline, so I shrug and turn on my heel in search of something more to help take the edge off.

I'm almost to the kitchen when I feel my phone vibrating in my back pocket, and after ignoring it for the first time, the fact that it's ringing again probably means it's something important.

I walk to the end of the hallway, finding a quiet room to duck inside before pulling it out and answering when I see Mama's name on the screen.

"Mama? Is everything okay?"

A throaty sniffle echoes through the speaker, and she clears her throat. "Hi, sweetie. I just… uh, I wanted to call and let you know that Ron stopped by after you left earlier."

My stomach plummets at the mention of her slimy landlord. "What's going on? What did he say? Sorry if it's loud—I just got to my friend's house for the New Year's party." I walk to the en suite bathroom and step inside, trying to drown out some of the outside noise.

"Oh, it's not that important. He was just stopping by to remind me that if I don't have the rent payment for him tomorrow, the eviction process will be starting. He can't allow me any more time. I'm sorry, sweetie. I hate that I even have to ask you to do this for me..."

I'm going to throw up in this bathroom. Shit, I was hoping for a few more days to try and figure out a way to keep the money I saved for my dorm, some type of Hail Mary, but it looks like that's not happening.

"Okay, I know. I'm going to work on it, Mama."

She sniffles, and the sound sends another fissure into my heart. I felt so much guilt for leaving early, and now I feel even worse.

"Thank you, honey. I just feel so terrible, Viv. Like I can't do anything right, and no matter how hard I try, I just keep letting you down. I *hate* letting you down." More sniffles.

"Mama, it's okay. Please don't worry about the rent, okay? I'll get it handled. Should I leave and come back home? I can be there in a couple of hours tops. I hate that you're there alone."

"No, no," she stops me. "I'm okay. I want you to enjoy your party. I just got a little worried when he stopped by, so I figured I would call you."

It's just a kick right to the gut. I thought I had a little more time to try and make it work, to try to find a way to get some money. But now, I'm definitely fucked.

"I might be coming back home this week. I don't have a dorm this semester, and I haven't figured out what I'm going to do just yet. So, don't give away my room." I laugh humorously, like it will help lighten the mood at all. It's not funny, but if I don't laugh, I'll cry.

"I'm sorry, honey. I promise this year will be better. I'll try harder, and it's going to get better for us, okay? I'll try and find a new job and start saving money."

I let out a soft sigh. "I know, Mama. I'll talk to you soon, okay? Love you."

We say a quick goodbye after she reassures me yet again that

I don't need to head home for the night, and I end the call, resting my forehead against the bathroom door and taking a few deep breaths.

"Viv?"

The voice startles me, and I nearly jump out of my skin, my hand flying to my heart to stop its erratic beating. My phone clatters to the tile floor and makes a sound that I'm honestly now scared to see. My luck, it'll be broken after the week I've had.

Reese is standing near the desk in the corner of the room, the most serious look I've ever seen on his face.

"Fuck, Reese, you are entirely too quiet for somebody that's your size and ego. Jesus!"

He walks closer, bending down to pick my phone up off the ground, and hands it back to me. The top part of the screen is shattered, but it seems to still work, and that's all that matters. I shove it into my back pocket. "Great. Love this for me."

"What happened to your housing?" he says, not letting me brush past him.

"You were eavesdropping on my conversation?" I scoff. "*Of course,* you were."

His shoulder dips. "You're in my room, Viv. I came back to grab a shirt for a girl who fell in the pool."

"Everyone's knight in shining armor, that's you." I gag dramatically just to send my sarcasm home.

He bites his lip to suppress a smirk, and my eyes roll. Every time I insult him, it's as if I'm complimenting him. I do not understand what's going on in that tiny little brain of his. "I know you can't stop thinking about the night you rode my face, but stop deflecting the question, Brentwood. What happened to your housing?"

For a second, I'm silent as I try to figure out the right way to handle this situation. He's got the loudest mouth of anyone I know, and all I need is for him to go straight to Lane, trying to figure out what happened. Because Lane will immediately go to Hallie, and then everything will go up in flames.

I would rather no one know what happened. Part of me is ashamed and embarrassed that we're in this situation, and the other part of me feels guilty for feeling that way in the first place. "It's really none of your business, Reese. Now, if you'll excuse me, I'd like to try and spend the rest of my night attempting to have fun."

I go to step around him, and he mirrors my step, causing me to run straight into his chest. Ignoring the delicious smell of his cologne, I tilt my chin up to stare at him. "*Move.*"

"Make me."

That's the thing about Reese. He has the ability to push my buttons, to push me to the point of insanity with little to nothing, and it's completely nerve-racking.

"Tell me, Viv. Are you dropping out? Does Hallie know about this?"

My gaze flicks to the door and back to him before I sigh and step around him, successfully this time, and shut the open door, drowning out the party.

"Can you please, for like once in your life, keep your mouth shut?" I say as I walk back over, rubbing my temples to alleviate the ache that's forming in my head.

I expect a flirty comeback in typical Reese fashion, but all I hear is crickets.

Fine.

"There's a situation at home, and it requires me to drain my savings, which means I can't afford housing this semester. I don't qualify for assistance, and even if I did, it would be too late get it." Exhaling, I drag my gaze to his. "I'm *only telling* you this because I don't want Hallie to know the actual reason I have to leave my dorm. I don't want to burden her with this, Reese, so I swear to god I will chop your dick off and feed it to you through a straw if you tell a single soul."

"Not how I imagined you touching my dick again, but heard. Why though? Why not talk to Hallie and stay with her and Lane?" he asks, his brow furrowing. "You know she'd lose her mind if she knew you were going through it and never told her."

"Because the last thing I want to do is move in with my best friend, who is newly in a relationship, who also lives with said new boyfriend. I'm not going to be the hang-on friend who has to interrupt the honeymoon stage of their relationship."

He nods. "Yeah, I guess I understand that. But I still think you should tell her."

Swallowing, I feel my pride swelling inside of me with every word. I hate being in this situation, and I hate even more that now he knows this vulnerable, exposed side of me that I've been hiding from the world.

Him. Out of all people.

"I plan to, but in the meantime, I have to figure out where I'm going to stay this semester, clearly it has to be my top priority."

He shrugs. "I mean, I have an extra room. Stay with me." My jaw falls to the floor.

He *has* to be joking… *Right*?

2 / reese

New Year, Same Girl

The words are out of my mouth before I even have time to think about them. To even really consider what I'm offering her. Which I clearly should have done *before* offering to let her move into my house.

It's no secret I'm into Viv—I haven't exactly pursued her quietly. But despite upping the charm and giving my best, and I mean my absolute *best*, efforts to secure a repeat of our October hookup, she's completely shut me out. No matter how hard I've tried. I'm not totally delusional, so I know inviting a girl I'm objectively attracted to to live with me when she can't stand me would be… complicated.

The type of complication I don't really need in my life this semester when I'm headed to the MLB right after graduation. But I *do* have a spare room, and if it helps to offer it to her, then fuck it. I may be reckless, but I'm not heartless.

Plus, I'm pretty sure she'd rather live *anywhere* but with me anyway.

Especially with how shit has been since that night at the bar when I went home with her.

The same night I've thought about every day since.

The night that we don't speak about and she does her best to pretend never happened. She does her best to ignore me when we're around each other and resorts to talking shit when she can't.

That happens when your best friends are obsessed with each other, and we're forced to tag along as third wheels everywhere we go. I kinda feel bad for Grant—he probably doesn't know what to do with the four of us.

A laugh bubbles out of her, and my brow rises. "Please tell me you're not serious right now? Even *you* aren't that insane, Reese."

Apparently so. Or at least that's how she makes me feel every time I'm in her presence.

"Damn, Viv, if I didn't know how much of a catch I am, you'd really fuck with a guy's ego." I pause, dragging my hand through my hair. "Look, I live in a house a few miles from campus. I have two bedrooms, and the other room is basically just a guest room. You could move in with me. Solves your problem."

"Yeah, so easy. Just move in with you, and all of my problems are solved." Her cheeks flush red as she says it, but then she scoffs. "You do realize offering me a room in your house is not going to magically make me want to sleep with you, right?"

I shrug. "You know, for someone who claims to not want my dick, you sure do bring it up a lot. Plus, you're the only one who hates me. Everyone else loves me."

"Right. The crowd parts for the great Reese Landry. How could I ever forget? Orleans University's all-star." Her jaw ticks. I can tell how much she hates being in this spot. Me knowing something about her she's determined to keep hidden.

"Listen, take it or leave it, that's up to you, but I have an extra room, Viv. Plus, moving in with me means that you won't have to tell Hallie why and make it her problem. Up to you. You want it, it's yours."

She pauses, her throat bobbing as she swallows, then shakes her head. "Appreciate it, but no, thank you. I'm going to figure it out tomorrow when I make it back to campus. I just… *please* don't say anything, okay? This entire conversation never even happened. I'd really just like to go back to pretending the other doesn't exist, okay?" As if I could pretend she doesn't exist.

When I don't answer, she steps closer, her blue eyes blazing. "Promise me, Reese."

"Sure. Fine." If she wants to keep her friends in the dark, then that's on her, but I did my good deed for the day.

With that, she brushes past me, wrenching the door open, and storms back to the party.

"FUCK YEAH." I groan, the vibration of the massage chair loosening my taut, aching, and overworked muscles. "Feels so fucking good. Like when you're getting your dick sucked and she accidentally uses her teeth a little, but it still feels fucking amazing, so you let her keep going."

"I agree," Grant adds from my right.

Lane sighs heavily, and if I didn't have my eyes shut, I'd see him probably roll his eyes. "Sometimes I wonder why I'm friends with the two of you."

"Because we're your best friends, and you love our bromance, duh." I grin, opening an eye to see him shaking his head. "Plus, who else would you listen to Taylor Swift in the car with? It's weird if you do it alone."

"*You* listen to Taylor Swift while you work out," he replies flatly.

Okay, true.

"Yeah, but it's only weird when you do it. I'm comfortable with my masculinity. Plus, you know that 'I Did Something Bad' gets me in the zone. It's my best pump."

This is also true, and he knows it. He just likes to give me shit where he can because that's what we do, but at the end of the day, we've got each other's backs through thick and thin. Ever since freshman year when I didn't know a soul, Lane and Grant have been there. It's always been the three of us, and now that we're halfway through senior year, real life is smacking me right in the fucking face.

Next year, everything will be different. We'll go our separate ways. Lane will stay here or follow wherever Hallie goes. Grant'll be a redshirt senior, and me? Well, I'm the number one draft pick overall.

I'm going to whoever has the first pick, and honestly? I don't give a shit where it is. It'll be a stepping stone to the majors and the dream I've had since I was a kid.

"What's up for this weekend? We hitting parties? The Redlight?" Grant asks, interrupting my thoughts.

I shrug. "I don't care, just as long as I can burn off all this extra energy I've got. I always get antsy before the season starts."

Lane's eyebrows rise. "Does that mean you're going to fuck your way through the dance team roster again?"

"Nope." The *p* pops on my lips. "I'm working on the debate team. You know how much I love a girl who loves to argue."

My phone vibrates in my lap, and a text message pops up from a number I don't recognize.

Unknown number: I'll probably regret this every day for the rest of my life, but can I… see the room before I make a final decision? Actually, I'm already regretting texting you.

• • •

A GRIN SPLITS my face as I scan the message again. Of all the shit I saw on my bingo card for this year, this sure as fuck wasn't on it. Vivienne Brentwood is texting me. After the other night, it's the last message I expected to receive.

REESE: ***Sorry, new phone, who dis?***

After typing a quick response just to piss her off, I save her number in my phone.

Vivienne: *eye roll emoji* Invite many girls to live in your house, Landry? Why am I not surprised?

Reese: Shrugs* You know me, always willing to lend a helping hand. Or finger. Or *eggplant emoji*

Vivienne: You're disgusting. I knew this was a bad idea, never mind.

Reese: Just a joke Viv. Not a dick, don't take it so hard.

Vivienne: I hate you.

Reese: 444 Boudreaux Ave.

"Who are you texting, grinning like that?" Grant asks, his eyebrow raised in question.

I guess now's as good a time as any to tell them that I might have actually lost my mind. It's not like they wouldn't find out the second it happened anyway. Not with chatty-love-pants over here.

"Wellllll, about that..." I say, trailing off. I already know I'm never going to hear the end of it from these two. "I think Viv might be moving in with me and taking my spare room."

Both Lane and Grant freeze, and dead silence fills the room.

Time ticks by, and I look between the two of them as they look back and forth between each other, and then Grant throws his head back and fucking loses it.

He's turning red with how hard he's laughing. No legible sound is coming from his mouth, just wheezes and fragments of words.

"I fucking hate you both," I mutter and turn my attention back to the massage chair, upping the intensity for my lower back.

"Let me get this straight," Lane says through his wheezes. "*Vivienne,* the girl who can't even stand to be in your presence for five minutes, is moving *in* with you. Into your *actual* house. *With you still living there*? Did you blackmail her? No, wait, she lost a bet, didn't she? Did she hit her head and forget that she hates you? Got amnesia?"

A long sigh echoes from my lips.

These two. Comedians. Someone give them a fucking Netflix special.

"Where else would I go, Lane? I'm not moving *out* of my house so Vivienne can move in. Be serious."

"Dude, I'm being fucking serious," he says, disbelief still written all over his face. "I'm just not understanding what is happening right now. I thought you were joking."

"Yeah," Grant says while still trying to gain his composure.

"Well, I'm not," I tell them both. "It's not even for sure yet, so don't say shit to anyone. I'm talking to *you*, Lane."

He flips me the finger and rolls his eyes. "I'm not saying anything because I want nothing to do with that shit."

"Yeah, okay, you tell your girlfriend every time you take a dump," I retort.

"Watch it."

My lips tilt into a smirk as I shrug. "True though. I love Hallie, you know that. She's my girl. But this is between me and Viv. Who knows, maybe she'll decide not to. Either way, I don't want you two saying shit."

"Hand on the Bible. But you do know I'm *never* going to stop giving you shit about this," Grant counters. "You're down so bad for that girl it's unreal, and having her living with you? A recipe for fucking disaster if you ask me. Dude, you literally just signed up for five months of blue balls with a girl that gets you hard when she *breathes*. And let's be real, you've got a better chance of fucking *me* than her."

"That's because you fuck anything that moves," I tell him.

"Fair."

I'M NOT surprised when there's a knock at my front door later that night. Before I even open it, I know Vivienne is on the other side of it. She wouldn't have texted me in the first place if she wasn't planning to take up my offer of becoming my new roomie. Which has put a pep in my step all fucking day.

A shit-eating grin flits to my lips as I grab the door handle and fling the door open.

"Please know if there was *any* other option, and I truly mean a*ny* other option aside from living in a tent under the interstate or becoming a college dropout before even finishing my first year, then I wouldn't be here," Viv says the moment I open the door and see her standing on the doorstep, her arms folded over her chest.

My eyes travel down the length of her body, taking in the tight black T-shirt and acid-wash blue jean shorts she's paired with an old, checkered pair of Vans. She's got on a black choker that looks like it's straight from the nineties or something, and her hair is loose, hanging almost to her waist.

She looks good enough to fucking eat.

I lift my arm higher while holding the door open wider, my lips turned up in a smirk. "Hi, Vivienne, it's so nice to see you too. Please, come in."

Her eyes roll, and she ducks under my arm, crossing the threshold into my house.

When I sent her my address earlier, I knew there was a small chance she wouldn't actually show. That she wouldn't take the bait I threw out. But if there's anything I've learned about this girl in the short time I've known her, it's that she doesn't back down. There isn't a chance in hell that Viv's going to roll over and give up. Nah, that's not who she is. She's ballsy as fuck.

It's part of the reason why I'm so attracted to her. That and the fact that she's easily the hottest girl I've ever laid eyes on, no question.

Add in the fact that she pretends to hate me, and my dick thinks it's the chase of a lifetime.

Viv walks around my living room and takes in the large cloud sectional and ottoman, then glances over at me, her eyebrows raised. "I'm surprised there aren't stripper poles and beer pong tables in the living room."

"Oooh, that's judgy, Viv."

"I'm judging *you*, not the strippers. I support sex workers."

I smirk. "Mhm. It's just a regular house, Viv. I mean… it's a bachelor pad because it's always just been me, but still. I keep my space clean, and I don't have parties here. *Ever*."

"Shocker," she mutters, walking further around the room. Her finger drags along the edge of the entertainment center below the eighty-five-inch flat-screen, and then she lifts it to inspect it like she expects to find dirt. She won't find any.

"Come on, I'll show you the rest of the house." I nod toward the hallway, then walk toward the spare room. She follows behind me, and I point out the bathroom with the Jacuzzi tub and waterfall shower, the kitchen, the outdoor area that has an outdoor kitchen, heated pool, and hot tub until we get to the end of the hallway where her room would be. I swing the door open and step aside so she can check it out. Her gaze drags over the bare cream walls, the plush carpet, and the metal-frame, king-size bed against the wall.

"I've got the master across the hall, and since there's not a bathroom in here, you'd have to use the bathroom down the hall."

Viv nods, chewing her lip as she walks over to the arched window and peers out of it. "You're so nonchalant about this, it's unbelievable. Look, I'm not happy about having to do this, okay? I feel like I'm backed into a corner because you and I both know that I don't have another option. If I did, I wouldn't be here. But… I really do appreciate you offering to do this. I hate inconveniencing anyone with my situation and definitely will not be bothering Hallie with it, so thank you. For keeping the reason why quiet, and for… you know, offering me your spare room."

"It's nothing. I've got the space, and you need a place to stay." I shrug as I lean against the doorframe and cross my arms over my chest. I want to make a comment about how I'm actually the one reaping the benefits of this arrangement if it means I get to see her walk around my house in those tiny shorts she loves to wear, but I refrain. Barely. This is the first time I think I've ever heard her be so… vulnerable. "As long as you don't, I dunno… murder me in my sleep or something."

Her eyes narrow as her brow quirks. "Don't tempt me, and that won't be a problem. But you should know that I absolutely know how to dispose of a body and have no problem getting my hands dirty."

"Yeah, I know exactly how dirty you can get, Viv." I chuckle when she rolls her eyes. She pretends to hate my constant flirting, but I know better. Just like I knew better the night I took her home and showed her just how good it could be between us.

"As much as it pains me to admit this… this place is really nice and honestly probably way out of my price range. Money is… tight for me for a while, and I need to know how much half the rent is so I can see if this is even financially doable," she says, deflecting from my suggestive comment.

"Ah, I don't even know. We can figure it out later. It's hella cheap because my parents own the place. When do you need to be out of your dorm?"

"Tomorrow evening. I don't have much to pack or move. Most of my furniture was provided by the school. I just have a few small things like my minifridge and my personal stuff. I was going to ask Lane, Eli, and Grant if they'd help. I mean… you know, *if* I decide to move in here."

I chuckle. "How about we just cut the bullshit and be real with each other, yeah? You need a place to stay, I've got a room, and now that you've seen that it's not a party house or some crazy sex dungeon like I'm sure you had envisioned, move in. Be my roommate. Don't let the fact that you can't resist me be the reason you pass up an opportunity to solve your problem."

Her lips flatten. "You're delusional if you think the reason I'm not jumping at moving in with you is because I can't resist you. There's no way you *actually* believe that?"

I shrug. "You tell me, babe. Because it seems like I've got plenty of room, and you don't have a lot of options right now, yet still some part of you is hesitant about what you already know is the right choice."

I can see the war waging inside of her, and I stand there silently, my arms crossed over my chest as her eyes scan what will be her new room.

"Fine. But know that it's because I have literally no other

option. I still hate you." She huffs as she crosses her arms over her chest, much like my stance.

"Never would've dreamed anything different, babe. Although, if I remember correctly, hating each other is much more fun."

3 / viv

Move In Day

You know what should actually be illegal?

Sweating… in January.

Not just sweating in January, but a shirtless, chiseled, and hot-as-shit *Reese Landry* sweating in January.

My gaze follows a rivulet of sweat as it slowly slides down his torso into the dip between the carved muscles of his abdomen.

Seriously, who has *that* many abs?

The black gym shorts on his hips are slung so low that it almost feels indecent.

No, that's definitely just the current thoughts I'm having about him.

"Hellooooo, Earth to Viv." Hallie snaps her fingers in front of my face, pulling my gaze from Reese. "Seriously, I'm starting to worry that you've been body snatched. I just watched an entire documentary on this, and it is entirely possible. I mean… you *are* moving in with Reese. Blink twice if you need help."

When I don't immediately answer, she exhales, brushing her now frizzy curls from her face. "That's it. I knew you were an imposter in my best friend's body. I'm going to have to kick an alien's ass."

It's so ridiculous that I snort, my giggle getting stuck in my throat until it tumbles out, and then we're both laughing so hard that tears form in my eyes, and it feels impossible to catch my breath.

My best friend is so fucking weird, and I love every bit of her weirdness.

She's my other half. My inherently *better* half. And it's times like this, when she's this feral, unhinged, alien-loving, conspiracy theorist, that I know she's my soulmate.

Fuck a man being my soulmate. No, that's my best friend, who's been by my side through it all. Who's held my hair when I was sick or held me when my father died and who's been the person that's picked up the pieces when some douche broke my heart. Or at least *thought* he broke my heart.

I've never been in love, and I'm in no rush to lose my sanity over a guy.

It makes me feel so guilty for keeping these important pieces of my life from her, even if I'm only doing it for her good.

When I can finally suck in a breath, I turn toward her and place my hands on her shoulders, staring into her wide blue eyes. "Hal, I swear, it's me. No body snatching. Just me. Although it is reassuring to know that you'd take on an alien for me." I'm trying to divert the conversation by joking, but her eyes narrow.

"Viv. Seriously, are you *sure* about this?" she asks, her tone now serious, and any hint of teasing is gone.

My lies continue to fall from my lips, but… if it means protecting her happiness, then they won't stop. I plaster on a reassuring smile, linking my arm through hers. "Yes, babe, I'm sure. Look, yes, Reese… annoys me to the ends of the planet with his rich-boy, everything-is-handed-to-me attitude, and yes, I would have picked another place, but the truth is, he has a badass house and needed a roommate. I just so happened to also need a roommate, so it works perfectly. Sure, yeah, it's really fucking inconvenient that there was a housing mix-up and I no longer have a dorm, but it is what it is. It all worked out perfectly. Everything is good. Promise."

She eyes me warily, clearly not convinced with my acting. "You know you could always stay with me, Lane, and Eli? I mean… I spend more time in his room than mine now."

"As much as I love that you're having all kinds of amazing sexual experiences, space babe, I do *not* need a front-row seat. I love you though, seriously *so* much, and I appreciate the offer, but things will be fine here. Pinky swear."

Before she can protest, I pull her into my arms and hold her to me, squeezing my eyes shut to enjoy the moment of just the two of us. Lately, they feel a little few and far between, and I want to soak in this time with her.

"Love you more. My place is always open, and you know I'll always be here, Viv. No matter what. You know that, right?"

"Of course, I know, Hal. That's what best friends do. You've got my back, and I've got yours."

A string of guilt tugs at my heart, and for a second, I almost come clean and tell her how shitty my life is right now and how I wish that I hadn't ever kept it from her in the first place.

It's hard to even admit that to myself. I just keep telling myself that it'll work out and try more to look at the glass being half full than empty, but some days are harder than others.

When I pull back, I turn to the house and shrug. "I mean, I know his mommy and daddy pay for it, but this place is ridiculously amazing." Amazing is an understatement. This place is a *palace* for a college kid. Not surprising that his parents would pay for something this over-the-top for *just* him for only four years.

While it's not three stories like their vacation "cabin", it still screams luxury. Twelve-foot vaulted ceilings, marble countertops, expensive chandeliers. The pantry is basically the size of my entire dorm room… including the bathroom.

And speaking of the bathroom, this one has *heated* floors. Literally, this guy is living the life most of us only dream about.

She nods. "It is. I just *still* can't believe that you're moving in with Reese. It feels so… weird."

Tell me about it.

A second later, the boys finish up carrying boxes into the house and walk over to us. Go figure that everyone *but* my new roommate is wearing a shirt.

Reese's gaze finds mine, and he grins, showing off a row of perfectly white teeth and dimples that do something funny to my traitor of a vagina.

Clearly, I need to hook up. But never with him again, obviously.

I'm horny, and the last thing I need to do is be attracted to this man. My life is complicated enough as it is to add in hooking up with a guy I can't stand simply because he's hot. Especially now that he's going to be sleeping right down the hall and is my new, unwanted roommate.

"I think that's it," Reese says, lifting his water bottle to squirt a stream of liquid into his mouth. "Got all the boxes and your books. Anything else you need to grab from your dorm?"

I shake my head. "No, that's it. I just need to turn my key into the administration office on Monday, and I'll officially be moved out. Thank you, guys, for helping me get it done so quickly."

"You can thank me with a dance next time we're at The Redlight." Grant winks.

"Okay, Casanova, Lane and I carried just as much shit as you did today," Reese mutters, an unreadable expression on his face.

I refuse to let my gaze dip below his chin. All I need is for him to catch me checking him out, and I'll never hear the end of it. His ego truly can't handle getting any larger.

It's bad enough I remember how it felt to touch him, skin to skin.

It's bad enough that I had a moment of weakness, and now I know what it feels like to have him inside me.

It's bad enough that I can't forget that night, no matter how hard I try to push it out of my head.

"Yeah, but Viv would never dance with you because she hates you, so maybe I *will* shoot my shot," Grant retorts to Reese.

"Oh?" Reese says, his dark brows raised in question.

"Y'all are ridiculous," Eli interjects, wiping sweat from his brow with the hem of his shirt.

Lane shakes his head as he tosses his arm over Hallie's shoulder and drags her against him. "How about we go to Jack's and get pizza so I can feed my girl, then the two of you can take out a ruler and continue measuring whose dick's bigger?"

"It's mine," Reese says, shooting Grant the finger.

Grant just rolls his eyes and pulls his phone out of his back pocket when it starts to ring. "Hold on, I've gotta take this."

He puts the phone to his ear and answers with a gruff "Hello?" then walks down the sidewalk away from us.

Lane, Hallie, and Eli are ahead of us now, walking toward Lane's vehicle, when Reese falls into step beside me, bending his head slightly to whisper, "Think you can vouch for me? Since you know exactly how big my cock is, Viv?"

"Mmm, well, I'd only know if I see Grant's too. Maybe I should…?" I smart back.

I would be lying if I said a shiver didn't roll down my spine at his proximity or the low, hoarse sound of his voice. But I firmly tamp down the feeling in my lower belly and don't let his words have their desired effect on me or at least show him that they do.

I jog ahead and loop my arm in Hallie's, leaving Reese behind with his jaw agape.

I guess he didn't expect me to dish his shit right back his way.

AFTER A QUICK DINNER at Jack's and finally convincing Hallie that I was not actually body snatched by aliens and that I'm fine staying here, I shut the front door to my new house and lock the deadbolt.

Now I'm alone with Reese, and I have no idea what to expect. How to… exist in the same space with him. Especially after the time that shall not be named.

Walking into the living room, I flop down on the other end of the couch next to him, massaging my temples. All I want to do is take off my makeup, put on my favorite T-shirt, and climb into bed.

"Soo… wanna cuddle and watch a movie?" Reese asks nonchalantly from beside me.

For real?

It's been like two minutes since I sat down, and he's already testing the boundaries. I guess now is as good a time as any to *reinforce* them.

"No, Reese, I do not want to cuddle and watch a movie. The only way we are going to make this work is if you understand that there have to be boundaries. We're roommates… who also happen to have slept together once by mistake."

"It wasn't a mistake, Viv." He snorts. "It was the best sex of my life, and it wasn't a fucking mistake. Don't say that shit."

For a second, I'm actually speechless by his admission, but thankfully, I quickly recover and remember how to speak.

"It *was* a mistake, Reese. One that we will not be repeating.

Not only because my life is complicated enough without any other distractions but because we're roommates now. We can never cross that line again, alright? I'm serious. From this point forward, I need you to understand that or we will never work as roommates, and I *need* this to work. We're going to be two ships passing in the night. We're not hanging out, and we're not friends. We're the kind of roommates that just share space, that's it."

"That's what you want?" he asks.

"That's the only option there is."

He pulls his pillowy bottom lip between his teeth as he leans forward on his elbows, those deep brown eyes finding mine. Finally, after a few silent beats, he nods. "Fine. Strictly roommates, then."

Relief floods my chest, and I nod too. "Okay, good. Glad that part is settled."

His eyebrow quirks.

"I know we talked briefly about the rent, but we still need to figure it out. I may need a few weeks to get something together for this month. How much are we talking?"

A laugh erupts from his lips. The same ones I'm having a hard time dragging my gaze away from. Since when are a guy's lips a turn-on for me?

"I'm not fucking charging you rent, Vivienne."

"Oooh, my full name. Guess you mean business." I scoff. "I'm paying *something*, Reese. I'm not taking a handout from you."

"No, the fuck you're *not*," he hedges, his jaw set firmly.

My gaze narrows. I'm not backing down on this. It's one thing for me to be his roommate, and it's an entirely different thing for me to be his roommate, free of charge. I'm paying my way. I always have, and I'm not going to stop now. Plus, I really don't want to owe him or anyone anything. And I damn sure won't be his charity case. It's embarrassing enough that I have to even rely on him for a place to stay.

"I'm not arguing with you. I can't contribute much right this second because I just had to wipe my savings, and I'm trying to get out of the negative, but I'm paying you something, Reese. I'm not living in your freakin' house for free. No. Absolutely not happening."

Sighing, he falls against the back of the couch. "Look, I understand where you're coming from. I do. I'm sorry, but you're not fucking paying me rent. Doesn't feel right. How about you handle… I dunno, groceries or something? It's a fair trade."

"How is buying *groceries* a fair trade for like hundreds of dollars in rent?"

His lip quirks into a cocky smirk, and he reaches down and lifts the hem of his T-shirt, showing off his six-pack of abs. "Do you see me, babe? I'm a six-foot-three catcher about to go to the MLB. I eat like a fucking horse to keep this physique up."

My gaze lowers for only a second before flitting back up to meet his, a scowl twisting my lips at the same time. "Stop trying to take your clothes off, Reese. We literally just had the conversation about boundaries."

Rolling his eyes, he drops his shirt. "I'm sorry that you're so attracted to me you can't control yourself when I show a little skin. I get it."

If it wasn't for the teasing grin on his face, I might actually throttle him. "Back to the subject at hand. Groceries in exchange for rent? And what about utilities?"

"My parents pay the rent, and I pay the utilities."

I didn't expect that. Him sharing the responsibility with his parents. It's no secret that Reese is rich. I'm sure everyone on campus knows it by now. His parents are in oil, and that's why he's got everything he's ever wanted or needed. It's why he lives in this lavish house and drives a brand-new Range Rover. He's never had to want for anything, and that much is obvious, so hearing that he pays part of the bills is surprising.

Apparently, I'm wearing my surprise because he adds, "I've got some sponsorships for a few athletic brands that bring in cash. I help my parents when I can, but they don't necessarily need it, so…"

Of course, they don't.

"Alright, so I can pay for half of those," I offer.

"Nope, utilities are my thing. I insist. Groceries—final offer," he says with a sly tilt of his lips.

"Fine." I sigh. I don't feel like arguing with him about it. "I'll take care of the groceries and anything else that's needed for the house. If there's anything specific that you want, just let me know before I go to the store."

Groceries I can handle, I think as relief floods my chest. It takes one small thing off my plate, knowing that I can hopefully stack my savings back up while still contributing a little bit for my room here. I need a safety net to fall back on.

"Sounds good. Practice is starting this week, so I'll be out early and probably home late with study hall. And since we're talking about our… arrangement, as much as your verbal abuse usually makes my dick hard, can we wave a white flag and make the house a neutral zone? I don't thrive in hostility," Reese says with rare timidness as he pulls the baseball hat off his head and tosses it onto the coffee table in front of him. I'm so used to seeing him with a hat that I forget how unruly his hair is. It curls at the nape and around his ears, and it's so ridiculously sexy.

Who knew something so simple could be such a turn-on?

Why does he have to be so frustratingly sexy?

Although it's physically painful to admit…I guess he's right. I don't want things to be tense and awkward while I'm living here either. Even though he annoys me to no end. But he *is* doing me the biggest favor by letting me live here and keeping my secrets to himself. I shouldn't be a bitch to him when all he's trying to do is help. It's the least I can do.

I nod. "Okay. Yeah. That works, as long as you respect the boundaries. So… great. Everything's settled, then. Um, I guess I'll just take a shower and head to bed. Thank you for helping today. And for letting me stay here," I tell him genuinely.

"It's nothing," he responds simply.

But he's wrong.

It's everything.

4 / reese

It Ain't About How Hard You Hit

I'm a morning person.

I love waking up early and setting myself up for success by getting the things I need to do out of the way first.

It's something I learned from my dad. When I was little, he'd wake me up, and we'd have breakfast together before it was time for school. And even though he was heading into the office for meetings, our time together was never rushed. He actually gave a shit about what was happening in my life and always made a point to give me that uninterrupted time.

I cherished those moments as a kid with him, and as I got older, we continued our tradition. Except he'd wake me up even earlier, and we'd get some weights in or a run before having breakfast.

My pops is my best friend. We're close, and college is the first time in my life that I've been away from home, and fuck, I miss having him here for those early mornings. We still FaceTime a few times a week with Mom, but it's not the same.

I shoot a quick text to our family group thread that includes my little sister, Rosie.

Speaking of…

I click her contact and press Call, bringing the speaker to my ear.

A few rings later, her groggy, sleep-filled voice answers.

"You better be dying. It'll save me from having to murder you," she rasps. I can hear the sound of covers shuffling as she moves.

"What? You don't like my 6 a.m. wake-up call? It's Monday, baby sis. Time to wake up and take on the day," I say cheerily.

Oh, did I mention that Rosie is the exact opposite of me in almost every aspect possible?

I barely skate by with my grades, and she's a bookworm.

I'm a morning person, and she stays up till 5 a.m. reading one of her raunchy romance books that I will admittedly say are quite good when you get to the juicy shit.

I'm ADHD as fuck, and Rose is the most organized, punctual person I've ever met. She has planners and a full schedule on her iPad, where she checks things off daily.

I just write shit on my hand when I need to remember it.

When we were little, I struggled to focus in class, and even being three years younger than me, she researched ways to cope with ADHD without medication and taught me everything she had learned.

She's my fucking heart, that girl. I've always been the one she calls when she needs someone, and I hope that never changes.

When she grunts instead of answering, I laugh. "Let me guess, you stayed up all night reading?"

"Actually, I went on a date, thank you very much." My eyebrows rise. Dating isn't really Rosie's thing.

I wonder if I should play the cool brother right now or the protective one because I kind of think that he and I, whoever he is, should have a little talk if he's going to be spending time with my sister.

"Okaaaaay. Tell me more."

She exhales, long and dramatic, before scoffing. "*Total* tool. He asked me what my bra size was, so I asked him what his IQ was."

"That's my girl." I grin. "Want me to beat the shit out of him? I've been needing to burn off some aggression. Seems like the perfect opportunity."

"No, you big oaf. What? Are you going to start hopping on a flight to New York every time I go on a date that doesn't go well?" She sighs again.

"You know I'd go anywhere for you, Rosie. The Landry jet is always there when I need to visit." She knows that, but I tell her every chance I can get.

Especially since she's all the way across the country at Juilliard. It's her freshman year on a full ride for ballet, and I'm so fucking proud of her.

"I know. But that's extremely wasteful to the environment, and I cannot condone it." She laughs, then goes quiet for a moment. "I miss you so much. I was eating pizza with a few girls from my class, even though I probably shouldn't be eating pizza, but that's neither here nor there—anyway, it made me miss Jack's and my big brother hovering over me all the time."

I gasp. "I do not *hover*, Jellybean."

"Dude, I'm eighteen and you still call me Jellybean, and you legit just asked if you should beat up someone I had a bad date with. Point proven."

"Fine. But it's only because I love you, and it's my job as your big brother to protect you. Now, tell me about class. How's it going? Are you settling in for second semester?"

"Yeah." She pauses for a moment, her breath whooshing out. "I think the holidays just made me a little homesick? Don't get me wrong, I love New York. It really is the city that never sleeps, and there are so many cool bookstores it's literary heaven. But… I miss Mom, and Dad, and you, and my room, and my friends."

I stand from my bed and walk over to my dresser as she talks, throwing on a pair of sweats and a T-shirt to head to the gym. I haven't heard Viv this morning, so I'm assuming she's still asleep.

"I get it. I feel like that sometimes, but you know I'm here night or day for you, Jellybean. If you need me to hop on the jet, I'm there. Just like when we were kids and I'd always sleep on your floor when you had nightmares. I might be further away now, but I'll sit on FaceTime if you need me." If there's one soft spot I have, it's my family. I'd do anything in the world for them. I wouldn't be here today if it wasn't for all the sacrifices they've made for me. Especially when it comes to baseball. I owe it all to them.

"I love you. Thanks for calling me, even if it is 6 a.m. I didn't get home until late from the date from hell, so is it okay if I call you later today?"

"Of course." I grab my gym bag off the hook on the back of my door and my wallet off my desk. "I'm headed to the gym, then class, but I'll be home later. I guess I should mention that I got a roommate…"

Her breath hitches. "A roommate? Is he hot?"

"Rosie," I grunt. "The only thing that is hot to you is soup and bathwater, remember? We've been through this."

"Stop trying to protect my virtue, Reese. I'm eighteen, and I'm a woman. Plus, I lost my virginity when I was sixteen in the back seat of a beat-up Toyota. There's nothing left to protect."

A sigh blows past my lips as I shove my wallet into the pocket of my sweats. "I'm going to walk into oncoming traffic now."

Rosie laughs, and even though my ears are currently bleeding, I do too. "My new roommate's a girl. I'll tell you all about her later."

"A girl?" She gasps. "No way. Oh my god, you cannot just

tell me you moved a girl into your freakin' house and then get off the phone. That's unacceptable, Reese. Wait, did you tell Mom and Dad? Is she your girlfrie—"

"Bye, Jellybean. Talk to you later. Love you."

I press End and hang up before she can finish her third degree. Serves her right for the virginity comment.

Immediately, my phone vibrates with a text that I already know is her without even looking.

Rosie: This conversation is not over, mister. I expect a detailed report this evening and don't you dare leave out any juiciness or I'm not speaking to you for at least three days!

Chuckling, I open my bedroom door quietly and make my way to the kitchen. I'm all but fucking tiptoeing, which is hard to do for a guy that's six foot three and two hundred pounds.

It's only been one night that Viv has been here, and I'm still trying to get used to cohabitating with another person, especially one that I want to sink my cock inside twenty-four hours a day.

Not sure what the proper etiquette is here.

The kitchen is quiet, and when I walk to the cabinet to pull my protein out, I notice a handwritten note on the back of a takeout menu from Jack's.

Thanks again for letting me be your roommate. Breakfast on me.
Don't worry, I didn't poison it.
... Maybe. ;)
-Viv

I can't hold back the smile that quirks my lips as I reread the note. Right next to where the menu was is a protein bar. I pick it up, rip the packaging open, and all but scarf it down in .2 seconds, and then I realize...

She's put out an olive branch, and fuck… *I'm taking it.*

AFTER A LONG-AS-FUCK DAY of class and practice, I don't make it back home until after nine that night.

Exhausted, sore, and fucking starving, I feel like I could eat the entire house at this point. Usually, I'm better about grabbing a bite at the commons or packing something protein-filled in my bag, but I was distracted this morning by Viv's note. She's been on my mind all day, and I'm doing my best for her not to be.

I shut the front door behind me, then hang my keys on the hook next to it and waltz into the kitchen.

I'm already dreaming about the ground turkey I'm going to make. Which admittedly doesn't taste that great, but I've gotta fuel my body, and I can't do that with junk. My stomach growls almost on command. Making a beeline for the fridge, I reach to open it and stop when I get a whiff of my armpit.

Shit, that's rank. Okay, shower first, *then* food.

When I round the corner to the hallway, I run directly into Viv, who screams at the top of her lungs and nearly jumps out of her skin.

Things happen so fast that I barely have time to recover from the fact that my eardrums might actually have fucking ruptured before a fist is flying toward my face, hitting me directly in the nose.

"Fuuuuuck," I groan, clutching my nose, noticing the wetness already coating my hand and realizing that it's fucking bleeding.

Viv just gave me a bloody nose with her Rocky right hook.

Fucking Christ.

My eyes are watering, and pain radiates from my nose to my cheekbones. I already know I'll have a black eye tomorrow. I can feel it throbbing in sync with the blood pumping in my head.

"Oh my god, Reese! What in the hell are you doing? Shit, are you okay?" Viv cries, and I can hear the genuine concern in her voice. Only then do I pry one watery eye open and see her pulling her earphones from her ears in a frantic jerk. "Oh god… you're *bleeding*."

Her face is ghostly white, and suddenly, her entire body sways.

Fuck, she almost broke my nose, and *she's* about to pass out? "Sorry… I'm not great with blood." She covers her mouth with her hand and drags her gaze from mine. "I'm sorry! I… you… My earphones were in, and I didn't hear you. I'm *actually really* sorry, Reese. I thought you were an intruder an—"

"Viv. Babe. As much as I appreciate the apology, can you please get me a towel before I bleed all over the floor and ruin the carpet?"

She glances back at the blood coating my hand and then swallows visibly and nods before darting off to the kitchen.

How does someone *so* tiny have that much power in their swing?

She flies back into the hallway with an armful of kitchen towels and thrusts them toward me. Some of them fall at my feet, but a few manage to land in my outstretched hand.

"Motherfuuuuucker," I groan when I tilt my head back and press the towel to my nose to apply pressure to stop the bleeding. This bitch hurts. "So much for that white flag, huh, Viv? Damn," I tease.

"You can't just sneak up on women, Reese," Viv mutters in self-defense. "It was a fight-or-flight reaction, and I just… *reacted*!"

Not sure who looks more worked up right now, me or her, and I'm the one with the bloody nose.

"Well, I do *live* here, so I wouldn't consider me walking to my room sneaking up on you." Leaning against the wall, I let my head fall back. "But I'll be sure to give you a smoke signal before I enter the room."

She rolls her eyes, then huffs. "Look, I was engrossed in the lecture I'm listening to for *Spaced Out*. Sorry. You surprised me, and I'm just a little on… edge."

"Yeah? What's this week's episode about?" I ask because I genuinely am interested.

She and Hallie have a weekly podcast where they talk about all things supernatural. As often as Lane talks about how proud he is of his girl, I feel like I've listened to every episode, even though I haven't heard a single one.

I'm planning on changing that soon. I wanna know as much about my new roomie as I can, and it seems like the place to start.

"Leprechauns," she says with a grin.

My eyes widen slightly, and when she notices, she laughs, soft and so sweet that for a second, I forget that I'm bleeding everywhere.

Goddamn, I love her laugh. And I feel like I haven't heard her do it enough these days.

Shaking my head, I wince when I put too much pressure on my nose. "No fucking thank you."

"Aw, Reese, are you scared?" Her lip pokes out in a mock pout, and my gaze narrows. "That's cute."

"Puppies are cute, Viv. I'm hot. But scared? Nah. Creeped the fuck out? Absolutely. Listen, I do not fuck with the universe like that. Law of Attraction and all that. And I do not want some tiny redheaded little leprechaun fucking following me."

Her laugh, throaty and low, cuts through the air, and even though it hurts like a bitch, my lip tugs into a grin.

"So you're a big baby, got it," she teases. "But for what it's worth, I really am sorry. I'm not a violent person or anything."

"Says the girl who *might* poison me," I joke. My shoulder dips, and I pull the rag away from my nose, then glance down at it. "Thanks for breakfast, by the way. It's fine. I'm an athlete—I've had much worse. I once took a cleat to the cheek when someone was sliding into home plate, and I needed ten stitches. Now, *that* was a lot of blood."

That's only one injury on a list a mile long, but it never deterred me. Baseball is in my soul.

Viv's nose scrunches as a shiver runs down her body, and she rubs her hands along her bare arms. "Ouch. I can handle a lot of things, but blood is not one of them. In movies, it's fine, but the real thing makes me queasy and light-headed."

"Yeah, well, that's me with ghosts, demons, and apparently… leprechauns," I admit. "Hard no for me."

Seems fitting that I'd move a girl in my house who's obsessed with that shit. Rosie's going to love that.

"I'll keep that in mind. Uh, sorry again for almost breaking your nose. I'll try to keep my research to a minimum when I'm home alone," she says with a lazy grin.

Pushing off the wall, I shake my head. "By all means, don't let me stop you from your creepy research."

Her eyes twinkle in amusement, and she nods as she pulls her plump lip between her teeth. "Night, Reese."

"Night, *Rocky*."

5 / viv

A Murder a Day Keeps Reese Away

It's been just over a week since I moved in, and I'm finally ready to admit that living with Reese isn't *quite* as bad as I expected it to be. Don't get me wrong, I'm still not happy to be sharing a living space with him, but I am appreciative that he was crazy enough to offer.

It helps that since the night I accidentally punched him in the nose, we've barely seen each other. Like true roommates. Our schedules are totally different.

Except ever since I left him that protein bar, we've been leaving each other breakfast in the mornings.

And it's kind of… cute, even though it physically pains me to admit that. I'm warming up to the idea of us being roommates, but that's exactly it. *Warming up.*

This morning, he left me a strawberry yogurt and a note that said, ***"Those jeans you wore yesterday? Yougurta be kiddin' me, Viv. ;)"***

I wonder how long it took him to scroll on Pinterest to find that dad joke.

"I can't believe the two of you actually made it an entire week together, and nobody died," Hallie says around a mouthful of Sour Punch Straws. We're not technically supposed to eat in the library, but we're rebels like that. "Now I owe Eli twenty bucks."

My eyes widen in disbelief. "You two *bet* on us?"

She nods unapologetically and shrugs. "I mean, it's you and *Reese*, Viv. You can't even be in the same room without going at it, and not in the good way."

I blink as I bite down on the inside of my cheek to hold in what I wish I could say. That going at it with Reese was by far the highlight of my freshman year so far and that I came twice before he ever got inside me.

Those are the things I wish I could share with my best friend, but that secret is never seeing the light of day. I'm keeping it tucked away exactly where it belongs. It would make things ridiculously awkward for everyone, and I'm pretty sure if our friends knew what happened, I'd never live it down.

I slept with the guy I claim to hate… I mean, what does that say about hating him?

"Fine, you're right. But…" I bend my head over the table, closer to where she sits across from me. "It's not *as* bad as I thought it would be. So far. It's only been a week though, so he could still be the roommate from hell like I expected him to be. Don't tell him that, but it's fine so far. He's gone a lot for baseball, and I'm usually working, studying, or in my room working on *Haunted Homicide*."

Hallie's eyes light up at the mention of my book, and I smile. Right now, it's one of the only constants in my life. The ability to lose myself in the fictional world that I've created. Nothing brings me comfort the way that spending a night at my computer with my characters does. It feels like home.

Hallie and Eli are the only two people who even know that I'm writing a book. It's not really something I'm ready to share with the world yet. It feels too personal, like a piece of me that is vulnerable and raw. Something I want to keep for myself until it's one hundred percent ready to be put out there.

"How's it going? God, I can't wait to hear more about Graves and Mica. I swear, I'm still dreaming about the scene I read with them at the spooky mansion."

"It's going good, just kind of slow right now. You know, with moving and picking up extra shifts here at the library, I just haven't had as much time to write. I plan to put my murder board up tonight and do some digging into the second act. But I'm so proud of it, Hallie," I tell her, swallowing down the swell of emotions that threaten to burst from my lips. To tell her that it's giving me an outlet that no one knows how desperately I need.

Hallie picks up her pen and brings the tip to her mouth before responding. "*I'm* so proud of *you*, Viv. Sometimes, I don't know how you do it all. School, work, and working on your novel, plus the time and research you dedicate to *Spaced Out*."

"It's my Type A personality." I laugh, gesturing to the color-coded planner in front of me, along with my notes from our last lecture.

"Well, I was thinking, since we're working so hard, that we deserve a girls night. Maybe this weekend or next weekend? A sleepover at my place or yours?"

I nod. "Definitely. We can work on our next episode too. Oh god, did I tell you that I almost like… broke Reese's nose the other day?"

She chokes on the Sour Straw she was eating, sputtering, "What?"

"Yeah, well, I was listening to a creepy lecture on leprechaun lore, and I had my earphones in, and he rounded the corner in the hallway and scared the actual shit out of me. It was a reflex."

Her jaw hangs open.

"There was blood everywhere. It was gross, and I did actually feel really bad. He just scared me, and I reacted."

"Wow. I can't believe Lane didn't mention it to me. He did say he had a mysterious black eye. I just figured he talked shit to the wrong someone."

"I guess that self-defense class my dad made me take freshman year of high school paid off? Reese is like six foot three, and I'm pretty sure he cried." I giggle.

I probably shouldn't be laughing at that, but it was a tiny bit funny.

Tiny.

"God, I would've paid money to have seen that happen. I mean, honestly, I expected this to happen way before now."

Gasping, I clutch my chest in mock offense. "I am *not* a violent person, Hallie Jo. Jeez. It was one hundred percent an accident. Trust me, if I was planning on hitting Reese Landry, I would have long before then."

She laughs so loud that there's an echo of shhh's around the library, and we both have to cover our mouths to keep quiet.

"I needed that. God, I miss you, Viv. I'm excited for our girls night. As much as I love being with Lane, I need some girl time. Your house or mine?"

Glancing down at my phone, I see the screen light up with a missed call notification from my mom. Crap. I start to gather my textbooks and tell Hallie, "I've gotta run. I need to call my mom and finish this paper for English. Let me check with Reese about this weekend. It feels so weird to call his house home, and I don't just want to, like, assume he's cool with me having people over. Ya know? I'm definitely not used to all this yet. I'll let you know tonight?"

"'Kay. Love you."

After shoving everything in my old JanSport backpack, I grab my phone from the table and tell Hallie bye. "Love you too, space babe. Text you later."

Once I make it outside of the library, I find Mom's contact in my call log and then bring it to my ear.

It rings and rings, but no answer. I try once more while walking to my car, but she still doesn't answer.

Opening my messages, I send her a text.

> Hey mom, sorry I missed your call. I was studying in the library with Hallie. Call me when you see this?

After a short drive to the house, I unlock the front door and step inside. It's completely quiet, which means Reese is probably out.

Perfect. Peace and quiet to get my murder board set up while I wait to hear from Mom.

I walk straight to my new bedroom and shut the door behind me.

The sun is setting, and the massive arched windows let an ungodly amount of natural light in, bathing the cream walls in warm rays. The room itself is as stunning as the rest of the house, and it makes me wonder if Reese realizes just how lucky he is to be able to have a place like this.

Most college kids live in a shitty, small dorm and survive on ramen noodles.

It's me. I'm that college kid, so the fact that I'm now currently living in this massive house with a walk-in closet and a Jacuzzi bathtub is still a little unbelievable. The soft, plush carpet. The recessed lighting and automatic shades. It's like it all hasn't *truly hit* me yet.

Part of me feels guilty not being able to afford my dorm and ending up here in this amazing house while my mom is stuck in our run-down, shitty two-bedroom apartment, struggling.

Maybe when I get all of my things set up and my murder board on the wall, it'll start to sink in and really feel like… home away from home.

I walk over to my computer and pull up the music app, then click on my favorite band. The deep, folky beat thrums through the speakers as I start pulling out everything for my board. It takes a second to get the space measured and then the actual board on the wall, but I manage to do it without hurting myself.

Once it's up, I start working on putting up the photos, research, and various stickies for the plot and character organization for the book that I've been working on since high school.

Being a writer has always been my dream ever since I was a little girl, typing away on an analog computer from the literal nineties, crafting stories about ghosts and things that go bump in the night.

I'll never forget that computer. My dad was on his way home from work one night, and he passed by it on the side of the road, sitting on top of a garbage can. Someone had put it out with the trash, and while it was completely out of date and had very few capabilities, it was perfect for a twelve-year-old me.

The screen itself was black, the letters a neon green, and it lagged every time I pressed the backspace key, but it was *mine*.

I cherished it because it gave me a new space to write the stories I had been penning for so long on scraps of notebook paper.

It helped me see my dreams as reality, and when I sat down in front of that computer, I wasn't just a little girl who one day hoped she could be an author like the stories she had been reading for so long. I *was* a little girl who was an author, who prayed one day she would be able to publish her stories for everyone to read.

I'm still that girl today. Just a little more jaded from the world and missing my dad with every breath.

And just like every day before this, I wish for just five more minutes with him. I'll never stop wishing for that.

He died when I was a junior in high school. Driving home from his shift at the local paper factory, a drunk driver swerved into his lane and hit him head-on. He was killed on impact. Or at least that's what they said.

My life changed instantly. Not only was I a child who lost her hero and her best friend, but in a way, I also lost my mother that day.

She's never been the same, and not only have I grieved him, but a part of me grieves the mother she was. In the beginning, I was too caught up in my own mourning to realize it, but it quickly became apparent that she'd been swallowed by the same grief.

For most people, time makes it a little more bearable, but for her, it only seemed to get worse until she could barely pull herself out of bed. Until she lost her job, and then another, and then another. She couldn't even see a television show with a car on it without having a panic attack. I found myself taking care of one grieving parent while I still grieved the other.

It's been a constant cycle, with neither of us being able to break free from it.

I swallow down the emotion and reach for the frame on my desk, swiping my finger over the glass. A photo of Dad and me when I was nine at my first father-daughter dance. The picture has faded over time, but I still remember it like it was yesterday. Still remember dancing on his feet in the prettiest purple dress that I felt like a princess in. Giggling when he spun me around the dance floor.

"Miss you, Daddy," I whisper, setting it back down on the desk. "Always."

Grief is an emotion that never wanes. It's constantly there in different shapes and forms, a reminder that no matter how much time has passed, you'll still ache.

I spend the next hour repinning and placing everything back on my murder board to busy my mind, keeping my sadness from taking over. Burying my feelings, like always, because I don't have time to fall apart. Not now, not later. So I do what I've gotten really good at… pretending that I'm not a mess.

Pretending that everything is going to be fine, even when it feels like it's not.

"Okay," I say to myself, blowing out a breath as I stand back and take in the entire board. The bright red strings connecting the plot points are back where they should be, and now I just need to make sure that it aligns with the second part of the story. I've been working on this so long I lost track of time, and now, darkness sits like a blanket outside my window. Black, inky

darkness.

My favorite time of day.

I'm working on pinning up my latest plot points when suddenly, my bedroom door bursts open and Reese barrels through, wearing nothing but a white towel slung impossibly low on his hips. He's soaking wet, rivulets of water dripping down his chest, torso, and legs onto the floor. Clearly, he's just come from the shower, but *why* is he in my room half-naked?

Before I can even ask him what in the hell is happening and why he's panting like he just ran a marathon, he all but yells, "What's in the pink bottle? In the shower?"

Pink bottle?

What?

My brow furrows. "First of all, why are you making a puddle on my carpet, and hello… have you heard of something called knocking? God, we just had a discussion about boundaries like two weeks ago, Reese!"

White flag, Viv. White flag. You can think it, but you can't say it. Woosah.

"Viv, for god's sake, please bitch at me later. Pink bottle. Tell me, now," he grunts.

"No, we can't talk about it now. There are boundaries in place for a reason."

He clutches the towel tighter around him when it loosens slightly from his grip, and my mouth runs dry.

God. Why is he so stupidly hot?

It's a crime against humanity. Truly. Being in the same room with a half-naked man that looks like him and you're not allowing yourself to touch. And really shouldn't even be looking…

At the little patch of hair below his belly button that leads to what I know is the best dick on the planet. He's so annoying even his dick is perfect.

"Viv. Fucking focus, *please*," Reese pleads, his voice rising a pitch. "I need to know what is in the pink bottle in the shower, right. Now."

"Um… exfoliating body wash? I think? I mean, I can't really remember offhand, but why are you even showering in my bathroom and not your—"

He cuts me off with a pained groan. "Look, tell me right now, whatever the fuck is in it… is it going to make my dick fall off?"

"*What*?" I screech. "What do you mean fall off?"

There's a pause, and then he sighs, dragging his free hand through his wet hair to push it off his face. "Is it?"

I'm so confused.

"Why would you be worried about your dick falling off? Wait, why are you even worried about *my* shower products? It's just bo—" Then, it dawns on me.

Why he's standing in front of me with a panicked expression and asking me if it's going to make his dick fall off.

My eyes widen, and I groan, "No. No, Reese. Tell me you did not."

His expression changes slightly, a look that is almost... guilty passing his face.

"You used my body wash to... *jack off*?" I sputter. "Are you serious right now?"

Shit. Now I'm imagining Reese in the shower, steam fogging the glass as he stands inside, one hand on the wall holding his weight as he strokes his cock to the scent of my body wash, his face morphed in pleasure.

Stop it right the hell now, Vivienne.

Now, I'm turned on.

"Fuck, my dick is actually tingling right now. And not in a good way. I think it's going to fall off, Viv. This is serious. My dick can't fall off. It's my best feature."

My gaze drops to the noticeable bulge beneath the towel, and I let it linger for only a second before dragging it back to his face. "I can't believe you used *my* body wash to jerk off. Maybe your dick should fall off. Serves you right."

"I'm sorry, okay? Shit! I had soap in my eyes, and I just reached for something." He shifts from one foot to the other, then brings his hand to the bulge, adjusting it. I *try* not to look. Really, I do.

Scout's honor.

"Should I call my mom? I don't even know my health insurance. Fuck, this is bad," he mumbles.

I let him suffer for a few more beats before rolling my eyes and crossing my arms over my chest, mostly so he doesn't see my hardened nipples poking through the thin fabric of my T-shirt.

I do not need to encourage him. Boundaries.

There are boundaries for a reason, even if I want to say fuck the boundaries right now.

"Chill. Your dick is not going to fall off, Reese. Just go wash it off, and it should stop. It has mint in it. Probably why it's tingling."

Relief floods his face. "Are you sure? Stop fucking laughing, Viv. This shit is not funny. My dick is important."

"Sure it is. I mean, not a hundred percent, but I guess we'll see, won't we?" I smirk.

This is a tad bit satisfying. And I don't mean the fact that he chose my body wash to use but because he's actually panicked that his dick is going to fall off.

He sprints out of my room, and I hear the bathroom door slam shut, so I go back to my task of finishing my murder board until I hear him walk back in.

When I turn to face him, he's still shirtless, go figure. But now, he's wearing a pair of gray sweatpants. The black band of his Calvins peeks out the top, and he's using a towel to dry his hair.

"I'm assuming you were able to save your dick?" I ask.

He grins and shakes his head, water droplets spraying me in the process. I step back and hold my hands up. "Okay, okay, stop! God, you're annoying."

"Yes, my dick is perfectly safe. Wanna check for me?"

"You wish." I turn back to the board, hoping he gets the hint and leaves, but of course, I couldn't get that lucky. "You never answered why you were showering in my bathroom and not yours. Boundaries, remember?"

"My shower isn't draining right, so I have to use yours until the plumber can come out."

Joy. More sharing. Just what I need right now.

"Ummmm..." he starts from behind me, then walks over and stands next to me, eyeing the board in front of us. "Are you plotting my murder?"

"Burst into my room again without knocking and yes, I am. I

told you I know how to hide a body. Did you think I was lying?" I drawl with a shit-eating smile.

His grin broadens. "God, you're *vicious*. I love it. Tell me what it is about you, Viv?"

"That I'm the one girl who doesn't throw herself at your feet?"

Ignoring my response, he reaches out to touch one of the sticky notes, and I slap his hand away. "No touching. You know, now that I'm thinking about it, Reese makes for the *perfect* name for the first victim in my book."

The words are out of my mouth before I really even think about them, and he turns to look at me. My eyes drop to his lips and the small beads of water still clinging to the top. I can smell the lavender minty scent of my body wash mixed with his scent, fresh citrus and pure man.

"What? You're writing a book? That's fucking amazing, Viv," Reese says. He looks at me for a moment, then back at the board. "You did all this?"

Shit.

I didn't mean to say that out loud. It just kind of… came out. Apparently, I have a problem with being brutally honest around this guy, and that is dangerous. For so many reasons. He keeps bulldozing in when my guard is down, and I end up telling him things I normally wouldn't tell anyone but my best friends. It's becoming a pattern that I don't like.

I clear my throat as I tuck a piece of my hair behind my ear. "Uh, yeah. I am. But I don't really want anyone else to know, so keep that information to yourself. Only Hallie and Eli know."

"Always with the secrets, Viv. No worries, I'm a vault, don't worry about it. But… why keep it secret? It's fucking incredible. You should want to tell everyone."

"I don't know," I say, pausing to contemplate if I want to continue this conversation with him. Even though we live together now, he's basically a stranger to me. But he's staring at me with a look that makes me feel strangely… confident.

"I don't know. It's not nearly finished, and I just want to keep it to myself for a little longer, I guess. It's nice to have something that's just mine. Less pressure when no one expects anything."

Reese nods, walking down the length of the board, his eyes scanning all of the pinned pictures, papers, and sticky notes. "I'm amazed. I mean, the detail that you've put into this. It's fucking incredible. Aren't you majoring in, like, English or something? Clearly, you should change it to criminal justice. Crime Junkie has nothing on you."

"Thanks," I say.

"It's some type of murder mystery?" he asks, nodding to the crime scene photo that I downloaded off a stock photo site for inspiration, less the actual dead body, of course.

I nod. "Yeah. It's called… *Haunted Homicide*. It's about a detective that can see the victims' ghosts and uses that paranormal sight to help solve their murders."

"Fuck yeah," he says with a wide smile. "Your secrets are safe with me. *But* I think you should tell the world, Viv. You shouldn't hide your talent from anyone. It deserves to be seen."

It shouldn't feel so good to hear him say things like this, but it does. I can't even believe I told him all that, something that I've been keeping quiet for so long. It's just kind of… easy to talk to him? Surprisingly.

"Thank you. Maybe one day."

Before he can respond, his phone begins to ring in his pocket, the sound cutting through the silence between us. He reaches in and pulls it out, glancing down at the screen and then dragging his deep brown eyes back to me. "It's my sister, and she'll call back ten times if I don't answer. I guess I'll let you get back to plotting murders?"

I nod and offer him a small smile. "It's a tough job."

He laughs, then slides his fingers across the screen and brings the phone to his ear. "Jellybean, what's up?"

I watch as he disappears through my bedroom door, and then glance back at the board and try to push away how easy it feels to open up to him.

6 / reese

Fine = Not Fine

The scent of fresh garlic hits me the second I walk through the door and set my bat bag on the floor after practice. I toe off my cleats and hang up my keys, then make a beeline for the kitchen.

The first thing I notice is the giant pot on the stove and fresh garlic bread on a baking sheet next to it, still steaming from the oven.

Fuuuuuuck yes. I'm hoping that Viv likes me enough today to let me have some of it.

I can't remember the last time I had something home-cooked except maybe whenever I went back home to visit my parents, and we honestly eat out a lot with how everyone's schedules are.

"Oh, hey," Vivienne says, looking up from the textbook she has on the counter next to the stove. The black, ripped jean shorts she's wearing hug her thighs and ass in a way that has my mouth watering for an entirely different reason. The food's completely forgotten, seeing her bent over the counter. Her dark hair falls almost to her waist, and it makes me remember the night that I had those silky locks wrapped around my fist as I pounded into her from behind.

I'll never forget it as long as I fucking live.

"Hey. Smells fucking delicious," I say before dragging my eyes off her and walking to the fridge. I open it and grab a sports drink for the electrolytes, twist the top off, and then down almost all of it. If I don't, I'll cramp up, and that shit is miserable. Not something I feel like dealing with tonight. "Please tell me I can have a bowl? I'm so hungry I could eat the house right now."

"Yeah. It should be done soon. I'm just letting it cook down for a bit," she says, and I notice she looks off. Not her normal, sassy, give-me-shit-for-existing self. Her lips are pulled in a frown, and there's a wrinkle between her brow from furrowing them. Her eyes look tired.

I walk over to where she's standing and pick the spoon up, dipping it into the pot of spaghetti and casually asking, "Everything good?"

When I glance over, her gaze is on me. "Yep. Why?"

I shrug as I bring my index finger to the sauce and dip it, then bring it to my mouth.

Goddamnit, that's incredible.

"You just seem a little off. Wanted to make sure you were okay. You know, what any good roommate would do."

She rolls her eyes, looks back down at her textbook, and mutters, "Yep. Just trying to study for Chem."

She's staring at the textbook like it's the most interesting thing she's ever laid eyes on, and even though she's saying "yep" every five seconds and that she's fine… I can tell that something is off. Plus, growing up with Rosie I know firsthand that when a girl says everything is fine, it is in fact… *not* fine.

"Ooookay." I set the spoon back down on the counter, walk to the kitchen table, and sit. If she wants to pretend nothing's wrong, then fine. I pull my phone from my pocket and scroll socials, then respond in the family group chat to all of the messages I missed while I was at practice and class today.

There are ten messages from my sister demanding to know more about my roommate.

Even though she knows the basics at this point, I've been holding out on her, and if I don't give her something juicier soon, she's liable to show up at the front door.

Jellybean: I'm starting to rethink the whole "best brother in the world thing." 🙄

Jellybean: Only someone who didn't actually love his baby sister would be keeping their new roommate from a meet the sister Facetime.

Jellybean: Seriously though, I promise no third degree. I just want to meet her. That's all.

Jesus fucking Christ, Rosie.

I laugh out loud, scrolling through the remaining messages, then quickly type a message back that I promise to call her later and try to set something up. Clearly, now isn't the time.

"Dinner's done," Viv mumbles from the counter, slamming her textbook shut.

Okay… so are we angry now?

When I stand, the chair scrapes across the floor, echoing around us. Even the break in silence can't seem to cut through the tension in the room.

Grabbing a bowl from the cabinet, I load it down with spaghetti and grab three pieces of garlic bread, then join Viv at the table.

Her eyes widen at the amount of food on my plate, but I just shrug. "Athlete, remember?"

"How could I forget when you remind me ten times a day?" Her retort is sharp as it slices through the air between us. Damn, I thought we were past all the hostility? Shit-talking banter, nah, we're still balls-deep, but this?

"Okay, spill. What the fuck is up, Viv? And before you say

nothing, something is obviously wrong because your claws are even sharper than usual. Quite frankly, I want to enjoy this bowl of food because I'm fucking starving, and I can't do that when you're shooting daggers at me with your eyes."

Sighing, she pushes a meatball around her plate before dragging those deep blue eyes up to meet mine. "I am not shooting daggers at you. You know… not everything is about you, Reese. Although, you seem to believe it is."

Alright, so we're deflecting. Back to being closed off.

Cool. Buuuut I'm not giving up so easily. I wanna know what's got her like this, what's bothering her.

I care, even though she acts like she doesn't want me to.

The spaghetti in front of me wafts to my nose, and I grab the fork, digging in and shoving a forkful into my mouth, groaning with my lips wrapped around the utensil.

Holy shit. This is fucking good. Not even good, but amazing.

I swallow it down before responding.

"Nah, I know this isn't about me because if it was, you would've already torn me a new one. What's happening, Viv? You should know by now that I'm persistent, and I'm not giving up until you tell me what's going on."

Her eyes narrow, and she drags her gaze back down to her plate. "Nothing. I'm good."

"Lie to everyone else, but don't lie to me," I say and cut my eyes to her over my bowl. "I live here, remember? So I'm not going anywhere. So just tell me. Who knows, maybe I can help."

"You can't." She sighs dejectedly, then rolls her eyes, so I wait her out. After a few minutes of hesitation, she says, "I'm just feeling really overwhelmed right now. With my schedule, my job." Lowering her voice, she whispers hesitantly, "And my mom. And on the way home from work today, my car started to make this sound, and I'm sure that's going to cost an arm and a leg to fix. There you have it. All my problems laid out for you. Happy?"

After another bite, I say, "Well, my sister, Rosie, used to tell me growing up, tackle the smallest problem first. I always really struggled with my ADHD, and she was constantly trying to find ways to help me cope with it, and it was one of the things she taught me. Take the smallest problem and chip away at it, then move on to the next."

Viv leans forward after setting her fork down and props her elbows on the table. I notice the thin chain bracelet on her wrist that has a little ghost emblem on it and how it feels perfect for her. "How old were you when you were diagnosed with ADHD?"

"Seven? Maybe. I don't really remember exactly when. My parents got me tested at my pediatrician, and I was on medication for a while, but I started playing tournament ball when I was twelve, and it was making it fucking impossible for me to keep on weight, even when I forced myself to eat, so we decided to take me off of it. My grades suffered when I did, so I struggled for a long time. Until Rosie started to help me with managing it."

"She sounds amazing," Viv says, a soft smile on her pink lips. "Your sister."

I nod. "She is. She's my best friend. Okay, so take the smallest part first, and see what you can do to work on it. Maybe take off a few shifts and give yourself a chance to catch up on schoolwork. What about your car? Let's go drop it off at the mechanic and get it fixed."

For a second, she says nothing, and then a grimace passes over her face, and she laughs humorously, shaking her head. "Yeah, well, obviously, I don't have the money for that, Reese."

Ah, so maybe I can help? Money is the one thing I *can* seem to contribute to this.

"Okay, no problem. What's your Venmo? I'll send you some, and if it's more than that, I'll call the shop and take care of it."

"Don't do that. *Don't* offer to pay for my stuff, Reese," she says. The mask of coldness drops back in place. "I'm not your charity case."

"Why can't I give you some money?" I ask. "It's the one thing I can help with, and if it takes shit off your plate... It's *just* money. I've got plenty of it, and I'd rather not see you stressed over something I can easily fix."

Silence greets my question until she stands, a bitter laugh bubbling from her lips as she takes her still mostly uneaten plate to the sink. "Of course, it's *just* money, right? Toss it at whatever problem for it to magically disappear."

My brows pull together as I try to figure out what just happened to set her off like this.

"Yeah, Viv. It's just fucking money. Why are you making it a big deal?"

She whips around, her blue irises ablaze. "Because it is a big deal. Maybe not for you, but it is for me. It's not a big deal to you because you have it just lying around to fix anything and everything that comes your way. Thank you, Reese. Thank you for reminding me of *exactly* who you are. I seemed to have forgotten for a moment. I needed that reminder."

Her cheeks are red and flushed with anger, and I'm just fucking lost. Standing from the chair, I walk over to where she's standing. "Fuck, Viv. I was just trying to help. Clearly, you need it. You don't seem like the girl who would cut off her nose to spite her face."

"I don't *need* your help. For anything. I've made it eighteen years of my life without someone handing me everything on a silver spoon shoved into my mouth, and I don't need that now." Her words drip with venom. "God, everything is just *so* fucking easy for you. Throw money at it, and the problem disappears.

Well, you know what, Reese? Contrary to what you believe, money doesn't fix everything. In the real world, where regular people live, money isn't the answer to all problems. There are things that money could never solve. Stupid me for thinking I could confide in you. I forget that you don't have real problems." With that, she tosses her bowl into the sink and storms out of the room, leaving me feeling like a complete and utter asshole for even trying to help in the first place.

Fuck.

7 / viv

BitterSWEET Apologies

I'm still upset from last night.

And also feeling slightly… bad that I lost it on Reese the way that I did. After yesterday being an absolute shitshow with a scheduling mix-up at the library, causing me to have to cover a last-minute shift, and then a distraught phone call from my mom on the way home to my car making that god-awful noise and driving weird and knowing that it just sounds like it's going to cost money I don't have to fix, I feel like I'll never be able to get back on top of my money situation and rebuild my savings. Combined with the weight of trying to appear like everything is fine in my life to everyone I know, I just didn't have the energy to pretend anymore. I'm emotionally exhausted, and I was completely on edge, and as always, Reese has the ability to get a reaction out of me, whether intentional or not.

Of course, when presented with a problem, he thinks that throwing his trust fund at it like that will solve everything.

Just when I was maybe starting to believe that he's an actual genuine guy and not the spoiled little rich guy that he acts like ninety percent of the time.

Ugh.

I pull the pillow over my head to block the light out and groan into the fabric.

Universe, anytime you want to send me a break, I'm here to accept it with open arms.

Sighing, I toss my pillow to the side and reach for my phone.

Two missed calls.

Shit, I must have slept through the ringer. It's barely 6 a.m.—I didn't expect anyone to be calling this early.

I quickly call Mom back, and after a few rings, her voice slides through the speaker.

"Viv?" I can hear the distress in her voice, and I'm immediately on alert.

"Mama?" I sit up in the bed, tossing the covers to the side. "Are you okay? What's wrong?"

A watery whimper is all that I get in response, and now I'm in full-blown panic.

"You're scaring me. Are you okay? Are you hurt?" My words come out in a rush as I start throwing on a pair of black leggings and the first T-shirt I can grab from my drawer.

"Oh, honey, I'm fine. I just took a little tumble when I was walking to the bathroom. Apparently, I forgot to eat yesterday, and I had a little fainting spell. I know better—I just didn't have much energy to even get out of bed yesterday."

I bring my hand to my chest to somehow lessen the erratic pounding of my heart. She's okay.

Everything's fine, Viv. Take a deep breath.

I follow my own instructions and suck in a deep breath, then exhale.

"I'm a little banged up, but I'm okay. I've got a large bandage on my arm. I seemed to have scraped it some. I'm okay, honey. I just wish you were here."

My forehead presses against the cool wood of my door, and my eyes drop shut. I know she doesn't do this purposefully, the guilt trips. The comments about how she wishes I was there or that I didn't choose to go to college away from home.

But every time she says it, guilt eats away at me.

"I know, Mama. I… I can come out there today and make sure you're okay. Check on you?" I offer, even though I can't afford to. Not just because my car is possibly going to break down but because that means I'll have to miss a day of school, and I'm trying to stay on top of my classes.

Not that I'll tell her that. Even if I did, she wouldn't truly understand.

"I'd love that, sweetie. I'm running low on groceries, and Mrs. Henderson offered to let me borrow her car to go to the store yesterday. I made it all the way outside, to the car this time. I… I just sat in the front seat, and everything about it reminded me of your dad. I couldn't do it, Viv." She sniffles.

It's been two years since his accident, and she's never driven. Never even started a car, which has really limited her job opportunities. It's all work-from-home positions, and on the days where it's hard for her to get out of bed, it makes it even harder for her to keep a job.

I understand she's terrified and that everything about driving sends her into a state of panic. I feel the same way. My hands still shake sometimes when it's late and dark, and I get in my head.

"That's okay, Mama. You tried. That's what matters, remember? It's going to be okay. I'll be there soon, and I'll take care of everything. I promise," I reassure her.

Another sniffle. "Okay, honey. Thank you for doing this. I'll see you soon."

I mutter a goodbye and stand straight, glancing around the room. If I make it through this week, it's going to be a miracle. A message notification vibrates my phone, and I glance at the screen, seeing another message from Hallie.

I honestly haven't had the mental capacity to respond to her texts over the last couple of days, and I feel horrible about it.

We're supposed to have a girls weekend, but I didn't have a chance to discuss things with Reese since we got into an argument instead.

Hallie: Wanna meet for lunch? I've got a break today between algebra and European lit.

I gnaw at the inside of my cheek as I try to figure out how to respond. Obviously, I can't meet for lunch today since I'm going to be driving home to meet my mom.

But I can't exactly tell her that I'm having to make an emergency trip home in the middle of the week because my mom is barely able to take care of herself.

I tap at the screen, responding to her message.

Viv: I'm totally swamped today working on my English paper, but still on for this weekend! Reese is good with it.

I don't actually know if he is or not, but I'm not asking him. Not after our fight. I don't have it in me for a repeat of yesterday. Reaching for my keys, I grab my things and shove them in my backpack, then swing my bedroom door open and head for the kitchen. I don't have time to cook anything, so I'll just grab a banana or something.

I reach for the fruit, but a note next to the bowl stops me in my tracks. Since moving in, this has been our thing. One day, he leaves me something, and the next, I return the favor.

Like one that said "You're the gOAT" with a packet of oatmeal. Or the boiled egg that said "I hope your day is Egg-citing." It's cheesy and ridiculous, and I just didn't expect it to happen after our fight from last night.

There's a cereal bar on the counter—marshmallow, my favorite—and a note.

Sorry I'm a dumbass. Forgive me?
SinCEREALY,
Reese

My laugh echoes around the empty kitchen, and I bring my fingers to my lips as I scan the black ink scrawled on the paper again.

I guess if there *was* anything to make me forget last night happened, it would be my favorite cereal bar and a bad breakfast pun.

THINGS WERE EVEN WORSE than I anticipated when I got to my house. Mom didn't just scrape her arm; she gashed it open and probably should've gotten stitches or had it checked out by a doctor, at the very least.

I disinfected it, put two butterfly bandages on the cut, and put in a call to her primary care physician for a video call. He said to keep an eye on it, and if it seemed to not be healing, then to come in.

"Mama, you have to start taking better care of yourself," I tell her, sitting beside her on the old couch. I've spent the remainder of the day cleaning up empty cups and dirty bowls, washing laundry and sheets, and then grabbing a few staples from the local grocery store to hold her over until I can come home again.

I'm so worried about her, and every day it feels like instead of taking one step forward, we're moving two steps back.

What if she had hit her head and passed out? I wouldn't have even known anything was wrong, and my worry is making me question my ability to stay at Orleans U, over two hours away from home.

"I know, honey. I am. I promise," she replies, like she always does. Always empty promises to prioritize herself, and it never happens.

Turning to face her, I take her thin hands in mine. "I'm serious. You have to, Mama. I'm too far away at school, and if something happens to you, I don't know what I'll do."

Tears shine in her eyes, and my heart feels like it physically aches.

"I'm not going anywhere, Viv. I'm here. Some days are just so hard, baby. It feels like it's impossible to even open my eyes. It used to be so easy to be happy. Before…"

Depression does that to you. It steals who you used to be and wields your joy against you like a weapon. A constant reminder that you're a shell now, empty and hollow.

I've never hated anything more in my life.

"You have to. Not just for you but for me. Because I need you. And I need you to take a shower, and eat more than once a day, and take your vitamins."

She nods, leaning forward to rest her head on my shoulder. "I will. I promise."

I want so badly to believe her, but if there is anything I know about history, it repeats itself.

Together, we settle on the couch and watch a rerun of *Friends* until I hear her breathing even out and feel her go lax in my arms.

Only then do I realize how late it's gotten. It's dark outside, and with everything I've done today, time got away from me.

Carefully, I move her off my shoulder and onto the cushions, then grab the blanket off the back of the couch and pull it up to her chin, tucking it around her.

She sighs in her sleep, her lids fluttering as she dreams. I hope they're good dreams, and like I do every day, I pray that she finds peace.

She *deserves* peace.

She deserves more than the shitty hand life has given her, but only she can pull herself from this. As badly as I wish I could, I can't do it for her. I've been trying to get her to get help, whether it be someone who makes house calls or even a Teladoc therapist. I think she needs professional help that I can't give her.

After finishing tidying the rest of the house, I grab my backpack and my phone and leave, locking the front door behind me.

It's almost 11 p.m., which means I won't make it back to campus until well after midnight.

I'm exhausted, mentally and physically. By the time I get home, I'll be too exhausted to work on *Haunted Homicide*.

Lately, the things that make me happy have been taking a back burner, and it makes me feel even more drained.

When I get in the car, the first thing I do is put on a podcast, and then I pull out onto the highway in the direction of campus.

The drive passes quickly because I'm engrossed in the podcast and not my exhaustion, and before I know it, I'm pulling into my parking spot in front of the house.

I quietly unlock the front door and push it open, tiptoeing through the house so I don't wake Reese. Which is apparently a moot point because I find him on the couch, reading a book.

"Hey," he says, glancing up from the pages.

"Hi."

I swallow, shifting from one foot to another. This is slightly awkward. The last time I spoke to him, I was incredibly mean, and now I feel bad, especially after his breakfast punny apology.

"About the—" "I want to—"

We both speak at the same time, and he laughs when our sentences run together.

"Sorry, you go first," I say as I walk to the opposite end of the couch, set my backpack down, and then flop onto the cushions. It's so soft that my body practically melts into it. A moan escapes my lips before I can stop it, and out of the corner of my eye, I see Reese shift and then clear his throat.

"I'm sorry about last night. I was trying to help, and I realize it came off like I was trying to use my money to fix everything. Like yeah, I do have money, and I wish you'd let me help you when you need it, but I understand that it's not going to fix everything and that it was insensitive. I just… if you need me, for anything, Viv, I've got you, okay?"

I nod. "Thank you. I'm sorry I was so harsh. I was having a really shit day, much like today, and I just lashed out. I appreciate you offering to help, and it was really… sweet."

His lip tugs up in a grin, and he shrugs. "It was nothing. And I wasn't like waiting up for you tonight or anything. I mean, I was, but only because I was worried and I wanted to apologize for accidentally being a douche and I wanted to make sure you got home okay. Not like in a weird way or anything."

He's rambling like he's nervous, so my brow quirks. "Apology accepted. I *cerealously* think the breakfast helped, ya know?"

Immediately, he catches the pun and lets out a raspy laugh. "Liked that, didn't you? Bet you didn't know that under all of these ridiculously handsome good looks and witty charm, I'm actually a master of puns. Specifically of the breakfast variety."

God, he is such a cinnamon roll.

"You're really on a *roll* with breakfast puns, Reese. I'm impressed." I can hardly even finish my sentence because I'm laughing at how absolutely stupid that sounded, but he joins in, and suddenly, my stomach hurts from laughing.

I'm chalking it up to deliriousness from how exhausted I am. "Why'd you have a shit day?" he asks when we finally catch our breath. My eyes search his dark eyes, and I swallow at the genuine sincerity I see shining back at me.

In a way, Reese is the only person in my life right now that I can be honest with and not worry that it's going to disrupt his life. I don't have to protect his feelings or worry about him hovering over me like a mother hen. He's the only person that I don't actually feel like an emotional burden. He's the only person I don't feel any pressure to be "okay" around, and by chance of fate, he's the only one who knows that I'm not.

I guess that's why I find myself telling him.

"Just some family issues. I had to skip classes today so I could go home and take care of it, and I'm just kind of emotionally drained." It's vague, but it's more than I've given anyone lately.

He nods. "I get it. What's your comfort movie?" My brow furrows.

"Comfort movie?"

"Yeah, like, what's the movie you put on when you just need to feel some familiarity? When you're having a shit day and need comfort."

"I didn't even realize that was a thing. I mean, now that you say it that way, I guess I do have a comfort show, but I've never really heard it explained like that."

Reese leans forward and grabs the streaming remote off the coffee table and extends it to me. "My sister and I have the same comfort movie, so we'd always go down to the theater in our house and put it on. Don't ask me how, but that shit is magical."

I take the remote and pull up Netflix, then put on the same movie I've watched more times than I can count ever since I was a kid.

"*Matilda*?" he asks, surprise lacing his tone. "Shit, I remember that movie. The books."

"Yep. I always imagined I was her, except instead of reading books, I was writing them."

"Not gonna lie, I expected it to be *Texas Chainsaw Massacre* or *The Shining* or something," he teases.

I reach over and push his arm, the hard muscle of his bicep not moving a single inch.

"Just because I love all things creepy and supernatural doesn't mean that I don't like other things too," I respond.

I'm exhausted and hardly able to keep my eyes open, but I guess now we're watching a movie. As it starts to play and baby Matilda appears on the screen, I find myself feeling less anxious. More relaxed. Even more sleepy.

I sink back into the couch and rest my head against the back as we watch.

Somehow, amid our conversation and settling in for the movie, we've each moved from opposite ends of the couch to somewhere in the middle. He reaches behind us to pull the thick cream blanket off the back, unfolds it, and hands it to me, his arm brushing against mine.

There's nothing remotely sexual about it, but it still makes me shiver, and my heart picks up speed.

We probably shouldn't be this close on the couch, watching a movie.

Not when we have firm boundaries in place. That's not something two people who are *just* roommates should do.

But, I guess… it's *just* a movie. Movies are harmless.

I pull the blanket tighter around me, my head dropping back against the couch, and my eyelids grow heavier by the second.

The last thing I remember before falling asleep is that I don't think that it was the comfort of the movie that I needed after all.

8 / reese

Sweet Tart

I woke up in the middle of the night with Viv's head in my lap and my arm slung over her waist like it belonged there.

Her silky, dark hair was spread out like a halo around her as she slept.

Fuck, I loved it more than I should have.

It felt better than it should have, and I should've gotten up and gone to bed since my arm had been asleep for I don't even know how long, but instead, I stayed exactly where the fuck I was without a second thought.

But, of course, when I woke up for the second time this morning with sunlight streaming in the windows, she was nowhere to be found. I was late for class because I slept through my alarm, but it was absolutely worth it.

I got a workout in after class, then went to practice, and now I'm lying in bed, staring at the ceiling.

I know Viv's home because I hear the shower running, and I'm trying my damnedest not to think about her in there.

Naked. Soapy…*Wet.*

Groaning, I reach down into my gym shorts and adjust my hardening cock.

I truly did not think this whole roommate thing through.

Obviously. I'm pretty sure I've been walking around with a permanent semi for the last few weeks.

To distract myself, I reach over and grab the book off my nightstand, opening it to the page that I dog-eared and picking up where I left off.

I'm so engrossed in the pages that I don't even hear Viv knock, but then my door opens, and suddenly, a shadow falls over me, causing me to almost jump out of my fucking skin and slam the book shut.

Shit. Shit. Shit.

I try to shove it under me before she sees what it is, but she snags it out of my hand before I'm able to.

Damnit, she's *quick.*

"Another book?" Her dark brow quirks, and her lips follow suit. "Wow, Reese, you've been holding out on me."

"I— It's…" I stammer, unable to think of a fucking excuse other than that I picked up the stupid thing because I wanted something to talk with her about. Common ground. And I know she's into this shit.

I've been having nightmares for three days, so I haven't decided if it's worth it or not yet.

"The Supernatural: Why the Unexplained Is Real," she reads aloud. "Never took you for a reader."

Sitting up, I snatch it back out of her hand and shove it under my pillow. "Well, that's because you don't *actually know* me, Viv. I'm a multitude of things that you don't know about. Lots of layers. *Complicated* ones."

She laughs. "Oh?"

"Yep."

Her eyes flick around my room, stopping on the bookshelf full of trophies and medals. She walks over to the shelf and drags her purple-painted finger over the nameplates.

"You've got a lot of awards. Mmm. Most valuable player?"

She picks up one of my Little League awards and turns to me, waving it in her hand.

"Ah, yes, that one was from the fourth grade. There are about six more up there if you were wondering."

Her blue eyes roll. "I wasn't, but as always, your ego makes itself known. Thank you for that."

"I'm confident. Not egotistical. If I had to guess, baseball is to me what your writing is to you."

Her nostrils flare at the mention of her secret. I'm not saying it to throw it in her face but to compare its importance.

Baseball is my life and my future. It's something I'm proud as fuck of. Sometimes it feels like she thinks I'm just a dumb jock, and I fucking hate that shit. If she would stop pushing me away at every turn, we might actually be able to get to know each other beyond the assumptions we have. We could at least be friends.

"That's fair. Sorry, I wasn't judging you. I know how important baseball is to you."

I nod, tossing her a grin, playing it off. Part of me wants to bring up last night and ask if she wants to do it again, but she's clearly avoiding the topic. And I already know the answer.

"So, I'm going to go grocery shopping," she announces as she sets the trophy back in its spot on my shelf. "Wanna come?"

"Wow, Vivienne, are you asking me on a date? Pretty bold of you."

"Sorry, I don't pick out fruit together until at *least* the third date. Way too intimate for a first date."

I love that her lips curve into a smile and that she rolls her eyes at my harmless flirting. But what do I love more? That as much shit as I give her, she gives it right back to me.

"Touché. I would love to go grocery shopping with you. But I need to know if you're the crazy type to make a list and actually shop from it?" I drag my hand through my hair and push it out of my eyes. It's getting long as fuck, but I can't cut it until after our first game.

I'm too superstitious for that shit.

Viv brings her hand to her chest and gasps. "Only psychopaths do that, Reese. I'm more of a *shove everything that catches my eye into the basket as I go* kinda girl."

"Oooh. My kinda girl," I retort without thinking.

Her cheeks heat and a blush spreads along them. Damn, I think that's a first.

I made Vivienne Brentwood fucking *blush.*

"Okay, well, I'll, uh… just grab my bag. Do you want to drive, or should I?" she asks.

"Is your car still making a weird noise?"

Pulling her lip between her teeth, she nods. "Yeah, I'm going to try and get a quote this week."

Not if I can fucking help it. It's not safe for her to drive around in a vehicle that may break down on her on the highway.

I just have to find out how to make it happen without repeating the other night.

"I'm driving, but none of your *judginess* about my playlist."

"TAYLOR SWIFT? Why am I not even a *little* bit surprised?" Viv says, her eyes sparkling with amusement when I turn on my Range Rover and "Style" plays through the speaker.

"Listen, she's an icon, and I'm a fucking fan. It doesn't make me any less of a man because I'm a Swiftie, alright?"

People can say what they want, but I don't give a shit. I paid an assload of money for VIP tickets for me and Rosie and even wore fucking friendship bracelets, that's how comfortable I am with my masculinity.

She holds up her hands in surrender. "Never said it did. I'm glad you feel so passionately about it. I'm not really a fan, but I respect her as an artist."

I pull out of the parking lot, then onto the highway, and glance over at her. "What's your vibe, then?"

"Nineties alternative. Blink 182, Nirvana, Matchbox Twenty, Train. The classics." She glances down at my phone in the console between us and swipes it. "No passcode? That's brave of you."

I shrug. "Nothing to hide."

She doesn't respond, just hums and taps away at my phone screen. A second later, the station changes from Taylor to Sugar Ray.

"Okay, I do fuck with this. One of my faves," I tell her as "Fly" plays through the truck speakers.

"I can't believe you have your playlists *public* like this. That's like showing everyone your nudes. A peek inside your soul," she mutters, dragging her gaze toward me.

"Are you slut shaming me right now?" I ask, my brow raised.

Her lips curve into a sly grin. "Maybe. I mean, you should at *least* make them work for it."

"So, you don't give up the playlists until the fourth date? After the grocery trip, of course. Bananas are *very intimate*, I get it."

This makes her laugh, and it floats through the cab of my truck, making me grin in return.

I love her laugh. I love *making* her laugh. I want to be the one who earns a laugh from her.

"Exactly. You understand. I just think some things are meant to be held close to you. Music happens to be one of them."

I turn into the grocery store parking lot and find a spot near the front. "I get it." When she reaches for the handle, I put my hand on her arm, stopping her. "Nah, let me."

She pauses for a second, blinking, but then nods and takes her hand off the handle.

Sorry, but I'm not letting a girl ride in my truck and not opening the door for them. Especially Viv.

Hopping out, I walk around to the passenger side and open it, offering her my hand. She slides her palm into mine, and I help her out of the truck while she mumbles a quick thank-you.

Something tells me it's not a thing she's used to, and I want to kick whoever treated her any differently.

We walk in comfortable silence into the store, and she stops once we're inside. "Where to first?"

I grab a cart and wheel it over to where she's standing. "Breakfast food, *obviously*."

She smirks. "Good choice."

Together, we walk over to the fruit section, and she picks out her favorites, and then I pick out some strawberries, grapes, and watermelon. I fucking love fruit, and since I can't have a ton of sweets in my diet, it's my vice.

"So... is your dad around?" I ask casually, pretending to be very interested in the twelve different versions of jelly on the shelf in front of me. She's talked about her mom before, but I've never heard her mention her dad.

I feel her stiffen slightly beside me, and my gaze darts to hers. She's frowning, and I suddenly want to stick my foot in my mouth. The expression on her face is sad, and immediately, I'm kicking my own ass for bringing it up.

"Sorry, not trying to pry. I was just curious. You don't have to answer if you don't want to."

"No, it's okay," she says quietly as she tucks a piece of hair behind her ear. "My dad passed away my junior year of high school."

Damn it. I knew I shouldn't have asked. No wonder she looks so sad. I can't even imagine losing my dad or any of my family, honestly.

My gaze softens. "I'm sorry, Viv. I didn't know."

"I know. It's okay. He… was killed in a car accident driving home from work one morning."

"So it's just been you and your mom for a while now?" I ask quietly.

She nods while emotion flickers in her eyes. "Yeah. It has. What about you? Are you close with your parents?"

We continue walking across the grocery store, but neither of us has really looked at anything besides each other in a while, and honestly? I love getting to know her.

"I am. My dad's my best friend, and I'm mom's baby." I give her a small smile. "And my little sister, Rosie, is my heart. I'd do anything in the world for her. If she asked me to streak down the street in the middle of rush week, I'd probably do it."

Viv laughs. "Of course, you would, and you'd probably enjoy it. It's good that you have each other though. I always wished I had a sibling growing up. And a little black kitten, but unfortunately, I got neither. My parents really only ever wanted one child, and my dad was allergic to cats, so it was just me." She pauses, sadness morphing her features. "I really miss him."

I feel so fucking bad for her now that I know about her dad. I want to hug her. Wrap her in my arms and just hold her if she wouldn't try to probably break my nose again.

Before I even have the chance to answer, she squeals, plucking a box of candy from the shelf and turning to me. "My favorite. I will physically fight you over a SweeTart."

That's exactly who Vivienne is. Sweet as fuck when she's dripping on my tongue, but tart and prickly the rest of the time. Good thing I like it both ways.

"I only like the red ones."

"Well, good because I like them all except the red ones." She chuckles. It's obvious she's changing the subject, but it did get pretty heavy in the middle of the grocery store.

"Now that it's settled, we need granola bars," I tell her and grin when she shakes her head enthusiastically.

"Yes! And cereal."

It feels oddly… domestic walking around the grocery store with Viv, and I can say it's something I never imagined doing, but fuck does life have a way of surprising you.

"Shit," she mutters when we get to the cereal and she stands on her tiptoes, trying to peer at the top shelf.

"What?"

"There's only one box of Cookie Crisp left, and it's pushed all the way to the back."

My gaze moves to the top shelf, and sure enough, the box is butted against the very back of the shelf. Stepping forward, I try to reach for the box, but it's just out of my grasp, even with my height.

"Ugh," she groans, a small frown on her lips. "I need that Cookie Crisp, Reese. *Need*."

"You and your affection for breakfast food," I tease. "C'mon, get on my shoulders and grab it."

She cuts her gaze at me, blinking. "Uh, no. We're in the middle of a grocery store."

"So?"

Her gaze darts from one side of the aisle to the other like we're about to be caught doing something we shouldn't be, and I want to laugh.

"You scared, Viv?"

"Of course I'm not scared," she scoffs.

My shoulder dips. "Prove it."

Another scoff, followed by an eye roll, and my grin only grows. She's never backing down to a dare.

That much I know about her.

"I don't need to prove anything. We're in the middle of a grocery store full of people. It'll cause a scene."

"If you're scared, then just say you're scared, babe." I'm goading her, but I know it's working, judging by the way her jaw ticks and her gaze on me narrows.

Her eyes flick to the shelf, then back to me, and she rolls her eyes again. "Fine. But *only* because I really fucking want my Cookie Crisp, Reese. *Not* because of your stupid dare."

"Sure. We'll go with that."

I round the cart, walk over to where she's standing, then crouch down, and in one swift motion, I've got her on my shoulders with my hands wrapped around her thighs to steady her.

She yelps, and her fingers fly to my hair, threading through the strands as she holds on.

"Reese! Don't you *dare* drop me." Her thighs clench around my head, and fuck, I wish it was because I was on my knees between them with my tongue buried in her pussy.

I chuckle, shaking my shoulders and making her grip harder. "Have some faith in me, woman. I could legit hip-thrust your entire body and not break a sweat. Have you seen these thighs? Catcher thighs, baby."

Her entire body shakes as she giggles, and it's fucking infectious.

I take a few steps as she leans forward and reaches for the box. It takes her a couple of tries, and she's practically bouncing on top of my shoulders in the process, but finally, she nabs it.

"Got it!" she says between laughs as I pretend to sway, spinning in a circle. One of her hands is still fisted in my hair, the other clutching the cereal box, and then she smacks me in the fucking face with it.

"Watch it," I growl, bringing my fingers to her inner thighs and tickling them. "Don't play with fire unless you're willing to get burned, baby."

An older couple walks by us, pushing their cart, a knowing smile on their lips, and I lift my hand and wave.

"Young love. So sweet!" The lady smiles. "I remember those days."

I can hear Viv squeak from above me, and then she's tugging at my hair. "Okay, goods secured. Let me down."

"Nah, I think I'll just keep you up here with only a box of Cookie Crisp to defend yourself with."

"Rude."

Smirking, I bend slightly and lift her off my shoulders by her thighs, and her back slides down my front as her feet touch the ground. My fingers brush against her pussy by accident, and her breath hitches. Slowly, she turns to face me. Our gazes hold, and I watch her throat bob as she swallows.

We're in a fucking grocery store, but all I want to do is pull her to me and kiss the fuck out of her.

A throat clears behind us, and Viv blinks, the spell suddenly broken.

We both turn to the hipster guy standing behind her. He doesn't look the least bit sorry for interrupting us when he asks, "Is that the last box of Cookie Crisp?"

"All yours," she squeaks, thrusting it into his hands and sprinting down the aisle.

Well, fuck.

9 / viv

Not Your Valentine

"Hallie, I love you, but I am *not* going out to dinner with you, Lane, and Reese. On *Valentine's Day*. You know it's for couples. Love Day. Which means that sounds an awful lot like a double date of some sort, and I am *not falling* for that trap." I shoot my best friend, who has obviously lost her mind, an incredulous look. "Nope. Not no, but hell no."

Especially after… whatever happened during our grocery store trip. It was weird and made me feel… *weird things*.

But in a *maybe I actually liked it* kind of way?

Hallie groans. "You have to. Look, every day is basically Valentine's Day with Lane, and I am tired of not seeing you. I miss my best friend, and I am using my best friend card."

Sighing, I slide off my headphones and put them on the desk in front of me. We've spent the entire afternoon recording a new episode of *Spaced Out*, and I've been soaking in time with my girl.

She's right. Life has been too crazy lately, and I miss her too. But I also know that going on even a "not" date thing with Reese is bad news. Things have been surprisingly… good between us. We're almost like friends now, and I just do not want to fuck that up in any way. Even if he did almost kiss me in the cereal aisle.

I'm pretending it never happened.

Just like I'm pretending the night at my dorm never happened either. Even if it's impossible to forget. Because I still want to climb him like a tree, and that is a whole problem in itself. I'm horny, and I want to have hot, sweaty, rough sex with him.

And I cannot.

To be honest, I'm not even sure how I'm resisting him at this point. He never wears a shirt. It's like he has a strong aversion to clothes, and I'm obviously the one doing the suffering. I swear, he does it on *purpose.*

Walking around the house in those stupid sweatpants that sit low on his hips, with all his stupidly *stupid* muscles on display.

Last night, I may or may not have used my vibrator and thought about us the night I rode him.

It was a weak moment, and I've decided that it's never happening again. I'm only looking toward the future.

"Plus, it's not a date. It's just friends, hanging out. Very casual. Verrrry un-date-like," Hallie adds. She clasps her hands together in front of her and gives me her best puppy dog eyes.

Shit, why are they working?

Am I *seriously* even considering this?

Hallie takes my silence as a chance to continue trying to convince me.

"We can just go have dinner somewhere yummy—casually, of course—and then go to the Kappa's Sweetheart Soiree. The theme is lingerie, and obviously, I wasn't even considering *actually* wearing it because Lane would probably rip out someone's eyeballs, but it would be really fun. Dinner and a party. Sounds like any other Saturday night, except it won't be at Jack's."

I *could* use a night out, and I could definitely use some tequila.

I've been so stressed lately that I haven't been as social as I normally am and being around my friends and people fills my cup in the best way.

Sighing, I begrudgingly nod. "Fine. But if there are any date vibes, I'm out. It's bad enough I have to live with the guy. I'm solely in this for the food, tequila, and QT with you. That's it."

What I don't add is that living with him isn't actually all that bad, but she doesn't need to know that my new roommate is growing on me in a way I'm not ready to admit.

Add it to the list of things I'm pretending don't exist.

"Yes," she screeches, clapping her hands. "Now, the real question. What am I supposed to get Lane?"

"Sex?"

Her eyes roll. "A given, Viv." She starts typing on her computer, and whatever she finds has her brow furrowing as she leans closer to the screen.

"Sometimes I forget that you're this... *sexual goddess* now."

I'm teasing her, but the truth is, Hallie *is* completely different from the girl who started at Orleans U. She's more confident and happier. She's completely blossomed, and I love seeing it.

I love seeing her this way.

"Edible underwear? That sounds like a UTI waiting to happen," she quips, scrunching her nose. "Flavored lube? God, it just gets worse. Why would you even need flavored lube?"

"Blowjobs. Duh."

"Yeah, but *why*?" Her cheeks turn the brightest red as she continues. "I love the way Lane tastes. I don't need some weird-flavored lube. Ugh, I don't know what I'm going to get him. This is hard. It's our first Valentine's Day together, and I want it to be the best."

As if she has to worry about Lane not being into whatever she decides. They're so obsessed with each other, that guy would rope the moon if she asked him to. Literally. She could get him a gremlin for Valentine's Day, and the guy would name it, then stick it next to his bed.

He's obsessed.

And I love that for her.

But… I'm going to stay over here in my very single, very available lane and let those lovebirds do their thing.

"You could get him matching sweaters. He'd probably love that," I tell her jokingly.

"You know, it's so funny that you said that because he tried to convince me to wear a sweater to the Kappa party."

Of course, he did.

I KNEW this was a bad idea.

I absolutely *knew* that I had no business doing this tonight, but I did it anyway.

And I'm immediately regretting my decision to go when I walk into the living room, and my mouth runs dry when I see Reese standing next to Lane.

He's got a black button-down on, with the sleeves rolled up, of course, showing off the tan, corded muscles of his forearms, and a pair of black slacks that are molded to his thick thighs and ass. His dark hair is still wet and curling around his nape from his shower.

I swallow, giving them a small smile and an awkward wave.

I'm not trusting myself to speak right now as I stare at him. "*Holy shit,*" Reese mutters so low that I almost don't hear him at all. "You look… *incredible,* Viv."

Hallie squeals when she sees me, leaping up from the couch, then tossing her arms around me once she's in front of me. "For once, something we can agree on. You look so good, Viv! Oh my god, that dress is killer. Everyone at the party is gonna have eyes on you tonight."

"This old thing?" I tease. My gaze flits to Reese, whose jaw works, not looking very happy about her comment.

The dress has been in my closet forever, but I never really had a place to wear it to. Anyone to wear it for… until tonight.

Not that I'm wearing it for Reese.

Okay, I'm lying. I'm one hundred percent wearing it because I knew he'd like it.

The pale purple satin hugs my body like a glove and stops midthigh, showing off just the right amount of leg without being indecent. I'm wearing my best bra, the one that makes my boobs look bigger, and I used my old curling wand, doing a few loose curls to go with the dramatic, smokey eyeshadow I applied. I'm even wearing heels, which is not something I do often.

It's not a date, I tell myself again for the tenth time tonight.

It's just an opportunity to wear this amazing dress and look hot as fuck.

From the look on Reese's face, it paid off.

"Thank you," I say. "But you're the one that looks hot. That skirt? Perfection."

Hallie glances down at the black skirt she's wearing with a white bodysuit with pink hearts on it tucked into the waist. It's the cutest outfit I've ever seen, and no one could pull it off the way she could.

"You girls ready?" Lane says, walking over and sliding his hand into hers. "I made a reservation for six. Just in case it was packed."

She nods, then looks over at me. "I'm ready if you guys are. Let me check on the Uber."

While she's checking on the car, I walk over to Reese to break the ice. For whatever reason, I'm slightly nervous.

Being nervous makes me feel… out of control of the situation. Lately, it's all I've been feeling. A lot more than I'd like seems out of my control. I never usually feel like this when it comes to a guy, but for some reason, my palms are clammy, and my stomach flutters like there are thousands of butterflies swirling in the pit of it.

It's not a date.

"You know this isn't a date, right?" I say.

"Trust me, you'd know if it was, Sweet Tart," he replies, shooting me a playful wink that makes me want to press my thighs together.

"In your dreams," I say with feigned confidence that I am not at all feeling right at this moment.

"Just two roommates, going out with friends. Plus, a Valentine's date feels like at *least* a ten-date kind of thing. Way after the playlist reveal. Light-years beyond bananas."

A smirk plays on my lips.

"Uber's here!" Hallie says, interrupting us.

"Let's do this," Reese responds. "Ready?"

As I'll ever be.

We walk out to the car, and I take the front seat instead of squeezing in the back. I could practically feel Reese's eyes on me the entire time, and my body feels hot to the touch. I'm flushed, and we haven't even made it to the restaurant yet.

The entire ride there, I'm quiet. I stare out the window, watching the city fly by.

Mostly because I'm trying to convince myself that I'm the only one who's on edge about tonight. Hallie's right. It's just friends, going to dinner and then a party.

Nothing more.

Tonight's about having fun and trying to unwind from the last couple of weeks of nonstop stress. I *need* this. And if I keep being in my head about things, then I won't be able to enjoy it.

The restaurant's packed when we make it inside. Apparently, this is a hot spot tonight, but I can totally see why. The vibe is very chill, cozy, and intimate without feeling overly stuffy and fancy.

The kind of place you can enjoy your dinner and not worry about which fork comes first. Thankfully, I feel less anxious now that we're here. Partly because in the last half of the ride, Reese told a story about his sister, Rosie, from when they were younger, and it was hilarious.

It's honestly adorable seeing how much he loves her.

The waiter takes us to a round booth that's tucked into the back corner of the restaurant, and of course, I end up sitting next to Reese.

He grins, and I ignore him by picking up the menu and pretending to be very interested in what's on it, even though I'm not hungry.

Jesus, why does he have to smell this good?

I can't even concentrate on the words in front of me because his stupid cologne is turning me on.

I'm too horny for this.

He reaches past me for the other menu, brushing along my chest when he does.

"Can you not?" I hiss quietly.

Smirking, he opens the menu. "Can I not what? Please be more specific, Viv."

Exist? *Breathe* in my general direction because it turns me on when it shouldn't?

I glance over at Hallie and Lane, who are bent together over one menu like the lovesick couple that they are, before dragging my eyes back to Reese. "Sit so close to me? I feel like I can't breathe. You're suffocating me."

God, is it hot in here?

He doesn't respond to my remark, only continues to gaze

down at the menu like he's trying to decide on his future, and not what entree to get.

"Mmm. All of this sounds delicious." He muses with a tilt of his lips.

I feel his leg brush against the bare skin of my thigh beneath the table as he moves in his seat, and I almost groan out loud.

Why did I agree to this? This was the worst idea, and I have no clue how I'm going to make it through the next hour sitting this close to the man I want to throttle, and bang at the same time.

10 / viv

The Party Pirate

Unintentional self-sabotaging is a thing.

And apparently, it's the only thing on my agenda from the moment I walk into the Kappa house after dinner. Where he drove me absolutely insane, until I felt like I was going to dry hump his leg at the table or something nuts that is *very* unlike me.

You know what's worse than wanting to have sex with your roommate who never wears a shirt and has stupid muscles and is the most annoying person you've ever met?

Being drunk and jealous while said roommate is across the room laughing at a fun-sized cleat chaser wearing nothing but Barbie-pink lingerie.

Clearly, it's the absolute funniest thing in the world, judging by how hard he's laughing.

My lips tighten in a scowl when she leans in and puts her perfectly manicured hand on his bicep and bats her eyelashes.

Well, what a bunch of *comedians* they are.

Of course, the girl he's talking to is the epitome of perfection with her tiny little scraps of lingerie that are leaving absolutely nothing to the imagination. I'm pretty sure if she bends over

even slightly, her vagina lips would be hanging out of the dental floss she's wearing.

Normally, I am a girl's girl. I'm all for the women in the room.

Do your thing, babe.

But don't do it next to Reese. Do it somewhere else. *Anywhere* else.

I get that my feelings are one hundred percent irrational, but guess what?

Try telling my alcohol-blurred brain that.

This stupid, foreign feeling inside of me intensifies with each giggle and touch.

I'm extremely busy shooting daggers at him when another girl clad in red lingerie walks by with a platter of shots, and I reach out, snagging one in each hand.

Perfect. More cheap tequila. The answer to all of my problems.

I quickly toss it back, letting the burn bring me back to the present and out of my state of jealousy. I'm just about to shoot the other when I hear Hallie call my name.

"Viv?"

Dragging my gaze from Reese, I look over at her. "What?"

"Are you… um, okay?"

"Of course. Why wouldn't I be?" I say, willing myself not to glance back at Reese. Hallie's looking at me strangely, probably because I *am* acting strangely.

I mean, Reese is single.

We're not together. I actually don't even like him. Right? Right.

He has every right to fuck every girl on this campus if he chooses to, and it's not my business.

"I'm great. *Phenomenal*, really."

She's eyeing me warily, her brow quirking. "You look like

you want to murder Reese. Even more than usual. Did something happen?"

I spent the majority of the dinner convincing myself this wasn't a date and it was no big deal, and now that we're here, I'm tipsy, and horny, and jealous.

An absolutely terrible combination.

Fuck Valentine's Day, and fuck relationships in general. There, I said it.

"Nope. Clearly, I'm the third wheel again for the night," I joke lightly.

Her gaze cuts through me. She's not at all buying my attempt to avoid this conversation. I sigh, then toss the other shot back, shivering as it sets my entire body on fire. "If I tell you this, I need absolutely no judgment. I mean none."

In typical Hallie fashion, she holds up her hand in the *Star Trek* sign, and I giggle. The Red Bull and vodka from earlier, combined with the two shots I just downed, are flowing through my bloodstream, relaxing me and making my limbs feel loose.

"I think I *may* want to have sex with Reese… again."

For a second, silence hangs between us. Completely the opposite of what I expected, and I think I may have shocked Hallie into a coma.

She's not moving. Not even blinking.

"Hal?" I wince. Maybe she's actually going to be upset about me keeping this from her.

"Oh my god," she whispers, her eyes going comically wide. "There is no way you just dropped this nuclear frickin' bomb on me in the middle of the Kappa house. Actually, there is no way you didn't frickin' tell me that you and Reese had *sex*!"

Not my finest moment, but I'm tipsy, and I really wish I could've told her before now. I really have hated keeping so much from her lately, and thanks to my alcohol-inspired word vomit, it just came out.

"I'm sorry I didn't tell you." I loop my arm over her shoulder and pull her to me. "I'm *sincerely* sorry from the bottom of my heart. I just… I didn't want *anyone* to know. No one will ever let me live it down if they find out. Plus, it was a mistake. One that I never intended on ever repeating."

Hallie blinks, trying to process everything that I've told her, and I'm kind of scared of what she'll say once she has. It's part of the reason that I've kept the secret for so many months.

"I think my brain is broken," she mutters before taking a deep inhale. She repeats it a few times. "You had sex with Reese. Reese Landry."

I nod, staying silent.

"I *knew* it!" she all but screams. It's more of a very enthusiastic whisper-yell, but still. It feels like every eye in the room is on us. Every eye except the guy that we're talking about, and that just annoys me. "God, I totally knew something was going on between the two of you! Seriously, I told Lane that I was picking up on some weird vibes, and he said that you guys wanted to bang each other. Ha! Joke's on him—you were *definitely* banging."

I gave her a second to ramble, but I stop her at that. "It was a *one-time* thing. One and only time, Hal. I was weak, and I promised myself it would never happen again. That I wouldn't fall for his stupid, charming smile."

Against my will, my gaze drags back to Reese across the room, and Hallie follows my eyes to the culprit.

"Viv, I need more details. I feel like I'm in an alternate universe right now, and normally, I'd be all about that, but I feel like you've been keeping me in the dark. When, where, *how*? And most importantly, if it was a one-time thing, then why do you want to do it again?"

Guilt kicks inside of me at her comment, and my stomach twists. She's right, and I hate it. There's nothing I hate more than keeping things from her, and of all the things I'm keeping a secret right now, this is low on the list.

"I know, Hal. I'm sorr—"

She holds her hand up, stopping me before leaning forward and looping her arm in mine, then tugs me against her small frame. "Don't apologize. It's okay. You had your reasons. I just need you to know that I'm *always* here, Viv. I don't want you to ever think you can't talk to me about something. If we have to hide a body, you already know where to find the pigs."

My head falls to her shoulder as I laugh. "I know. Ugh, I'm just confused. I want to bang him, but I also sometimes want to kick him in the balls."

"Pretty sure that's normal," she says cheekily. "I think it's just the way relationships are."

"He walks around our house with no shirt all the time, and I mean, honestly, Hal, how am I supposed to resist him when he looks like that? I think he does it on purpose because he knows that I want him. I don't *want* to want him, but it's like I just can't stop it." I'm annoyed at myself for it. "Anyway, let's talk about my… dilemma later. I want to do more shots and forget about Reese."

And the rest of my problems.

An hour later, and I am preeeetty drunk. Actually, I'm teetering on the edge of *too* drunk. I've lost count of how many tequila shots I've had, but that's perfectly okay because it just means you're doing it right.

"Viv, you *cannot* go up there!" Hallie giggles. She's not much of a drinker, but even she had a drink tonight. Just one, but still. Lane, of course, has been keeping a very watchful eye on us all night like the dutiful boyfriend he is. I mean babysitter. I mean boyfriend.

I hear my best friend tell me that I can't go participate in the Jell-O wrestling competition, but what I think she *actually* meant to say is yes. Definitely, you're meant to be the champion.

The best idea I've had all night. Maybe all week. Aside from coming to this party, that is.

"Sorry, babe. But it's calling my name, and I must go where the Jell-O takes me. Like the sea, mate!" I announce like a pirate, and I have no idea why. Okay, yeah, I'm drunk.

But I'm happy, and my arms already feel like wiggly noodles, and I haven't even looked for Reese in fifteen whole minutes. He could be in a room with his tongue down Playboy Bunny's throat right now.

And guess what? I don't even care.

What I do care about is getting first place in this Jell-O wrestling competition. I'm gonna take a hoe down. Respectfully, of course.

"This is insane. You are insane!" Hallie cries as I thread my hand in hers and pull her toward the middle of the room, where there's a toddler-size blow-up pool in the center full of red Jell-O.

Ouch, I wonder how long it took the pledges to make all this. "I'm insane, but I'm fun, which makes it all alright, space babe. Plus, you know that I'm overly competitive, and I am taking home that trophy," I say, pointing to the gold trophy on the top of the table that's a girl's naked torso. The boobs look like porn star's with very pointy nipples, and it has a plaque that

reads "Jell-O Champ." It's already mine.

Hallie just shakes her head and giggles, her black, curly hair all over the place from the last hour of dancing with me.

I needed this night so badly, and now I never want it to end. I feel like a free bird, without a single care in the world.

"Okay." I blow out a breath and stretch my neck with my hands. "Hype me up. C'mon, you're my cutman. You gotta get me ready for my match."

I start bouncing on my toes, my grin widening when Hallie clutches her hand to her mouth to stifle her laughter.

"You are *ridiculous,*" she says between laughs. "I can't believe you're actually going to do this."

I'm definitely doing it, and I hope Reese Landry and his stupid grin and even more stupid muscles sees me up there, and I hope that he regrets finding his Playboy Bunny tonight.

Actually, I'm going to make him regret it.

"Last call for entries. I repeat, last call for entries," the speaker booms with the last-call announcement, so I shoot Hallie a grin and turn toward the makeshift stage.

"Go get 'em, Rocky!" she yells behind me as I go.

When I get to the stage, there are several other girls waiting, of course, all in lingerie. I'm the only one actually fully clothed up here, much to the disappointment of most guys in this room, I'm sure.

"You signing up, gorgeous?" a tall blond guy with bright blue eyes asks me. He's got the mic in one hand and a clipboard in the other. "We're about to start."

I nod, plastering on a smile. "Yes. I am."

"Awesome. Here, sign this waiver here, please." He passes the clipboard over to me, and I sign without reading. I already know the gist. There will be Jell-O and wrestling, and they're not responsible if anyone gets hurt.

Got it.

Not worried.

Tequila plus me equals bad bitch.

Wow, do I even need Hallie right now? I'm hyping myself up. Once I take my place in line next to the other girls, Blondie turns the mic back on and faces the crowd before announcing, "Okay, ladies and gentlemen. We have our warriors. These beautiful, incredible ladies will be wrestling it out for the trophy. Even though they are all so wonderful, there can only truly be one Jell-O champion."

The crowd erupts in cheers, clapping, and yelling as he attempts to quiet them down. My eyes search the throng of people, and I finally spot Hallie standing next to Lane… and Reese.

Seems like he ditched his new plaything.

I smirk, my eyes narrowing when he catches my gaze. His expression is unreadable, but I don't miss the way the muscle in his jaw flexes.

Hm.

"And now, we have the lovely Vivienne Brentwood. She's currently majoring in creative writing, loves horror movies, and could *never* pass up Jack's Pizza."

I lift my hand in a dramatic wave, and when a few guys in the front row whistle, I blow them a kiss and wink.

I'm currently feeling like a real bad bitch, so I refrain from glancing at Reese again. He can eat every bit of this up.

"First up will be Vivienne and Santana! But oh, Vivienne, you know this is a lingerie-themed party, right? Unfortunately, you'll have to lose that dress if you're wanting to get into the pit."

I rack my brain to remember if I picked out a matching set today and decide that even if I didn't, oh well.

It's not like we're going to be completely naked. It's just… a little skin.

My eyes find Reese again in the crowd, and he glares back, his eyebrows raised as if to say, "Are you really about to do this?"

I lift my chin higher, reaching behind me to the zipper, and then I lose him in the crowd.

Because he's moving. Actually, he's pushing his way through, and not gently.

I get the zipper to the very bottom of my waist, ready to have it pool at my feet, and then he's there, standing in front of me with a tense jaw and an expression that says I probably shouldn't say anything right now.

Good thing I don't give a single shit.

When he leans down to throw me over his shoulder, I bristle. "Don't you da—"

I'm cut off when he hoists me up and tosses me over like I weigh next to nothing. His hand holds my dress shut as he carries me off the stage, all while I'm hitting his back and demanding to be put down.

"You did not just throw me over your shoulder! How dare you rob me of my title!" I cry, my head spinning from my new position. God, is my head spinning because I'm upside down, or is it because I'm *that* drunk?

He doesn't immediately answer, only pushes through the crowd and carries me toward the exit. Clearly, there's no use in trying to get him to put me down since he's ignoring me.

"Bye, Viv! Love you!' I hear Hallie yell just as we bust through the front door of the Kappa house and out into the cool night air.

"God, put me down, you big idiot," I mumble, squeezing my eyes shut.

"Are you going to keep your fucking clothes on?" he grunts.

Sighing, I counter, "Maybe. Are *you* going to start wearing shirts? Funny how you didn't mind Barbie not having her clothes on in there."

"Oh ho ho," He laughs as he finally, fucking finally lowers me to my feet. "You're cute as fuck when you're jealous, Viv." His taunting tone washing over me as his hands come to my hips, steadying me when I sway slightly. Everything is still spinning, so lovely.

It's turning out to be a swell evening.

My hand finds his arm as I try to keep my balance in my

heels and fail miserably. I am *not* jealous. I'm annoyed. But I also don't feel like fighting right now since I *did* do it to provoke him.

Consider him provoked, I guess.

"I'm bringing you home. You're drunk as shit, Sweet Tart." He reaches behind me and tugs the zipper of my dress up with his jaw tense.

Sweet Tart… That's new. Doing nicknames now, are we? My eyes roll. "Well done, Captain Obvious."

His dark eyes narrow, and he pulls his phone out of his pocket, assumingly calling an Uber.

Since my legs are as wobbly as a newborn foal at this point, I walk over to the ledge of the flower bed and flop down, almost losing my balance and falling backward into the flowers if it wasn't for the hand that slid around my waist at the last second.

Shit.

Reese stands in front of me with an amused expression on his face as he holds me close to his chest. I'm not even attempting to push him away as my hands fist into the front of his button-down since it's probably the only thing keeping me upright.

His dark hair falls in his eyes, a mess of curls that I want to run my fingers through. Just the way I did that night when he was between my thighs, sucking on my clit like it was a lollipop. Groaning, I push him away and sit back on the ledge. Carefully this time.

This man was made simply to tempt me, and god, I am so tired of fighting it.

Maybe it's the tequila talking. Aka Violet, my drunk alter ego. Clearly, she's just as horny as I am because all I want to do is kiss him. Fuck him. Have all his babies.

"Stupid muscles," I mutter.

"What was that?" he asks, his eyebrow arched in question. "Didn't catch that, Viv."

Well, obviously, because it wasn't meant for you.

"Nothing." I sigh. I'm about to ask where the Uber is when a black Cadillac pulls up to the curb and comes to a stop in front of us.

"Of course, you'd pay for the most expensive Uber there is to go three miles."

I brush past him toward the car, but my legs are still so shaky that I only make it three steps before he's sliding his arm around my waist and helping me walk to the car. He opens the door, and then picks me up off my feet, causing me to yelp.

"God, Reese! You pick me up like I'm a damn rag doll," I groan when he deposits me onto the seat, then reaches over me to fasten the seat belt.

He chuckles, and like the drunken idiot that I am, I inhale the scent of him, pressing my thighs together when a dull throb forms. It's like the close proximity reminds my clit of the dirty things he did to it with his wickedly talented tongue.

"That's 'cause you're fun-sized. Now, sit back and keep the seat belt on." With that, he shuts the door.

Why is it so hot when he gets all growly and demanding?

When he opens the other door and slides in beside me, he and the driver exchange pleasantries, and we're pulling onto the highway toward home.

I let my eyes drop closed so I don't puke in the back seat of this man's car. I don't get carsick often, but my head is still spinning from earlier, and I do not trust my ability to keep it together. We're only a ten-minute drive from Kappa to our house, so it feels like a minute later we're pulling up.

That's probably because my perception of time is as tanked as I am right now.

"Let's go, Viv," Reese says softly in my ear as he unbuckles my seat belt and helps me out of the car. I didn't even hear him get out with how I was trying to calm my stomach.

The car pulls away, leaving us on the curb, and he stops me from falling over. "C'mon, up you go."

He squats in front of me, giving me his back. I definitely do check out his ass in this position. Holy shit. All of that squatting has clearly paid off.

My eyebrows shoot up. "Um, you are not giving me a piggyback all the way inside."

"Yeah, I am, or I'm gonna throw you over my shoulder again. Either way, I'm getting you in that house. You're about to break a fucking ankle in those things."

Glancing down at my shoes, I wiggle my toes. Okay, that's fair. I'm one step away from becoming one with the pavement.

"Fine," I sigh, then walk over to him and place my hands on his shoulders as he hikes me effortlessly onto his back, his hands holding the back of my thighs.

He's walking toward the house when he says, "See how easy things can be when you aren't being a brat?"

"Don't make me kick you, Reese."

Chuckling, he carries me up the driveway and to the front door of our house before depositing me gently on my feet, then unlocking the door.

Once we're inside, I toss my purse onto the counter, then hobble toward the couch to try and remove these monstrosities from my feet. Whoever said shoes were a girl's best friend lied. "Thank you for the piggyback ride."

He walks over to where I'm sitting and bends down to his knee, stopping my fumbling hand from unbuckling the strap of my heel. "What else are my muscles for?"

Well, I could think of at *least* five things.

A shiver passes through me when his fingers dance along the skin on my ankle as he unbuckles the strap of my heel. His face is a mask of concentration as he works, and it's possibly the sexiest thing ever, seeing him on his knees in front of me being so… sweet and helpful.

Christ, this has to be the tequila talking.

"I think I told you once that pink was my new favorite color," he rasps, dragging his gaze to mine and making my cheeks run hot. He said that to me when he had me in nothing but my favorite set of pale pink lace, his eyes burning with need so brightly that I still remember it.

I feel the familiar lick of heat inside of me right now, the throb in my clit pulsing in time with my heart.

"But I lied. I think it might be this exact shade of purple," he says, eyeing my dress.

My throat feels tight, arousal prickling beneath the surface as I swallow roughly but remain silent. He quickly makes work of my shoes and carefully pulls them off my aching feet.

"Thank you," I whisper.

He nods. "Do you need anything else?"

Your dick? Preferably balls-deep in me while I ride you? Your tongue inside me?

"Nope. I'm good. Thank you, again."

His grin is still light, and when he stands in front of me, then twists in the direction of his room, I'm immediately regretting not telling him what I actually want.

11 / reese

Boo Bitch

Fuck. Me.

Groaning, I drop my forehead to the tiled wall of the shower and squeeze my eyes shut, desperately trying to push thoughts of the dark hair, blue-eyed seductress currently living in my guest room out of my head.

How the hell did I get myself into this?

It seems like every day is getting harder and harder not to drop to my knees in front of her and beg her to let me touch her.

It's that fucking bad.

And tonight? My already sinking ship has sprung a new hole, and now the entire damn thing is underwater.

When she walked out of her bedroom wearing that dress, I was speechless. She looked like a goddess bathed in purple satin, and it was a punch directly to the gut with a reminder that said *you can't fucking touch.*

Viv on a regular day is the hottest girl I've ever seen, but tonight? I couldn't keep my eyes off her.

No matter how hard I tried.

I wish I didn't know what she tasted like, or the little sounds she makes when she's about to come, or how it feels to sink inside of her and lose myself.

Because then, I wouldn't know what I'm missing. I wouldn't have to walk by her in the hallway and get a whiff of the mint-scented body wash she lathers on and remember the faint taste of it on my tongue.

I would undoubtedly still be attracted to her, but I wouldn't *burn* for her the way that I do. Like every fiber in my body is on fire when I'm in the same room as her.

I'm fucked. That's all there is to it.

My hand lifts from the wall to reach for my cock. Maybe if I relieve some tension, then I won't feel so out of my damn mind. Doubtful, but I'm desperate enough to try anything at this point.

Fisting my semi-hard cock, I pump it once, a groan rumbling from my chest.

BOOOOOM.

The fuck?

I drop my hand and turn the shower off when I hear another loud noise, followed by what sounds like a herd of fucking elephants coming from my bedroom. Stepping out of the glass door, I grab the towel off the rack and then hurriedly wrap it around my waist and rush out into my room.

Shit, it's dark as hell. In my haste to get in the shower, I forgot to turn my lamp on, and I can't see shit but make it in the general direction of my nightstand, then flick the lamp on.

The light illuminates the room, and that's when I see Viv standing at the foot of my bed, wearing nothing but a black baggy T-shirt that hangs to her thighs with a ghost on it that says BOO BITCH, her eyes wide like a deer caught in headlights as she shuffles from one foot to the other.

"Viv, fuck, you scared the shit out of me. Are you okay? Were you moving furniture?"

She rolls her lips together, holding back a giggle, and nods.

"Uh, yes. I mean yes, to the me part, not the furniture part. I… It… It was dark."

My brow arches. Who's Captain Obvious now? I keep my retort to myself and do my best not to let my gaze drop to the creamy expanse of her bare thighs because I've got nothing but this thin-ass towel on, and my dick has been on its worst behavior lately.

"What's up?" I ask, walking to my dresser and pulling out a pair of briefs to sleep in. When I turn back to face her, I catch her staring at my ass, and I grin. "Anything I can help with?"

Her gaze drops to the briefs in my hand, and she immediately covers her eyes so I can slide them on. Like she hasn't seen all of it before.

The towel hits the floor, and I put my feet in and am dragging them up my hips when I see her peeking through her fingers. It's so fucking funny that a laugh escapes me before I can stop it.

"Viv," I say, walking over to my bed and sitting on the edge. "What's going on?"

Silence meets my question. I watch her blow out a breath, and then she's placing her hands on the bed and crawling toward me, causing my throat to tighten.

Fuck.

"Viv, what—"

She makes it to me and then pushes on my shoulders, shoving me back on the bed, flat on my back.

"Stop talking," she rasps. Her voice is low and so fucking sexy as she swings a leg over and straddles my lap. The T-shirt creeps up her thighs when she does, revealing a pair of purple boy shorts that are molded to her pussy.

Goddamnit. This cannot be fucking happening right now.

Dear God, it's me. Reese. Tell me this is a joke and I'm not about to have to do what I have to do because of my moral compass.

She rolls her hips over my erection, and I groan.

"Viv, baby, stop. Stop," I say against her lips as she tries to kiss me. I plant my hands on her hips in an attempt to stop her.

"No. I want you, and I'm so tired of fighting it."

My heart falls to my ass at her words, and fuck, I have waited so goddamn long to hear her say that. Every fucking day since we first hooked up, I have wanted to hear her say that she wants me as much as I want her.

She slides her hands from my shoulders up to my neck, and her fingers tangle in my hair. Her favorite spot. When she kisses me again, this time, her tongue sneaks past my lips, tangling with mine, and my fingers dig into the soft, fleshy skin of her hips.

I have to stop this.

With superhuman strength I don't know how the fuck I'm possessing, I tear my lips from hers and pull back.

"We can't do this. Viv, you're still drunk, and it would feel like I'm taking advantage of you."

Rejection shines on her face, and immediately, her lips tug into a frown. "Are you kidding me? You don't *want* me?"

"Listen to me," I say, leaning forward to slide my hands along her jaw, staring into the deep blue pools of her eyes. "You think I don't want you, Viv? Fuck, I want you so bad I'm losing my goddamn mind. There is nothing more I want in the fucking world than this."

The expression she's wearing says she doesn't believe what I'm saying, but damn, I can't in good conscience fuck around with her knowing how much she's had to drink. And with how wishy-washy she's been about her interest in me, I'm getting whiplash a little, and I don't want her to regret it.

Do I want her? Fuck yeah, I do.

But I'll wait until she's sober and there's no question about what she wants from me. No hesitation. No doubt.

I flex my hips, brushing against her, my brow arching when her breath hitches.

"Does it *feel* like I don't want you, Viv?" After a beat, she shakes her head.

My thumb grazes her jaw as I speak. "Exactly. When the time comes for me to touch you—and trust me, it fucking will—it'll be when there's no question about your consent."

"Ugh, why is the room spinning?" She blinks. "Oh shi—" she starts but stops abruptly, closing her mouth and swallowing visibly. Her face has gone green, and I sit up, gathering her in my arms. "I don't feel so good."

Oh hell.

Suddenly, she scrambles from my lap, slapping a hand over her mouth as she sprints to the bathroom. Jumping from the bed, I follow behind her just as she makes it to the toilet bowl and falls to her knees. Her small frame drapes over the basin, and then she vomits so hard her entire body shakes.

Without hesitation, I gather her hair in my fist and pull it back from her face as she retches.

Every time I think she's done, she heaves again. Fuck, I hate this.

Not because I can't handle puke—I don't give a shit about that. I've seen enough puke and blood in my lifetime playing ball that I'm completely unfazed by any type of bodily fluid.

But because I can't do anything more than this while she's miserable. It's the nurturer in me, or whatever Rosie likes to call it.

I hate feeling helpless in any situation with the people that I care about.

Finally, when she's finished and sits up, I drop her hair, watching as she sags back against the wall, a look of pure exhaustion on her face. Her usually bright eyes are dull, and there are dark circles under them.

Even though she looks like she feels like shit, she's still so beautiful it makes my chest tight.

"You didn't have to do that," she says quietly. "Watch me puke. I can't imagine how unsexy I look right now."

Getting the alcohol out of her system seems to have sobered her up a little, and now she just looks tired.

I shrug, reaching into the cabinet and pulling out a washcloth to wet it under warm water from the sink. "Not the first or last time I've seen someone puke, Sweet Tart. And for the record, you still look sexy as fuck right now."

She takes the rag from my extended hand and pats her mouth with it.

"There's a spare toothbrush in the drawer right there if you want to brush your teeth. I'll leave you and let you get cleaned up."

When she nods, I give her a small smile, leaving her to it.

Ten minutes later, she comes out of the bathroom, looking less pale as she walks back towards my bed. "I know you said we can't do anything tonight, and I understand. I've had too much tequila, clearly, and just tried to climb you like a tree. But…" She trails off, her gaze dropping to the rumpled bed. "Could I sleep with you? *Just* sleep? I just don't really feel like being alone right now."

I'm already pulling the covers back for her when I nod. "Of course. C'mon." I'm surprised as fuck that she's even asking, but she keeps surprising me, giving me exactly the opposite of what I think's going to happen. It surprises me that a girl who keeps trying to hide things from everyone keeps giving me the gift of her vulnerability.

Her warm, soft body slips beneath the covers next to me, facing me with her hands tucked under her head. The heat of her body radiates, and our eyes are locked.

Moments pass with neither of us saying a thing, simply… breathing.

Without thinking, I reach out and twirl my finger around a piece of her hair. Her eyes drop closed, and she makes no move to stop me, so I run my fingers through the soft strands, gently playing with her hair.

"Mmm," she murmurs. "Keep doing that, please."

Not that I had any intention of stopping. So I continue dragging my fingers gently over her scalp, scooting my body just an inch—okay, three—closer to her.

I can't remember a time where I've done this before. Laid in bed with a girl that didn't involve sex. Usually, girls want to fuck me, and then we're exchanging pleasantries and they're out the door. They know the score before it happens, and I'm always up-front and honest that I'm not looking for a relationship or anything like it. It's always been that way.

So this is a first for me, and it's a little scary that I like it so much. It's even scarier that I think that it's solely because it's *Viv*.

"When I was younger, my mom used to do this for me."

"Play with your hair?" I ask.

She nods against my hand. "Yeah. Back before… everything happened. She would come into my room at night and talk to me about my day and play with my hair. Sit with me for hours and talk about absolutely nothing at all, but it always felt like everything. I miss it sometimes."

The sadness in her voice makes my chest ache. I don't really know what's happening at home, but whatever it is, it's weighing on her.

I wrap my arms around her body and pull her to me, her face burrowing into my bare chest, without even thinking about it. I just want to fucking hold her right now, and I hope like hell she doesn't give me shit.

Her body tenses for a second, and then she melts into my arms.

"Thank you," she whispers. "For everything tonight."

"Always, Viv."

Neither of us moves, only the sound of our breathing filling the room, and in what feels like only seconds, I hear her breathing even out, and she's asleep in my arms like it's the most natural thing in the world.

And truthfully? It feels like it is.

12 / viv

Everything Changes

My entire body is on fire. Not literally, but it feels like I'm wrapped in the warmest, fluffiest cloud surrounding every inch of my skin. And that's what pulls me from sleep. I crack one eye open and immediately regret doing so when the entire room is entirely too bright, bathed in the morning sunlight.

It's too early to be awake right now, and my skull throbs in reaction to the rays. My eyes drop shut to block the light.

Wait.

Both of my eyes snap open this time when I see the bookshelf full of trophies and realize I'm not in my bedroom. The warm, fluffy cloud that I feel all around me? It's definitely not a cloud.

Carefully, I pull the covers up and see the tan, muscled, veiny forearm slung around my waist, tucked under my side.

Reese. I'm in his bed, and he's got me hauled against the front of him, all of him. Every hard inch.

Last night comes flooding back in a wave of embarrassment and regret.

I was *so* drunk.

Sloppy, make a fool out of myself drunk, and I literally threw myself at him. Right before I puked in his bathroom and he held my hair because, of course, throwing myself at him wasn't mortifying enough already.

Reese shifts behind me, and I feel his thick cock hard against my back. My teeth bite into my lower lip as I stifle a moan. God, I'm so embarrassed I want the ground to open up and swallow me into it, but this also feels good. Entirely *too* good. Being held tightly in his arms, surrounded by his scent, feeling him pressed into me like this.

Waking up… *not* alone.

As the memories start to flood back, what I can't stop thinking about is how he took care of me last night. When I was the definition of a hot mess express, he treated me with kindness and compassion. With respect. For the first time in as long as I can remember, I was completely vulnerable with someone. I needed someone to look after me for once, and instead of him throwing it in my face or making a joke about it, he took care of me when he didn't have to.

He held my hair when I was sick and pulled me into his arms when I felt the walls closing in around me. When I crawled on top of him and propositioned him, he turned me down gently. Most guys would've taken advantage of the situation when I threw myself at him, but he didn't. He was a gentleman when he didn't have to be.

And instead of pushing him away, I let him in. I asked for his comfort. I let him past those walls that I've spent years building. Just for a little bit. That feels like a completely different version of Reese than what I had convinced myself that he is.

And I think I might have been wrong about him. Truthfully, I think I've known that for a while now, and I've just not wanted to see it. But last night proved that without a doubt, and now I'm entirely unsure what to do with this new realization.

I sigh, burrowing further into the covers, into his warmness, and when I accidentally rock against his cock, he lets out a deep groan that vibrates my entire body to my core. My thighs press together of their own accord, and my clit begins to pulse.

I'm too horny to be half-dressed in this guy's bed with his cock digging into my ass as he spoons me.

His arm tightens around me, pulling me even closer against him, and I squeeze my eyes shut when I realize he's awake, not quite ready to face him.

I feel the pad of his thumb brushing against the exposed skin of my stomach where the baggy T-shirt I threw on has ridden up. My mind drifts back to last night when I told him how tired I was of fighting my attraction for him and how every part of it was true.

What's the saying… drunken words are sober thoughts? Should I make an excuse that I have to go to the bathroom so I can flee, or do I ask him for the second time in twelve hours to have sex with me?

Because honestly, both options seem great right now.

I want him in the dirtiest, filthiest way, and I'm aching for a physical release. I'm aching for a repeat of the night that we spent together, and it's only because of my liquid courage last night that I could stop overanalyzing and overthinking for five seconds to ask for it. That and maybe a bit of jealousy that drove me to the tequila.

Even though we're both awake, neither of us moves aside from his fingers grazing my skin. Neither of us wants to be the one to make the first move, but I'm done holding back. I'm so turned on right now from the barest of touches that I feel like I'm going out of my mind, and I want to say fuck it for once.

Let my body make the decision and not my brain.

My hand moves over his on my stomach, and I slowly inch it lower, holding my breath the further it goes until his fingers sweep along the edge of my panties.

This is as close as I'm going to get to asking for him to touch me. It's a clear go-ahead, and now I'm leaving it to him.

For a second, his fingers don't move, and neither does he.

They rest above the waistband, but he doesn't dip his fingers inside. My heart is racing inside my chest as beats pass.

I'm about to flee with what's left of my pride when I feel his lips near my ear. "Is this what you need?"

His voice, hoarse and gravelly from sleep, combined with the brush of his lips against the shell of my ear, causes an involuntary shiver to rack my body, straight to my aching clit.

God, I'm so wet that it's almost embarrassing.

But after last night, I think we're past the point of embarrassment.

Or maybe I just don't have it in me to care anymore. I want this, and of all the things I deny myself, this isn't going to be one.

Swallowing roughly, I nod, and that's all it takes. My sober consent is all he wanted to give me what I need.

He slides two fingers beneath the waistband of my panties and dips into the wetness pooling between my legs, grunting when he feels how ready I am.

"Fuck, you're drenched, baby." His lips press against my neck, and another shiver rolls through me as my hips rock, desperate for friction. Anything to dull the throb. "I bet it aches, doesn't it?"

He pinches my clit between his fingers, and my back bows, spots dotting my vision as pleasure snakes down my spine and blooms inside of me. My nerve endings feel on fire with each stroke of his fingers. It feels so good, and I feel delirious with desire, delirious with need for him.

"Let me take care of you, baby. Let me give you what you need," he rasps as his fingers circle my clit roughly. "Fuck, Vivienne, do you know how long I've been dreaming about this? How many times I've fucked my fist and thought about sucking on your needy little clit again? How many times I've come with the thought of your tight cunt wrapped around my cock? I'm going out of my goddamn mind for you."

I'm already teetering on the edge of an orgasm just from his fingers on my clit and from the filthiness of his words. That's how tightly I'm wound, ready to snap at any given moment.

Pathetic, really, but I'm no longer in control of my body. It belongs to Reese and Reese alone.

My legs begin to tremble as they fall open giving him better access to strum his fingers along my sensitive clit. He's not being gentle, which is exactly what I asked him for that first night. The fact that he remembers that and is so good at playing my body like an instrument surprises me.

Every touch is purposeful, and it feels euphoric.

His fingers slip down to my opening, then circle my entrance before pressing inside, immediately finding my G-spot. A whimper sounds from the back of my throat, a desperate, needy sound that would normally embarrass me, but I'm too out of my mind for him, for the orgasm that's only just out of reach.

"Just like that, baby," he groans, fucking me hard with his fingers as his lips nip at the sensitive spot beneath my ear. The sound of his fingers slapping against my skin fills the room. The filthiest sound, and I want more. I reach down and rub my clit as his fingers reach deep inside of me, over and over, our movements both sloppy and frantic yet so hot. "Be a good girl and come on my fingers so I can lick it all up. I've wanted to taste you again for so fucking long. Give it to me."

That's all it takes to send me careening off the ledge into a state of bliss. My orgasm rocks through me, pleasure overtaking every inch of my body, and I give myself over to it. I feel the wetness coating his fingers, sticky between both of us as I come, and the feral groan I hear in my ear as I do prolongs my orgasm. He's wringing every ounce of pleasure out of me as I continue to rub my clit until it's too sensitive to touch, and my body's bucking against him.

Only then, when I'm able to open my eyes as my chest heaves and my entire body falls limp, does he pull his fingers out of me. I hear him suck them into his mouth greedily, and it sends an aftershock of pleasure through me.

It's so dirty and *so* fucking hot.

"You taste so damn good I could eat you every fucking day for every meal and still never have enough."

Shit. What did I just do? Does he think now that we're going to… like, be together? I just… didn't realize how much I needed… *physical touch* until today. And that scares me.

"Don't get used to it. You know we're good at one-offs, but that's all it is, Reese. A onetime thing," I smart, trying to make light of what we just did.

He stiffens behind me, and I hear him scoff. "Don't do that shit. Don't act like you don't want me as much as I want you, Vivienne. Not while my fingers are still wet with your cum."

I sit up, pulling my T-shirt back down as I turn to face him. "So what? It was a purely physical thing. Look, don't complicate this."

I hate that he's heavy lidded, the ultimate picture of bedroom eyes, and so unbelievably sexy with his hair sticking in twelve different directions. No one should wake up in the morning with bed head and morning breath and be that effortlessly sexy.

"Who says I'm complicating it? Why do you keep pushing me away at every turn when it gets to be too much for you? Seems like *you're* the one making it more complicated than it is."

Inside my head, I'm rebuilding those walls I've so carefully crafted brick by brick, trying to push him back out from the space he's taken up inside them.

Where all of my vulnerabilities are safe, and so is my heart.

Tossing the covers back, I swing my feet over and am out of

his bed in a single beat. "Whatever, Reese. I'm not doing this. Thanks for the orgasm."

I swing his bedroom door open, then slam it shut as I stalk into the hallway. I know I'm being a bitch, but I don't know how else to put my defenses back up.

To make sure he understands that just because we have this physical attraction to each other, it doesn't mean he gets to bulldoze in like he tries to do with everyone else.

Once I'm back in my bedroom, I grab a change of clothes from my dresser and stomp out to the hallway and into the bathroom, shutting the door behind me. I hate that I can still smell him on me, so I'm glad to peel off the T-shirt that has his scent clinging to it and my panties that are still damp from his fingers inside of me.

Stupid, talented fingers. Stupid muscles. Stupid. Stupid.

Stupid.

It's better this way, I tell myself as I turn the knob on the shower and water begins to spray from the showerhead.

Just as I'm about to step under the spray, the door flies open, and Reese busts in. His expression is determined as he makes his way over to me.

"Oh my god, I'm *naked*!" I say, making a feeble attempt at covering myself. Although, it's not like he hasn't seen it before. More than once at this point. "What the hell, Reese?"

"Fuck. This," he says, closing the distance between us, grabbing my face between his big hands, and slamming his lips on mine. My protest dies on my tongue as he kisses me like a man possessed.

I should push him away. I should yell at him to get out and to pretend earlier never happened. To insist we reinstate our boundaries. I know exactly what I *should* do.

But I don't.

His tongue licks at the seam of my lips, demanding entry,

and then he's sucking on my tongue and kissing me ravenously, until my knees feel weak. Until my heart is pounding so hard against my chest that I feel like I might actually faint.

A minute later, he pulls back, panting, a wild look in his eyes.

"Do you fucking *see* why I'm not going to let you run, Viv? Because if it was a mistake, or if it was wrong, then it wouldn't fucking feel like this. It wouldn't feel so goddamn good."

I swallow as my hands drop to my sides. I don't know how to respond because even though I want to run and pretend it's all bullshit, I want him despite all the reasons I shouldn't.

I'm trying to gather the strength to pull back, but I can only focus on the way his thumb grazes along my chin and the way his dark eyes are holding mine. How his chest is heaving at the same rate as mine from a kiss that felt like the world stopped spinning for a moment.

"You feel that, Viv?" he murmurs against my mouth, bringing my hand to the front of his boxers to feel how hard he is beneath them. "You feel this? This isn't fucking nothing. This is me *aching* for you."

His dick jerks in my hand as I close my palm over him, and he's so hot that my brain feels like it's short-circuiting. It's impossible to think around him when he's doing things like… touching me.

Existing.

Making me a wet, needy mess.

"Reese, I can't—" I shake my head. "I can't do a relationship. My life is a fucking wreck, and I can't take on anything else right now. So I can't give you that."

"I'm not asking for a relationship. I'm asking for you to stop denying what we both so clearly want. I'm asking for you to let your body have what it fucking wants, Viv," he grunts, hand trailing down my body, disappearing between my thighs. "I'm asking to come home from practice and eat this cunt as a post-workout meal. I'm asking to fuck you until your cum is running down my cock."

My legs tremble when he brushes a thumb over my clit. I'm beginning to realize how sincerely fucked I am when it comes to this man.

He has the ability to get under my skin like no one else.

Effortlessly.

Pulling his hand from my clit, he brings it to my mouth, where he traces his finger that's glistening with my wetness along my bottom lip before pushing it into my mouth. "Taste how badly you want me."

It might actually be the dirtiest thing that's ever happened to me, and I feel every ounce of it between my legs, the wetness dripping out of my pussy. I level my gaze, holding his eyes as I suck his finger into my mouth and swirl my tongue around the pad.

It's at this moment that I decide I'm done running. That I'm going to give him exactly what he's asking for. For me. And no one else.

His eyes darken, the corner of his lip tugging up into a cocky grin. "Friends with benefits, baby. That's all I'm asking for."

I reach up and pull his finger from my mouth. "*Roommates* with benefits. Friends is laying it on a *lítttttle* thick, don't ya think?"

"I've had my tongue on your pussy, babe. I think that makes us friends."

God, his mouth.

He's crude, and Jesus, so fucking sexy.

"Whatever. We're roommates who want to fuck each other who may *one day* be friends. Easy. Uncomplicated. Exactly what I need."

He nods, his shoulder dipping with it. "Sounds good to me."

Steam billows around us, and only then do I realize that the shower has been running the entire time. "Okay, perfect. Glad we got that out of the way. Now, if you'll excuse me, I'm going to take the shower that you just interrupted."

His gaze drops to my breasts, his eyes flickering with desire as his tongue darts out and he licks his lips. "Oh, you mean *we're taking* a shower? Get your fine ass in there, woman."

13 / reese

Friends who shower together

I feel like I'm in a fever dream, and Vivienne is the main character as she steps into the shower and under the spray, puffs of steam billowing around her.

I've got to still be asleep and having the best fucking dream of my life.

"Well, are you coming, or are you just going to stand there and watch?" Her teeth rake over her bottom lip as she taunts through thick, dark lashes, her hand traveling down her slippery torso and disappearing between her thighs.

My gaze follows her hand before I drag my eyes back up to meet hers and shrug. "I guess that depends on if you're going to show me how you've been fucking yourself when you think about me."

She can tease all she wants as long as I get a front-row seat.

Have at it, baby.

"So cocky. Who says I was thinking about you?"

"I do. Now, show me exactly what I've been dreaming about."

Viv's eyes darken and turn heavy lidded with desire at my demand. She leans back against the tiled wall and begins rubbing languid circles on her clit, a soft moan falling from her lips.

One hand reaches up and cups her breast before she pinches her nipple between her fingers and rolls. She continues to rub her clit and tug at her piercings, the winning combination that sends her barreling toward an orgasm, but I'm not letting her come that easily.

Nah, I wanna drag this out. Edge her until she can't fucking move. Taste her until her legs are trembling and can't hold her weight, and then I'll carry her into my bedroom and make her come on my face again.

I've waited so long for this, I'm in no hurry to stop.

"Good girl. Now, sit on the bench and spread your legs wide for me," I instruct as I quickly shed my briefs and kick them to the side, then reach for my cock and wrap my fist around it, squeezing tightly. A bead of precum seeps from the slit, and my balls feel heavy with the overwhelming need to come.

When she sees me stroking my cock, she pulls her lip between her teeth. A hazy, unfocused look flares in her eyes before she steps backward and lowers herself to the bench.

My brow arches. "Does it make you wet watching me fuck my fist, Vivienne?"

She nods, and I watch as her fingers dip down to her entrance, teasing her hole before one slips inside. Her eyelashes flutter, and her eyes drop shut, her head falling back against the tile.

Fuck, I could come just like this, watching her slide her finger knuckle-deep in her pretty pink little pussy.

I watch her play with herself until I can't take another second of not touching her. Even if it's the hottest thing I've ever seen.

She's the hottest thing I've ever seen, and she's spread out just for me like a present to unwrap.

Like she's mine.

That might not be true, but fuck, one day…

I step into the shower and stop in front of her, pumping my cock slowly. When her gaze drops to my hand and she licks her lips hungrily, I feel arousal tugging at the base of my spine.

I want to make it last all fucking day, but the way she's looking at me, laid out on this bench, has my control slipping. There's no way I can last without tasting her, touching her. Making her come.

I drop to my knees between her thighs, my eyes level with her pussy. "Use your fingers and spread yourself open for me, Vivienne. I want to see all of you."

Her throat bobs, and she swallows roughly and follows my demand like a good fucking girl. Apparently, the only time she *doesn't want* to be a brat is when I'm between her thighs.

Guess I'm going to have to spend more time here, making her come so she can't use her smart mouth for anything other than moaning my name when my tongue is buried in her pussy.

"Good girl," I rasp as she uses her pointer and middle finger to spread her lips open, giving me exactly what I want. I reach beside her and grab the showerhead and turn the setting up to where the water is a steady spray. "You know what happens to good girls, baby?"

"What?" she breathes.

I bring the showerhead to her clit, letting the water pulsate against it. Her back bows, and her hand darts out, needing something to grasp against the slippery shower wall.

"Oh god."

She's squirming, panting, writhing, and I've only just started.

Her legs fall open further, beckoning for more.

"Look how pretty you are, Viv. Your cheeks flushed almost the same pink as this pretty little cunt."

I pull the showerhead back and lean forward, circling my

tongue on her throbbing clit before latching on and sucking, rolling it in between my lips.

The sound that leaves her lips is needy and desperate, and it makes me fucking crazy. It unleashes something primal inside of me, something possessive, the part that wants to mark her and make her mine.

I lap at her clit feverishly, then flatten my tongue and drag it from her asshole back to the sensitive nub.

"You taste so fucking good. I'll never have enough of you. I'm obsessed with your pussy, and I have been since the first night you let me have it," I mutter hoarsely. My dick is weeping, I can feel my balls tight and ready for release, but right now, Viv's all that matters. I want to make her come, and I want it dripping down my fucking chin once I'm done feasting on her pussy.

Her pleasure is my priority. Always.

"Hold this to your clit while I fuck you with my tongue, baby." I hand her the showerhead, watching as she brings it to her clit. The spray pulsates against her flesh, causing her hips to roll against my mouth. My tongue teases her entrance before I delve inside, fucking her with it, relishing in the wanton sounds she's making.

That's my girl.

So fucking responsive.

When I replace my tongue with my fingers, sliding them deep and hooking them up, she whimpers shallowly, her chest heaving with pleasure.

"Eyes on me, Vivienne," I demand.

Her eyes snap open, connecting with mine as I seal my mouth over her clit once more, savoring the taste of her on my tongue. I flick it once, then again before saying, "I want to watch you come on my tongue. Let me taste your cum, baby."

My fingers slam into her roughly, her back arching even

further as she cries out. Her legs quiver against my head as she explodes, and her hands fly to my hair, yanking almost violently while she bucks against my mouth.

"Reese, oh… Reese. Fuck. Fuck. Reese." She's chanting my name like I caught the winning pitch and she's the only person in the stands.

I continue fucking her with my hand, swiping my tongue on her clit, curling my fingers, and massaging her G-spot until they're covered in her arousal. And I lick every fucking drop up like a man starved. When I can't take it another second, I reach for my cock with my free hand, fisting it roughly while I pump my fingers inside of her cunt, dragging out her orgasm until she's limp.

My muscles are taut, balls aching as I thrust into my fist, my hips punchy and erratic from the buildup and prolonged edging. "I want to make *you* come," Viv says through a heavy-lidded

gaze.

"I'm good. This was for you, Sweet Tart." My fingers slip out of her, and I place a soft kiss against her clit and a few more lingering kisses along her thigh. "I didn't do it expecting anything in return."

She sits up, and my gaze drops to her chest at the glint of metal through her nipples that catches the light.

I still can't fucking get over how sexy it is.

"I want to. Can I *please* make you come, Reese?" she says wickedly, her cheeks still flushed from the orgasm I just gave her.

Fuck. Jesus Christ, I almost come just hearing her *say* that. Fresh arousal pricks beneath the surface of my body as she pulls me off my knees and flips us around, pushing against my chest until my ass hits the cool tiled bench.

She climbs over me, settling in my lap, my cock hard and

straining between us, then leans forward, dragging her lips over mine in a teasing kiss.

Just barely, but enough for my dick to twitch between us.

"I forgot how huge your cock was." She blinks, her eyes lingering on my erection as she reaches between us and wraps her small fist the best she can around me.

My eyes almost roll back in my head with how good it feels to have her touch me. She swipes the pearl of cum from the slit with the pad of her thumb and spreads it over my head. She pumps me slowly, her teeth raking over her lips as she eyes my cock hungrily.

She seems to be enjoying this as much as I am, and I'm fucking mesmerized watching her stroke me. She twists her hand in controlled motions, taking her time working me.

My head falls back against the tile with a thud, and a groan tears from the back of my throat, my eyes dropping shut.

It feels like fucking heaven.

"Harder," I rasp, my eyes still closed as I bring my hand around hers on my cock, squeezing tighter, showing her what I like. She pumps me harder in a steady rhythm until my hips are flexing and I'm fucking her hand.

I can't hold back any longer. Her entire body lifts with my hips, and I decide here and now that I'm never hip thrusting at the gym ever again in my life. I'll do my workout right the fuck here with Viv on top of me.

"Fuuuuuck yeah. Just like that, baby." I shudder when her thumb brushes the underside of my head, chills racking my entire body. "You're perfect."

I'm a fucking goner the moment she brings her other hand to my balls and rolls them in her palm. Pure, white-hot pleasure jolts through my body as she does.

My hands fly to her thighs, fingers digging into the soft flesh as I come so hard I think I might actually pass out. Thick, creamy ropes of cum cover my stomach and her hands.

"Vivvvvv, *fuck,*" I groan, my hips still pumping as she wrings the orgasm out of me until I'm completely spent. And when I'm finally able to pry my eyes open, I see her grinning down at me, a devilish smirk on her lips.

She scoots back on my thighs, leans down, and drags her tongue through the cum covering my abs, her gaze locked on mine. Then, she swallows it down and licks her pouty lips like it's the best fucking thing she's ever tasted.

And now, I'm ruined.

Ruined for this girl.

"YOU REALIZE that even though we're... hooking up, it doesn't mean that I'm going to stop giving you shit, right?" Viv says from her spot beside me on the couch. Her hair's still damp from our shower, and the T-shirt of mine I insisted she wear, purely for selfish purposes, pools around her legs.

She protested about the T-shirt, but finally, I pulled it over her head and sealed my lips over hers, promptly shutting her up.

What she didn't argue about is the pair of wool socks she swiped from my dresser and slipped her ice-cold feet into. They almost come up to her knees, and the sight still has me snickering. "My favorite thing about you is your mouth, Viv. Why would you ever stop trying to make my dick hard?" I arch my brow in question.

"I think there might *actually* be something wrong with you." Her tone is light, playful.

My shoulder dips in a shrug as I stick my hand in the bag of

Veggie Straws in her lap and then toss a few into my mouth. "So, I think now that we've decided to bang on the regular, we should get to know each other. The basics, at least. You know, the important stuff."

"Okay…Why?"

"Just humor me. Nothing too personal, I promise." Finally, she nods.

"Ghosts or aliens?" I ask with a serious expression.

Viv tosses her head back and laughs, and a grin curves my lips up.

"*That's* the important stuff?"

I nod, swiping more straws. "Yeah, of course. You and Hallie are into your… creepy things, so I need to know what you prefer."

For a second, she contemplates between bites. Her fingers are dusted in seasoning, and when she sucks the tip of her thumb between her lips, my dick jerks.

"If you keep doing that, I am not responsible for my dick poking you in the ass, Sweet Tart."

She holds my eyes as she continues to suck her fingers, not stopping until they're clean. "Behave. We're supposed to be *getting to know* each other. And… ghosts. Aliens are definitely more Hallie's thing. I mean, I love all things supernatural, and I'm fascinated by them, but I'm definitely a ghost kinda girl."

It's what I figured. Before I can respond, she continues. "You know the old theme park? The one that's been abandoned since the flood? It heavily inspired a lot of *Haunted Homicide*. It's owned by the city now, but it is said to be one of the most haunted places in the country. Built on a burial ground or something?"

I notice how her entire face has lit up at the mention of her book. I can tell how passionate she is just by talking about it. It sparks my curiosity, and I want to know more.

"My friends and I snuck out in high school and tried to get in, but the cops ran us off. Ever since then, I've been researching it, trying to find out anything I could about its history. It's so eerie and creepy now. I love it. Anyway, it's where one of the victims in my book dies, and so it's a pretty important location."

"You and your scary shit." I shiver dramatically. No fucking thank you. Yes, I am a man who does not fuck with ghosts. "Can you contact the city to try and tour it? For, say… educational purposes? You're an author."

She shakes her head. "Aspiring author. And no, I tried over the summer, but the city never even responded. It's closed to the public, so I'm sure that's the reason they didn't respond. But anyway, what about you? Aliens or ghosts?"

There's a teasing smirk on her lips because she already knows the answer to that question.

"Uh, neither. Moving right along. What's your favorite food? Besides SweeTarts. That's an addiction."

She laughs softly until her brows pull together, and sadness flickers across her face. "My dad… he used to make the best gumbo. It was my favorite. He used to spend hours in the kitchen when I was growing up, always cooking for me and mama. Our fridge was always overflowing with Tupperware. It used to drive my mom crazy."

I reach out and pluck the bag from between her legs, then drag her into my lap. I can't fucking take it, seeing the raw vulnerability, the haunting sadness in her eyes, and not touch her.

"He sounds like my kind of guy," I say, tucking her hair behind her ear. "You know, you can always talk about him to me. Even if it makes you sad, Viv. It's okay to be sad."

The conversation has grown heavier, and I know that scares her. Anything below the surface makes her clam up and push me out, but I fucking care, and I need her to know that. Even if all she wants is to fuck me and nothing more, I still care.

I know she's got Hallie, but I want to be there for her too. "Thank you." She pauses and clears her throat, then crawls back over to her spot, avoiding my gaze entirely. "What about you? What's your favorite food?"

I shrug. "*Food*. I'm not picky—I'll eat just about anything. But if I had to choose a favorite, probably pizza from Jack's or this little sushi place deep in Manhattan. They've got the best sashimi in the world. It's me and my sister's favorite. Last year, she and my mom had it flown in for my birthday because I couldn't get there because of baseball."

Viv scoffs. "Why am I not surprised? I can't even *imagine* how much that must have cost."

"I think it's Rosie's way of bridging the distance between us. It's not about spending money but trying to do things that make us feel close together, even though we're thousands of miles apart. She always has my favorite sports drinks sent over before a game, and sometimes she'll just call to sit on FaceTime and watch a movie together. She's always been on the sidelines rooting for me no matter what I do."

"I think I'd like her," Viv announces once I'm through talking.

"Yeah? She's been asking non-fucking-stop to meet you on FaceTime."

Her eyes widen. "Really? Why?"

Nodding, I roll my eyes. "Yeah, she's convinced we're in love and harboring a secret baby or some shit. I don't know, she reads too many romance books and talks about tropes, which I do not understand in the slightest. She's a menace to society."

"A fellow book lover? Say less. Let's call her. Right now." Well, shit.

I expected Viv to feel, I don't know… *weird* that my sister wanted to meet her since we're, you know, *strictly* roommates, so I'm a little surprised that she's being so agreeable.

"You sure?"

"Yes, duh. Call her, *All-Star*."

I swipe my phone off the arm of the couch and unlock it. Rosie's generally always the first person on my call log, so I quickly press her name and wait for her to answer.

A few seconds later, her face comes into view. She's upside down, her hair hanging off what looks like the side of her bed, judging by the bright yellow comforter beneath her.

"Save me from this misery," she bellows dramatically, and then realizes that I'm not alone. She flips back upright, and her eyes widen. "Wait. Please tell me that you are the mysterious Vivienne that my brother has been hiding."

Viv laughs and nods, lifting her hand in a wave. "It is I. Nice to meet you."

"Nice to meet you too. I feel like I already know you with how much my brother talks about you," Rosie says, waggling her eyebrows.

And I'm going to kill her.

"I do… not… talk about you all the time," I tell Viv before clearing my throat. "I mean, I've mentioned a few things to Rosie, but it's not like I just sit around talking about you twenty-four seven or anything."

I drag my eyes from Viv's to Rosie and widen them slightly in a way that says, *Please shut up before I throw myself off the roof.*

"Don't worry, I already know he's obsessed with me," Viv says and reaches out, pinching my nipple like the menace she is.

God, these two are fucking perfect for each other. Menaces.

I swat her hand away as she turns back to my phone and says to Rosie, "I hear you're a book lover. Tell me some of your favorite authors."

"Oh god, I could talk about books for days!" Rosie says excitedly. "Ummm, okay, so I'm a *huge* romantasy fan, so probably Kerri Maniscalco?"

Viv squeals, plucking the phone out of my hand and bounding off the couch with it in tow. "Please tell me you've read her latest? I've been dying to talk about it! I swear I stayed up all night turning the pages like a freakin' fiend."

Taking the bag of Veggie Straws with her, she walks toward her room, leaving me on the couch, watching her go. Rosie starts talking a mile a minute about different authors and something about knotting, whatever the fuck that is, just as Viv's door closes.

Damn. This girl just stole my phone, my sister, *and* my snacks.

Why the hell do I like that so much?

14 / viv

Take Me Out To The Ball Game

Reese and I have fallen into a comfortable routine over the past week. Even though our schedules are still all over the place, the few times we've seen each other, it's been…

explosive.

That's the only way to describe it.

Living with someone who can't keep their hands off you is fun, and god, it's *so* hot.

The moment Reese sees me, he's on me and tearing my clothes off, hoisting me onto counters and kneeling before I can even get a single word out.

The man loves to eat pussy.

One of the many things I've learned intimately in the past week.

But… we *still* haven't had sex. At least not since I moved in. All he's done is give and give and give, and I never thought I'd say this, but I would like to reciprocate. Or at least have wild, sweaty sex with him on every surface of our house. But for some reason, we haven't.

"Yes! Strike out, baby!" Hallie yells, jumping up from her seat. "Let's go, babe!"

"Woo, go team!" I cheer with fake enthusiasm. I'm not a

sports fan, and while I'm not a total idiot and get some of the basic fundamentals, I'm still lost the majority of the time. I can count on one hand how many times I've been to a sporting event, and all of them have been because Hallie has dragged me with her to watch her boyfriend play. Because prior to her and Lane dating, we would've never chosen to watch baseball for fun.

She flops back down onto the stadium seat with a laugh. "I can't believe you *actually* came today. With zero grumbling and little to no bribing."

Yeah, me either, I say to myself but offer her a shrug. "I had some…free time."

"Mhmmm," she hums. "So it didn't have anything at all to do with your whole *friends with benefits* with the catcher?"

"Of course not. I'm simply here to support you, supporting Lane," I say. Although… I think we both know that's a lie.

Besides, baseball is suddenly growing on me. At a rapid rate. And it's definitely due to the fact that we're sitting behind home plate, and I've got the perfect view of Reese's ass while he squats behind the base.

Never in my life did I think I would be attracted to someone's ass in a pair of tight baseball pants, but here we are, and I am one hundred percent a fan if it means this is my view every time I come.

"Whatever you say," Hallie says, turning to face me with a smug smile, amusement dancing in her eyes. "I am so invested in this. I mean, part of me can't believe the two of you are… doing it, and the other part of me is kind of excited because it means we can double-date! I wanna know all of the details. Tell me everything."

She claps her hands in excitement, and I reach out, placing my hands on hers, stopping her. "*Waiiiiit* a minute. You're getting ahead of yourself there, friend. First of all, there will be no double 'dating.' That would imply dating, and we are not, ever. Neither of us wants a relationship. Second, the things this man can do with his mouth would make your cheeks turn as red as those socks they're wearing, babe."

Hallie would sink into the floor and disappear if I told her that he licked my asshole last night.

My girl is still too modest to hear about things like that, even though she's loving exploring things with Lane.

But sex is still new to her. Me, on the other hand, I am perfectly okay doing the filthiest things imaginable and have zero shame.

"Fair." She sighs, sitting back against her seat and crossing her arms over her chest. She somehow managed to talk me into wearing an OU baseball jersey tonight, but I downright refused when it came to wearing Reese's jersey. I am not encouraging that. That's definitely a couple thing.

Hallie wearing Lane's number 22 jersey clearly proves that I was right.

Instead, I opted for Grant's. I may or may not have posted a photo on Insta of me and Hallie wearing the jerseys and the field behind us… Maybe because I wanted Reese to see it.

"I'm just saying, it's weird. But kind of in a good way?"

Laughing, I shake my head and loop my arm around her shoulder, pulling her to me. "I love you, space babe. It's *just* sex. It's not like you and Lane. We're not making it a big deal, and neither should you. 'Kay?"

"Okay, but you promise the moment that it's more than just sex, you'll tell me, right?" she says optimistically.

I nod. "Of course. But don't get your hopes up because it isn't happening. Oh, look, another field goal. Go team!"

Hallie rolls her eyes and corrects me. "You mean strike." Whoops.

She stands and cheers for her man, because duh. It stays that way for the majority of the game, her leaping to her feet to cheer and then sitting back down with flushed cheeks in excitement.

I love that she's such a fan now. I love that she's so crazy in love with this guy. I love that she's so happy.

When a foul ball is popped in the air, Reese yanks his helmet and mask off, letting them drop to the dirt as he holds his glove above his head in anticipation for the catch. It lands directly in the center with a pop, and the horde of people around us erupts in cheers.

Not gonna lie, that was kind of hot.

Seeing him in his element, doing something he's so passionate about, is inspiring. And not only that, but he's *really good* at it. It comes naturally to him. His movements were precise and controlled, instinctual even.

While I was on the edge of my seat waiting for him to make the catch, he didn't seem the least bit fazed. Totally at ease.

Wow, I think I love baseball.

"That's ballgame!" the umpire yells, and the entire stadium goes wild, cheering, chanting, and hollering the guys' names. The announcers are officially calling the game, with OU taking the win 9-4.

We won. Reese just won the whole game with his catch… I mean, the *team* won.

I stand with Hallie and cheer, sharing in her excitement genuinely for the first time. We're clutching each other and screaming like these guys just won the championship, and I… love it.

I love sharing this moment with her. Way more than I ever expected to.

Reese turns toward us behind the plate, covered in red dirt from the field, his eye black smeared from sweat, hair sticking to his forehead, and in the middle of a stadium going wild, he looks directly at me, those deep, dark brown eyes holding mine and somehow drowning out all the noise.

Then, he winks. And suddenly, I'm the *only* person in the stands. Or at least it feels that way.

My insides flutter with butterflies, and my face feels hot from his stare. His gaze drops to the Hellcats name stretched across the jersey on my chest, and the corner of his lip tugs up.

As if he likes seeing me wearing a baseball jersey.

"God, the way he looks at you, Viv," Hallie sighs loudly in my ear over the crowd. "That boy is sooooo smitten."

Quickly, I brush her off with a scoff. "Girl, you are *seeing* things. He's just down to fuck. That's all. Now, c'mon. Ready to go?"

She nods and laces her fingers in mine, standing and pushing her way across the crowded row until we're making our way down the stairs.

Thankfully, most of the noise is still in the stands, so I can actually hear Hallie.

"I'll admit, this was actually more fun than I thought it would be. Definitely more exciting."

Hallie laughs and wiggles her eyebrows suggestively. "Gasp. Does this mean the Hellcats have a new fan?"

I laugh. "Maybe so. But as much fun as I've had, I'm anxious to head home. I think I've finally, freaking finally, figured out the problem with chapter 27, so I'm ready to go work on it."

I'm anxious to try and make some progress in my manuscript.

"When can I read? I'm dying to read. I feel like I already know the two of them, and I want to know the conflict. I think I'm more excited for your book, Viv, than Rebecca Yarros's new book."

When she mentions our favorite author, it reminds me of my conversation with Rosie.

"I forgot to tell you. I met Reese's sister. Sort of?" I interject.

Her head whips toward me as her eyes widen. "Ooooh, tell me more. Meeting the family already? Seems kind of… serious? I mean, for… just friends." She wiggles her eyebrows suggestively.

"Shut up. She just wanted to meet me because I'm Reese's roommate and because they're really close. *That's all*. But she's a reader, and of course, we immediately bonded over our love for romance books. I actually really like her. Clearly, Reese is the only Landry with the annoying gene." My phone goes off in my back pocket, and when I pull it out, I see it's a text from Reese.

Gotta meet with coach after press. See you at home.

"Okay, I'm going to head home and work on *Haunted* for a while. Thanks for asking me to come today. I had fun. *Surprisingly*," I tease.

She nods, bouncing on her feet. "Yes, and so I can finally read. I'll see you this week?"

I agree, giving her a quick hug before heading back to the house.

Hours later, I'm sitting on the couch in a pair of old sweats, my favorite ratty Nirvana T-shirt, with my hair on the top of my head in a ghostie scrunchie and my laptop in my lap, surrounded by notecards, notebooks, and thesauruses when Reese walks into the living room.

It's only been a few hours since the game, but I've spent the entire time glued to my computer, letting my fingers fly. Now that I've broken past whatever invisible wall there was in my manuscript, I feel like I can't get the words out fast enough, and it has me in the best mood.

I pull my earphones out of my ears as he sets his wallet and keys on the table and turns to me.

"Good game today. I *guess* now I can see why you're the all-star," I tease.

The corner of his lips tugs up slightly, definitely not his normal cocky grin. He seems more broody, a little quiet, which is *very unlike* him.

"Thanks for coming." Flopping down in the armchair next to me, he stares at the TV screen. I shut my laptop and put it on the couch next to me, my eyebrows arching.

"Everything good?"

He nods. "Yep. Everything's super." There's a hint of sarcasm in his voice as he speaks.

Clearly, everything is *not* super. "Are you upset about something?"

For a second, he's quiet, his jaw tense, and he shrugs. Then, a beat later, he turns to me, and his eyes are so dark they're almost black.

He pulls out his phone and scrolls as my brows tug together in confusion, and then he turns the screen around to face me.

"Saw this on Insta in the locker room after the game." It's the photo of me and Hallie at the game in our jerseys. Oh *shit*. So he *did see* it.

Excitement flutters in my stomach when his jaw works, and he laughs humorlessly.

I'll admit that I was poking the bear by posting that photo.

Maybe just a *little*.

"Wearing *Grant's* jersey," he adds before dropping his phone in his lap.

I rake my teeth over my lips. "Grant's my friend…"

"Your friend, huh?"

I nod. "Yeah, he doesn't get on my nerves like some of the other players."

I'm taunting him, hoping that he'll bite.

Lowering my voice to a whisper, I say, "Why? Did that make you mad?"

I hope it did. I hope he's so mad that he wants to angry fuck me right here on this coffee table. Finally.

"Fuck yeah, it did, Viv. I played that entire game with the taste of your cunt still on my tongue, and seeing you in another man's *jersey*? It made me fucking… insane," he rasps.

God, he is so fucking hot when he's mad. All growly and possessive.

I stand from the couch, walk over to him, and step between his spread thighs, only stopping when my knees bump the chair. I lean down, my hands on each armrest, until our lips are a breath apart. My heart is pounding in my chest because I already know I'm playing with fire, and I *want* to be burned.

"Why did it make you mad?" I breathe against his lips. Not kissing him, just… a small taste.

His nostrils flare, his jaw ticks, and he reaches out, dragging his thumb along my bottom lip as heat burns in his eyes.

Come on, Reese, play with me.

His eyes flare. "Because the only fucking jersey you should be wearing is *mine,* Viv. The only name on your back should be *mine.*"

Holy shit.

I swallow, my throat thick with anticipation. "And now you're angry? That I wore another guy's jersey?"

"Yeah, baby, I'm fucking *angry,*" he grunts against my lips.

Pulling back, I slowly drop to my knees between his legs and gaze up at him through my lashes. "Then, let me make it up to you."

My hands slide up his thighs, brushing over his hardening cock.

"You wanna make it up to me?"

I nod and tug his black shirt up, exposing the hard, sculpted plane of his abdomen. My nails rake down the muscles, each one contracting beneath my touch.

There's so much tension in the air I can taste it, and my thighs press together in response. I'm so wet, so turned on by the exchange, I feel the dampness on my sweats.

"Then make it up to me, Vivienne," he murmurs roughly, then laces his fingers behind his head and stares down at me. I can see the arousal swirling in the depths of his dark eyes, and it makes me hungry for him.

Hungry to have him in my mouth, to taste him.

It's the one thing I've never done with him, and I'm desperate for it.

On my knees between his legs, he watches me tug the waistband of his gym shorts down. He lifts his hips so I can work them down until they're pooling around his feet, leaving him in nothing but a pair of tight, black briefs. The fabric is molded to his cock, and I swallow. Only a tiny, minuscule bit of hesitation flits through my mind when I think about how I'll fit his cock into my mouth.

I wasn't stroking his ego when I said his dick was huge. He's thick and long, and my fist barely fits around him.

"Take my cock out," he whispers low, the commanding tone of his voice making my clit throb. "And make it up to me with your pretty little mouth, Vivienne."

Oh god. I'm so turned on right now I'm an aching, needy mess.

I grasp the fabric of his boxers and tug it down his hips until his cock pops free, bobbing between us. The head is thick and straining, with a little pearl of precum already beading on the slit.

Veins snake up the length to meet the broad head. He's perfectly manscaped, with a small mat of hair at his pelvis matching the dark hair of his beard.

Our gaze locks as I curl my palm around him and tighten my fingers into a fist, milking more precum from the tip. My tongue darts out and swipes the bead away, inciting a groan of approval that I feel all the way to my core.

I suck the tip of his cock into my mouth and swirl my tongue around the head, my hand twisting and pumping in tandem. My tongue travels the length of him, tasting him, teasing him, driving him crazy.

I edge him the same way that he loves to edge me until I finally suck him into my mouth. I breathe through my nose as I go deeper, until his cock hits the back of my throat, causing me to gag. He's so big he fills my throat in the most delicious way.

"Fuuuuuuck."

My eyes water, but I hold him there until I have to pull off and suck in a ragged breath.

He levels his gaze at me, then reaches up and tugs the scrunchie out, letting my hair fall in a curtain around us. "I like it down. I want to wrap my fist in it while I fuck your throat. Are you going to choke on my cock, baby?"

I nod eagerly, wanting to please him. To hear him praise me.

To be his good girl.

His fingers tangle in my hair as he gathers it into his hand and wraps it around his fist.

Even though I'm the one on my knees, there's no doubt who's in control. Just the way I want it.

"Tap my thigh if it's too much," he demands, and I nod, closing my lips around his head again, hollowing my cheeks out as I suck him deep.

He guides my mouth up and down his length languidly, in no apparent hurry. I reach up, palming his balls and rolling them in my hand, something that I know sets him off. They're sensitive, I remember from the last time I touched them.

I feel his fingers tighten in my hair when I let his cock slide down my throat, holding his gaze until my nose is pressed against his pelvis and I'm gagging around him again.

He drops his head back, exposing the thick column of his throat as he chokes out a mixture of a guttural groan and a pained whimper. His hips flex as he presses deeper, and I breathe through my nose, trying to relax my throat while he thrusts.

Tears blur my vision, and I can feel him throbbing deep in my throat.

I never knew I could be so turned on by a guy fucking my throat like he would my pussy, but it's the dirtiest, most obscene thing I've ever done, and I'm so wet that it's almost embarrassing.

This powerful, gorgeous man, completely gone for me.

Unhinged and never sexier.

"Your throat feels so fucking good. You're doing such a good job," he praises, opening his eyes and holding my gaze as he reaches between us and drags a finger from the base of my throat up over his cock, seeing just how full I am. "Are you ready to take more?"

I moan around his length, and he rocks his hips over and over, the head of his cock hitting the back of my throat with each thrust.

"You take my cock like you were made for it, baby," he grunts while his chest heaves and his fingers tighten in my nape. "I'm going to come down your throat, and I want you to swallow every drop, Vivienne. Okay?"

He pulls me off for a moment, a string of saliva trailing from my swollen lips to his cock, and I nod as I suck in a breath. "Please."

His eyes darken more, and he guides me back to his cock, where I slide my mouth down until I'm choking on him again, desperate to take him even further.

"Next time you think about wearing someone else's jersey, I want you to remember how it feels to have my cock down your throat."

His thrusts turn erratic as he delves deeper and groans, the muscles in his stomach rippling as he comes. I taste the salty, musky cum down my throat, swallowing it all. I slowly slide off his length after he empties himself into my mouth. I trail my tongue from the base of his cock, along the vein that runs up his length, cleaning all the cum off him, not wasting a drop.

This was so obscenely dirty I can't even handle it.

"Fuck, Viv, I think you just fucking killed me," he chokes out hoarsely, dragging his hand through his hair.

I smirk, climbing into his lap and straddling his hips. "Does that mean that you're not mad anymore?"

He grins, bringing his hands to my jaw and cradling it. "Well, depends, I guess. You gonna kiss me now?"

For a beat, neither of us moves. The only sound in the room is our harsh, heavy breathing. It feels… intense.

I smile, then lean down and whisper against his ear as I untangle myself from his lap. "Maybe if you *catch* me first, All-Star."

I'm up and gone, sprinting out of the living room into the hallway with him heavy on my heels.

15 / viv

More Than Flowers

It feels weird to be spending the weekend back home, and I think it's because the apartment no longer *feels* like my home.

Reese's house feels like home now.

And that terrifies me down to my bones.

It was only supposed to be a means to an end, a solution to a problem I never expected to have. But I feel so comfortable there. I feel at ease, like *myself* again. That scares me. It makes me feel like maybe the walls I've built up so carefully to keep him out are beginning to crumble as if they're made of something so incredibly brittle.

I've been at my mom's since Friday, after Reese insisted on dropping me off because he didn't trust my car to go so far without being looked at by a mechanic. Of course, I told him that he was insane and didn't need to drive me over two hours each way, but he claimed he was going to be out this way.

Highly doubtful, but at least this time, he didn't try to throw money at fixing my car and looked genuinely worried, so I let him drive me.

And now, after two days, I'm itching for the solace of my own space and the familiarity of my home at his house.

The nagging voice in the back of my head asks, *Or is it Reese I'm missing*?

I tamp down the thought and force myself back to the present because I'm not even going to try and unpack that right now.

"Mom, I think there's legitimately something growing in here," I mutter, raising my shirt to cover my nose like it will somehow lessen the stench radiating from inside the fridge.

I glance over at her sitting at the bar, picking at a piece of laminate that's started to peel from the countertop. She looks even smaller than the last time I saw her, which was just a couple of weeks ago, and it makes my stomach feel heavy with worry.

I feel like I live in a constant state of anxiety and stress lately. Except for those few stolen moments with Reese.

"I don't even smell it," she says, and my eyebrow arches in surprise.

"God, it's rank." I slam the door shut and walk over to the cabinet where we keep cleaning supplies and start searching for a pair of gloves. Maybe some goggles?

I'm going to need five showers after this. After rifling through bottles for a minute, I finally find a pair of latex gloves shoved to the very back.

Thank god.

"I was thinking, maybe we could go for a walk this afternoon?" I say, turning back to face Mom, now armed with the proper gear to take on cleaning out the fridge.

Her shoulder dips. "Maybe later? I'm not really feeling like getting out right now."

My lips fall into a frown, but I nod. I have to get her out of this house, get her out in the fresh air and some sunshine on her face.

"Okay, later, then. Before I leave."

Emotion flickers on her face, and the gnawing feeling in my gut returns, an almost permanent feeling at this point.

I hate leaving her, but I don't know that staying would even help at this point. And every time I offer, she almost seems more upset, insisting that I go back to school. I want to broach the subject of her seeing a therapist again or getting some professional help, but every time I do, she completely shuts down.

We're not taking steps forward at this point, only steps backward.

I quickly power through getting the fridge cleaned out, throwing out old, moldy food, and disinfecting it from top to bottom. The entire time, I rattle off to Mom about school and how classes are coming. She asks an occasional question but mostly stays quiet and lets me do the talking.

"Let me go throw this out. I'll be right back, okay?" I hold the trash bag in front of me, away from my face, still not believing that she's been living in here with that smell for lord only knows how long.

Most of my weekend was spent cleaning and washing the piles of laundry from the past two weeks. It doesn't seem like much but I feel like this is the only way I can help. I know that if I'm doing it, then she'll have fresh clothes and towels and a clean space.

Once I'm back inside, I walk to the couch and pick up the throw blanket that's rumpled on the cushions and begin folding it when there's a knock at the door.

My brow furrows. "Are you expecting anyone, Mom?"

She shakes her head and pulls her cardigan tighter around her. "No, sweetheart."

I set the blanket on the back of the couch and walk to the front door, swinging it open.

"Reese?" I sputter in shock.

What is he doing here? He's not supposed to pick me up until later.

"What's up, Sweet Tart?" He grins lazily, and my gaze drops

to his pillowy lips. The baseball hat on his head is turned backward and matches the red Hellcats T-shirt that is tight around his broad chest. I continue drinking him in, down to the worn jeans that are hugging his muscled thighs.

I know now just how much power is in those thighs, and I don't mean when he's behind the plate wearing catcher's gear. Although, that might be just as hot.

Almost as hot as he is with that hat turned backward. "Hi. What are you doing here?" I squeak.

"I tried texting you, but you didn't respond. I had to run an errand for my parents, so I was out this way early."

Shit, my phone. I reach into the back pocket of my jeans, pulling it out and frowning when I see the screen is blank.

"I'm so sorry, Reese. It must have died, and I was busy around the house." I turn the screen to face him, showing him it's dead. "I hope I didn't mess up your plans?"

"Nah, babe, you're good," he says with a smile, pulling a huge bouquet of flowers from behind his back. "I got these for you and your mom."

Holy shit. They're beautiful.

Pale purple roses with a mixture of baby's breath and lavender pieces throughout, tied with a beautiful lace ribbon.

And the bouquet is huge. Like the kind of flowers that you see celebrities or famous people receiving. Lavish and full, with perfect purple petals that look fresh and newly bloomed.

They probably cost a fortune.

"Reese… you didn't have to do that," I say quietly, trying to sort through the emotions running rampant inside of me.

Not only did he go out of his way to buy flowers… he picked an arrangement in my favorite color.

He dips his shoulder. "No big deal. My mom always said you don't show up to someone's house empty-handed."

"Vivienne?" Mama's voice comes from behind me, and I

whirl around to see her standing in the living room, questions swirling in her eyes.

Well…

I guess this means that Reese is meeting my mom. I can't just shut the door in his face without being rude or causing more questions from Mama.

I turn back to face him and ask, "Do you, uhm… want to come in?"

We never have company anymore, and I'm thanking the stars that the house is clean and that Mom is out of bed today.

He doesn't hesitate even for a moment, only nods, pushing off the doorframe. "Of course."

My smile is strained, but I swing the door open and step back for him to come inside. Once he's in the living room, I shut the front door behind him and face them both.

It's beyond strange seeing Reese in my house, something I truly never imagined happening. I'm not even really sure if I'm ready for Reese to know about… all of this. Everything that's happening with my mom and my home life. It's something inherently personal that I've kept close to my chest, and we're still building this trust with each other. It's… hard for me to be vulnerable.

"Mama, this is my… roommate, Reese. Reese, this is my mom, Belinda."

Reese's smile is blinding as he steps forward and offers Mom his hand. "It's nice to meet you, Mrs. Brentwood. I brought you and Viv these."

He hands Mom the flowers, and she blinks in surprise and takes the bouquet from him, a small smile flirting to her lips. It's so rare to see her smile it makes my chest ache.

"Oh goodness, these are so beautiful, Reese. Thank you so much."

Of course, she'd be just as charmed by him as I am. As

everyone is. He's the most charming guy I've ever met, and look how well I resisted him.

Not well. *That's* how well.

Every time he does something like this, I feel those walls crack just a bit, creating fissures that make my defenses more unstable by the second.

My gaze meets Mom's, and she looks like she has so many things to ask but just smiles at Reese again and offers him a seat on the couch.

"You have a beautiful home, Mrs. Brentwood," he tells her as he sits on the old, worn couch.

He's lying through his teeth, but the look of pride on Mom's face when he says it makes me want to kiss him.

And never stop.

He's thoughtful, and considerate, and kind, and nothing like I believed him to be. He's shown me that little by little, every single day since I moved into his house, and I feel like a total bitch for treating him the way I did. For assuming he was just some rich, playboy asshole.

"Please, call me Belinda. And thank you. It's simple, but it's… ours," she says.

I join Reese on the couch, sitting close enough that our thighs brush together, but not nearly as close as I want to be. Inhaling, I breathe him in, and the apprehension inside me slowly stutters to a calm.

He casually slings an arm over the back of the couch, right above my shoulders, and I wish that it was around me, hauling me against his side like he would if we were at home.

"What if we watch that new movie you've been talking about, Vivienne?" Mama says, breaking through my thoughts.

"Hmm?" I hum.

Reese chuckles next to me. "Let me guess… something horror related?"

I elbow him lightly in the ribs, rolling my eyes. It's like he knows me or something.

Mom looks between the two of us, something new twinkling in her eyes, and she nods. "You obviously know my Viv very well, then."

"Yes, ma'am, I think you could say that." I hear the amusement in his voice, and it makes me laugh.

Honestly, aside from Hallie, it feels like he knows me better than anyone lately. This is the first time I've really admitted that even to myself, and I don't know how to feel about it.

"If it's okay with Reese and he doesn't mind staying a couple of hours, it's fine with me."

Reese nods. "Yeah, that sounds fun. I don't have anywhere else to be."

"Okay, it's settled, then." Mom smiles and reaches for the remote, clicking the movie on and settling back in the armchair.

The opening credits begin to play, and Reese's arm drops along my shoulders, and he gently tugs me into his side. I all but sink into the embrace, letting my eyes fall shut for a brief moment as I savor the moment.

I'm scared of the feelings that are taking root in my heart. Actually, I'm *petrified*, but I'm also too selfish to walk away. He's the only place in my life where I feel safe enough to *be* selfish.

Before I realize it, he's shaking me awake. I groggily open my eyes and see the end credits of the movie scrolling across the screen.

"God, I'm sorry, Reese. I didn't mean to fall asleep," I whisper when I glance over and see Mom asleep on the armchair next to us.

"Don't apologize, babe. Clearly, you needed it," he says as we stand from the couch. I stretch my arms over my head, trying to shake off sleep before grabbing the throw blanket and covering my mom with it.

Reese waits by the front door, scrolling through his phone while I grab my overnight bag, laptop, and things from my bedroom. I write Mama a quick note, telling her that I didn't want to wake her and to text me whenever she wakes up, then set it on the end table next to her phone.

"Ready?" I ask him with a small smile, and he nods, reaching out and taking the bag from my shoulder and transferring it to his.

I double-check the lock once we're outside, and we walk to his Range Rover, which sticks out like a sore thumb in the run-down apartment complex.

It isn't lost on me as he holds my door open for me to slide inside that I've spent so much time trying to make him out to be a spoiled rich jerk in my head that I didn't see who was right in front of me.

He's the guy that has more money than anyone I've ever met and is about to be drafted to the MLB but spent the night watching a movie with me and my mom on an uncomfortable, springy old couch in an apartment that is the size of his *kitchen* and didn't once make either of us feel like it wasn't good enough for him. He treated my mom with kindness and compassion.

"I'm sorry if I shouldn't have shown up like that, Viv," he says once he's behind the wheel and we're pulling out of the parking lot and onto the highway. "I shouldn't have just assumed it was okay."

"No, no, it was okay," I reassure him. My eyes follow the slope of his cheekbones, to the scruff along his jaw, down to the thick column of his throat as he drives. Emotion feels thick in my throat as I go to speak. "You know… it's been a really, really long time since I've seen my mom the way she was tonight."

"That's great, Viv. How so?" he asks, dragging his gaze to mine.

I hold it for a moment, unsure of what to say next but feeling the urge to open up to him. To tell him what the last few months —years, really—of my life have been like.

He's a safe space to land, something I've not had since losing my dad.

"My mom… I-… I think... she's sick, Reese," I finally say. My throat feels tight, almost as much as my chest. "She's undiagnosed, and I'm pretty sure it's depression but I'm not a doctor so what do I know? It's been like this since my dad died. It's just gotten worse since I left for college. She refuses to see a doctor. Claims she's fine."

Tears sting my eyes, and I pause, sucking in a breath to calm the storm brewing inside of me.

"Viv, baby, you don't have to—" he starts, but I shake my head.

"No, I want to. I need to tell someone… I need to tell *you*."

Nodding, he reaches out, lacing his fingers in mine and squeezing reassuringly. A small gesture, yet it feels powerful at this moment. The comfort that I'm craving but not used to asking for.

"When my dad passed away, I was halfway through my junior year of high school, and it was the hardest thing I've ever had to go through. Not just losing my best friend but… the aftermath. *Everything* changed. My entire life changed in the blink of an eye. All because a drunk driver hit him head-on."

"Shit, Viv," Reese curses, remorse heavy in his voice. "I'm so, so fucking sorry."

"It's okay," I start but then stop, dragging my gaze from him out to the passing tree line, biting my lips. "Actually, it's not okay. That's a lie, and I'm so tired of lying, Reese. My dad died, and my mom is so depressed that she can't hold a job or even get out of bed some days, and sometimes, the weight on my shoulders feels like too fucking much to even *breathe*." My words come out in a rush, and I just keep going like I'm not on the verge of tears. "And I'm lying to everyone that I love about what's happening because I can't bear the thought of burdening them with my shit. I'm so tired of feeling alone, even though I'm the reason that I'm that way because I keep it all to myself. I'm overwhelmed, and everything feels so out of control. I'm trying to take care of my mom, hoping that things will somehow get better, and most days, I feel like I can't even take care of myself. I feel like a wreck. Like everyone is living their lives around me, the college dream, and I'm just pretendi—" I stop abruptly, sucking in a shaky breath, wiping at my eyes, trying to get ahold of my emotions after dumping all of that on him because I couldn't stop it. I just couldn't hold it in anymore. Silence fills the cab, and even though I just put everything out on the table, vulnerable and raw, I feel… lighter. For finally being able to speak it out loud to someone and not feel so alone with my thoughts.

Reese pulls the Range Rover off the highway onto a dark, quiet road and then cuts the engine. Before I can ask him what he's doing, he reaches over and unbuckles my seat belt, then drags me over the center console and places me in his lap. His hands cradle my face as he looks into my eyes, his own so dark and stormy, full of an emotion I can't quite place.

"You are not fucking alone, Viv. Do you hear me? Not anymore," he says in a breath against my lips, holding my gaze. "We're roommates, we're *whatever*. But at the end of the day, we're friends, and I care about you way fucking more than I'm supposed to. You are *never* going to be alone again."

The tears that have threatened to spill fall from my eyes onto my cheeks, and he reaches up, brushing them away with his thumbs.

"I see you, Vivienne. I see you trying to hide yourself from me, from all of our friends. But I'm going to be here, even when you push me away. Even when you hate me for how annoying I am, for threatening those walls you've put up. I'm not going anywhere, baby. Even if all you need from me is to be your punching bag. You are *not* alone."

I nod, burying my face in his neck and whispering, "Okay."

I don't even really know what that means for us, but I'm not questioning it. I don't want to right now. Because I need his comfort.

"It wasn't… it wasn't this bad until recently. Until I left for school," I say, shaking my head. "I don't think either one of us realized just how much she relied on me before then. And I feel so fucking guilty, Reese. For leaving her. But she doesn't want to hold me back. And if I don't get my degree and get a job, then how do I take care of her? Because what if… she never gets better? What if she can't ever find a job again and it's up to me?" I'm sobbing now, full-on, fat tears, hiccups, probably snot, probably soaking his shirt, but I don't even care.

Reese gently lifts my head and wipes the tears away, just patiently listening to me get it all off my chest, and it's more than I could ever ask for right now.

"I just want my mom to get better and to not have to worry all the time. That's all I want." I sag against his chest as his arms snake around me, clutching me tightly to him. "I just want to be a normal college girl, Reese. As fucked-up and selfish as that sounds. Because I can't even imagine how hard this is for her too."

"It's not selfish, baby. Your feelings are valid, and it's okay to want to be able to live your life too," he says against my hair.

I'll probably regret this later, but for now, I want to stay right here and pretend that somehow, when I wake up tomorrow, all of these problems will magically be gone.

"That's why I had to move in with you, you know. I had to use my savings to cover rent because she lost her job again. She was getting evicted, and if I didn't use the money I'd saved for my dorm fees, she would've lost the apartment."

He curses, his chest vibrating beneath my ear as I listen to the sound of his heartbeat, a steady, comforting rhythm that somehow helps me feel calmer. I count each beat, one by one, until my tears have dried and I'm feeling more in control of the rampant emotions inside of me.

I guess that's what happens when you spend so long bottling all of them up. They explode out of you in a rush, desperate to break free from the confines of their captor.

"I understand why you didn't tell me, but fuck, Viv. I wish I would've known. That *someone* would've known," he says after a while. "Why not tell Hallie and let her at least be there for you? I know she would be."

"It wouldn't have mattered. I wouldn't have let you help. That's why I haven't told Hallie either. She has this big, bleeding heart that wants to fix everything, and she can't fix this, Reese. All she'll do is worry herself sick, and that's the last thing I want. She's my best friend in this world—I just feel like every aspect of me is heavy, and I don't want to be the friend who only takes and takes and leaves nothing in return because my life is such a mess. Especially now that things have settled for her, that she's living her best college life. I just… I needed to get that off of my chest." I sit up, staring down at him. "I'm hoping that my mom will be willing to get help soon. I keep trying to convince her. I'm hoping that if I just keep pushing on and doing the best that I can to get through this rough patch, eventually, everything will fall into place and get better."

Reese sighs, dropping his head back against the seat rest. "I know I can't fix it, Viv. And even if I could, I know it's not my place, but I just hate seeing you go through this and not being able to do shit to take any pressure off of you."

I shrug, leaning forward to press my lips against his softly.

"Thank you for listening. Honestly, what I need right now is this. Exactly how things are right now. Okay?"

Finally, he nods. "Okay, Sweet Tart. Whatever you need from me."

"As much as I love being in your lap and whatnot, it's kind of creepy out here in the dark," I tease, trying to lighten the subject after sobbing on this guy's chest like he's more than just my roommate.

He chuckles. "Ah, so *now* you're scared of the dark? Babe, you literally spend eighty percent of your time watching scary movies, writing about scary shit, reading scary shit, and making podcasts about scary shit, and you're afraid of the dark?"

"I-I didn't say I was *scared*, All-Star. What I said was *it's creepy*." I bite the inside of my cheek to stop my smile.

"Oh, listen, before we go, I wanted to talk to you about something," he says, rolling his eyes when my eyebrows shoot up. "Jesus, Viv, you should see your face right now. I'm not asking you to marry me. Fuck."

My heart thuds in my chest. Obviously, I knew that. I did. I'm just still worried that he's going to… try and change things between us when we're finally at a place that works.

"I wanted to see if you would come to a Mardi Gras ball with me? My parents are part of the krewe, and it's basically just a big-ass party. But I'm supposed to bring a date, so…"

"So… you want *me* to go with you?" I ask.

He nods. "Yeah. Rosie's gonna be there, and I know the two of you are besties now."

Hmmm.

"Reese, you know I can't really afford a dress and al—"

Reaching up, he stops me with his thumb along my bottom lip. "I've got it covered. You'd be doing me a favor, being my date, so I'll take care of everything. All you've gotta do is show up and look pretty on my arm."

A big Mardi Gras party does sound like fun, and knowing Reese, even if it wasn't, he'd make it entertaining. Maybe this is a good diversion from all the heavy things happening right now.

"Okay, fine. On one condition."

His lips quirk. "Name it."

Leaning forward, I brush my lips along the shell of his ear and whisper, "I keep my heels on when you fuck me after the ball."

He answers me by capturing my lips in a kiss that leaves me breathless, for reasons I'm not ready to admit.

16 / reese

Date Date… Date?

SWIFTYBOYS4LIFE

Reese: I need advice.

Grant: Did you accidentally use Viv's body wash again?

Lane: Lmao. Still can't believe you put that shit on your dick.

Reese: It was an honest fucking mistake okay. Don't act like you both haven't grabbed some random shit in the shower to beat off with.

Reese: Back to the advice. I need it.

Grant: Hit me.

Lane: I feel like I need to ask first if this is something I have to keep from Hallie because I don't like doing that shit.

Grant: Dude, what happened to bros before hoes?

Reese: Oh shittttt

Lane: First of all, my girlfriend and the word hoe better never be used in the same sentence again if you want to remain breathing. Second, doesn't exist when you're in a serious relationship.

Reese: I support you 100% Lane. Fr.

Grant: Wow Reese. Can you also suck his balls while you're down there on your knees for him?

Lane: Nah, but he can suck yours. While you listen to Taylor Swift together.

Reese: I'd be flattered but no thanks.

Grant: 🖕🖕🖕🖕🖕🖕

Reese: What would you do if you had a date to the ball? It's not a date date, but… if it was a date. If I wanted to say, win my date over to actually have a real date date.

Lane: Why are you saying date so much?

Grant: 😂 Not a date, but a potential date for… dating

Reese: I hate you both. I'm better off calling fucking Rosie for advice.

Grant: I mean, I could call Rosie if you want. I am her favorite for a reason.

Lane: OH SHIT. 😱

Reese:…

Grant: Just kidding, Pookie.

Grant: So let's just pretend you're not talking about Viv and say "hypothetically" you want to woo the girl. AmIright?

Reese: Are we just gonna move past you trying to call my sister?

Lane: Seems like it.

Grant: Be attentive, treat her like she's the only girl in the room. Spare no expense at making sure she's having the best night of her life. Just be you, and the rest will fall into place.

Lane: Wow. That was actually solid advice.

Grant: 🙌 I mean this is why I get all the girls. Just sayin'

I still can't even believe Viv agreed to come to the Mardi Gras ball at all, let alone as my date. Because of obvious reasons.

But something changed between us that night in my car. She flayed herself open wide and bared it all to me. The last thing I expected from her, but I'm fucking taking it.

However I can have Vivienne Brentwood, I'm taking it.

Whatever little pieces she offers me.

Now that I said I would take care of every detail for the ball, I'm feeling a little, tiny bit of pressure. Good thing I thrive under pressure.

Right now, it feels like I'm in a stadium with ten thousand people and the entire game is riding on me to make the play.

I want to make this a night she remembers, and I want her to have fun. I want her to not have to worry about a single thing for the entire night. I want to spoil her and make her feel special.

Picking my phone up off the center console, I press Rosie's contact on FaceTime, praying she's not in class.

Thankfully, she answers after a few rings. She's completely soaked, wearing a bright red raincoat, standing under an umbrella on the sidewalk.

"Hello, my darling brother."

I roll my eyes and chuckle. "What's up, Jellybean? Look, I

don't have much time, but, um… I need to go in this store and pick out a dress, and I need your help."

I'm sitting outside a dress store, and I feel like a fish out of water, and I haven't even walked inside.

"Did you ask her?" she says excitedly.

I nod. "Yep. She said yes. And I told her I would take care of everything, so… I need your help finding her a dress. She sent me her dress size and shoe size."

Pulling off my hat, I drag my hand through my hair when I think of all the shit I need to accomplish this week leading up to the ball.

Rosie taps her chin as she thinks. "Yeah, and that means that there's no time to have the dress altered, so it needs to be something she can put on and go. Alright, let's do this. I have to be at the studio in twenty minutes, so bring me in."

I grin. "What would I do without you, Jellybean?"

"Play baseball and have absolutely no fashion sense. Get to moving!"

Surprisingly, finding Viv a dress was easy. Way easier than I thought it would be, even with my sister's help. I spotted the perfect dress after only being inside the store for all of five minutes. Easy to do when it's Mardi Gras and her favorite color is purple.

She always looks incredible when she wears it, so when I showed Rosie the dress and she squealed, it was clearly the one.

Rosie picked out the shoes, and that was that. She got off the phone with me to go to class, and now I'm waiting for them to put it in a bag.

Fuck, I can't wait to see her in it.

The glass counter in the front of the store is full of jewelry, so I browse while I'm waiting, my eyes scanning the display until something stops me in my tracks.

"No fucking way," I mutter.

The lady behind the counter chides, raising her brow when she hears me.

"Sorry, uh, can I see one?" I point to the silver necklace that I can't believe I'm seeing.

"Of course. Yes, this piece is on sale since it's out of season." She hands it over the counter to me, and I flip it between my fingers as I look it over.

It's perfect. Holy shit. "I'll take it."

Her eyes widen as she hesitates. "Would you like to know the price?"

"Nope. Doesn't matter."

Fate doesn't happen like that twice.

"WHAT DO YOU THINK ABOUT A LIMO?" I turn toward Grant where he sits in the leather chair next to me while the tailor measures my thighs.

I'm getting fitted for a new tux, and I dragged him with me because it's my least favorite thing to do.

He lifts his eyes from the magazine he was staring intently at and shrugs. "I mean, kind of a flex? But also a comfortable luxury, so it could go either way."

"I mean this with sincerity, that is absolutely zero fucking help, Grant," I retort.

The tailor tightens the fabric around my thighs and pushes a pin through while I try and remain as still as possible so it doesn't end up in my leg.

It's been three days since I picked Viv up from her mom's and asked her to come with me to the ball. Three days and I've barely seen her. She's had shifts at the library while I had a game and then a conditioning session with the guys, so we've been passing each other in the hallway with no time for anything more than a quick kiss and small talk.

Needless to say, I can't fucking wait to take her to the ball, and I can't wait to see her in that dress.

"So… you and Viv…" Grant says, trailing off.

"Me and Viv are… *roommates*. Just like I told you."

He scoffs. "Come on, dude. Admit it, you're down bad for her. Hell, even if you don't, we're your best friends. We see it."

Pulling my hat off my head, I sigh as I drag my hand through my hair. "It's complicated. She's… skittish, dude. Like a feral cat that'll claw you up the moment you get too close."

"I mean, you're comparing her to a cat, so I can see why it's complicated," he adds cheekily with a smug grin, stroking his chin. "But continue."

"Fuck off. You know what I mean. Yeah, I like her, and yeah, I want to be with her, but the second she feels like I'm getting too close, she backs off. It's why I'm nervous about the ball. For one, because I've never really… wanted to be with a girl like this. I've never wanted a relationship until Viv. And I want this to be real, me taking her out, a *date date*, and not just under the guise of me needing a date."

"Annnnd here we go again. I get it. You want to *date* her." I flip him the finger and sigh.

"Look, you want my advice?" His elbows meet his knees as he sits up and props his arms, continuing when I give him a stiff nod. "Give her what she needs. If it's time or taking things slow, do it at her pace. If she needs you in just a physical way, then be that for her. If you want to date her, then make yourself worthy of dating her. Be the person she needs, and the rest will just happen the way that it's supposed to. Let it flow and be patient. It'll pay off if she's feeling anything like you are right now."

My brow arches. Hmph. That sounds… like it's exactly what I should be doing.

"Damn. You know, G, I think you're secretly a romantic."

I'm starting to think he secretly writes poetry in his spare time and definitely listens to "Cardigan" on repeat while he does it. He has way too much *solid* relationship advice for a guy who's never been in a serious one.

He shrugs. "Women aren't complicated if you simply pay attention. Listen, I don't really know Viv all that well. But it seems like she's the kinda girl who needs to have some control. So let her set the pace, and you follow."

The tailor finishes my measurements and tells me I can take off the tux, so I step down off the fitting platform and go sit in the chair next to Grant. He's right… that's exactly who Viv is. Being in control makes her feel secure when everything around her is chaos.

"Thanks for the advice," I tell him, reaching out and giving him a bump of my fist.

"It's what I'm here for. One of us three has to be the one with all the brains."

I scoff. "Yeah, and I'm definitely the hot one, so…"

Shit, I guess since I've got him here, now would be the time to talk to him about the other thing that's been on my mind lately.

"I have something serious to talk to you about."

"What?" he says, crossing his arms over his chest.

"Should I get Viv a cat?"

17 / viv

Laissez les bons temps rouler

I suck in a deep breath to calm the jittering nerves inside me as I drag my clammy palms down the soft material of my dress, peering into the mirror in front of me at my reflection.

There aren't many times in my life that I can remember being this nervous, or maybe ever at all. I've never been to a fancy party, and most definitely not an extravagant ball that *billionaires* like Reese's family attend. A combination of nerves and a flutter of anticipation weighs heavily in the pit of my stomach.

But my dress for tonight is… *perfect*.

It's exactly what I would've chosen for myself had I been the one to choose, except I didn't. Reese chose it all on his own.

And somehow, he picked a dress that feels more like me than anything I've ever worn.

My heart thunders wildly in my chest as I scan my reflection again for the hundredth time. He chose a trumpet-style gown with a shimmery, almost sheer bottom in the most gorgeous shade of purple, a mixture between lilac and lavender that complements my skin tone and dark hair without being over-powering. It made doing my makeup effortless tonight, a simple neutral palette with just a pop of color on my lid and a slightly shimmery gloss on my lips.

I drag my eyes back up to my hair, which is falling over the bare slopes of my shoulders, and sigh. I *feel* as beautiful as this dress looks.

When I called Hallie earlier and showed her on FaceTime, she squealed so loudly she actually dropped the phone in her excitement.

"Oh my gosh, Viv, you look like a *literal* princess right now." I don't know about that, but I sure *feel* like one.

Smiling, I quickly grab my clutch and walk out of my bedroom into the living room, where I already know Reese is waiting.

My heels are quiet on the carpet, so he doesn't immediately notice that I've entered, giving me an uninterrupted moment to appreciate him in a tux.

Holy. Hell.

How is it possible for the floor to feel like it's actually fallen out from under my feet at the sight of him?

His dark hair is still damp and curling around his nape and ears, and he didn't shave, which means that his sharp jaw is covered in the delicious stubble that I love so much. The tux is perfectly tailored to every inch of him, and as I watch him fiddle with his cufflinks, my throat suddenly feels tight. He's always sexy, but in a suit, he's *devastatingly* handsome.

I feel like I'm swaying in the doorway as I admire the view.

It's at this moment that he looks up, his espresso-colored irises connecting with mine.

He opens his mouth to speak but then closes it as if he's trying to find the right words.

"Vivienne…" he starts as he steps forward to slowly close the distance between us. "Fucking Christ, you look…*breathtaking*."

I glance down at my dress and laugh softly because I'm feeling all kinds of strange, new feelings tonight. Feelings I don't quite understand, that I'm scared to examine too closely.

"Well, you picked a beautiful dress. I can't even imagine what it cost."

Reese makes a noise in the back of his throat as he shakes his head. "Doesn't matter because I would've paid any cost to see you in this dress, Viv."

His eyes do a slow perusal that makes me hot everywhere, sliding down every inch of my body and leaving a trail of arousal in its wake. He reaches for me, gently tugging me until I'm pressed tightly against his front, his hands splayed along the bare skin of my lower back, where his thumb caresses me with slow strokes.

There's nothing sexual happening between us, yet I feel every breath down to my core. I feel every graze of his finger along my skin.

"I wish I could kiss you right now. I know you probably don't want me to mess up your makeup, but just know the second you tell me I can, I'm kissing the *fuck* out of you, Sweet Tart."

His silly nickname does something to those butterflies in my stomach, causing chaos. I tell myself the same thing I have every single day since the night I cried in his arms.

This is casual. We're casual. Roommates who sometimes hook up.

Nothing more.

Casual is easy. Fun. Uncomplicated. Safe.

I reach up and adjust his bow tie, which is slightly crooked. Once it's straight, I drag my gaze to his and swallow. "You look handsome. Ridiculously handsome." I roll my eyes for good measure, but lately, it feels more like an act than anything, and it's hard to admit, even to myself, that things feel different between us.

Which is why I give myself the same spiel, over and over.

This is casual. We're casual.

"Thank you. Before we go, I have something for you."

My eyebrows shoot up in question as he pulls a black velvet jewelry box out of the pocket of his slacks.

"I know, I know." He winces. "You hate when I spend money on you, I know, and I'm sorry. But… I just couldn't pass this up. It's like fate put me at the right place at the right time, and it was meant to be yours, Viv." Carefully, he opens the box, revealing a dainty silver chain with a small charm hanging in the center. When I reach out, I realize the charm is actually a little ghost, and my legs almost give out, unable to support the shock cresting through my system.

Immediately, tears burn my eyes, and my hand shoots to cover my mouth.

"If you hate it, I can take it back, and we can forget this ever happened," he says with a slightly nervous expression, his throat working as he swallows. "I just saw it, and I know that you always wear the bracelet with the ghost, and they're so similar, and I know you love your ghosts…"

For a second, I focus on breathing through my nose, one steady breath at a time. He has no idea what my bracelet means to me, and that makes this even more… meaningful.

"Reese…" I start, but my voice breaks, and I reach out to brush my fingers along the delicate charm, trying to will the tears away.

"Fuck, did I fuck up, Viv? Shit, I'm sorry. I was ju—" My finger on his lips stops him.

"No, no," I choke out. "I just need a second, please."

He nods, reaching for me again, pressing me close to his front. The hard, unwavering planes of his body comfort me in a way that I never expected from him. And it's not lost on me that I've found comfort in his arms twice in the last week.

Finally, after a moment soaking in his quiet strength, I'm able to speak. "It's perfect, and I love it more than you know. I…I've had that bracelet for a really long time, and it's very special to me. It was a present from my dad for my twelfth birthday."

Reese's eyes widen, and a panicked expression passes over his handsome features. When he tries to speak, I shake my head. "I love it. I'm emotional because I'm just so happy, that's all. It's a very special gift. Thank you, Reese. I want to wear it tonight. Will you put it on me?"

"Of course." He opens the velvet box and pulls the necklace off its backing, then reaches for me, his hand gently sweeping my hair off my neck. I turn, and he places it along my collarbone, fastening it at my nape. His fingers linger to sweep lightly along the chain at my neck. "It's perfect."

His voice is a low, rough timbre that tugs at the heavy feeling in my stomach, and before I can even think about it, I'm whipping around to face him, my hands fisting in the lapels of his tux as I tug him to me, crushing my lips to his. He groans against my mouth as his fingers dig into the soft flesh of my hips. Right now, I don't care about the lip gloss or the fact that my lips will probably be a swollen, flushed mess after his beard brushes against them. I want to show him how much this means to me. To thank him for unknowingly getting me such a thoughtful, special gift that I'll cherish forever.

Our lips are frantic and messy, our teeth clashing together as our hands roam. It's a kiss that says more than words can, and right now, that's all I can give him. Because words feel like too much. And still not enough.

All I can give him is something physical in the only way that I know how.

I pull back, panting, my eyes holding his as the sound of our heavy breathing fills the living room. "Thank you. I'll never forget this, Reese."

I'm referring to the necklace, but the potential double meaning of my words hangs in the air between us. That it's not just the necklace. That I'm thanking him for everything he's done for me. For giving me a place to live, for keeping my secrets, for being a safe place for me to land for almost two months, for holding me while I cried, for making my mom smile, and for giving her a semblance of normal. For being there for me and not expecting anything in return.

For doing all the things that I never imagined he would. For being the person I refused to acknowledge that he was all along, yet he never stops trying to show me.

"Always." Sincerity shines in his eyes, and I nod, leaning forward and softly pressing my lips to his.

A car horn sounds from outside, and he sighs raggedly against my mouth. "As much as I think I'd rather stay here and have you to myself in this dress all night, we have to go, or we're going to be late."

"Ah, can't be late. I know how much you hate it."

The corner of his lip curves into a grin as he nods. "Yep. Also, I guess now would be a good time to tell you that I got us something else for tonight."

"Reese…" I warn, my gaze narrowing.

His hands lift in surrender. "I'ma need a pass for tonight. Look, this is how I show… that I care. It's not a flex. I just like to spoil the people that matter to me, and I know you don't like unnecessary, lavish things, so I'm keeping it to a minimum. But can I just take care of you for one night? One night of letting me do all the things you wouldn't normally let me do?"

I glance down at the beautiful ball gown I'm wearing and lift my hand to twist the charm of my necklace between the pads of my fingers. He's *already* gone above and beyond today; I can't actually imagine what else he has planned. I'm already feeling a little… weird that he's gone all out for tonight, but for whatever reason, this seems like it's important to him.

"Tonight. *Only* tonight," I finally say.

"Okay. I can work with that." With a smirk, he turns and walks to the front door, swinging it open. "Your chariot awaits, m'lady."

When I step over the threshold, past his outstretched arm, my jaw falls open at the shiny, black limousine that's parked on the curb in front of our house.

"God, you are so ridiculous. You know that?" His laugh is low, and raspy, and so fucking sexy.

I love it and how it always has the ability to affect me the same way.

With his hand on my lower back, he guides me carefully down the path to the limo, opens the door, and helps me inside. I scoot all the way across so he can join me on the seat, and when he climbs in, he turns to face me, leaning in until his pillowy lips ghost against the shell of my ear, sending a shiver down my spine. "I can think of several things I want to do to you in the back seat of this limo. You know, back seats seem to be our thing, Sweet Tart."

His fingers trail up the exposed skin of my thigh through the slit of my dress, and I capture his hand, holding it in place. "If you actually want to make it to this ball, then behave. Besides, I don't want to get this gorgeous new dress dirty… yet."

"I can't help it. You look good enough to fucking eat." His eyes flick with desire, and I swallow roughly.

How does he have this much power over my body?

"I'll behave. *For now*."

MY AROUSAL IS REPLACED with nerves once more when the limo pulls up to the front entrance of the venue. I'm still trying to wrap my head around the fact that Reese got a *limo* to take us tonight like that's a totally normal thing, but if there's anything I've learned about him, it's that he has no problem being the most extra person in the room. And I did give him one free pass for tonight only.

"Viv?" he murmurs my name as he stands in the doorway of the limo, jostling me from my thoughts.

Eyes cast upward, I give him a smile. "Sorry, yes?"

He helps me out of the car and then adjusts his tux before speaking. "Don't be nervous, okay? It'll be a blast. I promise."

"Who says I'm nervous?"

Chuckling softly, his shoulder dips in a shrug. "Just saying, if you *are* nervous about being my date, meeting my parents, whatever, don't be. There's no pressure. Just a fun night out."

Of course, he knows that I'm nervous. He has the uncanny ability to read me even when I'm doing my best attempt at concealing my emotions, and it makes me feel exposed, raw, and completely vulnerable.

Feelings that I don't handle very well.

I paste on a bright smile, tamping down my anxiousness as he shuts the limo door behind me and slides my arm into his. "I'm good. Excited. Can't wait to stuff my face with king cake."

Reese laughs. "I'm looking forward to dessert too, but not the cake."

He's incorrigible, and I tell him that as he leads me up to the entrance of the ballroom. Everything about this place is bougie. The heavy, black double doors with ornate gold embellishments that look like it's out of a movie where the place requires a password to enter. The gas lanterns flickering on each side. The glitzy Hollywood-style purple carpet we follow toward the entrance. The maître d' checking coats in the entryway.

It screams old money.

I feel like a fish out of water, even in this new dress and on the arm of a guy whose family could probably buy the building and everyone inside of it, but when he tightens his hand in mine, it reassures me that this is where I'm supposed to be. Whether I belong or not.

"Good evening, Mr. Landry." The maître d' greets Reese with a level of familiarity, gesturing us through the entrance with a sweep of his arm.

I don't even hear Reese respond because I'm too busy gaping at the ballroom in front of me.

"Holy shit," I breathe, mostly to myself, but out loud.

The inside is even more opulent than the outside, and the level of ornate detail… it's *mind-blowing.*

Seriously, I'm so shocked right now that I'm rooted in place.

Tables are scattered around the room with lush tablecloths and lavish centerpieces of purple, green, and gold flowers accented with a mixture of masks, fleurs-de-lis, and jesters. The ceiling above is draped in a tasteful gold chiffon and organza.

There are champagne towers positioned throughout and two bar stations stocked with only top-shelf liquor. Plush green and purple couches with feather pillows and fancy glass tables covered in more flower arrangements are tucked along the walls. The band takes up the entire back wall of the venue, and a photo booth with what looks to be a professional photographer is nestled into the corner.

I'm pretty sure I've only seen this kind of thing on TV, and even that doesn't come close to what it feels like to experience in person.

I can only imagine how much time and money went into making this ball happen.

"It's a little over-the-top," Reese says, his eyes raking over the room much like mine are. "They take it very seriously around here. My mom is on the committee, and my dad always donates every year, hence why my attendance is generally *not* optional."

Now I see why having a fancy dress is such an important part, and I'm even more convinced now than I was when I first put it on that it's absolutely perfect for tonight.

"Oh, there they are. C'mon, let's get the introductions out of the way." He laces his fingers in mine and gently tugs me after him.

My stomach flips the entire time it takes us to walk across the room, and when he stops in front of his family, I plaster on a bright smile.

Of course, they are just as attractive as he is. His dad is an inch or so taller than him, with the same deep brown eyes and stubble lining his jaw. The same unruly hair and a dimple that pops when he smiles at me as he bypasses my outstretched hand, opting to pull me in for a hug instead.

"You must be the infamous Vivienne that we've heard so much about." He chuckles. "Nice to meet you, darlin'. I'm Nate."

Reese groans. "Dad, Jesus."

His mom and sister laugh as his dad lets go, and I nod. "I guess that's me. I'm so glad to meet you both. Thank you so much for having me."

"Oh, we're so glad you're here, Vivienne. I'm Sera."

His mom is around my height, with deep auburn hair and striking green eyes. It's not lost on me that both of her children are the mirrored image of her husband. Even Rosie has Nate's same dark hair, with a slightly lighter shade of brown irises.

"And obviously, no introduction needed." Rosie beams, stepping in to hug me tightly. My eyes drift down to her dress. It's a soft, shimmery gold that makes her look like she belongs on a throne somewhere.

They're all so stunning and elegant, and even though I'm anxious and feeling a little overwhelmed, to be honest, I'm still excited to be here.

I just hope they don't notice my clammy palms. "The decorations are gorgeous. Truly," I say. "It's obvious how much time went into planning this."

Sera's eyes twinkle. "Thank you. It's… a labor of love, to say the least. But all proceeds of the auction will go to charity, so that makes it worth it. Plus, I get to spend time with these two, and that is few and far between these days." She lifts on her toes and puts an arm around both of them, pulling them against her.

It's obvious even just from these first interactions that their family is very close, and it makes my chest ache a little. It makes me miss having my family all together.

Reese laughs, affection evident on his handsome face. "I'm gonna go grab us some drinks. Viv, want anything?"

"Uh, maybe just water for now?"

"Yes, while my brother gets drinks, you and I can dance," Rosie interrupts before looping her arm in mine. "*Laissez les bons temps rouler*, baby. Let's get this party started!"

When Reese walks off to get drinks and his parents excuse themselves to meet with their friends, Rosie and I head straight for the dance floor.

We dance until we're breathless, both of us laughing as she tries to do the sprinkler but just looks like she's twitching instead. We're in desperate need of water when Reese appears on the dance floor with our drinks in hand.

"Jellybean, Mom's looking for you," he says to Rosie, who nods.

"Be right back," she adds breathlessly over her shoulder, leaving us alone on the dance floor for the first time tonight.

A slow song begins playing through the speakers, and the crowd starts to thin at the perfect time.

We stand there for a moment, his eyes raking down my body. "Finally, I get you all to myself, Sweet Tart," he murmurs with a smirk, pulling me to him and anchoring me tightly to his front with his palm against the small of my back. The lights dim, and we sway to the slow, sensual beat. "You look so fucking beautiful, I haven't been able to take my eyes off you all night."

I slide my arms around his neck and clasp them at his nape, dragging my fingers through his hair. "Thank you for inviting me here tonight. And for this dress, and for making me feel... like I *belong* here. With you and your family."

His brow pulls together. "That's because you do belong here, baby. I know you were... apprehensive about tonight, but you still agreed to come with me, and that's what you do. You put everyone before yourself. No matter if you're scared or anxious. I see you. I see *you,* Vivienne. I wanted to bring you here tonight so you got to be the one being taken care of for once. So you could wear this dress that makes me fucking ache, and so you could maybe let go of all the shit you've been carrying around for a little while and just breathe."

I'm willing myself not to cry for the second time tonight as I sway in his arms, soaking in the feeling of... him.

I'm in deep, and I don't know how to stop it.

How is it so hard for me to be vulnerable with everyone else yet so easy with him?

"Tonight has already been perfect," I whisper.

He reaches up, cupping my jaw in his hand and dragging his thumb over my cheek as he stares down at me. "That's all I wanted. I don't want you to worry about anything. I want tonight to be about you."

His head dips and captures my lips softly, my eyes fluttering shut. I melt into him as the room fades out around us. My only sensations are the security of his arms wrapped around me, the feel of his mouth taking mine.

I don't even know if the music is still playing or if we're standing out here alone, I'm so lost in Reese Landry.

Everything about him.

He kisses me like I'm the answer he's been searching for,

holding me as if I'm precious to him, until he tilts my head, sweeping his tongue into my mouth, the kiss turning hungry in an instant. He groans against my lips, and his hand tightens on my jaw.

I'm panting when I pull back, Reese's eyes molten as he holds mine. And when he licks his lips, I feel my resolve beginning to fade.

It's impossible not to want to fuck this man every minute of the day.

"Come with me somewhere?"

"Where?" I whisper breathlessly.

He leans forward next to my ear. "I've waited the entire night, and I can't wait another fucking second to taste you, Viv."

18 / reese

Getting Caught is Half the Fun

"You're *insane,* Reese Landry," Viv pants as I tug her along the empty hallway. She's trying to keep up in her heels, and I want to throw her over my shoulder and carry her caveman style if it means I can get her there faster.

"You made me insane wearing that dress all night, baby."

She laughs, her hand woven tightly in mine. We're like two teenagers sneaking away from our parents, looking for a room to make out in. Except when I get her in that room, I'm doing more than kissing her.

She's so beautiful it makes my chest ache.

Earlier, when I told her she was breathtaking, I meant in the literal sense that seeing her walk out in that dress actually made it hard to breathe. My throat felt tight.

The thing about Viv is that as beautiful as she is on the outside, the inside matches. She's empathetic, resilient, strong, selfless to a fault. She puts everyone above herself. Their feelings, their happiness.

She's a breath of fresh air, especially when she's busting my balls, and I'm feeling things that I'm not supposed to, but it's too late.

I'm too far gone. I'm falling for her. I'm falling like a lovesick idiot because I know those feelings are one-sided, and I'm firmly in the *friends who sometimes fuck* zone.

And I know that she set these boundaries to protect herself, to keep me at a distance, to keep what we have surface level.

But it feels like more. It feels like it's been a slow descent since the moment I met her into something that I can't turn off. Even if I tried.

Finally, we make it to the end of the hallway to the last door, and I quickly punch the numbers on the keypad to gain entry. Thank fuck they haven't changed it since the last time I was here. Pushing the frosted glass door open, I hastily pull Viv inside, shutting it quietly behind us. It's dark inside but not pitch-black since the bathroom light is on, casting a shadowy glow around the room. It's enough to see Viv in front of me, her chest rising and falling heavily from us sprinting down the hallway, her pouty pink lips parted as she stares up at me. Her gaze follows as I drop to my knees in front of her and trail my fingers lightly up the bare skin that peeks out of the slit of her dress.

I can feel her pressing her thighs together, and I grin, bringing my lips to her knee and pressing a soft kiss there, then another on the inside of her thigh. The bottom of her dress is poofy as fuck and in my way, so I tug it open at the slit and slip beneath it.

Her breath hitches when my teeth graze the inside of her thigh, and then I bite down, leaving a slight indentation. I lick the mark when her back bows, a whimper tumbling from her lips as I slowly make my way up to the apex of her thighs.

Fuck, I can feel the heat of her pussy and smell how wet she is when I drag my nose along the pale purple lace that almost matches her dress.

"What if we get caught?" she pants when I ghost a finger across her clit that pushes against the fabric.

Smirking against her skin, I tease, "That's the fun part, Sweet Tart."

I wish I could see her face right now, but this fucking dress makes it impossible to see anything but purple poofy shit, and as unbelievably fucking beautiful as she looks wearing it, I'm regretting my choice for the first time tonight.

I tug the lace of her panties to the side, revealing her bare pussy. Despite the dim light, I can see her already soaked and glistening, her clit peeking out from her lips, and my mouth fucking waters.

Apparently, the thought of getting caught is just as thrilling to her.

Fuck yeah. That's my girl.

"I'm going to need you to be quiet for me while I eat this pretty little pussy. Can you do that, baby?"

She hums, and that's all I need before I dip forward and sweep my tongue against her clit and begin circling it, flicking it again and again until I feel her legs begin to tremble. Reaching down, I lift her heel-clad foot and place her leg over my shoulder, pressing her back against the wall and supporting some of her weight.

We're not in a rush, but I feel ravenous after spending the entire night desperate to taste her, so I quicken my pace, using my finger to tease her entrance as I suck her throbbing clit between my lips and roll it.

"Oh god," she whispers, rocking her hips against my mouth at a frantic pace while I suck her clit roughly and slide two fingers into her pussy.

I can already feel the flutters of her orgasm coming, her walls beginning to tighten around my fingers. Her hips rock harder and faster as she chases her pleasure unabashedly.

"I—about to… come." Her head thuds against the wall. *"Reese."*

I fuck her harder, increasing my pace. My fingers make a sloppy, wet sound that fills the room as I push two fingers deep and curl them, massaging the spot inside of her that has her thighs clamping around my head and her entire body trembling. She's about to fall apart when I hear footsteps echoing down the hallway. A click of heels and conversation that is just far

enough away that I can't make it out.

Fucking Christ. We might *actually* get caught.

"Come for me now, baby. Right now," I demand, sucking her clit into my mouth again and letting my teeth graze the bud.

A second later, she shatters, flooding my tongue and fingers with wetness that I greedily lap up. The voices are getting louder, and I realize that there's a chance they're going to see me with my tongue buried in her pussy. My dick's impossibly hard as I lick at her cunt, cleaning her mess up.

"Someone's coming," I rasp against her clit, taking one more swipe of it before I pull back and slide my fingers out of her.

She squeaks, "What? Oh my god. *Get up here! Hurry up!!*"

I quickly lower her leg to the ground, but the heel is caught in the layers of fucking fabric from the dress, and somehow, I'm caught in between it. I try to stand, but it tugs at the front of her dress, almost knocking us both over.

Jesus Christ.

"Reese, what are you doing? You're going to get us caught!" she whisper-yells as she tugs at the dress at the same time I do, and we're getting absolutely nowhere.

"I'm trying, woman! This damn dress is caught in your heel." I'm fumbling around in the near dark, trying to untangle her heel from the fabric.

The voices are outside of the door now, and I can see the silhouette of someone on the other side of the glass. "I'll grab more cups, and then we can head back."

Just as the numbers beep on the keypad, I free her foot and all but crawl out from under the goddamn dress. I grab Viv's hand, and we run for the bathroom, closing the door behind us.

She's pressed against the wall, chest heaving as the first burst of a giggle falls from her lips, causing me to place my hand over her mouth. My fingers are still wet from being inside of her, and I almost come in my pants when I feel her tongue dart out and swipe along my fingers.

Dirty fucking girl. *My* dirty girl.

Our eyes lock, and my brow arches, and I'm two seconds away from saying fuck it and fucking her right here on the sink in this bathroom when I hear the door shut outside.

I drop my hand from her mouth, and she rolls those pink lips together. "Well, *that* was exciting."

"Yeah, and I need to get you home. Right the fuck now," I tell her, grabbing her hand. "Let's go say goodbye to my parents and Rosie, and then we're going. I'm not nearly finished with you, Vivienne."

Turns out, my plan to get Viv home and naked is quickly derailed when we join my family at the party. Rosie takes one look at Viv's flushed cheeks and my disheveled hair and grins, shaking her head.

"You two are *so* busted," she whispers to us both, low enough that my parents don't hear. "Sneaking off for a secret romp. This is romance book coded!"

Viv laughs while I just shake my head. "Anyway. We're going to head out soon."

"Uh, no, sir. We haven't even had the second line yet," Rosie says. "No way. It's the best part of the ball—well, aside from the drinks, dancing and beads. Oh! Here are yours for the second line. Hankies too."

She hands us both purple beads to go around our necks and

gold handkerchiefs. We put the beads on, and even though I really fucking want to get Viv home and be alone with her, I also want her to have fun and have the true experience of a Mardi Gras ball, therefore… we're staying. *For now.* This is my favorite part, after all. Rosie's right.

I dip my head to Viv's ear. "The moment this is over, I'm taking you home."

She rises on her toes and grasps my jaw as she whispers, "You still have my one and only condition to fulfill tonight, All-Star."

The heels.

And now I'm imagining her in nothing but those heels as I sink inside of her.

"Fuck, Viv. Don't make my dick hard in front of my sister," I groan.

My parents walk over at that moment, and thankfully they do because my resolve is gone.

Not a single fucking strand of restraint left.

Rosie squeals, twirling her handkerchief in the air with fervor. "Let's gooooo! I've been waiting all night for this," she yells when the music starts. She loops her arm in Viv's, and Mom joins them. They take off in the line, leaving me back with Dad.

I can't take my eyes off Viv as she laughs, dancing until her cheeks are flushed red.

I love seeing her so happy.

I'm enjoying this entirely too much. Seeing her blend in so seamlessly with my family, ingraining herself in a tradition my family has had for as long as I can remember. It feels like she fits, a perfect piece of the puzzle.

"You told her yet?" Dad says with a smile as we walk. My brow furrows.

"Told her what?"

He chuckles, his deep brown eyes that are the same as mine flickering with something I can't place. "That you're crazy about her."

"Dad…" I start but trail off because I don't know *what* to say. It's not like he knows about our arrangement and how it's supposed to just be friends with benefits. Not a conversation I really want to have with him. Because I want more than just sex with Viv. I want it all. Do I admit that I'm falling for her?

"Never seen you like this with anyone, son," he says, a soft tilt to his mouth. "You don't have to talk to me about it if you're not ready, but I see the way you look at her. You look at her the way I used to look at your mom when I was your age."

Part of me is afraid to feel this way about Viv. To have such strong feelings about a girl who may never feel the same way. Not only that, but I'm graduating in May and headed to the minors. I don't know where that would leave us, even if she did want to be with me. And given all that's happening in her life, I know Viv needs security right now.

I'm scared I'll fuck it all up.

"What happens when I leave? What happens if she never feels like I do?"

He shrugs. "You make it work. That's what you always do when you love someone. You put in work and show up even when it's hard. That's what sets a relationship apart. Being vulnerable is part of what love is, son. It's trusting another person to take care of your heart. It's scary, the unknown, but it has to be a risk that you're willing to take. That's up to you to decide."

I nod as my gaze flicks back to Viv, watching her holding my mom's and sister's arms as they dance.

"I think I know the answer," I tell him, and he nods. I'm falling for a girl who may never feel the same.

It's not like I can stop just because she might not ever feel the same. Because this doesn't feel like a *choice*.

Dad claps me on the back, pulling me in for a quick hug once the second line ends, and Viv walks up, completely out of breath from dancing.

"God, my feet are going to fall off," she whines with a pained look on her face. "I am *not* normally a heel kind of girl."

Bending down, I reach under her dress and close my hand around her ankle, lifting it to unbuckle the strap from around it, then slide it off.

She sighs in relief. "Oh god. That feels so much better already."

I do the same with the other shoe, dropping a chaste kiss against her ankle before grabbing both heels in one hand and reaching for my phone with my other. "Ready to head home? I'll text the driver."

"Yes. I wanna go say goodbye to Rosie first, and your parents."

After texting the driver we're ready, we walk over to Mom, Dad, and Rosie and say our goodbyes. They hug Viv and make her promise that they'll see her soon, and fuck, I hope it happens.

We're walking toward the exit when I turn to her. "Hop up, Sweet Tart. I'll carry you out so you don't have to walk on the concrete with your feet hurting."

"Stop being so sweet. It makes me want to fuck your brains out." She smirks and climbs on my back, looping her arms around my neck while I hike her higher. I feel her lips against my ear when she murmurs, "I've been thinking about it since you ate me out in that room."

She licks the shell of my ear and giggles when a deep groan sounds from my chest.

This fucking girl.

"Just wait until I get you home, Sweet Tart. You'll be tapping out after the second round. I've got lots of plans for your pussy."

"Promises, promises, *All-Star*."

19 / viv

The Second First time... Come again?

We barely make it through the front door before Reese is lifting me off my feet, my legs wrapping around his waist as his mouth slams against mine frantically, his fingers threading through the hair at my nape.

On the ride home, he touched me *everywhere* with steady purpose. Dragging his fingers up my thigh, stroking my jaw, whispering all the dirty things he planned to do to me when he got us home, how beautiful I looked tonight, and how he can't believe that he gets to touch me. He drove me to desperation with the small touches and promising words.

I was panting when he helped me from the limo. Even his hand brushing against the small of my back as we walked was enough to make my clit throb. My head feels dizzy with a lust-filled haze. He's surrounding me, infiltrating every part of me, and I don't want to walk away. I don't want to stop this feeling.

We bump into the edge of the couch and almost end up on top of it, but he catches us at the last minute with his strong arm behind my back, his lips never leaving mine.

His tongue thrashes with mine, stroking, exploring, claiming, and I'm writhing in his arms by the time we make it to his bedroom.

He tosses me onto his bed and yanks at the bow tie around his neck, unfastening it and letting it hang open, all while his gaze stays zeroed in on me.

God, he looks fucking unhinged. Wild, heated eyes that travel down my body and make me feel strung up with electricity.

I'm so wet that I'm probably making a mess on his bed and ruining this beautiful dress.

"You make me fucking crazy, Vivienne. I'm worried I'll be too rough…" he grunts, low and raspy, fingering the buttons of his shirt, and I feel it in my core.

"I want rough. All of it. *All* of you, Reese," I promise, reaching up and pulling at the buckle of his belt, his pupils darkening when I flick the button of his slacks open and slowly drag the zipper down.

He works the buttons of his shirt free until the white fabric hangs open, revealing his broad chest and sculpted abdomen. He's staring down at me with so much intensity that it feels tangible, draping over every surface of the room, making the air between us thick with tension. His pants are open, the bulge of his cock straining against the thin fabric of his briefs.

I stare up at him while dragging my fingers down his erection, palming him through his briefs, his cock twitching in my hand from the motion.

He reaches down and drags his thumb along my bottom lip before pushing it inside my mouth and groaning when I suck the digit deeper and swirl my tongue around it.

"Are you going to suck my cock like the good girl I know you are, Vivienne?"

I nod around his finger and rake my teeth over the pad, causing him to hiss. Only then do I slip my hand into the waistband of his briefs and wrap my hand around his length, pumping him once, and then again.

Circling the head with my thumb, I feel the slit leaking with cum, and I can't wait another second to taste him, so I pull off his finger and lean forward, closing my lips around the tip of his cock, hollowing my cheeks and sucking hard.

My hands grip the base of him as I take him deeper into my mouth until he jerks against the back of my throat.

"Fuuuuck," he chokes out raggedly, his fingers flying to my head, threading through the strands. "My girl loves to suck my cock, doesn't she?"

I answer by sucking him deeper and holding until I'm gagging around him.

He loves it when it's messy, and I've learned that I love pleasing him. I've never wanted to hear anyone's praise more than I do his.

I pull off his length, rubbing the saliva that trails from his head along my lips, holding his gaze.

When I drag my tongue along the thick vein down his cock, he *whimpers*. It's the sexiest noise I've ever heard coming from the back of his throat as he tightens his fingers in my hair and his head drops back, exposing the thick column of his throat.

My mouth closes around the head of him, and he guides me up and down his length, torturously slow, setting a languid rhythm. I watch as his chest heaves and his breathing becomes erratic, hitching when I deep-throat him again.

I've never felt so powerful in my life, watching this gorgeous, fierce man losing control because of *me*.

It's both filthy and beautiful at once.

Heat pools in my belly, so I reach beneath the slit of my dress and slip my fingers into my panties, pressing my fingers against my swollen clit. I'm throbbing unbearably. Desperate to dull the ache. Desperate for *release*.

I'm so turned on sucking him that I could come with just a few more brushes of my fingers.

Except he stops me, his fingers grasping my wrist and pulling my hand out of my panties, holding it up for him to inspect. My fingers glisten with the evidence of what he's done to me, how wet and desperate I am for him.

I slide my mouth off his cock and lick my lips, watching him intently.

Eyes penetrating mine, he dips his head and sucks my fingers into his mouth, noisily licking them clean. His groan vibrates around them, and when he pulls back, his pupils are blown, so dark they're almost black.

Suddenly, he hoists me off the bed, flipping me around until my hands brace against the mattress, my back to him.

I feel his finger ghost down my spine, trailing lower until he's tugging at the zipper, and then the dress is pooling at my feet, leaving me in nothing but my strapless bra, damp panties, and the heels he put back on after I begged him to fuck me in them.

"So fucking beautiful," he murmurs, sweeping my hair aside and pressing his lips to the top of my spine in an achingly tender kiss.

It feels intimate in a moment that's been driven by lust and desperation.

I look over my shoulder at him and watch as he uses one hand to unclasp my bra, freeing my breasts. The fabric ghosts along the hardened peeks of my nipples, and I shiver, a full-body response to the stimulation.

My body is in overdrive, the sensations heightened to new limits from how turned on I am.

His lips trail along my spine and across my shoulders, forging a path to the spot below my ear where he sucks and nibbles along my hypersensitive skin.

I feel hot, everywhere. It burns inside of me, a white-hot flame that licks my veins.

"I nee—" I pant breathlessly.

His voice is hoarse with desire as he speaks. "What do you need, baby? Tell me."

"Make me come, please," I beg, reaching back and closing my fingers around his to drag them to my pussy. He cups me through the fabric of my panties, and I moan unabashedly.

"Do you need my fingers? You need me to make your sweet, needy little cunt stop aching to be filled?"

Oh my god.

The mouth on this man. I can't even handle how filthy it is. My legs are shaking on the floor, threatening to give out.

I nod, whimpering when he slips his hand beneath the lace and sweeps his fingers across my clit.

The barest of touches, but it's still enough to have my back bowing against him. His cock brushes against my ass, and he flattens his hand against my pussy and tugs me backward, molding me to his front. Every hard inch of him is pressed tightly against me, and I can already feel my orgasm winding inside of me, making my limbs heavy.

By now, Reese has memorized every inch of my body, committed all of it to memory, and uses it as a tool. I've never felt so in tune with another person, so effortlessly in sync.

"I'll *always* take care of my girl," he breathes against my neck as he circles his fingers on my clit, then pinches it at the same time his teeth rake across my skin roughly.

That's all it takes for me to come, my legs shaking as my muscles go taut and my head falls back against his shoulder, unintelligible moans falling from my lips. Pleasure rocks through me in heavy waves.

He continues to strum my clit as I come against his hand, wringing every ounce of pleasure out of me until I collapse against him, trembling from the intensity of my orgasm.

"You're so fucking beautiful when you come, Viv," he praises. He turns me to face him, his heated stare singeing through me, and slants his lips over mine, sucking and nibbling before teasing the seam with his tongue.

I just had one of the most powerful orgasms of my life, and I'm *still* wanton for him.

I want him again and again until I'm too spent to move and my muscles are aching from exertion.

Tearing my lips from his, I hook my fingers into the waistband of his pants and boxers and start to work them off. "I need you inside me. Now."

I'm done waiting.

He shrugs out of his jacket and shirt as I tug his pants down until he's fully naked in front of me, fisting his cock and stroking it slowly.

I can't even get over how hot he is, no matter how many times I've seen him like this.

His body is truly a work of art. Broad, chiseled shoulders with a dust of dark hair covering his chest. Row after row of sculpted abs with a thin line of hair trailing down to a thick cock and heavy balls.

Who knew *balls* could even be sexy?

Without a word, he stalks forward, grabbing my jaw with his hand and slamming his mouth back on mine roughly. I whimper against his lips, my hands sliding around his shoulders as he carefully lowers me to the mattress and tears his lips from mine to kiss down my neck to my chest.

His lips ghost across my collarbone, then down to the valley between my breasts, moving to my nipple. He uses his tongue, circling the taut peak before pulling it into his mouth and rolling it roughly between his teeth. The sound of his sucking and his teeth hitting the metal of my piercing sends a shiver down my spine and a new flood of arousal to my pussy.

Reese is absolutely a tit guy, and he seems to love my piercings. Every time we hook up, he gives them his undivided attention until I'm squirming beneath him.

He sucks, bites, and nibbles at my breasts, scattering marks across them before he kisses down my stomach, lower and lower, but still not where I'm aching with need.

"Please fuck me," I plead.

I'm a foreplay girl like any other, but I feel empty, and I want him to stuff me full of him.

His deep, dark eyes meet mine as he gazes up my body. "I love hearing you beg, baby."

I'm so wet I feel it coating my thighs.

I try to press them together to give myself friction, anything to ease this ache, but his fingers slide along my thighs, keeping them open. I know how much he loves to eat me, and as much as I love it too, I'm too delirious with desire to wait for him to be inside me.

"Such a needy girl. Desperate for my cock," he murmurs against my skin.

Another kiss along the skin above my panties before he reaches up and tears them off my body in one swift, rough pull.

My breath hitches, and he smirks wolfishly.

He fits his hips between my thighs, hovering over me until my nipples brush against his chest, and his lips are a whisper above mine.

I can feel him heavy and hot against my pussy, and when he rocks his hips, hitting my clit with his velvety cock, my eyes drop shut.

"So good," I breathe. "More. Please."

Answering my plea, he fists his cock and drags it through my pussy, coating himself with my wetness as he nudges my clit with his broad head again.

It feels so good my toes are curling in my heels. I wrap my

legs around his back as he continues rocking his hips until I'm squirming.

I'm losing my mind.

Pulling back, he drags his gaze down to where he's lining up with my pussy, pressing against my entrance, and slipping inside an inch, causing us to both groan in unison.

"Fuck," he says, stiffening. "Condom."

I shake my head, hooking my legs together around his back. "No, I want all of you. I'm clean. I… haven't been with anyone. Since…" I trail off, suddenly feeling self-conscious.

I haven't had sex with anyone since the night we spent together.

"Neither have I," he counters, and my jaw falls open. I can't hide the shock in my expression at hearing that. I thought… I mean, I never expected anything from him, but… wow. "I didn't want anyone but you, Vivienne. Not then and not now. It's only been *you*."

I'm overwhelmed with how good it feels to hear that, even if it's something I never thought I'd want from him. And something he definitely doesn't owe me.

"I'm still on birth control," I whisper, leaning up to sweep my tongue along his bottom lip, giving him any permission he's seeking.

Without another word, he presses his hips forward, slowly sinking inside of me inch by inch until he's buried to the hilt and my clit is brushing against the soft mat of hair at his pelvis, as deep as he can go.

I've forgotten just how big his cock feels inside of me, and he reads my pained expression.

"Shit, I'm sorry." He pauses, giving me a second to adjust, dipping his head to suck my nipple into his mouth and flicking the tip of his tongue over the pebbled peak.

Quickly, the small bite of pain turns into pleasure, and I feel my body relaxing.

"You okay, baby?" he asks softly, so sweetly that I feel like my heart could burst. Not only does he make me come like no one ever has, but he's attentive. Deliberate. Affectionate.

While sometimes he's unhinged and slightly feral, the other times when it calls for it, he's soft and sweet.

I nod. "I just want you to move."

I *need* him to move. I need to feel him hitting that spot again.

His hips rock tentatively hitting that spot inside of me that has my eyes rolling back and pleasure surging through me in a torrent. Once I'm raising my hips to meet his, he withdraws until his cock is only barely inside, then thrusts hard, his hips slapping against my thighs, hard, deep strokes that I swear I can feel in my lower stomach.

So deep that he's bottoming out, the head of his cock hitting my inner walls, and when he does, he slowly rolls his hips. The muscles of his abdomen flexing with each swivel.

When he does it twice in a row, I swear to god, I see stars, little black bursts dancing behind my vision. I don't think I've ever been fucked this way. Not even that first night we were together.

So purposeful, like he's trying to leave a mark on not just my body but my soul.

"Fuck, god… *Reese.*" I writhe beneath him, my back arching from the sheets as he pounds into me, fucking me so hard that I inch up on the bed.

Finding a rhythm, he places my foot on his shoulder and flexes his hips even deeper, nearly bending me in half.

He's so powerful. The muscles in his biceps ripple as they hold his weight, and he pounds into me like a man possessed.

I reach between us and circle my clit when my orgasm begins to swell inside of me, ready to burst.

Ready to catapult me into another universe.

Reese rises on his knees, slowing his pace as his gaze drops down to where his cock is slowly sliding into me, and a wild look flares behind his eyes.

I dip my fingers lower so they sit around his cock while he thrusts, feeling him sliding inside of me.

"I love watching your pretty pink cunt stretching around my cock. You're taking me so well," he rasps, his eyes locked on us. "Fuck, my cock is covered in you, baby."

I lift my fingers, which shine in the light, and he captures my hand, sucking them into his mouth as he surges forward, nearly folding me in half at the waist. His pace increases, fucking me harder, faster, deeper.

I clench around him, and he groans raggedly. "You want me to come in this pussy?"

Fuck, why is that *so* hot?

The thought of him filling me up with his cum is obscene and dirty but so fucking hot.

Raking my teeth over my bottom lip, I nod, and he curses.

He stops mid-thrust, pulling out of me entirely, then rolls us until his back hits the bed, and he's beneath me, his slick cock pressed against my soaked center. "Ride me. Make yourself come on my cock."

Lifting onto my knees, I line him up with my entrance and sink down until we're flush, my palms flat along his chest as I lift myself and then drop down roughly, earning me a groan of approval.

"Good girl. Just like that. Play with your nipples, tug on them," he demands as he brings his thumb to my clit and begins rubbing uneven circles.

My fingers find my nipples, doing just as he says, tugging and pulling roughly on the barbell through the center while I rotate my hips, fucking myself on his thick cock.

"I'm…" I pant, lifting and slamming down on him, bouncing, chasing the orgasm that's just a breath away. "I'm coming. Oh *god*… Oh…"

The combination of his cock and his strokes on my clit has me shuddering, trembling as I try to remain upright. My spine bows, and I moan his name over and over as arousal spirals inside of me, tightening my limbs, pulling my muscles taut.

It's a full-body experience, and I'm completely lost in it.

Completely lost in *him*.

He lifts his hips in a couple of shallow thrusts, then follows me, grasping and rolling my hips as he comes inside me with a deep, guttural groan.

"Fuuuuck."

My walls flutter around him, wringing every ounce of pleasure out of us both until I collapse on top of him, sweaty and sated. His heart races wildly beneath my cheek, our breathing erratic after what is no doubt the absolute best sex of my life.

His arm drapes over my back, and we stay like that for so long that I feel my eyes growing heavy as I listen to the steady rhythm of his heartbeat, lulling me. His softening dick is still inside me, our joint cum covering us both, but neither of us moves.

He's just… *resting* inside of me. That's a first.

I laugh, and I thought it was mostly inwardly until he asks, "What are you laughing about, Sweet Tart? Not great for my ego when I'm still inside you."

I lift my head and rest it on my hands, looking into his eyes. "Exactly… I was just thinking I've never… just had someone's dick inside me like this."

His brows shoot up. "You're keeping it warm. That's a thing, you know?"

"What?"

"It's called cock warming." He smirks. "But don't worry, if

you keep squirming like that, he'll be all warmed up and ready to go soon."

I throw my head back, laughing. "You're ridiculous."

"I can't help that my cock's favorite place to be is inside your pussy."

I love that even when things are… intense between us, it still feels easy.

Fun. Playful.

Being with him always feels like that, and I don't know if I love it or if it terrifies me.

20 / viv

Space Babe + Murder Maven

I'm still on a post-blissful-weekend high from the ball when my mom calls as I'm leaving the library after my shift Monday afternoon.

"Hi!" I answer brightly, shoving my notebook back into my backpack and making my way outside the entrance.

"Hi, sweetie. You sound chipper today. I'm guessing that you and Reese had a good time at the ball?"

That's because I spent the entire weekend feeling happier than I have in a really long time. Not just because of Reese, but because it felt like for the first time since I started college… I was *just* a college kid, with no responsibilities, no expectations. I was able to have fun, and let loose, and not worry.

I feel guilty for thinking those things, but it doesn't make them any less true. I feel lighter, refreshed even.

"Yeah, we did. It was incredible, and I can't wait to show you all the pictures. I sent one to your phone on Sunday. Did you get it?" I ask.

"I did. Gosh, Vivienne, you looked so beautiful." Emotion weighs heavily in her words as she speaks. "I wish I could have seen you in it."

"Me too. How's your day today? Is everything okay?"

She seems in much better spirits than the last time I talked to her, and that makes me feel a sliver of relief. I climb into my car and set my bag on the passenger seat as I wait for her to respond.

"I'm doing fine over here. I ate breakfast this morning, and I sat out on the patio and got some sun."

My jaw falls open in surprise. It usually takes me begging and pleading to make that happen, and so I'm really surprised to hear her say it.

"That's amazing, Mom. I bet it felt so good to be outside in the fresh air and to have the sun on your face."

"It was. I'm going to go take a shower, but I wanted to check in and see how the ball was. I love you, Viv. Always and forever, okay?"

Tears prick my eyes, and I suck in a deep breath to keep them at bay. "I love you too, Mom. I'll call you soon, okay?"

She tells me she'll talk to me later, and we say a quick goodbye. I wasn't expecting our phone call to go this way, and I'm suddenly feeling emotional. Partly because it makes me realize I've gotten into the habit of anticipating the worst, and I hate that about myself.

I'm so used to having everything in my life be a chaotic mess that now I just expect things to go wrong.

The entire drive home, I think about our conversation, and it makes me feel hopeful that there are brighter days ahead, especially for her. That maybe she's starting to get a little better. She deserves happiness. She deserves the world, and it's hard for me as someone who wants to fix everything to feel so helpless.

I pull into the driveway and walk inside. Putting my stuff on the barstool in the kitchen, I see a piece of paper on the counter next to a box of chocolate sprinkle donuts.

Another one of my favorites. I pick the note up and scan it.

Can't wait to be back home. See you Wednesday. Donut worry, Sweet Tart, you're the only thing I'll be thinking about ;)
-Your All-Star

Reese left this morning for an away game, dragging himself out of bed before the sun even came up after spending most of the night fucking me until I was too sore to move.

My muscles still ache from all of the delicious, mind-blowing sex we had this weekend. His stamina knows no bounds, and he honestly probably could've gone another round if I didn't threaten to kick him out and make him sleep in his own room because my poor vagina needed a much-needed break.

A problem that I didn't think I'd ever have, but then again, Reese makes me feel a lot of things that I never have.

I pull my phone out of my back pocket after setting his note down and pick one up of the donuts from the box, snapping a photo of me licking the chocolate off the top.

Me: Too bad you're not here to lick this off of me. Thanks for the treat 😜

Good luck tonight. I'll be watching and maaaaaybe wearing your jersey.

I can't stop myself from giggling as I attach the photo to my text and press Send. Teasing him like this is entirely too much fun, especially because he always gives it right back.

I love that about... whatever this is between us. It makes me feel lighter.

I'm surprised when I see the text bubbles pop up on our thread since his game should be starting within the hour.

Reese: That's one spanking for making me hard in front of the entire fucking team babe.

Two for the jersey comment. It better be mine.

And three, just because I love seeing your ass marked red.

Call you after the game.

And now I'm grinning like a lovesick fool, my heart squeezing with happiness… and I realize this is a problem.

A major problem.

God, when did this happen? When did he go from being this rich playboy that I spent so much time trying to hate to being the first person I want to text whenever something happens in my life? The person who makes my whole day with a sweet gesture and a flirty text. The person that feels safe, that feels like… home?

I'm so beyond fucked.

Before I second-guess myself, I text Hallie an SOS message, asking her to come by for girl time. I've not seen my bestie as much as normal lately, and after such a great day, I'm actually feeling brave enough to ask for some advice.

Hallie: On my way. I'm bringing backup

An hour later, Hallie and I are piled up on Reese's massive couch under a mountain of blankets, eating our favorite snacks and binge-watching *Unsolved Mysteries*, just like old times.

"Start at the beginning, and tell me what's going on," she says as she tosses another piece of candy in her mouth. "I want every single juicy detail."

I groan, dropping my head back against the couch. "I don't know, Hallie. It all just feels so… *overwhelming*. And not even necessarily overwhelming in a bad way, just overwhelming. Don't get me wrong, the way he makes me feel is incredible. He is incredible. I just feel all of these things that I don't really understand nor know how to even process. I've never really felt like this about anyone before."

Hallie sets the bag of Sour Punch Straws down and turns

toward me. "Okay, should we start with the easy part... Do you want to be with Reese?"

For a second, I'm silent, chewing on my lip before I finally answer, "Yeah, I think I do."

That's why this feels so overwhelming and so confusing. Because despite every effort not to, somewhere along the way I started to catch feelings for him, and now it seems impossible to ignore those feelings.

Hence, my SOS message to Hallie tonight. I desperately need to work through all of the thoughts in my head after his note from this morning. He's just so unexpectedly sweet, and I love spending time with him more than I should. The feeling he gives me... it's one that I'm not ready to give up.

"And you know that it's *okay* to like him, right, Viv?" she says. Her expression is serious but kind as she speaks. "Look, I know at first you weren't his biggest fan, and okay, that's understandable because he can be very... *in your face.* That's just who he is, and it's not necessarily a bad thing—it can just be a lot. But, Viv, from what you're saying, it sounds like things have changed between you two, and that's okay. It seems like you've gotten a lot closer since you moved in, and maybe whatever reason that you didn't like him in the beginning isn't the same anymore? Because you didn't know each other that well. It's okay... things change."

I gnaw away on my fingernails, the shimmery purple polish beginning to peel as I mull over her words.

"You're right, but also, it's *Reese,* Hallie. The last guy I thought I'd be interested in. And we made this agreement to be strictly roommates. I set these firm boundaries, thinking I could protect myself from his charm, but he completely bulldozed through them, almost effortlessly. Now, I have these feelings for him, and he's about to graduate in a few months and go to the minors, and I'm a *freshman* in college. Who even knows where he'll end up once he's drafted, and I don't even know if he even *feels* the same way. We're just having sex. That's what we said." My words tumble out in a rush that probably doesn't even make sense because they've been simmering inside of me for a while, but once I start, I can't seem to stop.

It feels good to say it all out loud and to finally admit how I feel to myself.

Groaning, I glance back up at her. "It's just I feel seen in a way that I've never felt before with him, Hal. It still surprises me, but somehow, he just gets me. I feel safe with him. I was *definitely* wrong about him at first. I know that now—he's shown me that over and over again. He's funny and kind and is so loyal to the people that he cares about. But I don't know… I'm just *scared.* For so many different reasons."

"Oh, Viv," Hallie mumbles, pushing the candy and blankets aside as she scrambles beside me and tosses her arms around my neck, pulling me tightly against her. "You really, really like him, don't you?"

I nod.

I *really* do.

"Yeah. And I think I have for a while, but I just wasn't ready to admit it out loud or even to myself. But after this weekend, after meeting his family, after all the things he's done to support me… I can't pretend that I don't have feelings for him anymore."

My gaze flits back to the counter, where the note from earlier is. "And we have this silly thing that we do where we leave each other cheesy, pun-y notes with breakfast. It started as kind of like a peace offering and a joke, but then it just… stuck." I laugh. "He left for the away game this morning, and when I walked in from my library shift, I saw a box of my favorite donuts and a note from him. God, Hal, it just made me so happy, and that's when I realized that *Reese* makes me happy. *Being* with him makes me happy. Coming home after a bad day and seeing *him* makes my entire day better, and that's not how you feel about someone who's only a fuck buddy or a roommate. But yeah, I'm scared to feel that way. I'm… scared because opening up to people is hard for me, especially the last few years. I know that he's into me, but what if it's just physical for him? What if it was just about the conquest? I don't know if I can handle that after I've let him in. I'm not sure I can put myself out there like that."

Her brow arches as her lip curves up, and she looks me in the eye with love. "Yeah, but what if it *is* more to him? You can't live your life with *what-ifs*, Viv. And you can't always hide your feelings from people."

"You make it seem so easy. The only thing that feels *easy* is how I feel when I'm with him. I feel like a different version of me. A happier, lighter, more carefree version of me. More like the me I was before…" I trail off, suddenly hit with the weight of my emotions.

"You don't have to talk about it if you don't want to, Viv. I know how hard it is for you." Hallie rests her head on my shoulder and takes my hand in hers to give me a reassuring squeeze. Cuddled up next to me, she waits out my silence, giving me space while I figure out if I want to continue.

She's my oldest and closest friend. My best friend. And she never left my side when my whole world shifted. She knows that my mom was devastated, that I was heartbroken, and how much has changed since my dad passed away. But even *she* doesn't know just how much my mom has been struggling or how much support she needs. I didn't really let *anyone* in on the downward spiral of my whole life since that moment. Living it has been hard enough, but talking about it? It just hurts too much.

The familiar weight of guilt feels heavy in my stomach as it does most days, but even more right now. The sinking feeling makes me question whether or not I'm making the right decision to keep the whole truth about what's been happening with my mom from Hallie or if it's going to end up hurting her that I didn't confide in her sooner.

I don't have all the answers. About Reese. About my mom. About Hallie. And right now, I've never wished more that my dad was still here. He always had the best advice about anything that was happening in my life. He always knew exactly what to say to make me feel better, and I wish that I could get his advice. Sometimes I wonder if that's why I have such a hard time opening up to people now because he was always the person that I ran to.

I debate about telling Hallie everything, but for some reason, I can't get out the words just yet. I've already unloaded so much on her tonight. Today's phone call with my mom made me hopeful that maybe things will be better soon, so maybe the conversation will be completely different when I do talk to Hallie. Why burden her with worry if things really are getting better?

I lay my head on Hallie's and sigh before steering the conversation back toward Reese. "I'm just in extremely unfamiliar territory, and I feel like I'm trying to see in the dark."

Hallie nods, handing me a Sour Punch Straw she swiped from the bag. "I understand, but honestly, Viv, the fact that you guys have this... *breakfast club* little thing together is literally the cutest thing I've ever heard of."

God, it seriously is. I never thought I would be the kind of girl to get so... giddy over things that a boy does, but I can't seem to stop when it comes to him.

I nod as I finish chewing. "I know. That's just it, Hallie. He's always like this. Charming, sweet, thoughtful. I even caught him reading a book about supernatural stuff, and the boy is a complete *chicken*. Seriously, it gave him nightmares for like a week."

"No, he did not! Wait… Reese can read?"

A laugh bubbles out of me, and she giggles before adding, "Just kidding. I think he's got it bad for you, just so you know. The way he acts with you is definitely more than roommates with benefits, Viv. And I think that you should tell him how you feel and give him the chance to reciprocate. How will you know he doesn't if you never tell him? He's surprised you so far, right?"

"When did you get to be so wise?" I say, leaning my head against her shoulder, and I feel it dip as she shrugs.

"Love does that to you, I think. It makes you see the world differently. I'm not an expert, you know that. But I do know that you're amazing, Viv. You're confident, and beautiful inside and out. You deserve love and you deserve feeling the way that you do with Reese. Don't miss the chance to experience it because you're afraid."

"Love you, space babe."

"Love you more, my little murder maven. I'm glad to know that you're happy here… you know I've been worried about you. I just haven't wanted to push you too hard because I know you don't like to talk about it, but I know you miss your dad. I'm always here for you, okay? No matter what. It's me and you. Always."

I nod. "Forever and ever."

Hours later, after we crashed from our sugar high and passed out sometime during *Unsolved Mysteries,* my phone ringing wakes me. I crack an eye open and quickly answer the incoming FaceTime call so I don't wake Hallie, who's snoring lightly next to me, her legs entwined with mine.

"Hello?" I whisper sleepily as Reese comes into view. His dark hair is wet and unruly, and of course, to absolutely no surprise, he's shirtless. The slight dimple in his cheek pops as he grins.

"'Sup, Sweet Tart. Missing me yet?"

My eyes roll, but I bite the inside of my lip to hold back my smile. "I miss you… *doing the laundry*. There's a whole pile right he—"

"Liar," he cuts me off with a sly grin. "You know you miss my co—"

I scramble up from the couch, almost tripping when the blanket gets caught in my legs. "Shhhh. Hallie is right here."

Snickering, he shrugs. "Not like she hasn't heard the word *cock* before, babe."

"Yeah, but I'd rather her not hear you talking about *yours* being inside of me," I say quietly as I tiptoe down the dark hallway and slip inside my room, shutting the door behind me. I turn the lamp on and lie down on the bed. The sheets still smell like him from the weekend we spent tangled in them, and it does make me miss him.

"Are you… wearing my T-shirt, Viv?" His eyes darken when they drop to my chest and see Hellcats Baseball Department stretched across it.

"I told you there was lots of laundry to be done. I didn't have anything else to wear."

He licks his lips and nods before dragging his gaze back to mine. "Mhmmmm. Guess I'm going to have to stop doing laundry if it means you'll start wearing my stuff. Or maybe you'll just have to be naked."

"*Caveman*," I tease as I tuck my hair behind my ear, then flip onto my stomach. "How was the game? I didn't catch it because Hallie came over for a sleepover."

"Good. We won, but the next game will be harder. It's against a team that's also 7-0, so it'll be a first loss for either team, but I'm confident that we'll take it home." I watch as he moves from wherever he was sitting and walks through the hotel room.

"Are you rooming alone?" I ask.

He shakes his head. "Nah, we generally always have a roommate during away games. Too bad he's not as hot as my actual roommate." When he winks, my stomach flips. How is he so attractive literally at all times? "Grant's my roomie for the night, but he went to grab us dinner. I'm fucking starving. You and Hallie have fun?"

"Yeah, we had a blast. I miss spending time with her. It feels like lately we've both had our own stuff happening, and I miss just being able to lie on the couch and binge-watch our favorite shows together. It was really good getting to spend time together, just the two of us."

After tonight, I made a promise to myself to prioritize spending time with my best friend like we used to, no matter what has to take the back burner.

I missed nights like tonight.

"That's great, babe. Listen, any time you wanna kick me out and spend the night with Hallie doing girly shit, like naked pillow fights, let me know. I'll crash on Lane's couch." He smirks.

I'm about to respond when I see the door open behind him, and Grant strides in, a bag of takeout in each hand. "Hey, Viv," he says with a wink, earning him a death glare from Reese and a giggle from me.

I lift my hand and wave. "Hi, Grant. Congrats on the win tonight."

"Appreciate it, babe."

"She is not your babe." Reese scowls at Grant as he flits the camera back to him. "I'm gonna hop off and eat, then probably crash. Just wanted to see your face before bed."

There are those stupid butterflies.

"Sounds good. I'll be piling the laundry up while you're gone so it's ready for you when you come home."

He laughs, low and deep, and I smirk as we say goodbye.

Not even a full minute later, my phone vibrates with a notification, and I see his name pop up on my screen.

Reese: I have a surprise for this weekend.

Me: Why would you text me that, and now I have to wait till then!?

Reese: Because I'm gonna need another free pass for this one.

Me: 🙄 Reese, stop buying me things.

Reese: You'll love this one, I promise.

Me: If it's ridiculous, you're returning it.

Reese: Well, I can't actually return it. See you Wednesday. Night babe.

Sighing, I set my phone on the bed next to me. What could he *possibly* have to surprise me with?

21 / reese

Operation: Cat Daddy

This is going to go one of two ways.

1. Viv's going to lose her shit.
2. She's going to fall in love.

And I hope like fucking hell it's the latter because I've already fallen in love, and clearly I've already lost my mind, so we might as well just go all in while I'm at it.

I text the guys again for the tenth time since I got home.

Reese: I'm fucking nervous. My palms are sweating. Even my balls are sweaty. We've played in sold out stadiums, and I'm more nervous about this.

GRANT RENAMES CONVERSATION TO: OPERATION CAT DADDY

Lane: 🤣🤣🤣🤣

Reese: Are you making fun of my child?

Grant: No, I'm making fun of you.

Lane: Hallie wants to know if you got the scratch tower for her?

Reese: Yeah, I got a bunch of shit because I panicked. I bought like ten different kinds of food because they were all organic and non-GMO and fucking confusing so I just bought them all.

Grant: It's a cat.

Reese: It's my child, you dick.

The front door opens, and I hear Viv walk through, shutting it behind her, so I quickly put my phone on the couch.

Shit, why is my heart beating so fast right now?

I'm not nervous or anything. Okay, fine, I'm a little nervous, but only because I really fucking want her to like my surprise.

"Reese?" Her voice comes from the kitchen.

"In here."

She comes around the corner and looks so fucking cute I want to walk over and kiss the fuck out of her.

Her hair is down and wavy today, with purple little clippy things holding it back from her face, and she's wearing a pair of acid-washed, holey jeans with a strappy purple tank top tucked into the front.

Purple. Because my girl loves purple. Fuck, I missed her.

She skids to a stop as her jaw drops, and her eyes widen. For a second, she just stares silently until she finally says, "Reese… what is that?"

"Um… a kitten?" I feign innocence. Clearly, it's a kitten, but… it's a kitten that wasn't here this morning.

Her eyes are wide as she speaks. "I see that, but *why* is there a kitten here… in your lap?"

I scoop up the little ball of fur into my arms, then stand and cross the room toward her. "Well, because I got her for us. *Surprise.*"

Her throat works, emotion flickering over her face. "You bought us… a cat?"

"Yep. I mean, technically, I didn't *buy* her. I adopted her from the shelter. But I guess we could always take her back if you really don'—"

"No," she interrupts me urgently. "No, you can't take her back!" Reaching out, she rubs the top of the kitten's head softly, and the tiny little thing twists in my arms to go to her. I *feel ya, little one. I always want to go to her too.*

I hand her over and watch as Viv snuggles her into her arms and kisses the top of her little head as emotion settles on her face. "She's really going to stay?"

I nod. "Yeah, Sweet Tart, she's gonna stay. If you want her to."

"I can't believe you remembered, Reese," she says lightly, her blue eyes full of emotion as she looks up at me.

Of course, I remembered. Because when it comes to her, I pay attention. To all of it. All the little details. I know that she hates when her socks don't match and that she loves the smell of books. Grapes disgust her, and she likes to paint her nails every week and really fucking hates the commercials on TV with the sad animals and that Sarah McLachlan song because they *always* make her cry.

And of course, I remember that growing up, she was an only child and always wanted a cat.

So I got her one.

Not just because I want to do anything in the world to make her happy but also because I've realized that I don't like that she's going to be here by herself when I'm on the road for games. And I don't know… I'll be on the road a lot when I'm drafted, and if we somehow end up together, if she ever wants more with me… I don't want her to ever feel alone again. If I can't physically be there with her, now she has our cat to be with her.

"I remember everything, Viv, and I've been thinking about it since you told me. I called Rosie to help me find a place that was at capacity, and when she did, I went there as soon as I got home today and adopted her."

I wasn't entirely sure if I was ready to be a cat dad yet, but the moment I saw this kitten, I knew she was the one and that I wasn't going to be leaving there without her. How could I when she is so fucking cute?

She was stretched out on the windowsill of the shelter, her black coat gleaming in the sun as she basked in the sunlight, and when I reached down to rub her head, she meowed and lifted her white-colored paw in greeting. All four of her paws are completely white, a stark difference to the rest of her body. She looks like she's wearing little boots.

"What should we name her?" Viv asks as she gazes down at her, scratching behind her fuzzy ear.

"What about… Boo? Short for boots because of her paws." I run my finger along her front paw, and she swipes playfully at it. She's purring like crazy, and I read online that means they're happy and content. Judging by the way she's immediately taken to both Viv and me, she was the perfect choice.

Viv nods, a small smile curving on her lips. "Boo. I like that. I think this is the one. God, Reese, I can't believe you got us a cat! She's so perfect."

Not as perfect as she is. But the kitten is pretty damn cute.

I'm committing this moment to memory in hopes that I never forget how happy Viv looks right now, how radiant she looks when she's content. How her smile fully reaches her eyes, how I feel like she's taken root in my heart and ensnared me since the first night that I met her.

I realize this makes me a simp, the way that I feel about her, and I also don't give a shit anymore.

I'm so fucked-up about this girl that I don't even care how whipped I seem.

I bought her a damn cat. That's how bad I've got it.

Granted, I fell in love with Boo at first sight, but still. I think it goes to show that she could ask me to rope the goddamn moon, and I'd somehow make it happen.

Because I want to. I want to be the one that makes her smile like this. I want to be the one that takes care of her the same way she takes care of everyone but herself.

"Oh my god, you even got her a little purple collar," she breathes, fingering the thin, bedazzled collar around her neck that has a little bell attached to it.

I mean, she should know by now that I'm going to spoil the fuck out of my girls. And Boo is now basically our love child.

Grant was talking shit, but I *am* a cat daddy now.

When her eyes lift to mine, she gently sets Boo to the floor, and we watch her hesitantly pad around the living room, her little tail swishing as she takes in her surroundings. It's a new place, so it'll take her a bit to warm up.

"Thank you. This might be the best thing that anyone has ever gotten me, Reese," Viv says, stepping into me, her lips tilting up into a smile as her arms slide around my neck and tangle into the hair in my nape. "I missed you."

Two days was too fucking long.

"Missed you too, Sweet Tart," I respond before dragging my knuckle along her cheek. "Never wanted to be back home so bad while on the road. It was a fucking killer."

She nods while rising on her tiptoes to pull my head down to meet her mouth, gently pressing her lips against mine.

It's chaste. Innocent almost.

Yet every nerve ending in my body comes alive as I kiss her, a live wire of current pulsing through my body.

This is what we do best. Communicate through touching, kissing, fucking.

Her fingers fist into the front of my T-shirt when I angle her mouth, deepening the kiss and slipping my tongue inside, tasting her for the first time in two days.

It's like coming home.

Her whimper rocks through me, and our kiss turns hungry, frantic even as our tongues tangle together, and my hands splay across her waist, anchoring her against me.

Not close enough.

"Fuck, I missed you," I murmur against her mouth, sliding my hands along her jaw and cradling it as I drop my forehead against hers. "Missed *this*."

How can *kissing* someone feel so… intimate? I could kiss her forever.

She gazes up at me, her lips swollen from our kiss, cheeks flushed, and eyes unfocused with arousal.

"You're so fucking pretty, baby."

"Stop being so sweet. You know it makes me want to climb you like a tree." Her voice is raspy, heavy with the same need that I feel. "I'm trying to have self-control."

A laugh rumbles from my chest. "How about we order Jack's for dinner? And then I can have dessert on the kitchen table and make up for lost time."

"It was two days, Reese," she says, giggling so fucking adorably. "You couldn't have missed me *that* much."

"You're sincerely underestimating how much I want to live between your thighs."

"*Caveman*."

We order our usual from Jack's Pizza and sit in the middle of the living room floor with the box between us as we eat, discussing her upcoming podcast episode and how her book is coming along. She asks me about how my training is going and what it's going to be like once I'm drafted to the minors and if I'm nervous. Boo, tired from all her exploring, lies curled up sleeping between our legs the entire time.

Once we're done, Viv walks over to the drawer in the kitchen and pulls out a card game and, with that cute little fucking smirk, challenges me to it like she's throwing down the gauntlet.

Except it turns out that my girl is a really sore loser.

"God, you are *such* a cheater!" Viv accuses, tossing her cards onto the floor between us, narrowing her eyes at me as she crosses her arms over her chest. "Admit it, you totally cheated."

Boo scampers out of the living room at Viv's sudden fit, and I chuckle. "Babe. It's UNO. How the fuck do you cheat at UNO?"

"I don't know, but you did. There's no way you won *four* times in a freakin' row, Reese Landry. I'm calling bullshit. You've got a stack of draw four cards hidden over there somewhere, I know it." She crawls over the cards to where I'm sitting and peeks around my back like I'm actually hiding something, and I take the opportunity to pull her into my lap. I capture her lips, swallowing her protests and replacing them with her moan. When I pull back, her eyes are heavy-lidded and unfocused.

"Stop trying to distract me from the fact that you're a cheater."

"Is it working?" I tease, kissing her again. My tongue traces the seam of her lips, slipping inside and stroking hers until we're both breathless.

I pull back and gaze down at her. "Remember when I said I had a surprise for you this weekend?"

"No way. I thought Boo was the surprise! *No* more surprises, Reese."

"Sorry, but my plan's already in motion, Sweet Tart. I need you to be free Friday night. Can you please do that for me?"

Silence meets my question until finally, her sigh stutters against my lips, and she nods. "Fine. But I just need you to know that you don't have to buy me things all the time, Reese. Even if it's available to you, I don't need material things. Please don't think I'm unappreciative because that's not it. I just don't want you to think you have to constantly do things like this for me."

"Baby, I do it because I love seeing you smile, not because of anything other than that. Alright? Plus, this surprise is… not *technically* a material thing. And I know that you'll love it. That's all that matters. Just be ready Friday when class is over, okay?"

"Okay." She leans forward and slants her lips over mine, whispering, "Can we make up for that lost time now?"

"I thought you'd never ask."

22 / viv

Boo! Look What You Made Me Do

In the days leading up to Reese's surprise, I don't see much of him. I've been at the library, both for my job and working on finishing a paper for English, and he's been putting in extra time in the bullpen with Lane, practicing for their upcoming spring conference tournament. Which, I hear, is a big deal in college baseball. Not that I would know, but I learn more and more every day. It's like a whole new world. Full of balls.

Literally and figuratively.

The only time I've really seen him is when he crawled into bed while I was writing, cuddled up with Boo against my side, and passed out the second his head hit the pillow.

Yeah, we've pretty much transitioned to sleeping in the same bed every night without ever officially making it a thing.

It kind of just happened, and I didn't want to question it because at this point, it would feel weird to be in the same house and *not fall* asleep with his warm, hard body wrapped around mine like a blanket.

He has to be touching me somewhere anytime he's in my presence, and I sometimes wake up during the night sweating because he's the equivalent of a human heater.

I've gotten used to the feeling of sleeping next to him though.

And I like it.

Glancing in the mirror once more, I brush my hair out of my face and scan my outfit for tonight. I have absolutely no idea what he has in store, so I wasn't sure what to wear, but he assured me that shorts and my Vans were fine.

I've gotta applaud the fact that he's held out this long. Despite my attempts at… convincing him. Turns out he's much better at keeping a surprise than I am. Even when my mouth's involved.

"Viv, you ready? We gotta ride," I hear him call from outside my bedroom door, and then he rounds the corner. "Gonna be late."

He's got on my favorite red baseball cap turned to the back with a black Hellcats hoodie and a worn pair of jeans, looking absolutely mouthwateringly delicious.

It makes me kind of want to stay home and ride *him* instead. "Stop looking at me like that, Sweet Tart, before we don't make it out of this door."

My teeth rake over my lip as I look up at him through my lashes. "I mean…"

His head shakes. "Nah. You would kill me if you knew what you'd be missing. Save all that energy for later—you're gonna need it. Maybe tonight will be the night I finally take that pretty ass."

I can feel the deep, raspy words in my core. I can't help but clench my thighs together at the promise in his words, and if there's something I've learned firsthand in the last few weeks, it's that he always keeps his word. I wasn't a virgin when I met him, obviously, but it's one of the only things we haven't done. Aside from his finger when he's fucking me from behind.

And I *want* it. I want to feel completely full of him there. To give him that part of me.

"Fuck, Viv," he mutters after my reaction to his words before closing the distance between us and tugging me to him, kissing me so fiercely that I have to hold on to the front of his hoodie not to lose my balance.

God, he kisses the same way he fucks. Unhinged and possessive. Like he's staking his claim every time he touches me.

"Let's go. Right the fuck now," he pants against my lips.

"Okay," I agree.

Yet my fingers stay entwined in his shirt, and he's clutching my waist like I'm the one who's holding *him* up.

A moment later, his Apple watch goes off, and he curses. "We have to go right now, or we're going to miss it."

Without him supporting the weight of my legs, which are still shaky from his kiss, I sway for a second, causing him to laugh.

"C'mon, Sweet Tart."

We quickly kiss our sweet *Boo-by* girl bye and then walk out the front door. I follow behind him to his Rover, and he helps me into the passenger side, then slides in behind the wheel and pulls out of the driveway onto the highway.

It takes over an hour to get to our destination, and the further we get, the more… confused I am.

I don't truly figure it out until we're pulling down the dark, deserted road, and I whip my gaze to Reese.

"No way."

His smile says it all.

"Oh my god," I squeal. "There's no way!" I'm so ecstatic that I'm squirming in the passenger seat, barely able to contain my excitement. I can't even imagine how in the world he made this happen.

And what strings he had to have pulled to do it. For me.

"I am going to suck the soul out of you, Reese Landry."

His laugh fills the car, and he reaches out and captures my hand, lacing our fingers together as we continue down the dark gravel road toward the one place I've been dreaming of visiting again since I was a little girl.

He's taking me to the abandoned theme park.

The one that is known as one of the most haunted places in America, a former historic tourist attraction that has been closed to the public for over a decade because of all the unusual things that kept happening there. Experts say that it's a hotspot for paranormal activity, and that's the reason why I've been dying to go back. Because ghosts are my thing, and this man made it happen.

I'm going to have a heart attack.

"How did you make this happen? It takes months to even get a response from the city, and it's literally always a no. This is crazy!"

"My dad's good friends with the mayor. She's been his friend since high school. I called in a favor. Promised her season tickets in return. But we can only go in tonight, and we've got to sign a waiver on our phones that releases the city from any liability."

"Done," I breathe excitedly. "I think I'm in shock right now. I can't believe I'm going to go back. Crap, what about flashlights? I'm not prepared. I should've brought an EVP recorder. Or a spirit box."

Reese pulls the car up to the dark entrance, and my jaw falls open. Holy shit. It's even scarier than I remember. Vines and moss wrap around the ten-foot fence, blocking out most of the park from view, but you can still see the silhouette of the abandoned coasters in the background. It's too dark to really make out what's beyond the fence, but I'm dying to see what's on the other side.

He reaches over me and opens the glove compartment, pulling out two flashlights. "Not even going to pretend I have a clue what you're talking about, Sweet Tart. But I did call Hallie when I put this together, and she told me to at least get this."

I glance down at the object he's pulled out in addition to the flashlights.

A camera.

I squeal, swiping it from his hand, and then I unbuckle my seat belt to lean over the console. "Thank you. Thank you. Thank you," I whisper against his lips.

I want to say more, like confess that I like him. Way more than a friend and nothing like a roommate. That all of these things he does for me, all of these thoughtful things that don't cost a dime, are my favorite. That I appreciate how he listens to me. How he gets me. That being with him makes me happy, and I wake up every morning with a smile on my face, knowing that I'll be with him.

I just… It doesn't feel like the right time. And if he doesn't feel the same, then I don't know what I'll do. I'm not ready for that.

"Are you gonna hold my hand?" His eyes shine with amusement. "'Cause you know I'm fucking scared of ghosts."

I nod. "Of course. Don't worry, *I'll* protect you, Reese."

He chortles, swiping the flashlight from my lap, and opens the driver's-side door, slipping out.

I do a little happy dance in my seat while he walks around and opens my door. When he opens it, I give him another quick peck on the lips before I hop out and turn on the flashlight and ready the camera.

"Okay, let's do this. We have to go to the fun house!"

Reese groans as he flips the switch on his. "Fuck me. Why did I do this again?"

"Mmm. I'm going to fuck you alright… and because you're amazing, that's why. Now, come on, you big chicken. Nothing's going to happen," I say, grabbing his hand and tugging him toward the entrance.

For my sake, I definitely hope we see a ghost, but for him…

"Yeah, that's what every single person in a horror movie says before they die, babe."

True.

But I think it'll be fine. The only thing in here we really need to worry about is the alligators from the nearby swamps.

Now, those *I'm* afraid of.

Reese unlocks the heavy padlock on the front gate and pushes it open, allowing us to slip inside. Pretty sure he's supposed to lock it back, but I think he's too afraid that he won't be able to get out if something's chasing him. He's looking a little panicked, to be honest.

As soon as we're through the gate, he's back at my side, fingers woven tightly in mine, so tight that it almost hurts.

The park is eerily quiet and creepier than I remember, which makes me excited. This is so my vibe, and I am loving it already, and we've only just walked through the gate.

There's no electricity, so it's completely black aside from our flashlights, and I am a little thankful that Reese got the good ones and not the ones where the batteries die within twenty minutes, because as excited as I am to be here, I do not want to get stuck in the dark in the middle of the night.

"You sure about this, Viv?" he whispers as we make our way past the ticket booth and further into the park.

I giggle. "Yes, I'm sure. We're already here. You know, for a six-foot-three, bad-ass collegiate athlete, you sure are a baby."

"I am manly as fuck, Sweet Tart. Do I need to remind you with my dick?" he says, glancing down at me, his expression still slightly anxious. "I just don't… fuck with ghosts. They're meant to stay on their side of the…"

"Veil," I volunteer when he trails off.

He nods seriously. "Yeah, that."

We pass by the dilapidated merry-go-round, now faded and crumbling from the exposure to elements since the flood. The rusted metal creaks and groans in the wind. It's eerily haunting, seeing so many pieces of the park still intact, like one day it just ceased to exist.

And I guess, in a way, that's what happened. Now, it's a ghost town. A moment stuck in time, untouched by the world.

We walk hand in hand down the sidewalk, passing by what was once the carnival games. There are old bottles with plastic rings still wrapped around the necks of them from a game of ring toss.

"This is so fucking creepy," Reese mutters, tightening his hand around mine. I tug him along the sidewalk when his stride slows.

"Come on, I think we're almost there."

The number one place on my list is the fun house. It's apparently where there's the most activity, some even caught on camera, and I have to see it for myself.

I've been studying maps of this place, old documentaries, and other media stories for years for *Haunted Homicide*, so even in the dark, I feel like I know it.

With only the beam from our flashlights to guide us, we make our way through the park, and finally, I spot the fun house up ahead.

"There it is!" I say excitedly, stopping to turn to Reese. His brow is furrowed as his eyes dart around us. "I just want to see this one place, okay? Then we can leave. It's good enough that I even got to be here. After dark at that. I promise, we'll go right after this."

Reese nods. "Alright. Let's do this shit."

I love the determined expression that passes over his face, and I bite the inside of my cheek to keep from laughing. I appreciate the sudden bravado.

The entrance of the deep red fun house is covered in various shades of graffiti and its faded original art.

"*Enter at your own risk*?" he reads out loud, groaning. "Damnit, Viv."

"It's *just* graffiti. It's okay," I reassure him.

He doesn't look the least bit assured, so I turn to face him, rising on my tiptoes and pressing my mouth against his in a sweet, chaste kiss that immediately turns heated when he grasps my hips and pulls me toward him, his tongue slipping past my lips.

I pull back and smile. "There, now you've got all the courage you need. C'mon, let's go."

His hand is tight around mine as we duck under the half sheet of plywood that covers the door.

Holy shit… The inside is even creepier than the outside, full of life-size clowns with terrifying faces and mirrors that distort your body. It's so dark in here, even with the flashlights, still not enough to counter the blanket of darkness. The floorboards creak beneath our feet, creating a creepy soundtrack the further we walk.

This is freakin' awesome.

I snap a few photos with the camera and then press deeper into the house with Reese on my heels.

Suddenly, there's a loud bang from the other side of the house, and he stiffens beside me.

"What the *fuck* was that?"

Turning, I shine my flashlight around us and see nothing. "It's just the building settling. This place is old and has been abandoned forever."

He's just on edge and thinking that everything is something coming to drag him away to the underworld. He's so close to my back that I can feel the heat of his body on me, his hand splaying on my hip, holding me in place.

"I don't like this sh—"

A loud crash causes us to both jump, cutting him off.

"Yeah, and tell me what the fuck that was, Sweet Tart," he whisper-yells.

My eyes widen. "Um… *a ghost*?"

He shakes his head. "Nah, fuck this. We're getting out of here. *Right the fuck now.*"

"Bu—" He cuts me off by bending down and throwing me over his shoulder in a single swoop. Without hesitation, he turns on his heel and carries me right out of the fun house in an almost sprint.

"Nope. I'm done. We came, you saw, and now we're getting the fuck out of here before something drags us down to hell."

I'm giggling so hard I might *actually* pee my pants. How is he moving so fast carrying a whole-ass person on his shoulder like a sack of potatoes?

"You can put me down now, you caveman!"

"Nope, not till we're safely out of this bitch," he mutters.

He is such a nut. I lift my head and watch as we pass through the quiet, dark park, and my heart squeezes at the thought of him facing his fears for me.

Reese did this despite the fact that he's terrified of all things spooky, just because it was something I mentioned and because he wanted to make me happy.

"Thank you for facing your fear for me tonight." I tell Reese when he's "safely" gotten me in the car, buckled me into the seat, and climbed in his side.

He glances over at me from the driver's seat and smirks, "Anything for you, Sweet Tart. But next time? Can we please just watch a movie about this shit so I don't have a heart attack at twenty-two?"

"Or maybe next time we bring actual ghost-hunting equipment so we're prepared."

His expression turns panicked, and I laugh. *"Just kidding."*

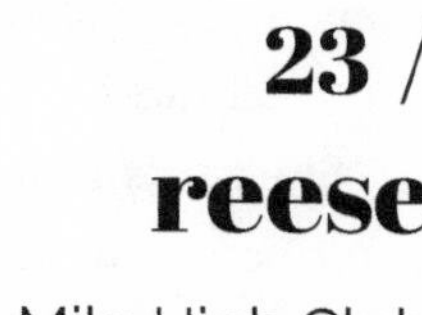

23 / reese

Mile High Club

"I can't believe you just... *own* a jet," Viv says from the seat next to me, staring wide-eyed out of the window at the sea of fluffy white clouds we're flying through.

We're somewhere over the Atlantic Ocean currently, with about an hour left in our flight.

I'm still surprised that she's even *here,* honestly. I figured when I casually threw it out that I wanted to take her away for a few days during spring break that she'd immediately shoot the idea down. So imagine my surprise when she said *maybe.*

That maybe eventually turned into a yes after she called her mom and discussed it with her. She's nervous about going this far from her even for only a few days, but her mom reassured her over and over that everything was fine and that she needed to go and enjoy herself.

Viv still wasn't convinced and ended up reaching out to a neighbor in her mom's apartment complex who has helped out before and asked if they would check in on her while she was gone.

Only then did she feel comfortable enough to say yes to going to Turks and Caicos with me.

On the jet.

It helped that she was able to spend a few days with her mom at the beginning of break while I had practice. I could only take off a few days, so I picked her up from her mom's apartment and whisked her away.

"Technically, it's my *parents'* jet, not mine," I counter.

She turns to look at me, leveling her gaze. "Same thing. Your *family* owns a jet. Which it's insane that you say it so nonchalantly. Normal people don't just *own* jets, Reese."

I shrug. "Always been my normal, babe. And my parents having a plane means that I get to take you to the beach and see you in that purple bikini that I've been dreaming about since you showed it to me."

Her laugh fills the cabin, and I grin. I'm so fucking happy she decided to come, and I can't wait to get off the plane and head straight to the pool. Not just because I'm eager to see her in that tiny bikini but because I wanna spend the next four days doing nothing but relaxing and being inside Viv every damn chance I get.

My schedule's getting more intense as we approach graduation, and I'm lucky that I was even able to take off a few days to bring her. I just want to spend all the time with her that I can before the season gets crazy and we're stuck stealing small moments just to have any time together at all. When we head to the championship this year, things will be crazy all the way until June.

I decided before even boarding the plane that I'm going to tell her how I feel while we're here.

It's time. I can't even pretend that I'm not crazy about her at this point, and truthfully, I'm done trying.

I fucking want her. *All* of her. I want her to be *mine*.

I want the whole world to know that she's my girl. After talking to Grant, I know that I want to be with her, whatever it takes… I just have to give her a little nudge and let her set the pace.

"I also can't believe we're going to Turks and Caicos," she says as she shuts her laptop. She's been writing for most of the flight, and I've been sneaking glances when I could. Apparently, her muse has been musing because she said she's polishing the last few chapters, and I'm hoping once she's done, I'll finally get to read it.

I know how important this is to her and how close she is to fulfilling her dream of publishing, and I just want to support and celebrate her the same way she has for me.

"Speaking of. I'm worried our signal might be a little spotty while we're there, so I think we should go ahead and call Hallie to check on Boo."

"God, I miss her already," Viv says, pulling her phone out of the pocket of the Hellcats hoodie of mine that she stole. Not that I'm complaining. I'd prefer if she exclusively only wore my clothes because I'm a caveman like that. At least when it comes to her.

"Me too."

Her fingers tap at the screen as she pulls up Hallie's contact info, and after a few short rings, she answers, filling the screen. "Hi!" Hallie smiles. "Wait, are you calling me from… *the* jet?"

Viv laughs sweetly. "The *infamous* Landry jet. Yes, I am. We're not sure if we'll have cell signal or Wi-Fi, so we just wanted to call and check on Boo?"

Before Hallie can even respond, I lean over into Viv's seat, my face hovering over the camera. "Hey, Hallie."

"Hey, Reese."

"How's my little Boo-bear doing?"

Hallie's cackle echoes through the air, and I feel Viv chuckling beside me. It's the new running joke between everyone… how much I love my cat. Whatever. If a parent doesn't love their child, what does that make them? A psychopath. And I am not a psychopath.

"Boo is *fine.* You are such a hovering cat daddy, you know that?" she chides before disappearing from the camera for a second, then popping back in, bringing Boo's sweet little face onto the screen.

"There's my girl," I coo. "I hope your Aunt Hallie is taking the best care of you."

Viv giggles. "Hi, my Boo-by girl. I miss you!"

I lean further over Viv and then take the phone out of her hand so I can talk to Hallie directly because this is important. "Oh, listen, did you warm her food up for her? Remember the instructions? She hates when it's cold."

"Yes, Reese!" Hallie retorts with an exaggerated eye roll. "I am perfectly capable of taking care of Boo while you're gone. I reassured you of that... at least ten times before you left."

I nod. "You did. Thank you for that, but I just wanted to make sure. And you got the new mouse toys I left for her?"

"All ten of them? Yep. Got 'em." She sighs, clearly over my shit.

I don't get what the big deal is. Everyone's so annoyed that I'm being an over-the-top cat daddy, but I can't help it that I love her. I'm not apologizing for it. I'm a proud helicopter cat dad.

Viv swipes the phone out of my hand as I protest and flits the camera back to her. "Sorry, he's spiraling. Thanks, space babe."

"Always. Byeeeee, have fun on your trip!" Hallie ends the call before I can say goodbye to Boo.

Rude.

"You would've never let her get off the phone!" Viv laughs as she reads my pouting expression. She climbs into my lap, settling over my now hardening cock before dipping her head to whisper, "I think it's so hot that you're being a doting and concerned cat daddy."

My lips tug into a smirk, and I reach up, brushing her long hair out of her face. "I'm glad. You should know, then, I even got these special organic treats from this French place that I found online that are supposed to help with digesting hair balls."

"Ooooh. I love it when you talk *dirty* to me." She giggles against my lips.

We land an hour later—after Viv stayed true to her promise and sucked the actual fucking soul out of me—at a private airstrip just outside of the city. I realize the irony that while we were flying through literal clouds, she had me on cloud nine with her talented mouth.

As we deboard the jet and head to our private car, I can already tell Viv's anxiousness is morphing into excitement.

Relief fills my chest. I was worried she might spend the entire time we're here stressing since at takeoff she was so visibly anxious and uneasy about both flying and being this far away from her mom. But the call with Boo and Hallie, and the call she made to her mom right after seemed to put her a bit more at ease. That and our introduction to the mile-high club.

I thread my fingers through hers, squeezing gently as we ride to my family's villa. She's staring out of the window excitedly, and I can't even fucking say how happy it makes me to see her like this.

To see the tension slowly slip out of her body. To see her smiling face lit up with excitement.

"Oh my god, look, it's a *coconut*. There are actual palm trees. This is insane. I can't believe we just rode on a jet, to another country!" she breathes, her eyes dancing with animation.

"Yeah, we did, baby." I laugh and slide my arm over her shoulders, pulling her against me and pressing my lips to the top of her head. Soaking it all in. Soaking *her* in. "We should be there any minute now."

I wish we had longer than four days. Selfishly, I wish that I could keep her here, all to myself, but I know that can't happen, so it just means that I've gotta make the most out of the time we have.

Maybe if things go well and we become a couple, I can bring her back for a few days this summer between games.

Or hell, maybe she and Hallie can come sometime this summer for a girls' trip. I think that would make her happy. Might even be good for her mom if she's comfortable enough to travel on the plane.

"No. Way. Holy fucking hell, Reese!" Viv whisper-yells. Glancing up, I see Viv eyeing my family's large white Spanish-style villa with wide-eyed wonder.

So yeahhhhh, I maybe "*forgot*" to mention that we're staying in a secluded luxury villa, but I know how weird she gets about money, and I didn't want that to be the reason she didn't agree to this vacation. It was enough that I got her on the damn jet without her having a heart attack about the cost. I just want her to be able to step away for a few days and enjoy herself.

Her arm flies out, smacking me against the stomach lightly, but I double over dramatically with an oof.

"Damn, woman, you just knocked the air out of me. We're back to this, Rocky?"

Her breath hitches as she tries to give me a once-over, then realizes I'm fucking with her. "I should've aimed lower. Please tell me that the driver has the wrong address and you did *not* book something this expensive, Reese. It's just the two of us—why do we need a whole freaking mansion?"

"I didn't book this house," I tell her, and she exhales in relief. "My… parents own it."

The car pulls to a stop in the circular driveway in front of the house, and I climb out before turning back to take Viv's hand, helping her out into the warm sun.

Her jaw is still hanging open as she surveys the grounds and house in front of us. I take in this house, trying to see it through Viv's eyes. The terracotta roof and the custom carved front doors, the large flower-covered balconies with wrought iron accents, and the limestone pathways with manicured grass lines. I can admit that it's beautiful, and for a minute, Viv is speechless.

"Reese. This is *crazy*. I realize that I keep saying that, but I think I'm in shock. How many more houses do you have?"

My parents have.... quite a few more houses, but none of them technically belong to me.

I shrug, shutting the car door behind us. "A few. I don't visit much with school and ball, so it's really my family and their friends that get to use all of them."

Honestly, my parents' wealth has never been a huge deal to me. Granted, I know I grew up extremely blessed and had access to things a lot of people didn't, and I'm thankful for that. For the opportunities I've had. But if it all went away tomorrow, then it would just... *go*.

And I would be fine.

Yeah, I'm aware money can make things easier. I also know how nice it is to not have to worry about paying for stuff, to be able to do shit like this for Viv and for my friends, but it doesn't define me. I've worked really fucking hard to set myself up to make my own money with my baseball career.

"Come on, I wanna show you the inside." I grab her hand and tug her toward the front door. I quickly get the heavy wooden doors open and bring her inside, giving her a second to look around at the entryway with the grand staircase and the mosaic Spanish tile flooring.

"This is fancy, even for you, All-Star," she teases before she pauses to admire the oil painting my mom had commissioned last Christmas of all four of us, mostly as a joke for Dad. But of course, he called her on the bluff and insisted we hang it, so now it's definitely... a conversation piece.

"Blame my mother and her sense of humor for that one. That thing creeps me out—the eyes follow you when you walk, I swear," I mutter, grabbing her hand once more and guiding her toward the sitting room.

I give her a tour of the house, including the kitchen, where I plan to have *her* for breakfast, lunch, and dinner, the theater room, most of the downstairs, and then the large patio with the pool. It's got a waterfall with a Jacuzzi and overlooks the ocean. One of my favorite spots in this house.

Then, I take her upstairs to show her the master bedroom that'll be ours while we're here.

"There's a bathtub, Reese. On the *balcony*."

I nod, my lips curving into a smirk. "Yup. And I can't fucking wait to get you in it."

She walks around the room, gazing at every little detail before approaching the king-size bed in the middle of the room and dramatically flopping down backward on it like a starfish.

Fuck, she's cute.

"I'm never leaving this spot." Sighing happily, she burrows into the mountains of pillows and the thick blue, down comforter on the bed until I crawl over her, covering my body with hers.

My gaze holds hers as I slowly start to tug her shirt up, then dip my head and drag my lips languidly along her jaw. "Don't worry, Sweet Tart. I'll make sure you're too exhausted to leave."

I'M NERVOUS AS FUCK. I feel like this is happening a lot lately, me being nervous about something. About something with Viv.

And it's not a feeling that I'm used to experiencing. I'm generally calm and collected under pressure. I've played in sold-out stadiums with crowds chanting my name. Held my composure and made key plays in high-stakes games. But this feels different.

This one conversation is going to change everything. Good or bad, it's going to shift things between Viv and me. I hope like fuck she feels the same way that I do. That we're doing more than just hooking up, but if she doesn't… I'm going to be heartbroken for the first time in my life.

That's a scary fucking feeling.

But I have to be honest with her before this goes any further, before I fall harder.

"Hey, can we talk about something?" I ask, trying to hide my nerves. We're sitting on the patio, listening to the ocean as we rock in the porch bed after having dinner on the beach. I always thought it was ridiculous that my parents had this thing installed when we moved in since we come here once, maybe twice a year, but right now, I'm thankful for it. It feels like the perfect place to tell her how I feel. The sun is painting the sky in shades of orange and blue as it sets. It's the perfect temperature, cooler at night than during the day.

Viv turns to look at me, her eyes worried. "What's wrong?"

She looks so fucking beautiful like this. Her hair is wild and blowing in the breeze, freckles scattered lightly across her nose from the sun, her skin slightly red after our time by the pool, making her eyes look an even brighter blue.

"Nothing. Nothing," I say quickly, reaching out and grabbing her hand, lacing my fingers in hers. "I just…"

The worried brow furrow I spent all day watching melt away starts to return as I stumble with my words.

"Reese, would you spit it out? You're freaking me out," she says, her eyes wide with impatience.

Fuck, even when I'm trying to confess my love for this girl, she's still giving me shit. Unknowingly, but if that doesn't describe how things are between us, then I don't know what would.

I chuckle. "I am, woman. Don't rush me." Turning more toward her, I bring my hand to her jaw, sweeping my thumb along her skin, needing some type of physical touch to calm my nerves probably as much as hers. I'm not great with words, and I have no plan on how to do this, so I just throw it out there with no preamble. "Viv, I don't want to… be friends who sometimes hook up anymore."

Her throat works as she swallows visibly, her body stilling. This would be the time where she throws those walls up, but I'm not going to let her push me out. I need her to be real with me. To be honest, if she truly doesn't want to be with me, fine, I'll respect that. But I'm not letting her walk away if the reason is that she's afraid of her feelings.

I'm fucking afraid too. But loving her… it's not a choice. I can't just turn it off.

"Reese…" she says quietly in a tone I can't decipher.

I shake my head. "Let me get this out, okay?" When she nods, I drag in a deep breath and continue, looking deep into her eyes. "I don't want to be friends who hook up anymore because I want to be *more* than friends, Viv. I want to be with you, for real. I want you to be my girlfriend, not just the girl I'm hooking up with. You deserve more than that. I like you, and I want us to be in a relationship."

Her hand tightens in mine as if she's holding on for dear life. Silence meets my words, and fuck, I'm *scared*. I'm scared that she's going to tell me to fuck off because she's not interested in being in a relationship. And if she did, she'd have every right to. She's the one who said from the beginning that she wasn't interested in more than this. Shit, at the beginning, she didn't even want to be around me.

I'm the one who fell for her, despite knowing all that.

I'm terrified that I'm going to lose her. That I've ruined everything between us and that she's going to run, and that this time, I won't be able to catch her.

She's quiet, dropping her gaze down to her fidgeting hands, and I'm fucking panicked.

"I… I think I want that too," she whispers, swallowing roughly, probably as nervous as I am right now. "I want to be with you, Reese."

Holy shit. Is this actually happening right now?

I've been so in my head about the fact that she might say no that I hadn't even really considered that she might say yes.

"Really?" I say in disbelief. Fuck me. I fist pump the air like an idiot who can't stop himself because Viv just told me she wants to be *my girl*.

She laughs, soft and sweet. "Yes. I want us to be together. I just… I don't know how we're going to make this work with you graduating and the minors, and I'm really fucking afraid of us messing this up, Reese."

And because I can't last another moment without touching her, I slide my hands around her waist and tug her into my lap and kiss her forehead, the tip of her nose, and then her lips before tucking her into my chest. "Hey, it's okay to be scared, baby. It's scary being vulnerable in a relationship with someone. I don't have all the answers, but what I do know is that we'll figure it the fuck out. Whatever it takes to make it work, we'll do it. What matters is that we *want* to make it work. I want to be with you, Viv, and I'm going to do whatever it takes to make that happen."

"But you're going to be drafted and move to a new state. You have no idea where you'll be, and I'm going to be here, still in college and dealing with my life…" She trails off, raking her teeth over her lips. "Long-distance relationships are hard."

I nod, taking that in. "Yeah, I'm sure they are. But they're worth it, Viv. *You're* worth it. We'll have FaceTime dates, and I'll fly you out to my games and visit home every chance I get. It'll be hard at times, but I want to *try*. I want to try, with you."

Viv lifts her head and leans forward, dropping her forehead against mine. Together, we just breathe for a few minutes, soaking in everything about this moment. "This is crazy. We're complete opposites. What if we never work together?" Her voice is barely above a whisper that I feel on my lips.

She's not wrong—we are opposites. There's never a guarantee with any relationship, and I can't guarantee the future, but what I do know is that I'm all in, and I'm going to do whatever I can to make it work.

"Yeah, baby, we are different." I laugh lightly, holding her gaze. "And maybe the only thing we have in common is how we feel about each other, but that's all that really matters. We can be night and fucking day, Viv, and it won't change anything. You come to my games even though you have no clue what's happening. I'm pretty sure you called it a touchdown the other day, which really hurt my fucking soul, but you showed up. And I'll take you to every haunted house in the damn country if that's what you want. I'll buy the ghost equipment and pretend I'm not ready to shit my pants if it makes you happy. You'll be my date to stupid rich people functions, and you'll act like you hate every second of it, even though I know you secretly like getting dressed up, and I'll be your biggest fucking fan. I'll send letters to every publisher in the country, Viv. Because I want you and whatever comes with it. It'll work because we want it to. Because together, we're better."

She laughs with unshed tears in her eyes and shakes her head like she can't believe we're having this conversation right now.

Hell, I can't either, but I'm so glad I decided to tell her how I feel. I couldn't keep it in any longer without being honest with her, and I feel a huge sense of relief that she wants the same things I do.

"Are you sure this is what you want? You're about to leave, Reese… I just don't want you to feel like I'm weighing you down or distrac—"

"Fuck no, Viv." I cut that shit off before it even comes out of her mouth. "I mean it when I say I want this, and I want you. There's no question. How I feel about you is not a choice, baby.

That's what I want you to understand. You're my priority." I lean in to press my lips against hers tenderly, wrapping my arms more tightly around her. To show her what I can't with my words.

Some things should be felt.

"Tell me that you feel this too. That I'm not alone."

Her lips move against mine as she nods. Her breath fans along my mouth when she speaks. "I do. You make me happy, Reese, and I do want to be with you. I just… might fuck this up somewhere along the way. I'm not good at feelings and being vulnerable and open, but I'm trying. I'm trying to communicate better and allow myself to rely on people. I just might sometimes need a little grace. Patience. For when I do it wrong or push you away."

My heart squeezes in my fucking chest at what she's saying. Like I'll give up on her because sometimes she may shut down or need a little space.

"Anything you need. We're going at your pace, however slow or fast that might be. Okay?"

She nods, a soft but genuine smile on her face. "Thank you. For being so *good*, Reese. I feel like I don't deserve it. I don't deserve you. I'm not sure I ever… apologized to you for being so mean and bitchy when we first met. For misjudging you so badly and getting so annoyed. I know now I just sometimes use that as a defense mechanism. That's not an excuse, and I'm sorry. You deserved better than that."

My face softens. "I told you that night after leaving your mom's that I wasn't going anywhere, Viv. I meant that. We all deal with shit in our own way, and if you need me to be the punching bag sometimes, then so be it. I'm solid fucking muscle, and I can take a few hits."

A tear escapes from her eyes, and I dip my head forward, licking it up. I kiss her reddened nose from the sun and then both apples of her cheeks. Her eyelids, her jaw, her cupid's bow.

Every inch of her I touch with my lips to show her that I'm here, that I'm not going anywhere. That I want all of her, even the sharp edges.

"Sorry I'm crying, ugh," she whines, swiping at the tears.

"Don't apologize for feeling, baby. You're human, and it's natural to have those feelings. And it means so much to me that you'll share them with me. I'm in your corner, always, Viv. Let's be together and figure out the rest as we go."

For a second, she's quiet, her watery eyes searching mine, and then she nods, leaning forward and pressing her lips against mine.

Her tongue swipes almost hesitantly at the seam of my lips before slipping inside and tangling with mine. My hands slide from her jaw to her hair, threading in the strands as I pull her in closer until she's squirming in my lap.

"Reese?"

"Hmm?" I hum against her mouth.

"I want you, *boyfriend*. Right. Now."

24 / viv

Don't Blink

Being with Reese is always amazing, but now it feels…*different*.

More intense. More intimate. More freeing.

It's on a whole new level, and I think it's because we both admitted how we've been feeling about each other. It feels like the final barrier that separated us has been dissolved, and nothing stands between us. Which feels crazy to say, considering we're still mostly clothed, but it already feels like everything has shifted.

His stormy eyes hold mine as he kisses my center through the thin fabric of my panties, nibbling at my clit gently until my back is arching and my hand is flying to his hair, fisting through the strands.

"I'm so fucking crazy about you, Vivienne. You have no idea." He pulls my panties to the side, exposing my pussy to his hungry gaze. "Crazy about this pretty little cunt that's always dripping for me."

Oh god. His mouth is so obscenely filthy, and I can't get enough of it. I expect him to rush things along with how desperate we both seem to be right now, but he doesn't. This won't be fast and dirty. He takes his time as he leans forward and drags his tongue through my center torturously slowly.

Languid, soft strokes that have me writhing on this makeshift bed. It swings gently from the wind, rocking me into his mouth on its own without my hips having to do the work.

My hands travel up my stomach to my breasts, where I yank my tank and the cups of my bra down so I can tweak my nipples between my fingers, rolling them roughly. The added sensation, combined with Reese's tongue, has my pussy throbbing, an orgasm already building inside of me, climbing higher and higher.

I'm hypersensitive tonight, and I'm not sure if it's because Reese and I are *officially* a couple or because he's just wickedly talented with his tongue.

Probably a combination of both.

"Come for me, baby," he murmurs, kissing my thigh before returning to my clit with his mouth. He slides his long finger inside of me and strokes my G-spot with expert precision.

It only takes a few pumps before I'm coming, falling over the edge. My entire body goes taut as my orgasm hits me, sending me into a spiral of pleasure that has my toes curling along his back and my fingers tugging at his hair so hard that I hear him hiss, sucking at my clit with fervor in response.

"Reese," I cry, rocking my hips against his mouth as he licks me through my orgasm, curling his finger inside of me to hit that *perfect* spot. I come so hard that I'm nearly in tears, my muscles aching from exertion as I tremble.

"So fucking perfect," he mumbles against my clit, pressing his lips to the sensitive bud before pulling his fingers out of me and crawling up my body with a trail of kisses, fitting his hips between my thighs.

He slides his hands underneath my shirt and makes quick work removing it, tugging it over my head and tossing it aside.

With his lip pulled between his teeth, he drops his gaze down to my chest at my pebbled nipples, which are pushing against the cups of my bra.

He's staring at me so reverently that it makes my heart skip. I rise up to my elbows and watch as he tugs his shirt off, pulling his shorts and briefs down, and kicks them away as he palms his cock. He strokes it slowly as he watches me, and I have to press my thighs together to dull the throb.

There's something so... addicting about watching him pleasure himself.

Carefully, he crawls over me, covering me with his body as he takes my chin in his hand and kisses me sweetly, languidly, as if he's savoring the taste. I feel like I'm melting in his hands. His mouth moves tenderly over mine as he reaches down, and drags his fingers through my core, playing with my clit until I'm writhing beneath him. His lips drag along my neck, nipping at my earlobe lightly, causing me to shiver.

He takes his time working me into a desperate frenzy until I feel like I can't take another moment of not having him filling me, buried so deep that I don't know where I start, and he begins.

"Reese, I *need* you," I whimper when his lips close around my nipple, sucking it into his mouth. "Please."

Sitting up slightly, he fists his cock and drags it through my folds to tease me, nudging against my clit with a surge of his hips, sending a bolt of pleasure down my spine.

"I'll always give you what you need, baby," he says as he lines the head of his erection up with my entrance, pushing in only an inch. The muscles in his arms ripple at the exertion of holding back, his chest rising and falling shallowly while he slowly rocks into me, his eyes locked with mine.

Inch by inch he moves until he's buried to the hilt, finally inside me.

His head dips and his lips are on mine once more, kissing the breath right from my lungs until my head feels dizzy, and I'm clenching around him. We're groaning against each other's lips when he finally withdraws and agonizingly slowly thrusts back inside of me. He's unhurried, but he's building a frenzy inside of me.

"You're mine now, Vivienne," he rasps, kissing the corner of my lips, slanting his mouth over mine and thrusting his tongue softly inside, filling me with promises. Promises I believe. "I'm never letting you go."

I nod, my hands grasping at his shoulders as he reaches between us to thrum my clit. A light swipe of his fingers that has my toes curling and my back arching against him in pleasure. Everything about his touch is tender and gentle. Full of meaning. Tonight feels different than any of the times we've been together, more intense and passionate. He's showing me that I'm *his*.

I'm already close when his hips roll, grinding his pelvis against my clit as he starts to thrust faster. When he dips his head to drag his tongue along the valley of my chest and capture my nipple in his mouth sucking on my piercing, I can't hold back any longer.

I fall apart, gasping and crying out his name as he thrusts twice more and follows me into bliss. I can feel his cum in hot spurts inside of me, filling me. *Claiming me.*

There is no doubt. I am wholly Reese Landry's.

He groans hoarsely as he pulls free, and I sigh into the fluffy blanket, my eyes falling shut as the sound of the ocean washes over my sated body. I feel the porch bed sway as he steps off, and when he returns he carefully parts my legs, and drags a warm cloth up my center, cleaning me. He kisses my stomach, below my belly button, my hips, the inside of my thighs.

"I'm obsessed with you. Every inch of you was made for me."

I feel his lips drag along my inner thigh as he continues to pepper kisses on my body.

Once he's done, he lies down beside me, looping his arm over my stomach and pulling me back until I'm molded to his front.

His lips brush along my shoulder, and then he kisses my head, holding me tightly against him. We lie there together, breathing, savoring the feel of each other, and the powerful moment that we just experienced.

I feel so peaceful, and so safe wrapped in his arms... I never want to leave.

"VIV. BABY, WAKE UP." Reese's faraway voice jostles me from sleep, but I'm so tired, and all of my limbs feel heavy. I don't want to wake up yet. It feels like I've just closed my eyes.

Hands wrapping along my bicep, shaking me, finally lifts the heavy fog of sleep, and I crack an eye open groggily. The room is still dark, and I'm confused and disoriented for a moment as I try to get my bearings. I realize we're in the king-size bed in the master suite so Reese must have carried me up here at some point.

"Your phone keeps ringing. It's not a saved number, and I think it might be important because they've called a few times." I turn my head to see Reese hovering over me, extending my phone to me, and only then do I register that it's ringing.

Shit, what time is it?

I grab my phone from his hand and swipe to answer it. "Hello?" My voice is hoarse and scratchy, probably from the number of times I screamed Reese's name tonight.

"Hello, may I speak to Vivienne Brentwood, please?" A

woman's voice comes through the speaker, one that I don't recognize, and it has me shooting up in the bed, holding the sheet to my naked chest.

"Yes, hi, that's me. Who is this?"

THERE'S A BRIEF PAUSE, followed by "Hi. This is Tara Givens. I'm calling from New Orleans Medical Center. Sweetheart, I'm calling because your mom has been admitted to the ER due to a car accident and we have you listed as her next of kin."

The room spins around me, panic flooding my chest so abruptly that it almost causes me to drop the phone. What?

Car accident? How? My mom doesn't drive.

I'm acutely aware of Reese moving from the bed, but I can't do anything but stare straight ahead in shock.

"W-what?" I stammer. Hot, fresh tears fall from my eyes, making the room blur further.

This call feels all too familiar, like the night that my dad died all over again. The memories from that night come rushing back in thick, fragmented pieces that seem to embed themselves in my skin.

Suddenly, I can't seem to take a full breath. My chest feels tight, like the air has been completely sucked from my lungs. I think I'm at the beginning of a panic attack. It's not the first time in my life that I've had one, but I've forgotten how debilitating it can be.

Reese's hand is on my back, rubbing soothingly as he says my name, but I can't even form a word right now. I'm too busy trying to suck in air.

"Breathe for me, baby. One in, one out." He places my free hand on his chest, helping me breathe in a slow rhythm with him. I follow his instructions and take a few deep breaths as the woman's voice in my ear calls my name, over and over, calling me out of my panic fog.

"Ms. Brentwood? Are you there?"

I swallow. "Y-yes, I'm h-e-ere."

Focusing on Reese's hand and the steady, soothing motion, I breathe, one in and one out.

"Your mother is stable, Vivienne, but she's sustained some serious injuries that will require further evaluation and possible intervention. Due to the nature of the trauma, the details of her status are evolving and not much more information can be given accurately over the phone as a result," the nurse says gently, a single sentence that has me clutching the phone so tightly my knuckles hurt.

A sob racks my body, and I seal my hand to my mouth to stop it from escaping.

She's okay. She's not gone. *She's still here.*

I just… I don't understand what's happening. Dread courses through my body, and I'm shaking so badly that my teeth are chattering.

"I know you must be scared right now, but she's in great hands here. The doctor believes she may have a broken collarbone and wrist. She has a gash on her forehead that required stitches, and they'd like to do an MRI to rule out any bleeding in the brain, but no life-threatening injuries. They'll know more once they complete the additional testing." She pauses, and I use the moment to suck in a desperate breath, filling my burning lungs. "She told us you're currently out of the country?"

I feel my chest tightening again. I'm in another country, and my mom… I left, and now she's hurt, and I can't be there. "I am…" I mumble quietly, guilt swallowing my panic.

"The jet will be ready in thirty," Reese says from beside me. "We'll be there in six hours."

I nod like the woman on the other end of the phone can see it.

I'm just… in my head. I'm not thinking clearly. I move from the bed numbly and start to search for my clothes, keeping the phone between my ear and shoulder as the nurse speaks. "We'll see you whenever you get here, Vivienne. It's going to be okay. Please travel safely. If there's an emergency or change in her condition, we'll contact you directly."

"T-thank you," I say, then drop the phone onto the bed. I don't even think I hit the End button in my blind hurry to find my clothes and start putting them on. I have to pack all of my things up and—

"Viv."

I glance up, and Reese is in front of me, reaching for me. Suddenly, I'm pulled against his body as everything inside of me spills over, and I begin to sob into the plane of his chest. Deep, heart-aching moans shake my body.

I could've lost her. I lost my dad, and I almost just lost my mom. I feel myself spiraling, falling deeper and deeper into that shut-down space in my head, and it feels nearly impossible to pull myself back out. I'm trying not to let it overcome me, but I'm so scared, and I feel so guilty.

I stand there frozen, unsure of what to do next, while Reese gets our bags together. I just need to get to my mom. It dawns on me that I didn't even ask what happened. Why was my mom in a *car*?

Reese kneels in front of me, sliding my underwear up my legs, followed by a pair of leggings, before gently slipping my sandals on my feet. He helps me into my bra and a clean *Spaced Out* shirt, then places a swift kiss to my forehead once he's gotten me dressed.

Because I don't think I could have done something so basic for myself right now even if I tried.

I hardly remember him walking me to the car and putting me inside. I'm still numb as I stare out of the window into the inky darkness. The landscape I found so exciting just yesterday now looks bleak.

All I can focus on is my fear and the growing guilt that feels like it's suffocating me.

I go through the motions as we deboard and drive to the hospital, my gut churning with worry and anxiety the whole way. It feels like I've spent the entire time trying not to get sick or worry myself to death.

We burst through the front entrance of the hospital roughly seven hours after receiving the phone call. Every moment since then has been torture. I know they said that she's okay, but I want to see her myself. I *need* to see her. Now that we're here, I just want to see her.

"Hi, we're here to see Belinda Brentwood?" I tell the front desk attendant, who gives me a sympathetic smile. "I'm her daughter."

She nods. "One second, please."

Shivering, I run my hands up and down my arms to fight off the chill.

Hospitals are always so mind-numbingly cold. It's something I've always remembered since the night I lost my dad. How I could feel the cold seeping into my bones as I waited to hear something, anything. I think all hospitals are probably this way.

I hate them.

Maybe it's irrational to feel that way about a place that's supposed to save lives, but they don't. Always save your life. My dad died here.

Reese grabs my hand and laces my fingers in his before dipping down and pressing his lips to my head, and for a second, I allow myself to soak in his steady, unwavering strength. I need it more than anything right now.

"Okay, it looks like she's on the tenth floor. Room 1082. You'll take that elevator to the left, and then hook two rights once you get to that floor. There should be signs to guide you towards the room."

"Thank you," I mumble, nearly sprinting toward the elevator. Once inside, I quickly punch the tenth floor, and we ride up in silence. Right now, I'm not capable of a conversation.

I just… I need to see Mom. I need to see that she's okay with my own eyes and try to figure out how this happened.

The door opens, and I step out, following the attendant's directions to find her room. I pass clinical white wall after white wall, the smell of antiseptic so strong in the air that I feel like I could choke. I'm willing myself to not have another panic attack, to not have an actual mental breakdown in the hallway of this place, but everything inside of me is threatening to spill over.

It's triggering just to be here, and… for the same reason. My heart races as we walk down the long hall, and I wring my hands in front of me, trying to convince myself that everything's going to be okay, that my entire world hasn't just been flipped upside down in the span of seven hours.

Like it hasn't crumbled into pieces. *Again.*

Finally, I see room number 1082 on the wall, and the door is slightly cracked. Just as I'm about to push it open and walk inside, an older nurse with short gray hair and kind eyes walks out wearing light green scrubs.

When she sees me, her brow pulls and she smiles warmly. "Hello. Are you Vivienne?"

I nod wordlessly.

"I heard you were coming. Your mom is sleeping. You can go in, but she's been in a bit of pain and drowsy from her medication, so please let her rest, okay? Her body needs the rest."

"Thank you. Can you tell me what happened?" I ask.

She shakes her head. "All I can tell you is that she was in a car accident and suffered trauma as a result. From her chart it says she's had an MRI and a CAT scan but any new updates or results will come from the doctor as he makes his rounds. I'm sorry I can't give you anything more definite."

She gives me a gentle smile as she heads to the room next door.

Quietly, I push the door open and step inside. In what feels like slow motion, the floor falls out from beneath me.

I don't think I was prepared for what the sight of seeing Mom's frail sleeping frame drowning in a hospital gown would *truly* feel like. The emotional impact that it would have seeing her hooked up to countless wires and tubes, her body covered in cuts and deep, purple bruises. Her arm's in a sling, secured to her chest, and she has a cut on her forehead that's been stitched shut. Seeing her like this…

It's so painful I feel it *physically*.

There's an ache in my chest that I rub my hand along to try to soothe as the hot tears spill from my eyes, wetting my cheeks.

I'm trying to hold it together, all of the uncontrolled emotions inside of me, but I'm breaking. I'm falling apart, and I don't think I can keep it together for another moment. I'm hurdling off the cliff inside my head. It all feels like *too* much.

My hand flies to my mouth, and I run out of the room before I do something selfish, like wake her with my sobs when she needs the rest.

"Viv, baby," Reese calls from behind me, but I don't stop. I can't.

I can't do this.

I can't watch her lie there because of my selfish actions. I almost lost Mom the same way that I lost my father. It happened all over again, and I can't process any of it. I wasn't here for her.

I sprint down the sterile hallway, pushing through the double doors without stopping as everything in my pathway blurs with tears. My lungs are constricted, burning from the fresh panic attack racketing my body, stealing every piece of me. I'm in the waiting room, doubled over with my hands on my knees as I pant, desperately trying to suck in even the smallest amount of air.

I'm so dizzy it feels like I'm suffocating. My heart is pounding out of my chest. I'm losing it.

"Fuck."

Black dots dance behind my vision, my head swimming with heaviness. Oh god, I think I might pass out. Reese tugs at my arms, pulling me against his body, which makes me feel more suffocated, and I can't do it. I can't do this.

I tear free, panting, "Stop. I… I can't handle this right now."

"Okay, baby, I'm here," he responds.

"No." I shake my head stiffly. "You should leave. Go back to the beach. Go home. Enjoy your break. I've got this. Let me handle this, Reese. Like I always have."

His jaw tenses, and he reaches for me, grasping air when I move back. "Viv, you don't have to do this alone. Let me stay and be here for you."

"No. No. I can't. This… It's t-too much. I can't handle any of this right now! I need you to leave. I have to focus on my mom, and I need you to go," I yell, my words a jumble as I speak because I'm just… spilling over.

"I'm *not* leaving you, Vivienne," he says quietly, emotion flickering on his handsome face. He doesn't try to reach for me again, but when I step back once more, he follows.

My chest tightens again, my breathing even more erratic, my nails cutting half-moons into my palms as I make tight fists at my side.

But I don't register any of the pain.

"I should have known better. God, I *knew* better than to do this. I'm the reason my mother is lying in that hospital bed, hurt and broken," I choke out. Hot tears coat my cheeks as I break down, determined to punish myself for what I've done.

"There was never going to be a time where I was going to just live my life carefree and happy… not without consequences. That's how things work for me. Everything will inevitably go wrong."

When I pause, he tries to speak. "Vivi—"

But I shake my head and cut him off, spewing everything inside of me because now I can't stop. "This is my fault. It was irresponsible of me to want so much for myself. If I hadn't gotten involved with you, this never would have happened. I knew better, but I was too fucking selfish to walk away. It's *my* fault."

I'm screaming at him in the middle of the hospital, my voice echoing around the waiting room, but I can't stop the venom from coming out of my mouth. Part of me is aware that I'm self-sabotaging right now, but there's nothing I do better than *this*. Hiding my real feelings. Pushing people away because it hurts too much to let them in, because it's too hard to let them get close. It's all I know how to do.

Defend. Deflect.

Reese is wrapped around my heart like thorny vines, embedded into my organs.

He's a constant reminder that I will never be good for him. I'll always be the girl who's got issue after issue, heavy shit that follows me. He doesn't deserve that. And… I can't handle needing someone as desperately as I need him. It terrifies me to *need anyone*.

"*Leave*. You're just making this harder. God, I can't do this. I can't need you this way because my mom needs *me*. You're a distraction, Reese. Please, just go." I brush away my tears and wipe my nose on the back of my wrist.

I'm such a mess.

His stormy eyes flare with emotion. "Viv, don't do this. Let me be here for you so you *can* be there for her. Lean on me. I'll do whatever you want, whatever you ask of me, but please just don't ask me to leave. I can't leave you. I *won't* fucking leave you."

I shake my head vehemently. "You don't know what this is, Reese. A real life p-problem. You don't know anything about those in your privileged little bubble."

I'm sobbing again, my trembling legs giving out, unable to hold my weight any longer, and I collapse to the floor, only for him to catch me at the last moment. His strong arms circle my body and hold me tightly against his broad chest, invading my space while I fight him, tearing at his shirt like a wild animal who's avoiding capture.

"Stop. Stop. Stop," I sob. "I should have been here with her. It's all m-my fault. If I was here, i-t wouldn't have happened. I should have been here to take care of her. I never should have left h–h-her."

My heart physically aches, and my sobs grow louder as my body shakes. He holds me tighter, so tight that I can hardly breathe. His lips are pressed against my head as I sob.

"It hurts, Reese, it hurts so bad. I was s-supposed to take care of her, and I failed. I *failed* her."

Giving in to my desperate need for his comfort, I sag against his chest, snot and tears soaking the fabric of his shirt as I cling to him. "I left her. And Dad left me. And it's all just t-oo-o much. I'm so scared to lose her. To be alone."

The painful, triggering memory of losing him in this very hospital feels like too much to bear. The heaviness is crippling, and my shoulders sag with it.

"It's too heavy, I can't… I can't hold it all anymore," I whisper dejectedly against his chest.

Reese tips my chin to him and holds it firmly between his fingers as he speaks, his eyes holding mine intensely with so much affection that I'm almost overcome with it. "I told you before, I'm not fucking leaving you, Viv. Not now, not fucking *ever*. Do you hear what I'm saying? I'm. Not. Leaving. Because I fucking love you. Do you understand that? I love you." He pauses, his eyes burning into mine.

"And this is what you do when you love someone. You stay. You show up for them." He leans in closer, still holding my gaze. "I will be here to hold the weight when it's too much. I'll be your strength when you have none left. I'll hold you, and I'll take all the shit you wanna give me. I'll be whatever you need as long as I'm with you. Let me love *you*, Viv. Let me be the one to take care of you and to be there for you so you're never alone. I love you so fucking much that I can hardly breathe sometimes. I just need you to let me love you."

His declaration only makes me cry harder, gut-wrenching sobs that I feel in the depths of my soul. It's as if everything from the last few months comes pouring out in a torrential wave of

pent-up emotion. A wave that I can't stop once it's started, one that I hope doesn't drown us.

He loves me.

So many months of hiding parts of my life from others, hiding parts of myself. Months of keeping everything inside until I was bursting at the seams with all the feelings I've been neglecting. Grief that I buried, crippling stress, feeling lost and overwhelmed all the time. Guilt. So much sadness. Everything I kept pushing away in hopes that they'd just… disappear. Except that's not what happens… it's what makes you quietly fall apart.

I see it all clearly as my emotions purge from my body in the flood of tears. "It's m-my fault," I repeat despondently.

He shakes his head. "It is *not* your fault, baby. None of this is your fault. You can't hold the blame for others' actions, and it's not fair to put this on yourself. Viv, you take care of *everyone*. You take care of Hallie, you take care of your mom, hell, you even take care of me. But you don't always take care of yourself. You never put yourself first. You put every-fucking-body's feelings above yours—their lives, their needs, *their* happiness. Fuck that, Viv. Fuck always putting yourself last. Let me take care of you for a change. Let me put you first. Let me fucking love you. I was made to love you, and I've never been more sure of anything in my life. Over baseball, over the minors. Over it all. This is what I'm sure of. I should have told you that last night, but I was scared to. I was scared that you'd run, that it would be too much for you to hear. But tonight made me realize that you run when the world gets to be too much, but I'm coming after you, baby. I'll chase you to the ends of the goddamn earth."

I feel the slow, soothing brush of his fingers along my back as silence hangs between us. I work to steady my breathing. Even just his words, the tone of his voice, calms me. He steadies me. He makes me feel anchored. Rational thought breaks through my mass of emotion, and I realize how much I just unloaded on him, unfairly taking *everything* out on him. Everything became too much, and I just…lost it.

I lost it on him, and I feel sick to my stomach about it. About hurting another person I love.

God, this is such a fucking mess. *I'm* such a mess.

"I'm so sorry. I'm fucking everything up," I whisper solemnly. "I shouldn't have said those things. I just… I feel so *guilty*, Reese. It feels like it's eating me alive from the inside. Not being there for my mom when I should have been. And I think the dam just burst with everything I've been dealing with. Trying so hard to hide what I've been feeling, lying to the people who care about me about how badly I've been struggling. Trying so hard to not burden anyone else with my shit."

His jaw works for a second before he speaks, the muscle rippling. "Viv, why do you not give yourself the same grace that you give others? Baby, you move *mountains* for those that you love. You'd do anything for them. You accept their mistakes and their flaws without a second thought because that's loving someone. But you never do the same for yourself. It's okay to need others like they need you. You're human too. We're all imperfectly flawed, we all have our baggage, and it's okay to have all the feelings. To be happy. To be afraid."

I *am* afraid. If there's anything I've realized in the last twenty-four hours, it's that I'm terrified to lose my mom.

And I *can't* lose her.

And Reese… I can't lose *Reese*.

"I'm worried I'm going to lose my mom. That I won't be able to hold her together. And I'm scared to lose you. That all this will be too much for you." My voice is barely a whisper into his shirt, his arms tightening around me as I say it.

"You're not going to lose your mom, Viv. And you're not going to lose me. I'm in love with you. I've never told a girl I love her until today. I've never *been* in love in my life. Maybe with baseball, but that hardly counts. I might not always get it right, and I'm sure there are going to be times where I fuck up and you get pissed and throw shit at me. And times where you're regretting your decision to be with someone who's constantly on the road. But I'm going to show up, Viv. Every fucking time. I know you're terrified that one day you'll push me away and I won't come back. But that's not going to happen. Because I love you. And I think that you love me too."

I blink away fresh tears that just seem to keep coming, sniffling as I snake my hands around his neck and clasp there. I press myself closer to his chest, my eyes holding his.

Those deep, dark, stormy eyes that are full of so much sincerity it makes it hard to breathe. I don't just hear what he's saying to me—I feel it. I feel it in the way he's holding me and how I didn't even have to ask him to bring me here—he already had the plane ready. I feel it in the way he bought me Boo simply because I mentioned once that I always wanted to have a cat of my own. I feel it in the way he goes out of his way to do sweet things to make me happy, how he supports my dreams and makes me feel proud of them. And I feel it in how he stood here and took every single awful thing that I threw at him because he knew I needed to lash out, that I needed to break. And he didn't walk away. Instead, he put me back together.

He hasn't just said those words to me; he's proven it, over and over again.

We are messy. And he's right, there will be times where I probably throw things at him, times that I frustrate him or push him away when it becomes too much. But he's too far buried into my bones to let him go.

His actions have proven that my fears are just that… fear.

"I love you too, Reese. And I'm sorry. I'm so, so sorry that I freaked out and said those terrible, hurtful things an—"

"It's okay. We're okay." He dips forward, dragging his nose along mine. "I'm just sorry that I had to tell you I love you here, in the middle of all this and not in a grand gesture kinda way.

You deserve grand gestures, baby. I want to be the guy that gives them to you."

I lean forward and lay my head on his chest, soaking in the sound of his strong, steady heartbeat. We stay like that, unmoving, his arms wrapped tightly around me for minutes. Just… existing together.

"All I need is this. All I need is *you*," I whisper.

"Then that's what you'll have."

25 / viv

A New Chapter

We're sitting in the waiting room, me still clinging to Reese like a lifeline, when a nurse approaches us. She's not the same one from earlier but a new one. She's younger, with auburn hair and is holding an iPad.

"Hi, are you Vivienne?"

I nod, untangling myself from Reese, only for him to grab my hand tightly in his, keeping me close as we stand from the floor.

Quiet strength. That's what he gives me in the times that I need it most.

"Your mom is awake and asking for you." She smiles.

"Thank you," I reply. I try to prepare myself as we walk to her room, knowing that seeing her in that bed again is going to upset me all over again, and I hope I can handle it better this time. I don't want my emotions to bleed out onto her right now.

I use the walk back to her room to try and mentally calm myself. When we get to the doorway, Reese turns me to him, his large hands cradling my face as he peers down at me. "You need this time with your mom, Viv. I'll be right here waiting outside. Even if it's hours, just take your time. Okay? I'm not going anywhere. I love you."

I nod, lifting slightly to press my lips to his. "I love you too." I don't think I deserve him, but I want to keep him anyway.

I want to do the selfish thing for once and keep him all to myself, even if I'm not worthy of it.

Pushing the door open, I step inside and shut it quietly.

Mom turns her head toward me, our gazes connecting from across the room. We're both quiet for a moment, just taking each other in. I see the very same love, fear, hurt, frustration… and pain in her eyes that I feel right now.

"Mama," I sob as I cross the room and sit on the edge of her bed, gingerly dropping my head to her non-slinged shoulder. "I'm so glad you are okay. I was so s-scared. I thought I was going to lose you. I tho—"

"I know, baby, I'm sorry. I'm so sorry, Vivienne," she cries, her eyes watery as she links her uninjured arm around mine, holding me against her. I'm so grateful to have the comfort of her touch, but I'm afraid to even breathe too hard, that it might hurt her already battered body.

"No, *I'm* sorry. This is my fault. I never should have left you. You needed me. I should have st—"

"Vivienne, stop," she says firmly, turning her head more toward me. I lift my gaze to hers, and she shakes her head. "You do *not* need to apologize to me. You did nothing wrong by living your life, sweetheart. That's all that I want for you."

She brings her hand down to capture mine in hers, squeezing it gently. "All I have ever wanted for you was to see you spread those beautiful wings and fly. You've always been my darling angel baby girl with so much imagination and excitement for life. Even as a little girl, you were so vibrant… so determined. Your father and I were always so amazed by everything you did…and you certainly kept us on our toes. We knew even then that you would be someone so special, Vivienne. And I'm not just saying that because I'm your mother. You were always meant to do great things." Her eyes flutter shut as she continues, a lone tear dripping down her cheek. "And I know I've been holding you back from doing those things."

"Mama, no, I—"

She shakes her head again, linking our fingers together. "I need to say this, Viv. Please let me. It's been a long time coming." More tears drip down her bruised, cut-up cheeks, and I wish with all my heart that I could take them all away.

My heart feels like it's been ripped from my chest and stomped on, but I stay quiet and listen.

Her chest stutters as she sucks in a deep breath. "I've been lost. For a very long time. Since losing… your dad. A piece of me went with him, Vivienne. And I can't seem to bring myself back. It feels like I'm split in two sometimes, with only one side of me still here. It feels like the best, most important part of me is gone… and what's left is sad, broken, and empty. The pain of losing him has consumed me. I know that, but it was never a choice to be like this… to feel like this. I want with all my heart to feel better. To feel like myself again. But… I don't think I can do that on my own anymore. I've tried to be strong, to not be this way… I've tried so hard to do that. Not just for me, but for you."

I can't stop the painful noise that sounds from the back of my throat, even when I bring my hand to my mouth and cover it.

"I think I've been lying about my feelings for a while. Telling myself I could just will myself to feel better with my mind. I've had a few good days lately. And this week, I had several in a row. It felt like so much progress, that I thought I could do something on my own, do something I haven't been able to. That's how I ended up here. I told myself that I was ready to try driving again. I was just going to drive the short mile to the grocery store, pick up a few things. I made it down the street, but as soon as I turned on the main road and saw other cars, I had a panic attack behind the wheel. I think I blacked out for a minute because they told me I swerved off the road and crashed into a tree."

Oh my god. I knew it was not going to be easy to hear her talk about it, but knowing how badly this could have gone…

"I could have killed someone, Viv," she cries. "Or myself. And I would never be able to live with that. Something way worse could have happened. I'm lucky that I was able to walk away relatively unscathed, with just a break and some cuts and bruises. That could have been completely different."

I nod. "I was so scared when I got the phone call, Mom. *So* scared."

She sighs as she swipes her thumb along my skin in a soothing motion.

"I'm sorry that I've been struggling so much. And that I've not been honest with you… or myself… about how bad it's been lately, Vivienne. I just… didn't want to burden you any further than I already was. I know it's caused you so much trouble with helping me, especially since you've gone to school. I don't think I realized how much you were holding us both together until then. But I never wanted to interfere with your life, and yet it seems like now I always am. I'm your mom—I should be taking care of *you*, sweetheart."

"Please don't apologize for any of that. And you're not a burden. You're my mom. I would do anything for you." I swipe at the tears on my cheeks and lean back against her shoulder gently so as not to jostle her. I feel her fingers running through the strands of my hair soothingly, just like she did when I was younger. It brings a fresh wave of tears because it reminds me how much I've missed having her act like my mom. She's been here physically, but I miss what our relationship was like before my dad passed away. I miss our movie nights and talking about boys and silly things until the sun came up. I miss reading books together, shopping, and doing all the things together because we were best friends. I miss laughing with her.

I miss the days when life was simpler for us, when things were easier.

"It's okay to need help. And it's okay to ask for it. I'm learning that every day. It's hard to lean on the people that I love for support when I feel weak. But I'm here, and I'm not going anywhere, Mom. I want to be there to support you. You're not alone, and we'll find a way to get you what you need to get better," I say sincerely. I've broached this subject with her before, but this time feels different. This time, she's asking for the next step, so I will do whatever it takes to make it happen for her.

Silence hangs between us, heavy and thick, as we lie together side by side in her hospital bed before she speaks again. "We've learned the hard way that life is shorter than you think, and today taught me that again. I want my life back. I want to get better. I need to face this, and I need help to do it."

Relief floods my chest as emotion tightens my throat. All I've ever wanted was for her to be happy and healthy. For her to start to live again. I hate that she had to have a big scare to be the push she needed, but all that matters is she wants the help. That she's aware she needs it. That she wants to fight for herself again.

All that really matters is *getting* her the help that she needs. "I never want to lose you, Mom." I sniffle.

"You're not, sweetheart. I promise that things are going to change. I know it won't be easy, and I'll never stop missing your dad. I'll never stop loving him and wishing that he was here with us." Her voice breaks, and she pauses to gather her composure. "I'm not going to get any better on my own. The doctor recommended some local therapists, but he also mentioned there are more intensive therapeutic recovery centers that help people struggling with their mental health conditions, some that even specialize in grief and depression. Given what happened today, he said it could potentially also be…PTSD. He recommended I talk to a therapist first to see what kind of treatment is best. I may even need to be put on some medication, but he thought something like that might be good for me. The centers are expensive, I'm sure, but maybe our insurance would cover a portion of it."

I nod. "We'll figure it out. Whatever it takes, we'll figure it out."

"I love you, sweetheart, and I'm sorry to put you through this," Mama says, regret lacing her tone.

I shake my head, sitting up on the bed so I can look into her eyes. "No more apologies. Okay? From either of us. We're doing the best that we can, and that's all that matters. That we're together and trying. Moving forward, we're going to be open and honest with our healing. Because I think we both have some healing to do."

As she nods, there's a soft rap on the door, and then a doctor steps inside. His white coat swishes around him as he makes his way over to us with a smile that crinkles in the corners of his eyes.

"Well, how're we doing in here? Mrs. Brentwood, this must be your daughter?" he says, extending his hand toward me to shake. "I'm Dr. Stephenson, your mother's admitting physician."

Immediately, I like him. His pleasant bedside manner. His trusting smile.

Mom nods as we shake hands. "Yes, this is my daughter, Vivienne."

"Hi, Dr. Stephenson, it's nice to meet you. Thank you for taking such good care of my mom."

He waves his hand through the air, smiling softly as he flicks his gaze back to mama. "It's my pleasure. I looked over the CT scan and the MRI results, and the good news is that there's no bleeding on the brain or any surgery needed. So she should be able to bust out of here to recover at home after a night of observation and pain management. You'll need to be sure you're getting a lot of rest."

Relief floods my chest. Thank god. I can't even fathom leaving her here alone, which means I'll be sleeping in this tiny little armchair near the window until she's released.

"I did have a couple questions..." I glance at Mom before dragging my gaze back to the doctor. "She mentioned that you told her about some treatment options for her mental health. Is that something we can go over in detail?"

"Absolutely. I'd be happy to help with a plan. My colleague Dr. Oliver is the psychiatric physician on call. Together, we can gather some options for us to discuss that tend to both her physical injuries and her mental health recovery." He grabs the chart off the table near the whiteboard and glances through it. "Let's take a look at all your vitals first, and I want to check a few of those cuts. When I check back later today, I can introduce you to Dr. Oliver, and we can lay out a few treatment plans so we can help with any next steps before you head home."

I can see Mom nodding out of my periphery. "Yes, that would be great."

She seems almost... *hopeful*? For the first time in a long time. And that makes me feel so happy my chest could burst. It's been a whirlwind of emotions since I woke up this morning, but I'm so thankful. Grateful more than anything that she's here... and ready to take the next steps toward healing.

Dr. Stephenson reviews Mama's chart and her pain scale, then looks over the cuts on her face. "Everything looks good. I'll check in on you later. In the meantime, if either of you have any questions, please let me or one of the nurses know. I'll let you get some rest," Dr. Stephenson tells her.

"Thank you so much," Mom says as he opens the door and

slips out of it. Before it shuts, a hand catches it, and Reese pokes his head in tentatively.

I give him a soft smile and gesture him in.

He strolls through hesitantly, his hands shoved into the pockets of his jeans and a worried smile on his handsome face. I want to pitch myself off the bed into his arms. His hair is disheveled, which tells me that he's been running his hands through it the entire time he was waiting, nervously if I had to guess.

God, it will *never* get old.

Those butterflies swirl in my stomach at the sight of him. He's been my strength through all of this, even when I didn't deserve it, even when I didn't think I wanted it, and… I… I just fucking *love* him.

With my entire heart.

"Hi, Ms. Brentwood," he murmurs, making his way over. "I'm so glad that you're okay. If you need anything at all, let me know, and I'll be there. Anything, okay?"

Okay, now I'm just a melted pile of goo for him. He's so sweet and thoughtful to my mama, and it makes my heart ache… in the best way. I feel like I can't even explain it, but god, I *feel* it.

I think this might be what being in love is. Being perpetually crazy about someone.

"Thank you, darling. Thank you for taking such good care of my little girl," she says, reaching out to grab his hand and hold it tightly in hers. "Thank you, Reese. I'm so glad she has you."

His dark eyes shine with sincerity as he tells her, "I'll always take care of her. I promise you." And then he gives me his trademark smirk.

Great, now I'm crying again, fat, heavy tears coating my cheeks as I watch the exchange between them.

He dips down and presses a sweet kiss against my head as

Mama says, "I think I'm going to get some more rest. I'm feeling a bit tired already. The medicine they gave me makes me drowsy."

I nod. She looks exhausted, and she needs sleep to heal her body. It's been an exhausting day for us all emotionally, and with all her injuries, I can't even imagine how drained she must be feeling. I help her lie back down and arrange her pillow and blanket around her so she's as comfortable as possible.

"Baby, when you're ready, I think you should go out into the waiting room for a minute. There are some people here who'd like to see you. I can stay here with your mom," Reese says once I'm done tucking Mom in.

This man is so sweet, so thoughtful and wonderful, I can't even believe that he's mine. I press my lips against Mama's uninjured cheek. "I love you, Mama. I'll be right back."

"Take your time, sweetheart. I think… I'm in good hands," she says groggily, already drifting off to sleep.

When I flick my eyes to Reese and see him grinning shyly, my heart skips in my chest.

"I think we both are, Mama."

WALKING out to the waiting room, I'm not sure what I was expecting. My emotions and adrenaline are still so high that I haven't had the mental capacity or time to think about anything other than getting to my mom and making sure she was okay.

So when I turn the corner and see all of our friends huddled up together on uncomfortable plastic chairs, my jaw falls open, and fresh tears well in my already red and puffy eyes. Grant, Eli, Lane, and Hallie are all here.

For me.

Without me asking for support or telling them anything about what I've been struggling with, they showed up for me.

Hallie lifts her head and sees me, then shoots off the chair and barrels towards me in a blur of curly hair. "Viv, oh my god!" She collides with me so hard that I almost fall over, her small arms wrapping around my body as she buries her face in my neck, squeezing me to her. "I was so worried. I've been going crazy. Is your mom okay?"

I nod and circle her body, hugging her back tightly. I've been keeping so much from her I feel like I don't deserve her kindness. Her love. "She's okay. She's pretty banged up and has a broken collarbone and wrist, but she's physically okay. Thank you so much for coming… I… I need to tell you so much. Can we talk for a minute?"

She pulls back, brushing her springy black curls off her face, and nods with an understanding smile. "Of course."

We move to the chairs beside us and sit. I can feel Lane's, Eli's, and Grant's gazes on us, so I peek around Hallie and give the guys a small smile as they sit down a few rows away, giving us privacy to talk. They quickly pretend they're looking around at anyone but us, and I roll my eyes. It's cute.

I capture Hallie's hand and squeeze as I turn to look at her deep in the eyes.

"My mom has been going through a really rough time. She hasn't… been like herself for a long time, and I've been hiding it from… everyone. She can barely take care of herself most days, but she hasn't wanted to get help. I've been doing everything I can to look after her, and I left the dorm because I needed to use the money I'd saved to pay for her rent when she lost her job. Most days, it's hard for her to even get out of bed, but today… she tried to drive for the first time since my dad died. She had a panic attack behind the wheel and was in a car accident. Thank god she's okay and didn't hurt anyone because it could have been so much worse..." Hallie's eyes widen with shock and concern as she waits for me to continue. "I'm so sorry, Hal. I should have confided in you sooner. I know that's not enough, but I need you to know how sorry I am for keeping this from you. That's not what best friends do, and I did it with the purest intentions. It's not an excuse, but I've just been struggling so much with everything. I didn't want to burden you or drag you down with all of the heaviness in my life. So I've just kept it all in. I'm so, so sorry."

Her eyes fill with tears, and she drops my hand, leaning forward to throw her arms around my neck again and pull me into another one of her bear hugs. "Oh god, Viv. I'm so sorry that you've been going through all of that. I knew things had been different with your mom since the accident, but I had no idea it was... like that. That has to be so hard for you both. I... just wish I would've known. I wish I could've been there for you. I *want* to be there for you."

"I know, and I shouldn't have kept it from you. It's... just hard for me, Hal. To put my shit out like this. I wish I could be more like you in that aspect, so willing to open up and let the people you love in. It's my favorite thing about you. It's just not as easy for me, especially since my dad died. I know it probably hurts that I wasn't honest with you, and I'm really sorry. I did have every intention of telling you what was going on eventually. At first, I held back because I thought my mom would get better, and then things started getting worse this year. And I just didn't want to bring you down from your love high."

Some more weight lifts from my shoulders now that she knows, another affirmation that I should have just told her things were getting worse a long time ago.

She pulls back, holding my arms in hers as she shakes her head at me. "Viv, you are my best friend, and I love you.

Nothing you ever go through will be too heavy for me, okay? This is what friends do for each other. We hold each other when it's hard. Real friends don't think your challenges are too much. You're never *too* much."

Hearing her say all this, reassuring me, hits me directly in the chest, and a sob bubbles over, spilling from my lips. I needed this. I needed my best friend, even if I don't think I deserve her forgiveness right now. I needed to hear that things would be okay between us.

"Thank you, Hal. And I'm sorry for not letting you in. I want to say it a billion times because it doesn't feel like enough." I pause, swiping away at a tear before continuing. "My mom… she's just been struggling for *so* long, and I've been so busy trying to keep both of our heads above water. But what happened today… it just opened her eyes and mine. She wants to get some professional help. Grief therapy or maybe a treatment center that specializes in grief and depression. I think things are *finally* going to be better. For real this time."

"That's amazing, Viv. I'm so happy to hear it. And I want you to know you can *always* come to me. No matter what. Please don't ever feel like you have to keep things from me because I can't handle it. I'm strong. I can handle it. I'm sorry if I've seemed distracted with Lane. You're so important to me, and I want to be there for you. No matter what is going on in my life. Okay?"

I nod. "Never again. I promise. I can't promise that I'm always not going to… retreat into myself because it's what I've always done. It's really the only way I know how to cope with all my thoughts and emotions, but I promise I'm making an effort to be better about it."

She loops her arm into mine and drops her head on my shoulder as her thumb ghosts along my hand. "It's me and you to the stars, Viv. We deal with it together. The happy, the sad, the fear, the pain. We have each other through it all. Because you're my best friend."

I rest my head on top of hers, soaking up her reassurance. Out of the corner of my eye, I catch the guys looking our way again, and my shoulder shakes with laughter, causing Hallie to sit up. "What?"

"The guys are dying down there. They want to come over so bad. I bet Lane is already getting separation anxiety. Should we put them out of their misery?"

Hallie giggles, nodding. "Yes. I swear they haven't shut up since we got the call. Everyone's been so worried about your mom… and you, Viv. We all love you."

I never thought I'd see this moment. I'm surrounded by friends who love me and a boyfriend who… treats me like I'm *precious*. My mom is going to be seeking help. And I'm finally in a place where I feel like I can be honest with the people I love.

My heart feels full in a way it hasn't for a long time. Since that moment in my junior year when everything was flipped upside down.

"Come here, you three," Hallie sighs, waving them over as we stand from the rickety chairs and face them.

Their expressions are so worried and nervous that I can't help but laugh a little.

"It's okay. My mom's okay. She's pretty banged up, but she's okay." The guys take turns each giving me a big hug. First Eli, then Lane, and Grant last. His tall, lanky body wraps around mine for a lingering squeeze.

Meow.

My eyebrow shoots up. Was that… did he meow?

Grant's expression turns panicked as he leans away to rearrange his hoodie carefully before flitting his gaze back to me.

Meow. Meow.

Oh my god. Is that an *actual* cat?

"Did you… sneak … Boo in here, Grant?"

The satisfied smirk on his lips is my answer. He darts his eyes around like he's checking to make sure no one's watching, then pulls the front of his hoodie down slightly, revealing my baby girl curled up on his chest, staring up at me with her wide yellow eyes. I can hear her purring from here.

My god, these guys are out of their minds. Who sneaks a cat into a *hospital*?

I reach forward and scratch her head lovingly.

"I figured you would wanna see her, and we didn't know how long we'd be here and didn't want to leave her alone. She's actually an angel, and I think she might love her Uncle G the best," he jokes. His long finger strokes her head, and she rubs it against him, eyes dropping closed. "Actually, I *know* she does."

"It is kinda weird how she's taken to him," Eli mutters, running a hand over his short blond hair that's slightly darker than his brother's.

Grant smirks, dipping his broad shoulder in a shrug. "What can I say? I'm a pussy *magnet*."

We all groan in unison at his terrible joke, and it only makes him smirk harder, a full smile that lights up his whole face. "What? You can call me a pussy connoisseur if you must. All the pussies love me."

"I'm done," Lane grunts. He steps in and gives me a slightly awkward but sweet pat on the shoulder. "You need anything, Viv, you know where I'm at, 'kay?"

"Yeah. I do. Thank you."

When he steps away, Eli sweeps in and gives me another quick hug before saying, "I'm sorry I haven't been around much lately, but you know I got you always. Except don't put me on the cat-sitting list. I don't think the cat likes me."

Hallie giggles, and Grant interjects, "Bro, you're *not* watching

Boo. You don't even know how to warm her food up just how she likes it."

Eli's eyebrow shoots up. "In… the microwave? Press Start?" He rolls his eyes.

"Yeah, but for how long? You'll burn her tongue if it's too hot. And she needs her favorite dish," Grant says, a dead serious expression on his face.

Jesus Christ.

"Okay, enough. No fighting over Boo," I tell them with a stern look, biting my lip to keep from laughing. "In all seriousness, thank you for being here for me. Thank you for showing up tonight."

"We got you, Viv," Grant says, still petting Boo discreetly.

"Yeah, we're family. It's what you do," Lane adds. When he reaches out to pet Boo too, Grant slaps his hand away.

Reese has created another cat daddy monster.

I feel Hallie slide her hand into mine and squeeze reassuringly. "We're here for you, Viv."

I nod.

From this point forward, I make a promise to myself, and to them, that I'm done shutting out the people I love when all they want to do is support me, especially when I'm going through hard things.

And for the first time in a long time, I *truly* don't feel alone.

26 / reese

That's all she wrote

"Mmm, you know how much I love when you play with my hair," Viv murmurs against my chest, where she's sprawled on top of me, her eyelashes fluttering shut as she burrows her face into my neck.

These are my favorite moments.

When everything's quiet, it's just the two of us and Boo cuddled up on our couch, reading one of her supernatural books together after a long day of school, baseball, and studying. It's not something that we can do every night since I have to travel for baseball games with the team, but it makes us appreciate the nights where we can spend time together doing something as simple as this.

Plus, the only way I'm reading this scary shit is if we're doing it together because I'm not voluntarily picking this up for fun.

I do it for *her.* Because I'd do anything for her.

"I think you only like me for my talented fingers, Sweet Tart," I chuckle.

She hums. "*And* your tongue."

My chest shakes with laughter, and I bring my fingers to her side, tickling her until she's squirming. "Always with that smart mouth."

"I thought you said that it was your favorite thing about me?" She lifts her head and props her chin on her hands, batting those thick, dark lashes at me innocently.

My girl is far from innocent. She's fucking wild, and I love every damn bit of it. Lately, she's been… lighter. Less stressed and anxious. More playful, happier.

And I think it's because things are steadily improving with her mom and she's able to breathe a little.

It's been three weeks since her mom's accident and fourteen days since she admitted herself into a voluntary treatment facility in Dallas. It's one of the top treatment facilities in the country for mental health recovery, and even though it's a little further away than Viv wanted, it was the best place for her mom's care. It helped that her mom was able to tour the place and get a feel for it before deciding to go. She assured Viv that she felt comfortable there, and she seemed really hopeful about going.

Belinda's insurance wouldn't approve covering the cost of the facility and only covered minimal mental health treatment at all.

But for the first time ever, Viv's let me help her with something money related without any protest. I wanted to make sure her mom was taken care of, getting the best possible care. So I asked Viv to let me take care of it, no matter the cost, and she agreed.

Which surprised the hell out of me, but honestly, I'm so glad that I'm able to help, that I can contribute in some way to make this easier for both of them.

And I want to do whatever I can, not just for Viv but for her mom. Because I care about them both.

Viv's the most important thing in my life, even more than baseball… *She's* my number one. She's my heart. "I did say that it was my favorite thing about you, but then again, there are many, many favorite things about you," I say, pressing my lips to her forehead. "Like… *this*."

I drop the book to the floor and trail my fingers down her side to cup her ass through the tiny pair of cotton shorts she's wearing, earning a sweet little moan from her. But when I slide my fingers lower, brushing over the heat of her pussy, she stops me.

"I really, really want you to keep doing that with those very talented fingers, but my mom is going to be calling any minute. Remember?"

Shit. I almost forgot. It's Thursday, and her mom calls on FaceTime.

"After, then," I promise, reaching down to pick up our book so we can continue where we left off. I will admit this only one time… that I'm a little invested in what's happening. And it's not so bad reading something spooky when I've got Viv's body covering mine, with her curled into my chest.

We read for another thirty minutes or so until it's time for her mom to call. She sits up, grabbing her laptop off the coffee table to set it up. When Belinda calls, she can't press Answer fast enough.

"Mama!" she breathes, smiling brightly.

Her mom's face fills the computer screen, and she's smiling, her eyes brighter than even last week. She looks good, and I know that Vivienne feels the same way because her deep blue eyes are filled with tears.

We've been talking a lot about her dad lately and the grief she's been experiencing silently, and I think it's been helping to talk about it to someone. She's also said she wants to start seeing a therapist to focus on unpacking some of the stuff she's kept buried.

"How are you, Mama?" Viv asks.

"I'm feeling good today. I had a session this morning with

my therapist, and then I went on a mile walk around the grounds. The flowers were blooming and so beautiful. This evening, we have art therapy in the garden, so I'm excited about that. Oh, hi, Reese!" Belinda laughs softly, waving when she sees my head in the corner of the camera.

"Hi, Belinda. Just wanted to say hi really quick. Oh, and I tried that recipe you told me about, the lemon pepper chicken? It was amazing."

Her mouth curves up in a smile and her eyes dance. "Good. I'm glad. It was one of Viv's dad's favorites."

The two of them share a look, a smile full of memories only they understand. It's heartbreaking that Viv lost her dad, and I hate it for her. For her mom. But they're working together on dealing with their grief, and keeping his memory alive seems to be bringing them both joy.

I love her so fucking much that I wish I could take all of her pain away, all her heartbreak. But since I can't, all I can do is be here to support her. Leaning to press my lips against the top of her head, I stand and give them some privacy, making my way into my bedroom to look through my email, checking on the surprise that I ordered for Viv. It's supposed to be delivered today, and I can't wait to give it to her.

After the call, she breezes through the bedroom door with a smile. "It was so great to talk to her today. God, Reese, she looks *so good*. Her cheeks had color, and her eyes were so bright. She couldn't stop talking today, and it's been so long since we have had such an easy conversation."

I nod. "I know, baby. I noticed too. I'm glad she's there and working on feeling better. Seems like it was the right choice for her."

"I think so too, and she said that even though her therapy sessions are hard, she feels like they're helping. To purge all of her emotions and talk with someone about it. She's meeting with the therapist daily, and she really likes him. I'll never stop saying it, but thank you. Thank you for helping me get her there. I know this is only the beginning, and it'll be a journey, but I already feel so much hope knowing she's got a whole team of people to help her through it."

Viv crosses the room and steps between my spread thighs at the edge of the bed, sliding her hands around my neck and giving me a sweet kiss. "Also, Hallie texted and asked if we wanted to all meet at Jack's, but we can stay home if you want…"

"Nah." I shake my head, bringing my hand to my stomach. "My stomach is growling, babe. I can't live in these conditions."

She laughs sweetly. "You're ridiculous."

Thirty minutes later, we're all crammed into the largest booth at Jack's Pizza, sharing a pizza, laughing as Eli tries to shove an entire damn piece of an extra-large slice into his mouth because Grant bet him a hundred bucks that he couldn't. Ari, Eli's girlfriend, rolls her eyes and just shakes her head at her boyfriend.

It feels… *normal*, being here surrounded by our friends, laughing about dumb shit. Only this time, I've got my girl tucked against my side where she's always belonged.

"Let me feed you, Sweet Tart," I rasp as I wave the piece of extra-cheesy pizza in front of her mouth. She rolls her eyes and laughs but opens her mouth to take a bite. When I pull it away, there's a long string of cheese hanging from her mouth to the pizza, and then we're both laughing as she tries to pinch it off and put it in her mouth, leaving a trail of pizza sauce on her chin.

Leaning in, I lick it off, then capture her lips, kissing her.

Yes, I realize it's… *cheesy*. But fuck, I'm in love. I'm a sappy, lovesick fool for this girl. The last few weeks have been a complete whirlwind, but I'm so glad that we can be here with our friends. To be officially together… *finally*.

"God, the two of you are worse than Lane and Hallie," Grant groans around his pizza. "How am I supposed to deal with this?"

Lane's shoulder dips. "Don't be sad that you're single, dude."

Viv and Hallie giggle as I stifle a laugh. "Yeah, you know you're always welcome to be our seventh wheel."

Grant rolls his eyes as he picks up another piece of pizza. "I'm not jealous. I'm just saying all of you are all lovey-dovey, and it's making me a little queasy. I'm trying to eat here."

"You sure that's not the *six* pieces of pizza you just put down?" Eli asks.

He's not wrong. The guy eats more than anyone I know, and that's saying a lot since we're all athletes.

"Yeah, that might also be it. But I'm pretty sure it's just all of you making googly eyes at each other. And I'm going to pretend that I don't know y'all are all getting handsy with each other under the table," Grant retorts. "By the way, when can I come visit *my* favorite girl?"

My eyes narrow, and when Viv sees, she elbows me in the side with a laugh. "Whenever you want. She's getting so big!"

What? I'm a little protective over my child. It's what cat dads do. Well, dads in general, but I'm not going to test that theory… *yet*.

Grant's smile splits his face. "'Kay. Cool. Maybe Thursday after the game? I need some cuddles."

I dip my head toward Viv and brush my lips along the shell of her ear. "Coincidentally, I don't think we'll be home during that time. Sorry, bro."

I'm joking, sort of, and Viv snickers, rolling her big blue eyes. "Stop hogging Boo from everyone, All-Star. It's rude."

Fine. These guys are my best friends, so I guess they can see her. But they still need to know their place when it comes to *my* Boo girl.

LATER THAT NIGHT, Viv's cuddled on the couch with Boo in a pair of my old sweats and my old practice T-shirt, watching *Ghost Adventures,* when I walk into the living room holding her newly wrapped gift in kraft paper that Hallie let me borrow. I'm fucking nervous again, and I'm worried my sweaty-ass palms might ruin the paper that took me entirely too long to wrap. It looks like a disaster, but hopefully, she cares more about what's inside of it than the shit wrapping job.

It might be the most important gift I've ever given anyone, so yeah, I'm *really* fucking nervous.

"Are you finally coming to watch Gh—" She stops midsentence as her gaze drops to the gift in my hands, and her brow furrows. "What's that?"

I close the distance between us, sitting down on the couch next to her, swallowing roughly as my pulse races. "A gift for you."

"Reese, we said no more gifts. You've already given me so much…" She trails off, sitting up and blinking.

I nod. "I know, but this one is… *really* special, baby." I hold it out to her, and she takes it with a slightly shaky hand.

The gift sits in her lap momentarily as she stares down at it and then agonizingly slowly begins to unwrap it.

"Sorry for the horrible job wrapping it. It's the first time I've ever actually wrapped anything," I admit nervously, sitting forward and resting my forearms on my knees as I watch her continue to tear off the paper to reveal the professionally bound book inside.

It's a purple leather hardcover with a gold inlay title.

Haunted Homicide By Vivienne Brentwood.

Her hand flies to her mouth, covering it as her face crumples and her eyes shoot to mine. "Reese. You… *you had my book bound*?"

I nod, reaching out and cradling her jaw in my hand as I sweep my thumb along her cheek. "I did. I wanted to be the very first person to have a copy of your book because I'm so fucking proud of you for following your dreams and finishing it." I press a kiss to her forehead. "But then I realized it's not me that should have it. This copy is for your dad. He helped inspire your dream. As much as I love you… he loved you first, Viv. I know that he's so proud of you. I know that he's looking down right now and wishing he could be here with you. And I know he'd want to celebrate this moment with you… finishing your *first* book."

Viv's shoulders shake as she starts to sob. She brings the book to her chest, clutching it protectively, and I drag her into my lap, my arms circling her body tightly. She burrows her face into my neck as she cries.

"I am so lucky that I get to love you, Viv. I am so goddamn *lucky* that you're mine, and I will never take it for granted. You're the best person I've ever known, and I know your dad is such a big part of who you are," I whisper against her hair. "I wish I could've met him. I wish I could've shaken his hand and thanked him. I wish he could be here to see you become a published author one day, to see your name on all of those bestseller lists. To go to your first signing event, to see you become everything he always knew you would be. I'd do anything to make that happen, baby, but I can't, so I wanted you to have this. So you could still share this moment with him. I thought you could maybe take me to meet him too? And you could show him his copy and tell him all about your story."

She's crying so hard that she doesn't speak for several minutes, simply clinging to me with the book clutched between us until she's sucking in a breath, trying to calm herself. I give her as long as she needs because I know this has to be emotional for her. Fuck, it's emotional for me.

"I love you, Reese," she says against my neck. "I love you more than I ever thought was possible, and I wish I could express how special this is to me, but everything I can think to say feels inadequate. I don't have words for how much it means to me. I'm not sure I ever will."

I shake my head as I drag my fingers through her hair. "I don't need them, baby. I can feel it."

It's what we do best—feel each other when words aren't enough.

That's how I know in my bones that Vivienne is the love of my life. We understand each other in a way that I can't even explain, and I know she's the girl I'm going to *marry* one day.

Because that's what love is, a connection that is deeper than words.

It's in my blood, coursing through my veins with each pump of my heart that belongs to her.

She pulls the book from her chest, brushing her thumb along the front as she stares down at it. "I wish that my dad could be here too. I wish he could be here for all of these moments in my life. To see me publish my book, to get married, to buy my first home. I think about that a lot," she whispers, dragging her gaze up to look at me. Her eyes are red-rimmed and puffy from her tears, and raw emotion swirls inside of them. I lift my hand and brush away her tears, holding her when she rests her cheek against my hand. "I know he would be so proud of me. I just wish that I could *see* it. I would give anything for just five more minutes with him. Just five minutes to tell him how much I love him and how much I miss him, to feel his arms around me just one more time. To hear him tell one of his horrible dad jokes that I always pretended to hate, but secretly, they were my favorite. I wish I could taste his cooking again and hear him yelling at the TV when the Saints were losing. I wish I could remember what he smelled like, Reese. It's been so long that I've forgotten. I'm scared that one day, I'll forget all of these things, and I can never have them back. I just need *five* more minutes."

She squeezes her eyes shut, overcome with emotion as she sucks in a shuddering breath and brings the book back to her chest. When she opens her eyes again, they're filled with tears. "Thank you for this beautiful, thoughtful, irreplaceable gift. I will cherish it forever, Reese. Thank you. And I would love for you to meet him. It would mean so much to me."

"Whenever you're ready, I'll be there." I lean forward and pull her to me, pressing my lips gently against hers, tasting the salty remnants of her tears. "I'm sorry that I made you cry."

"It's a good cry. I just miss him so much, and you gave me something so special that will forever belong to us. It reminds me that even though he isn't here, a piece of him is always with me, and I can never thank you enough for that." She kisses me tenderly, bringing her free hand to my jaw. "You are so important to me. I want you to know that. You're changing me, Reese, and I've never loved who I'm becoming more than I do now. Thank you for being my safe place to land. Thank you for helping me find myself again."

"Always, baby," I murmur.

I'll always be the place she can run to. I'll always hold her when the world around her feels like too much. I'll always put her first, even when she can't do it for herself.

I'll always take care of her and be her strength.

From the moment I saw her months ago, I wanted her. But I didn't even really know what that meant back then.

Mostly, I just loved when she busted my balls and gave me as much shit as I gave her.

I thought I had it all figured out, that my future was set in stone, and that I had everything I needed.

But all along, she was missing.

This beautiful, resilient, defiant girl who walked into my life and set my heart on fire. The one who challenges me, who pushes me to be a better man.

My equal in every sense of the word.

The girl I thought that I would never catch because every time I got close, she'd run even further away.

But we ended up colliding into each other in a way neither of us expected, and it turns out that *catching feelings* was the best choice we ever made.

epilogue

Viv

One Year Later

"You were amazing tonight! I can't believe you caught that ball," I shriek as I crash into Reese, sliding my arms around his neck and locking my legs around his waist as he lifts me off my feet. "God, it was *so* hot. I am *so* wet for you right now."

Seriously, seeing my man out there on the field like an absolute badass in catcher's gear is quite honestly the sexiest thing in the world, and I'm not even lying… my panties *would* be soaked if I was wearing any.

But he stole them off me when we were making out in the car like teenagers before his game.

"Yeah? Let me feel, Sweet Tart," he rasps against my lips, a devilish smirk curving on his pillowy mouth. I'm so crazy about this man that sometimes I feel like I just want to… I don't know, crawl inside of him because I can't get close enough. I'm obsessed with him. Every single thing about him.

I laugh. "Well, maybe if we weren't in a parking lot, but I would not like to end up on TMZ. You forget that you're basically a celebrity now, babe."

"I thought almost getting caught was the fun part?" he asks.

"Um, do you want anyone to see my p—"

He silences me with a growly kiss that has my toes curling in my old Vans and my hands tugging at his freshly showered hair. It's been over a year of being together, and we're still as ravenous for each other as we were since the days of sneaking around at Orleans U. You'd think that the honeymoon phase would fade, but if anything, it's only gotten stronger. We can't seem to keep our hands off each other.

"I am *so* impressed," I tell him as he sets me on my feet and unlocks his Range Rover, tossing his bat bag in the back. "I mean, babe, the way you slid under the ball and gloved it the second before it hit the ground? I was losing my mind."

Being in love with a professional baseball player means that you fall in love with the sport the same way you did with the man, and now I can admit that I'm a fan. Mostly of *my* man, but definitely the game too. I love watching him do what he loves, pouring his heart and soul into his career. And I want to support him the way that he supports me, which means I've come a very long way since the days when I thought home runs were *field goals*.

Slightly embarrassing, but life is all about growth.

"Your mom still coming in this weekend?" Reese asks as we walk to the passenger side of his car and he opens it for me. Something he always does, no matter what.

I nod, excitement buzzing inside me. I miss her *so* much. But I'm so proud of how well she's doing. "I think we have to pick her up at the airport at two on Sunday."

"Good. Got her a surprise." He grins, those deep brown eyes flaring lovingly.

I should know by now that he's never going to show up empty-handed, even though he knows I don't need material things to be happy. I just need him.

It's just not how he's wired.

I've learned that gifting things is *his* love language, and I hate telling him no or giving him a hard time about it. When we first started dating, it bothered me because I didn't understand, but now I know it's just his way of expressing his love.

Not because he wants to flaunt his wealth.

That's the exact reason Boo has four cat towers and a cashmere cat bed in our high-rise apartment that overlooks Seattle. I literally cannot imagine a more spoiled cat than ours, something that Reese takes entirely too much pride in.

I click the seat belt into the buckle as he slides into the driver's side and pulls the car out of the parking lot toward our apartment. We've lived here for three months now, and it still feels so new. New city, new apartment, new places to explore and people to meet.

I was so nervous when he got drafted to the Washington Wolves but even more excited because it's his dream to play professionally, something he's been working for his *entire* life.

That made my decision to go with him that much easier. I had already been on the fence when finishing out my freshman year about switching to online classes. I figured it would give me more flexibility to be there for Mom and would allow me to focus more heavily on getting my book out there. Querying agents and publishers. Revising, revising… and even more revising. So it was a no-brainer that if Reese was moving across the country, then so was I.

He never would've asked me to go with him because he wouldn't want me to feel like I was dropping my life in order to support his, but I didn't want to be without him. Reese is my home. Wherever he goes, so do I.

On our way home, we make a quick stop at the grocery store and grab things for dinner, including a bouquet of purple flowers because Reese is the most thoughtful man to ever exist.

I think about that a lot. How if there was ever a perfect definition of a man, he would be it.

"Smells *almost* as delicious as you," Reese mumbles as he walks up behind me at the stove, burying his face in my neck and inhaling. Of course, his first home game in a week means cooking his favorite… my dad's etouffee.

My head lolls when he drags his tongue along my skin, gently nibbling a path up to my ear. I can't help my eyes fluttering shut when I feel him rock his hips forward and press his cock against my ass.

"God, I missed you so much," I mutter, already breathless.

"What part? My mouth?"

I nod, abandoning the spatula on the counter as I flip around to face him. "Mhmm. And…" I slide my hand under his shirt to sweep my fingers along his sculpted abs and down the trail of hair leading into the waistband of his shorts before closing my palm around his hardening cock. His breath hitches as I fist him, dragging my thumb along his slit, gathering the precum on the pad.

Holding his gaze, I whisper, "This." I rise on my tiptoes and kiss him softly, tenderly sweeping my tongue along the seam of his mouth and slipping it inside to tangle with his.

"And your talented tongue," I pant against his lips as I pull back slightly.

"Fuck, baby," he breathes. "I missed you *so* fucking much."

"Ditto."

I'm two seconds away from dropping to my knees on the kitchen floor so I can properly welcome him home when the fire alarm goes off. Only then do we both realize that there's smoke filling the air, and the pan on the stove is sizzling.

We both spring into action as I pull what's left of the burnt roux off the stove and run to the sink, turning the cold water on. Steam billows from the pan at the temperature change.

I can't help but giggle that I literally burnt our dinner because I got distracted by his wicked tongue and almost gave him a blowjob in the middle of the kitchen.

Reese's leaning against the counter, a small grin on his lips while he shakes his head.

"Sorry I ruined dinner." I rake my teeth over my lips, scrunching my nose.

He stalks toward me, sweeping me off my feet and hauling me over his shoulder as he carries me to our bedroom. There's a hard swat at my ass that leaves it stinging deliciously and my clit throbbing for more.

"I want you to ruin dinner for me every fucking day for the rest of my life, Sweet Tart."

And then he tosses me on the bed and shows me exactly what I've been missing with his tongue, fingers, and cock until I'm a sated mess, draped over him like a blanket of bones.

"I love you," he says sleepily, pressing his lips to the top of my head as his fingers ghost along my spine.

"I love you more," I whisper, my eyes dropping shut as I savor the sound of his strong, steady heart beating beneath my ear.

And god, do I *love* Reese Landry.

I love him so much sometimes that it feels like my heart could actually burst.

I love him irrevocably to the depths of my soul. And I know I always will.

"GOD, this is *so sooooo* exciting, Viv. I can't believe we're at your freaking book tour!" Hallie says excitedly, bouncing on the balls of her feet. "You're literally a *New York Times* best-selling author."

I can't *actually* believe it either. Even standing here in a room full of people, preparing to give my first ever panel.

I knew that so many manuscripts never even make it to an editor's inbox, that it takes some authors years to get their work published. At times, it seemed and felt impossible. It took months of querying for me to even find an agent… and an embarrassing amount of tears and moments of wanting to quit.

But I finally did, and it's almost like the universe knew to save the best for last.

Anna is a literal angel, and I truly think that if it wasn't for her unwavering support and for believing in me the way that she does, I would've never found a publisher for *Haunted Homicide*.

And when it debuted at number five on the NYT Best Seller list, I cried for hours. Mostly in disbelief because it's a debut and because I had no expectations. I just wanted to publish my book into the world and hoped that someone would pick it up.

It's been a whirlwind that superseded every dream I've ever had.

Sometimes, it feels like I need to pinch myself because it doesn't even feel real.

"I can't believe it either," I say, scanning the crowd of people who are here because of me. It's truly unbelievable.

"Okay, okay, I have to take my seat. You are going to kill it, Viv. I'm so, so proud of you. I can't even put it into words how proud I am. I love you," Hallie says as she throws her arms around my neck, pulling me tightly against her. I also can't believe that she flew in from New York City just for this, but I'm so happy she's here to share this moment with me.

"Love you more, space babe."

She pulls back, giving me one more peck to the cheek, and

then takes her seat next to my mom and Reese in the front row with an empty seat reserved for my dad.

My biggest supporters. The reason that I never gave up on my dream. Because even when it was hard, they pushed me to keep going. They made it impossible to give up when I had them in my corner encouraging me.

Reese winks, blowing me a kiss, and I laugh. Even though he has an early game tomorrow, *of course* he flew across the country for less than twenty-four hours, just so he could be here.

And I thought I couldn't love him more?

I take the microphone from the bookstore employee and take a deep breath before stepping out from behind the curtain, lifting my hand in a wave. It feels like an out-of-body experience for people to be here with books of mine that they purchased for me to sign. An honor that I'll never take for granted.

"Hi, everyone!" I say, my voice tight with nerves. "Thank you… for being here and for your support for *Haunted Homicide*. It feels surreal that I'm standing here today, honestly. Only a year ago, I was just a girl with a dream, and now that dream is standing right in front of me."

I'm not only talking about my book but also about Reese in the front row. My number one fan. The man who read it cover to cover so many times he could practically recite it line by line. The man who bound my first copy in memory of my dad. The man who flies across the country just to support me without a second thought. The man who captured my heart when it was prickly and thorny. The man who never gave up on me, even when I was so desperate to push him away.

"I wanna talk for a minute about dedications. They're the first thing you read in a book, before the prologue and the foreword. Because they're the most important. The foundation of why. *Why* you wrote your novel. *Why* you put those words on the page. You're probably wondering why I have two? Because I dedicated it to the first man to ever love me—my father, who passed away when I was in high school. He's the reason I followed my dreams and started writing *Haunted Homicide*." I pause, sucking in a stuttering breath as my gaze connects with Reese's before continuing. "But it's also dedicated to the man who loved me last. He's my *why*. The reason this book ever made it to publishing. Because he believed in me more than I ever believed in myself. I have something I'd like to read to you that I wrote for him."

Reaching into the back pocket of my jeans, I pull out a folded piece of paper that has started to wear in places with the number of times I've read it, preparing for *this* moment. My gaze connects with his as I say, "Reese Landry loves me every single day in a grand gesture. He deserves a grand gesture of his own….

I love the way you wear a backwards hat and your big bleeding heart.

I love your tender touch and how you hold me when I fall apart. I love your strength and how you always put me first.

I love the way you see me, and sometimes I love you so much that it hurts.

But mostly, I love the way that you love me. How I always imagined love would be.

I love the way you caught me and the way you never let me go. I love you, All-Star, and I hope you always know."

I brush the tears off my cheeks then drag my eyes back to his as he stands from his chair, and stalks toward me. His strong arms circle my body and pull me against him as he captures my lips and kisses me with so much love, so much adoration, that my knees feel weak.

He kisses me in a room full of people like we're the only two here.

He kisses me with purpose.

With promise.

Because Reese Landry is my *endgame.*

WANT MORE?

Didn't get enough of Reese + Viv?
I get it, girl!
I've got the perfect bonus scene for you.
A super spicy scene that didn't make it into the book!

Click here to subscribe to my newsletter and you'll instantly get your hands on this spicy scene!

Ready for the next book in the Orleans University Series?
Grant's book, Walkoff Wedding, is available for preorder.
Click here to preorder your copy.

Start the series here with Lane and Hallie's book, Homerun Proposal.
Flip the page for a sneak peek of Chapter One!

chapter one

Hallie

"I'm pretty sure it's *staring* at me," Vivienne mutters, peeking through one squinted eye. "How is it possible that a…" She leans in and whispers like we're in a crowd of people and not alone in my room. "*Penis…* is looking at me like I owe it something."

I cringe when she uses the word "penis." I'm pretty sure, aside from the word "moist," that penis is the ugliest word in the entire English language.

"This was *your* idea," I remind her, not dragging my eyes away from the screen of my laptop, which currently has a man thrusting into a woman from behind as she moans obnoxiously loud. The sounds of their mingled breathing and skin slapping fill my room. Surely, *this* can't be what everyone raves about, right?

Sex.

Intercourse.

Lovemaking.

Something I know nothing about beyond the basic mechanics that I've learned in sex ed and movies and from the birds-and-the-bees talk with my parents, which I'm *still* scarred from.

I, Hallie Jo Edwards, am still *very* much a virgin, even though

I'm a freshman at Orleans University. Isn't college where everyone loses their virginity?

Eighteen years old and never been kissed.

How is that even possible?

Well, very easily, if you're *me*.

Me… the girl who chooses to stay home from a party just to finish a spooky cross-stitch and the kind of girl who has no less than thirty tabs of Dramione fanfic open at once. The girl who considers black and purple the only primary colors on the color wheel. The very same girl who survives on conspiracies, Sour Punch straws, and nineties alternative on an iPod shuffle. Talk about outdated.

Not exactly dickbait.

But I'm good with it. I'm totally comfortable floating to my own tune at the beat of my own drum.

I mean, I'm awesome.

And by awesome, I mean the never-been-kissed, college-freshman-virgin kind of way.

"I've seen lots of them, but this thing looks like an untamed dragon. Someone get this man a leash for this *beast*," Viv says as a shudder racks her body.

I shrug. "It is kind of… *wild*."

We both look at each other, then die.

Absolutely lose our shit, giggles escaping until we're both in a heap on my bed with tears streaming down our faces.

Out of all of the ideas that my best friend has ever had, this by far is the weirdest. It's one thing to watch porn on your own, but it's an entirely different ball game when you're doing it with your best friend who has the maturity level of a fourteen-year-old boy.

"Hal?" a deep voice calls from the other side of my door, and then it swings open, and Eli, my other best friend, strides through without waiting for a response.

I reach for my computer so quickly that I accidentally push Viv off the side of the bed in desperation to slam the screen shut before Eli realizes what we were doing. In my haste, I slam my finger inside my computer and squeal.

"Shit. Fuck. *Damnit*." I suck the tip into my mouth to dull the ache as I jump from my bed and push the computer all the way off the other side.

It lands on the floor with a thump.

Eli looks from me to Vivienne on the floor in front of him, who is desperately trying to hold it together, to the discarded laptop, then back at me, his brow furrowed in confusion. "Uhh… What's going on? What are you watching, and why did you just freak out when I walked in?"

Silence greets his question until Viv loses it. She's the first one to go, her laugh exploding out of her like a poorly timed bomb. She shakes her head as she pants between breaths, "We're watching porn. *Terrible* porn at that."

Her words are merely a string of wheezes somehow formed together into a sentence, and I groan as I watch a devilish smirk slide onto Eli's face.

Great. Now this is a *group* porn-watching session. I settle back onto the bed and wish momentarily that it would swallow me up so I could avoid the mortification I'm currently experiencing.

Without another word, he waltzes through the door, then slams it shut with his foot and steps over Viv, making a beeline straight for the bed.

He rubs his hands together in anticipation as he dives in next to me, putting his arms behind his head. "So, what we watching? A little girl-on-girl action? Maybe a little double penetration?"

My eyes widen as I stutter, "*D-double*?"

"Don't freak her out, Eli. Jesus," Viv mutters as she walks over to the side of the bed my laptop fell to, picking it up and reopening it. The screen resumes the poorly filmed and recorded amateur sex tape we're watching.

"Wow." Eli blows out a breath, squinting at the screen. "That guy's got some serious fucking stamina."

"Yeah, I mean, look at the muscles in his ass. You could crack an egg on those babies." Viv nudges Eli to scoot over, and she slides in beside him, crossing her legs. "If only this was actually how it went."

His chest rumbles with a scoff. "Just because *you've* had bad sex doesn't mean it's like that for everyone else, Vivienne."

That's right. I'm the only virgin left of my best friends, and I am painfully aware of the fact.

Viv sticks her tongue out at him and flips him the finger.

"At least you've had *bad* sex. I've had *no* sex, which is even worse," I mutter to the both of them.

Eli's gaze turns to me. "It's not a big deal, Hal. Tons of people wait for the right person."

I love him, I do. And I appreciate him saying that, but he just… doesn't get it.

Sighing heavily, I say, "I'm just over it. Being the tagalong, the sweet, 'aw, she's cute,' alas awkward and pathetically alone Hallie Jo."

Viv tilts her head. "Which is why I've got the *perfect* plan." She rises from the bed and spins to face me. "Hal, we're in college. We're freshmen at one of the best universities in the South. Together. We need to get out and *live*. Go to parties, drink way too much cheap liquor. *Kiss* hot boys. Get pointless tattoos that we never regret when we're old and wrinkly, despite what the boomers think. Be young while we have the opportunity. You know, before real life starts."

In theory, it sounds great. Easy even.

Like, technically speaking, how hard could it be to find a party on a college campus, cheap liquor in a red Solo cup, and a hot guy who's more than willing to stick his tongue down your throat?

That's not the hard part.

You see, it's got everything to do with me.

I'm just kind of… me. And I already know that I'm not everyone's cup of tea.

Honestly, I'm probably more like kombucha if I had to categorize myself.

Bitter at first taste but then slowly starts to grow on you after you hold your nose and force it down.

I mean, it is fermented bacteria that's good for you. Gross, but not bad after a while.

But Viv is right.

This is supposed to be the prime time in our lives. The time to sow our wild oats, to let our hair down and live it up before the societally imposed walls of adulthood close in on us.

"She's right, Hal. At least about living it up while you can. Get out, see what the world has to offer you. I'll come, too, and look out for you two. Make sure you're having fun. Safely," Eli adds.

I chew on the corner of my lip as I mull over what they're saying.

I know that they're both right… It just seems much easier to talk about than it actually is to do it. Putting yourself out there, forgetting the things that hold you back. Pretending you're not scared that the world will reject you for being yourself.

Finally, I drag my gaze up, flickering between the two of them. "You're right. Both of you. Let's do it." I exhale, letting the nerves go. "Tomorrow, we're going to go to a party."

Her eyes light up like I just told her we're about to meet Ed and Lorraine Warren back from the dead. "Really?"

I nod.

"We're going to a *frat* party, and we're not leaving until

you're no longer an eighteen-year-old college freshman who's never been kissed. Welcome to the first day of the rest of your life, Hallie Jo Edwards."

"This sounds oddly reassuring yet ominous all at once," I say at the same time "*Pizza's here*!" is yelled from the foyer, signaling our highly anticipated dinner is finally here. Together, we all get up from my bed, abandoning the laptop. "Now, can we *please* go stuff our faces with pizza? I'm starving, and I want to do more research for this week's episode."

Eli laughs, tucking his arm around my neck and dragging me against his side as we follow behind Viv to the kitchen. Sometimes I forget how much I need an Eli hug. It always makes me feel better, and admitting all of that out loud was hard, even if I don't want to show it. Growth is rarely ever easy.

Viv heads straight for the fridge and pulls out an orange Fanta, one of our many obsessions.

"I've been listening to a nonfiction book this week and taking a few notes in preparation. I think this episode will have more listeners than ever before, judging by the amount of hype it's getting on social media. Also, I've got to head out after this. Another calculus tutoring session, and go figure, the guy giving it is a complete perv," she says as she sits at the table and throws open the pizza box, reaching in for a large slice, then pushing one my way.

I grab my slice and take a giant bite, closing my eyes and moaning around the mouthful of extra cheesy, greasy goodness.

"Bigfoot this week, right?" Lane Collins's voice booms behind me, announcing his presence, scaring the absolute shit out of me to where I begin to choke on the mouthful of pizza.

I'm hacking, and Viv's eyes widen as I try desperately to get the food unlodged to no avail.

Holy shit, I'm going to die literally choking on cheesy pizza with black olives.

I'm going to die a *virgin*.

"Shit, are you okay, Hal?" Eli rushes over, tossing his still-empty plate onto the table and pulling me from my chair. His arms circle my waist as he begins to perform the Heimlich.

The piece of pizza that seemed much smaller when I was only chewing it and not choking finally becomes unlodged from my throat and flies out onto the ground with a disgusting squelch.

Air invades my lungs, and I sink back into Eli's arms as relief floods me.

I'm okay. I'm safe. I'm with Eli. It's okay.

I'm still trying to catch my breath when I look over at Lane, leaning against the counter, promptly sucking out all of the air that I've just managed to inhale after my near-death experience.

He has that effect about him, walking into a room and stealing everyone's attention and the ability to breathe.

Maybe he just has that effect on *me*, but judging by the number of girls that sneak out of our off-campus house in the middle of the night, it's *not* just me.

You see, for as long as I can remember, I've been harboring a small… innocent little crush on my best friend's older brother, and it's a secret that I'll likely take to my grave.

Because Lane Collins would *never* look my way.

I've only ever been his little brother's best friend, the one who's tagged along since we were kids. The annoying neighbor girl that he could never seem to get rid of, not even as he got older and his parents forced him to let Eli and me tag along to the movies, to the mall, to the field when he played.

I *cherished* those moments because even for just a few minutes, I was in his orbit. I existed right along with the girls that threw themselves at his feet. I would be the recipient of the dimpled smile he reserved for those girls, and I would hold on to those moments like it was a lifeline, simply tiding me over until the next second of attention I could steal from him.

"What's up, Hal?" He smirks, those damned dimples popping as he reaches into the cabinet and pulls out his favorite shaker bottle. I try not to notice that he's shirtless, and his wide chest is on display for my eyes to devour.

Try being the operative word.

It's impossible not to notice how perfectly defined his chest is and how the muscles in his arms flex and ripple every time he moves.

"She almost just choked to death on a piece of pizza," Eli says, shaking his head as he rubs my back. Clearly, he's well acquainted with the fact that my clumsy awkwardness truly knows no bounds.

Lane raises his all-too-perfect eyebrow. "So, just another Thursday, then?"

"Yep."

Assholes.

This is what I get for living with these two. Well, not that I really had much choice. Since I wasn't in any rush to live with a stranger in a tiny dorm on campus, my parents and the Collinses decided that the best place for me to live was right here with Eli and Lane, who already had an off-campus house. I wouldn't have to room with someone I didn't know, and they could look after me since this is the first time I've lived outside of my parents' house.

A situation that worked great for everyone.

Theoretically.

I spend most of my days trying *not* to fantasize about Lane and the rest of the time trying to focus on the ridiculous freshman course load I've taken on as a film production student. I got waitlisted at my dream school, NYU, so I opted for my second choice, and I'm hoping to get my prereqs out the way so I get accepted as a second-year transfer. Which means that I have to work extra hard to make sure my portfolio is ready and my GPA is high.

Reaching for the kitchen chair, I pull it out and flop down into it, blowing my bangs out of my face while doing so. My eyes drift to Lane at the stove, working on his protein shake, his gray sweatpants slung haphazardly low on his waist, revealing the Adonis belt of his hips.

Something tells me that he would look nothing like the man from today's *porn debacle*. That he would be the kind of guy who'd talk filthy to you while he did despicable things to your body. My face begins to flame as I imagine the two of us in that video, doing the things that the couple on the screen did.

The feel of his hands gripping my hips as he thrust into me, his eyes devouring me an—

"So, we still on for our Friday movie night, Hal?" Eli mumbles through a mouthful of pizza, mentioning our decade-long weekend tradition that jolts me from my dirty images of his brother.

Jesus Christ. My heart drops to my stomach as if everyone in the room can read my thoughts.

In the short time that I've been here, it's been a rare occasion for us to all be together for a meal since all of us have vastly different schedules. Especially since it's preseason and Lane is Orleans University's star pitcher.

When he's not working out, practicing, or in study hall, he's with his friends at a party or with his flavor of the night.

"Yep. Viv and I finished discussing things for this week's episode, so I should be good." I open the orange Fanta she slid to me and take another much smaller bite of the greasy pizza.

Some college kids love ramen, and then there's me. I'm surviving on strong will and Jack's Pizza.

Eli shoves another bite into his mouth, chewing quickly

before speaking. "Cool. I heard there's this new documentary called *Fantastic Fungi* that I think you'd like."

That *he* would like, and that will undoubtedly make me pass out within thirty minutes of the moment he presses Play, but whatever.

Honestly, who in their right mind would choose to watch a documentary on fungus growing out of the ground for *fun* on a Friday night?

Eli Collins. That's who.

"Can't wait," I say despite my true feelings, plastering on a wide smile. At the end of the day, I love to spend time with Eli. He's my best friend and has been since we were just toddlers, and if he wants to bore me to death during our weekly movie night, fine.

"What are you up to this weekend, bro?" Eli asks his brother, who's still standing at the counter.

Lane's tanned shoulder dips. "Coach wants me icing my shoulder, so I'll probably come back early and get some sleep. Who knows, might hit a party up. Find a cleat chaser to sneak out." He shoots me a pointed gaze, his lips tugging up in a grin.

And there you have it, ladies and gentlemen. America's *sweetheart*.

This is the guy that every single female at Orleans University would trip over their feet to have a chance with.

He's charismatic, even when he's being a douchebag, and that is a special skill that only guys like Lane possess.

"Shouldn't you be studying or, I dunno, doing something *productive*?" Viv asks.

A smug smirk sits on his lips as he taps his finger along his temple. "I don't have to study, Viv, not when I've got a brain like this."

"Runs in the family," Eli adds cockily.

Truly, how is Lane so smart *and* so attractive? It's not fair to us normal, average humans who actually have to apply effort in order to get a passing grade.

The Collins brothers share the same unruly dirty-blond hair and almost the same shade of brilliant emerald eyes. Both have strong jaws and tanned skin that is from genetics and not the sun. But that's where the similarities end. They couldn't be any more different if they tried.

Eli is more reserved and nerdy, while his brother is outgoing, cocky, and the life of the party. Both are handsome and smart, even if Lane likes to pretend he's just a dumb jock for the sake of his campus reputation.

I know better only because I grew up next door, and I see the side of Lane that he chooses not to share with the world. As Eli's best friend, I've spent as much time in their house as I have my own. I'm lost in thought, popping the bracelets on my wrist, when Lane turns toward me.

"Nice bracelets, Hallie Jo," he muses, then downs the glass of water in one gulp, the strong column of his throat bobbing as he swallows.

My cheeks immediately heat. He's being sarcastic and teasing me because of the beaded bracelets on my wrist that Viv and I make when we're binge-watching Netflix. Maybe it's childish, but we have fun doing it and seeing who can put the most absurd shit on them.

One guess who's currently winning that bet. The unhinged one. Aka *Vivienne.*

"Uh, thanks?" I say quietly, my eyes flitting to Viv, who's squinting at him. "They're just, uh… a silly thing we do for fun."

"They're cute." His smirk widens into a full-blown smile, and once again, it feels hard to breathe.

Cute. Lane Collins just said something on my body is *cute.*

Before I can even really begin to obsess over his comment,

Viv pastes on a mischievous smile. "Are you going to the Kappa party this weekend? Me, Hallie, and Eli are going."

"You two are going to a *frat* party?" he says, disbelief lacing his tone while his eyebrows nearly meet his hairline.

I roll my eyes. "Don't look so surprised. We're allowed to have a social life too, Lane."

Holding his hands up in surrender, he shakes his head. "Just wondering. Not really your scene, huh?"

I shrug as I drop my gaze. "I'm just… trying out some new things."

"Like hooking up with hot boys." Viv giggles as she wiggles her eyebrows suggestively. She stands from her chair and walks to the trash to throw away the plate. "Gotta run, or I'm going to be late for my tutoring session. Send me all the good vibes, please."

We all say goodbye, and I escape to my bedroom, where I shut the door behind me and head straight for the window. I climb out carefully, placing my foot onto the awning and then onto the flat slope of the roof.

Since starting at Orleans University, this spot has become my favorite place in the world to be. High enough that I can see the entire campus, and at night, the stars shine bright in a blanket above me.

I don't know how long I sit out here, my knees pressed against my chest, watching the sun fade into the clouds as dusk appears.

Long enough to where my butt has gone numb and I've twisted the little pink alien pendant around my neck into knots. A nervous habit.

A sound behind me pulls me from my thoughts, and I turn back to see Eli climbing through the window, and then he's joining me on the asphalt shingles, resting his forearms on his legs as he peers out at the glittering lights of campus.

Neither of us speaks for a minute, the sound of cars passing on the highway drowning out my thoughts. It's a comfortable silence, and that's part of what I love about my friendship with Eli. It just feels… natural. It's always been like this between us. *Easy*.

"Hal?"

I glance over at him, his piercing green eyes seeing right into my soul. Or at least that's what it feels like sometimes.

He bumps my shoulder with his. "You feeling weird after that conversation?"

Shrugging, I finger the bracelets on my wrist but say nothing.

"Viv was only joking, Hal. You know how she is. You don't *actually* have to hook up with anyone. Being a virgin isn't a big deal, you know? This is your life and something that's important to you. Things should happen when *you* feel ready, not because you feel like you need to prove something or to be anyone other than who you are."

"I know. I just feel… like, am I still a virgin because I'm weird? Am I really just that awkward?"

"Hallie." He blanches. "Fuck no. You're one of the most incredible people I know. You're smart and funny and beautiful. I mean… the whole package."

Tossing me a playful smirk, he reaches out and threads his hand in mine. Not in a romantic way, but in a comforting way. A way that has always just been… us. Something he learned early on, that physical touch is my love language.

"I'm just tired of blending into the wall like a glorified wallflower. I'm just *tired,* Eli. I want to experience all the things that I never have, and I feel this… I don't know, push inside me for more. Not just my…" I lower my voice, clearing my throat in hesitation. "*Virginity*. I mean just in life. I want to be more than a wallflower. I want to spread my wings and fly. Grow into the person I'm meant to be. Find out who I really am. You know, all the important things."

Eli's fingers tighten in mine, and he nods. "I know, and I support anything you decide, Hallie. I always have, and I always will. Just be true to yourself. That's all I'm saying."

"I know. And I don't think I could take on college without you by my side," I tell him.

"Anyone who is lucky enough to be a part of your universe will know exactly what they have from the moment you walk in."

And just like that, it hits me why it is that Eli Collins has always been the rock in my life.

Because he makes me feel like I'm the best version of myself.

Continue reading Homerun Proposal for FREE in KU by clicking here!

also by maren moore

Totally Pucked

Change on the Fly

Sincerely, The Puck Bunny

The Scorecard

The Final Score

The Penalty Shot

Playboy Playmaker

Orleans U

Homerun Proposal

Catching Feelings

Walkoff Wedding

Standalone

The Enemy Trap

The Newspaper Nanny

Strawberry Hollow

The Mistletoe Bet

A Festive Feud

The Christmas List

Orleans U

Homerun Proposal

Catching Feelings

Walkoff Wedding

about the author

Maren Moore is an Amazon Top 20 Best-selling sports romance author. Her books are packed full of heat and all the feels that will always come with a happily ever after. She resides in southern Louisiana with her husband, two little boys and their fur babies. When she isn't on a deadline, she's probably reading yet another Dramione fan fic, rewatching cult classic horror movies, or daydreaming about the 90's.

You can connect with her on social media or find information on her books here ➡ here.

www.ingramcontent.com/pod-product-compliance
Lightning Source LLC
LaVergne TN
LVHW042338070725
815584LV00029B/428

* 9 7 9 8 2 1 8 4 0 0 5 9 0 *